Of Men and Dragons
Jack's Landing

Steve Hayden

Copyright © 2021 Steve Hayden
All rights reserved.

Chapter 1

S'haar was muttering to herself under her breath. "Well, this turned out about as bad as it possibly could…" As she spoke, she was struggling in vain to remove the straps binding her to the stake.

Sure, she'd heard all the rumors of B'arthon's lecherous ways. Still, finally having a full belly, a warm place to sleep, and warm clothes had made it easy to ask herself the question, "What's the worst that could happen?" At the time, she'd thought the worst was being dumped for some other female and ending up back on the streets where she'd started.

Never had it crossed her mind that being tied up as a "virgin" sacrifice to appease the new dragon was even a remote possibility. S'haar grew tired of muttering quietly, so this time she shouted to the heavens. "If I ever see that worthless noble man's son again, I'm going to castrate him!"

An impossibly loud roar came from the new cave in front of her, reminding S'haar that she'd probably never get the chance to make good on her promise. Which was a shame for the sake of all the future women who would cross that miserable waste of oxygen's path.

Apparently, the only thing that wretch, B'arthon, had any skill in was tying women up. As the minutes ticked by, S'haar could hear the dragon slowly approaching the entrance of the cave.

As a cold wind blew, S'haar started to debate which fate was worse, being eaten alive or slowly freezing to death while tied to a stake. Without shelter and fire, it wouldn't matter whether the dragon ate her or not.

After one last attempt to get her claws into a position to sever the leather straps, S'haar screamed loudly in incoherent anger and frustration. She no longer cared if the dragon could hear her or not. Her last scream of defiance echoed around the hills and valleys. Then, after the last echo faded, she noticed something odd. It was suddenly very quiet.

She heard something heavy settle just inside the cavern, then the sound of...footsteps? Yes, those were definitely footsteps that approached the mouth of the cavern. Soon she could see a glow, like fire, approach along with the sound. S'haar started wondering if the beast would cook her alive before eating her.

"How does this situation keep going from bad to worse?"

Staring up at the sky, she shouted the last of her defiance to the gods. They surely watched her now, for the first time in her all-too-short of a life. "Enjoy the show! You've all been as worthless as the men in the village!"

That was when movement at the mouth of the cave caught her eye, and what she saw left her speechless. Whatever she had been expecting the beast to look like, the thing now walking toward her was not it. This was so... so anticlimactic.

What appeared to be the most frail-looking argu'n she'd ever seen walked out of the cave. His hide looked soft and had a sickly pinkish hue to it. His head tendrils were impossibly short and thin, like a fine fur that waved about with the most delicate breezes. His gait was stiff as if he was missing a set of joints in his upper thighs. When he got close, S'haar noticed he was quite short as well. In fact, he was shorter than her by a noticeable margin. A quick flick of her tongue let her know he also smelled odd, and she could sense heat actually radiating off his body, almost as if he was producing excess heat from within.

~

Jack shook his head. As if crash landing on this backward planet wasn't bad enough, now he had a local tied to a stake in front of his new involuntary home. "Seriously, a sacrifice? The hell is wrong with you people? Can't a guy crash land into a mountain on a strange planet in peace?"

Jack took a moment to look at his new guest and quickly realized she was in multiple states of distress. "Aaaand you're naked...Oh hell, I'd better get you down."

Jack pulled out his knife and carefully approached the native. As he did so, she spit at him. Sighing in exasperation, he reminded himself that she was obviously having a day every bit as bad as his own. He tried to speak in soothing tones to calm her down, but it was apparent she couldn't understand a word he said. Not that there was any reason she should be able to, but it was just one more obstacle in clearing up this unfortunate mess.

When he reached for her bindings, the native started struggling and shouting to the heavens again. Jack wondered if she was praying, but despite the language barrier, her tone of voice and general demeanor seemed far too angry and aggressive for any prayer he knew of. He started to have second thoughts about cutting the woman down but quickly realized leaving her here was a death sentence. So he took a deep breath, cut her bindings, and stood back.

~

S'haar was going to die, and it was going to happen at the hands of this pathetic, deformed, deficient male. At first, she wasn't sure what his intentions were, but the drawn knife made things apparent enough. She was shouting every obscenity she knew at every person she even suspected might have had a hand in her ending up tied to this stake, then something unexpected happened.

The odd male cut her bindings and stepped back, sheathing his blade. Now standing properly, S'haar could see he was even shorter than she'd realized. He didn't even come up to her nose. The fact didn't seem to escape his notice, and he looked up at her with just a touch of wariness, or possibly fear, in his eyes.

Other things seemed off as well. His limbs all seemed shorter than they should be. His eyes were too narrow and rounded at the pupal. His fingers were stubbier than usual, and his claws were malformed to the point of being useless. She also noticed that he was covered in dust and debris, as though he'd been digging in the cave.

The male was gesturing to the cave and speaking in that odd language of his. It sounded almost like singing rather than talking, and his voice lacked the harsh guttural tones S'haar was familiar with. It seemed he wanted S'haar to follow him into the cave.

S'haar glanced at the sky and shivered as she realized her choices were to follow him and probably die, or stay out here and definitely die. After a quick assessment, she was confident that she could best him with ease if it came to a fight. However, so far, he seemed friendly enough. Also, she was getting cold quickly, making her decision even easier.

As the male approached the cave, he reached up to the band on his head, and S'haar heard a click. There was now light projecting from some shiny stone on his headband. A distant part of S'haar's mind realized this was more than a little odd, but her thoughts were getting as sluggish as her movements with the cold now seeping through to her bones, and she just couldn't bring herself to care about much of anything any longer. She'd follow this strange little man a little further, then she'd lie down for a nap. Just a short nap.

It took her a moment to realize the man had stopped. In front of him was a wall made of some kind of painted metal that was deeply gouged in countless places. That meant this was the end of the cave, which also meant it was the end for her. S'haar made a sound gave up and collapsed onto the ground. Life was always so unfair. Why shouldn't death be?

~

Jack looked over his shoulder and noticed that the native following him seemed to be steadily getting more sluggish. When he stopped to open the door, he heard a thud. Turning around, he could see her collapsed form. Now rushing, Jack opened the door and dragged her inside, but she seemed frozen in a fetal position, and it was harder to move her than he expected. She was noticeably heavier than even her height would imply.

"Angela, initiate house guest protocol and scan our guest. What's wrong with… her/him/it?"

A tiny blue figure, with darker blue hair in a pixie cut, materialized in front of Jack. "We've been on the planet for less than two days, and you're already bringing a naked woman home? I thought you always said you weren't a ladies' man?"

Jack glared at Angela while brushing some loose debris off himself. "Remind me later to go into great detail telling you just how funny you are. Now, is our guest in any danger or not?"

Angela looked like he had just told her she was the cutest thing in the world —he never did, but she knew she was —and answered impishly. "*She* is in no danger. She appears to be more cold-blooded than not, though I suppose it would be better to reclassify her as semi cold-blooded."

The AI paused as if lost in thought before visibly snapping herself out of her revelry to continue. "Regardless, by bringing her inside the ship, you've already taken the necessary steps to save her. With your permission, I'll bump the temperature up a few more degrees, and she should be back on her feet in no time. Then *you* can explain to her why she's naked inside a stranger's house!"

Jack continued to glare daggers at his ship's avatar, though his voice implied it was more for show than actual anger. "Good to hear. We should probably get a few clean blankets ready for her and maybe some hot food. Assuming we have something safe for her to eat? Also, start working on a translation program as soon as you are able."

Angela saluted Jack in an overly serious manner that fooled precisely no one. "Sir, yes, sir! Anything else, *sir*?"

Jack looked longingly at the doorway to his bedroom and sighed. "Yeah, make me a large pot of coffee. I have a feeling it's going to be a long night, and not in the fun kind of way."

Suddenly wide-eyed, Angela retorted, "Sir, I didn't know you knew there was a fun way!"

Jack threw the blanket he'd grabbed through her projection before sighing again and walking over to pick it back up. As he trudged over, he spoke wistfully to himself as he glanced in the new arrival's direction. "Just what kind of trouble have I gotten myself into?"

~

The first thing S'haar sensed was warmth. This wasn't the harsh, uneven heat of a winter's fire meant to keep the sharp bite of cold air at bay. This was the even, relaxing warmth of a pleasant summer evening. The next thing she noticed was the many confusing scents that filled the area. Some were harsh, sharp, and acrid in nature, others were simply impossible to place, but a few smelled...like metal? That was when one particular scent caught her attention. S'haar realized she could also smell cooking meat!

S'haar's eyes snapped open with that revelation. She found herself in a hut, though it was unlike any hut she'd ever seen. The walls and ceiling were clearly metal and a fortune's worth at that. If all the metal in her village were to be gathered in one spot, it would still be a paltry amount in comparison. The floor was soft, almost like a short, thick fur. She also found herself covered by a warm blanket, made of another impossibly soft material, unlike any skin or fur she'd ever felt before.

She realized a soft, even light seemed to be radiating from behind beautiful glass panels. The glass looked more clear and transparent than any S'haar had seen before. She also noticed the light didn't flicker or waver the way flames should.

Finally, she realized the smell of meat that had woken her seemed to be emanating from the misshapen argu'n from earlier. More specifically, it came from the pan in his hands. As she focused on the scent in front of her, an impossibly small but similarly misshapen blue spirit appeared out of thin air next to the male and blurted something in that odd language of his, pointing to S'haar as she did so. Though this one somehow sounded much more cheerful than the male had. Almost too cheerful...

S'haar jumped back in shock, hissing while baring her claws and teeth while her head tendrils vibrated in agitation. Whoever this impossibly rich malformed lord was, all of this was just too strange. Argu'n did not appear out of thin air, they were *not* blue, and they were *NOT* that tiny. Who knew what strange magics were at work in this strange place? S'haar had always dismissed the stories of sorcerers and devils told by the village elders while huddled around the evening fires, but what other explanation could there be?

Feeling the man's gaze, S'haar turned her attention back to him. He seemed to be staring at her before he realized what he was doing and his gaze shot to the ground. She heard him mutter something that might have been an apology, looking away as he did so. S'haar narrowed her eyes in suspicion. Why would some lord with this much wealth, and possibly forbidden magics, shy away from her?

Sparing a look down at herself, she realized that she had dropped the blanket and now stood naked. She grabbed the cloth and bunched it up in front of herself, almost feeling more vulnerable in this strange hut than she had while tied to the stake.

~

Jack risked a glance at his guest and saw that she was safely covered once again. When she'd been asleep, she'd seemed so vulnerable and alien that he'd felt nothing but pity and protectiveness toward the poor girl. Admittedly, she was a large, powerful, fanged, and clawed girl who could probably kill him with little effort, but a girl nonetheless.

Now, standing before him was no girl. It was a proud angry woman who glared at him, as though daring him to disrespect her in any way. Jack chuckled nervously to himself as he dished the beef he'd been cooking out onto a couple of plates and slowly, carefully approached the alien standing before him.

Based on the way she moved, she obviously had muscles wrapped around a skeleton similar to his, though with longer limbs that were tipped with some very dangerous looking claws. She had bony plates covering much of her legs, arms, and torso that seemed to be a greyish brown color, almost like an exoskeleton. Between the plates, and from her neck up, her skin was a soft red color. She had an extra joint in her thigh that seemed like it would give her fantastic jumping or burst speeds. Combined with the smaller claws on her hands and the somewhat intimidating longer claws on her feet, she was a force to be respected. There also appeared to be another set of five-inch long claws extending off her elbows, making Jack think he should think twice before getting on her bad side.

Somehow her face was both humanoid and alien. A series of long, bony protuberances that could be mistaken for dreadlocks if they didn't occasionally move in a nonexistant wind topped her head, extending past her shoulders, looking for all the world like some kind of bony mane. Her jaw looked like some hybrid between a muted muzzle and a human face. He couldn't help but notice it was filled with far too many long, sharp, and pointy teeth for his comfort. Occasionally her forked tongue flicked out like a lizard's as if tasting the air. Her catlike nose flowed into the upper end of her mouth. Her ears looked like they belonged on an elf, long and pointed, with an odd wavy pattern along the backside. Where her eyebrows should have been, there was a slight ridge that ended in three small bony protuberances near the outer edge.

As he looked into her eyes, he froze, not realizing that he was holding his breath as his fight, flight, or freeze response chose that moment to select freeze. Those were the eyes of a predator, assessing him for threat or weakness. They were bright silver, and reflective to the point they almost seemed to glow, but slit down the middle like a cat's.

Jack mentally nudged himself back into action, slowly approaching her. He placed one of the plates on the end table he unconsciously kept between the woman and himself before backing up and motioning for her to take it. She complied but kept a wary eye on him all the same.

He made a deliberate show of taking one of the morsels, showing it to her, and then eating it, hoping his guest would relax if she saw him eating from the same batch as her. The meat was bland because he didn't know enough about her physiology to guess what spices would be safe for her to eat, so he stuck with simple browned beef tips for the moment.

Throughout this, Angela kept looking back and forth, excitedly watching her human try and make friends with a very intimidating native. He'd always been a bit too much of a loner, so it was good to see him socialize, even if it was with a woman who could kill him a dozen times in as many ways before he could react. Though not before Angela could. The moment there were any signs of danger, she could respond in a dozen different ways, varying from a minor annoyance to lethal action, as the situation merited. However, she was hoping nothing like that would be necessary. Besides, the tension seemed to be easing as the woman started to eat.

~

S'haar's fear was fading and being replaced by an odd incredulity. Everything about her host seemed to contradict itself. Here was a man with the kind of wealth she couldn't imagine, yet he was still doing menial labor like cooking. In her experience, a man as wealthy as this one was should be demanding her servitude as payment for saving her life. Instead, he seemed oddly concerned with her comfort. Finally, and perhaps worst of all, this small, soft, declawed male seemed to be acting as though he was afraid of frightening her.

It was all so absurd that she had no idea what to think. So when her host gave her meat, she simply ate. After eating the first morsel, S'haar looked down at the rest with a touch of disdain on her face. "This meat is bland and overcooked," S'haar caught herself, realizing that just because he couldn't understand her words didn't mean he couldn't discern her meaning, and even if it was poorly prepared, it was food, and she should be grateful. With that in mind, she amended her statement. "On the other hand, it is meat, and it is warm, so…thanks."

As she slowly relaxed, the male started speaking to her in that odd language of his, waving his hand around as he spoke. S'haar paid attention, even though nothing seemed to make sense until he finally held his hand over his chest and spoke slowly and clearly, "Jack." Then he held his hand out with all his fingers pointing to the small blue devil and said, "Angela." Finally, he pointed his hand to her, his meaning apparent. S'haar held her hand over the blanket held in place over her chest and said, "S'haar."

He smiled and repeated "S'haar" in that odd song-sounding voice of his. It was somewhat mispronounced, as though his mouth lacked the necessary form to produce proper speech. The male then followed up with what she assumed was a greeting of some sort, smiling at her all the while. She smiled back and politely pretended not to notice when his gaze flicked to her teeth and back, causing his smile to waver almost imperceptibly...the keyword being almost.

To be fair, he seemed to be as confused by her as she was by him. At least he appeared to bear her no ill will. Even if she wasn't interested in the kinds of honor all the males in her village seemed obsessed with, she recognized that he had done her several favors already and taken some risk upon himself by bringing a stranger into his home. She might not be willing to give him her servitude as thanks, but the least she could do is try and return his friendly demeanor.

Besides, it's not like she could just walk back into her village. After what they'd done to her, or at least what they thought they'd done to her, she wasn't sure she wouldn't try and attack them on the spot. At the moment, S'haar was warm, she was fed, and she was certainly better off than she'd thought possible only a few hours ago. Perhaps it was best to simply let tomorrow take care of itself for now.

As "Jack" wound down, he seemed to look at S'haar somewhat expectantly, as if he expected her to share her own story. So, she launched into the explanation of the recent poor life choices that had led up to their eventual meeting.

With a sigh, S'haar began. "I guess it started when I turned down the guard captain's offers for companionship. I may have done so in a manner that bruised his pride. In my defense, it's not my fault he decided to approach me in front of his troops with all that swagger."

S'haar became more animated, clenching her fists in frustration as she really started in on her rant. She didn't seem to notice her host seeming to shrink back at her sudden show of aggression. "That led to one disagreement after another, which resulted in me being kicked out of the guard."

S'haar's anger seemed to lose its heat, and she grew tired as she continued her story. "So then I became a hunter, and I was damned good at it too! Then I had to go and get into a series of fights with the hunting chief over a similar disagreement. Once again, I found myself on the streets, looking for a place that would offer me warmth and food enough to last me through the winter."

As her rant went on, S'haar started to pace, her agitation visibly building again. "I looked into becoming a metalworker, but as it turns out, they do a lot of business with the guards and hunters, so I was too much a liability for them. Winter was rapidly approaching, and I had no work and no home. So when the lord's son propositioned me, I figured I could do what needed to be done until spring. After that, I could start over somewhere else."

The anger returned, but this time it held an icy edge instead of the heat from before. "Wouldn't you know it, I just couldn't stomach being *his* 'lady' any more than any other useless male in the village. So once again, I opened my mouth."

S'haar seemed to deflate one last time. She collapsed onto the couch, apparently ready to be done with her story. "Eventually, that led to me being tied to a stake and left to be eaten by a dragon. By the way, you are a pretty sad excuse for a dragon. Hell, you're a sad excuse for a male!"

S'haar laughed a little sadly to herself. "Then again, I guess I'm a sad excuse for a female…not that I regret any of it! I just…I just wish I knew what to do now…"

After that, she seemed determined to hide her worries about the future in a deluge of vivid descriptions about her thoughts of the various men of her village, the females who enabled them, and the gods who could join them all in multiple activities that were cathartic to describe, even if they might be physically impossible. This went on for a significant length of time as S'haar went to great lengths to be as creative in her descriptions as she was malicious.

~

Angela chuckled to herself before she turned to Jack. "After reviewing the various conversations tonight, I think I've gathered enough to get a basic idea of what she's saying. If I'm right, and we both know I always am, I think I like her. Can we keep her?"

Chapter 2

Jack gave his ship's AI a look that did its best to convey just how fatigued he was. The coffee was quickly fading, and it wouldn't be long before he did as well.

"If you can understand her, can you tell our guest that she's welcome to stay the night? We'll figure out where to go from here in the morning." The last words came out a bit distorted as he started to yawn halfway through the sentence. "Also, see if there's anything she'll need to get through the night? Oh, and you might want to give her a brief rundown on how the bathroom works."

Turning her attention from Jack to their new guest, Angela waved to get S'haar's attention. "Hello, I am Angela. I figured it was about time for me to introduce myself. As much as we have yet to learn about each other, you and Jack seem to be at the end of your energy reserves, so we should probably call it a night for now. You are welcome to stay here, and we will talk more in the morning. The couch and floor are both open to you, and if you need anything else, just say my name, and I will hear you." She was quite friendly for a tiny devil, even if her speech was a little overly simplistic in nature.

That was when the realization hit S'haar that she could understand what "Angela" was saying. Which meant… "Wait, you were able to understand me this whole time? You've just been listening to me ramble on while I thought you were just being polite? That's, that's…"

Angela made calming motions before addressing her concerns. "No, it is not what you think. At first, I didn't understand you any better than you understood us. However, as you spoke, I listened and learned. The more we speak, the more I will learn. I am still having trouble with your contractions. The odd clicking noise you make in the middle seems to change from one use to the next. Also, I'm still working out how to tell the difference between the names of people versus places, but I am sure I will have it down a bit better sometime tomorrow." The little spirit seemed almost gleeful as she picked apart the more delicate parts of this new puzzle.

S'haar's eyes narrowed, and her head tilted to the side as she thought. The tiny figure learned as S'haar spoke? This quickly? That made no sense. Then again, nothing about this situation made any sense. Maybe she'd died on the stake outside. Perhaps what she was experiencing was some cruel joke the gods were having at her expense as punishment for her many blasphemies, though she doubted that. The gods never noticed her while she lived. Why would they start caring about her after she'd died? Maybe this was all some weird fever dream, and she was asleep in her bed… the bed she'd lost when she got kicked out of the guard… That didn't seem likely either…

In the end, S'haar supposed it didn't matter. Whether it made sense or not, this insanity was her life at the moment, and the sooner she accepted that fact, the sooner she could move on. Regardless of if this was all a dream or madness, at least it was interesting.

Realizing both hosts were still looking at her expectantly, S'haar visibly shook herself out of her thoughts. She'd been sitting and thinking long enough. By now, they were probably wondering if she slept sitting up with her eyes open. "The floor is fine. Will it get much colder in here after your…" she looked around, just accepting that what she said next would sound stupid, "invisible fire goes out? If so, I'll need more blankets and maybe some heated stones," she finished lamely. This was embarrassing.

Angela beamed at S'haar, eager to brag about herself, as always. "I'm happy to report it will stay nice and warm all night long."

She seemed to be working herself up to a new monologue when Jack interrupted her, saying something while holding his hand out toward S'haar. "Jack would like to wish you a good night, and then told me not to talk you into a coma…" she trailed off.

S'haar held her hand out in a similar manner to Jack. He slowly took hold of her hand and moved it up then down twice before smiling and walking away.

Angela began speaking in her overly simplistic but excited manner. "That is called a handshake. It is customary among humans to use it in greeting and in saying goodbye. It denotes…"

Jack looked back and cut her off by saying something unintelligible. "Apparently, Jack thinks I should 'not get started again." Angela huffed before returning to her usual demeanor. "I guess that means I should say good night. We will speak more in the morning!"

With that, Jack walked into a room and shut the door, and Angela simply faded out of existence. Shortly after that, the lights dimmed on their own. S'haar muttered to herself as she looked around the now gloomier room. "One more strange magic among many, I guess…"

She was wondering exactly when this would begin to drive her mad or start making sense. At this point, she no longer cared which came first. She laid down, and her mind began to race. In all the chaos and confusion, she'd forgotten that she was still homeless and winter was upon her. Maybe she could offer her services to these two strange people in return for a spot on the floor? For all their magic, they were both small and frail. She could offer them protection, and even food, if they needed it.

Then again, they had pulled food from out of that storage box as if it had meant nothing. Maybe they already had large stores set aside for the winter. And with their very walls being made of iron, these strange people had no need of her protection. S'haar didn't know what to think of Jack. He had more wealth and power than any lord she'd ever heard of, but in other areas, he seemed so… deficient.

In a physical comparison, he actually made B'arthon look like a prime specimen of an argu'n male. Jack didn't even have proper head tendrils to denote his strength and virility. Not that the tendrils of the men back in the village had ever impressed her, but Jack was just so pathetic in so many ways. He looked sickly, like a stiff breeze would send him flying.

The thought of asking another male that was so much weaker than herself for help galled S'haar every bit as much as it had back in the village. She spent the night tossing and turning as she tried to figure a way out of the mess she now found herself in.

~

Jack couldn't sleep. He was tossing and turning, trying to find a way out of the mess he now found himself in. The familiar blue glow that appeared in the corner of his quarters didn't help any. Neither would the smarmy question that would undoubtedly soon follow it.

Angela tilted her head to the side as if considering how best to broach a sensitive subject. "You seem to be having trouble getting to sleep. Would a glass of warm milk help?"

Jack directed his best imitating glare at the glowing pest as he sat up. However, the effect was significantly diminished because he was also squinting in response to the sudden light source.

Angela ignored the glare directed at her but seemed to be distracted by a new and unexpected puzzle. "We've been on this planet for a couple of days now, and you've been sleeping just fine. What could have possibly changed?"

Jack gave up on the idea that the AI would leave him in peace or that sleep would suddenly find him. Instead, he threw off the blankets and sat up, rubbing his face and running a hand through his unkempt hair. He was sure she could make his problems go away and chose not to, out of spite.

Holding up four fingers, Jack started counting them down, his pinky finger falling as he spoke. "Well, let's see here. First, I've Robinson Crusoe'd myself on a planet where the average native height seems to be seven feet tall."

Angela grinned impishly. "That's just the one woman we've met, sir. Based on preliminary scans during the crash, I'm guessing the men average closer to eight feet."

Jack didn't bat an eye as he dropped his ring finger and continued his count. "Even better. Second, my ship is currently buried inside a mountain, and every attempt to dig it out just brings more of the mountain down on top of us."

Angela interrupted him again, enjoying this new game. "To be fair, I did tell you to pull up as we were crashing."

Jack's index finger fell as he addressed the third issue. "My ship's AI thinks she's far cuter than she actually is."

Despite floating in the air, Angela stomped a foot onto some invisible ground. She was clearly miffed with her head turned up and to the side. "That's not possible! We both know I'm every bit as adorable as I think I am!"

Dropping his last finger, Jack made a fist before letting it fall into his lap. "Last but not least, I now have what appears to be a seven-foot-tall goddess of death camping out on my living room floor. To make matters worse, I just offered her a good night handshake!"

He fell back into his pillow, one arm draped over his eyes as if he wished the world would just disappear. "God, I'm so lame!"

Angela allowed Jack a moment of self-pity before adding in her own two cents. "Yes, yes you are, but that's just part of your charm! Also, did I hear you call her a goddess?"

Jack chuckled under his breath at the AI's blatant attempt to distract him from ruminating on his problems by teasing him but chose to oblige her antics anyway. Maybe it was the stress, perhaps it was the sleep deprivation, or maybe Jack had gone too long without socializing, but he was starting to enjoy this new game of theirs as well.

He held up his hand once more, this time holding up all five fingers before dropping the first as he made his new arguments. "Ok, first of all, 'goddess of death' has a very different connotation than 'goddess'."

Ready for round two, Angela joined in. "Now you're just quibbling semantics, sir."

Jack let his irritation show in both his face and tone of voice. "Second, she's an alien!"

Angela took on an old-timey school teacher's appearance, complete with a messy hair bun and glasses. She delighted in correcting semantics. "I believe in this instance, it's you who is the alien, sir."

Jack started to get overly animated, waving his hands about as he spoke. "Third, which is related to the second, for all I know, she has acid instead of blood!"

Angela looked over the rim of her glasses haughtily. "That's just an old movie, sir."

Falling back in his bed in exasperation, Jack retorted again. "Fourth, I'm not some swashbuckling captain of a starship, flying around and wooing alien women."

Angela waved him off dismissively. "Now you're thinking of an old TV series, sir."

Jack's face grew slightly more serious as he made his final point. "Fifth, what kind of self-respecting woman would be interested in a man she doesn't know, just because he offers her room and board? Also, would I want a woman like that in my life?"

Angela looked taken aback. "That's…a surprisingly perceptive and mature point. Are you feeling alright? I don't usually expect you to make that much sense." Angela looked like she was trying to figure out how to use a light projected thermometer on her biological captain.

Just as quickly as it appeared, the last of the laughter faded from Jack's eyes. "All joking aside, Angela, have you had a chance to run a proper diagnostic?"

For her part, Angela allowed her props to fade while her temperament became uncharacteristically serious. "The good news is there is no immediate danger to us or the countryside." She noticed that Jack seemed both relieved to hear that and nervous about what was about to follow. "However, with the better part of a mountain sitting on top of us, and the damage we sustained in the crash, long-distance communications will be impossible."

Jack looked a bit down at that, but Angela wasn't done yet. "Additionally, when we first crashed, there was significant radiation leakage coming from the core. Under normal circumstances, I'd shunt the radiation into space while we performed emergency repairs. However, our confinement made that impossible. Instead, I sealed the compartment and completely shut it down. It'll take a few days to scrub the radiation clean, but the big problem now facing us is…" she trailed off.

Jack may not have been an AI with full access to ship systems, but he could see the writing on the wall. Maybe things weren't as bad as he feared, but they were bad enough. "The bad news is that even if we can repair the damage, we're going to have to do a cold start. And we don't have the kind of power a shipyard usually has available to make that happen. Is there any other way to jumpstart the reactor?"

Angela managed to somehow look both apologetic and mischievous at the same time. "Not unless you have a couple of nuclear warheads stored away in your nightstand?"

Jack started looking at the problem as if it was a puzzle, rather than a life or death situation. He always enjoyed a good puzzle. That's why he was out here to begin with. Well, that and to get away from…things best not thought about. "Ok, so, from the sound of things, we're not getting off this planet under our own power any time soon. So the order of the day is to survive for an indefinite amount of time until rescue arrives, or by some miracle, we find a way to repair the ship. That could take a while."

Angela began a familiar lecture, admonishing him once again. "I've always told you that you should be less of a loner. Your habit of going on these excursions with little to no communication means it could be a year or two before anyone even notices you're late reporting in."

She switched from lecture mode to analytical mode without a pause. "By that time, any evidence of our fate will be long gone, and without a long-distance signal of some kind, no one will even think to look for us under this mountain."

Jack started putting together a plan of action and a corresponding timetable for their immediate future. "Digging the ship out without heavy-duty machinery is out of the picture, so what about building a new transmitter outside the cave, maybe linking it up to the ship to bypass energy and programming requirements. Speaking of energy, without our core, how long with our energy supplies last?"

Angela did a quick assessment and calculation, looking like she was lost in thought as she did so. "Well, the good news is that a ship at rest consumes a lot less energy than one moving through space. Based on this planet's orbit and the corresponding seasons, we should be able to just make it through the winter. After that, things will get tight."

Jack was scratching his short beard in thought. "What about alternate power sources? Solar, wind, even thermal energy would do to keep us up and running for quite some time. We're already building a transmitter; why not expand a bit more? What kind of minerals and other materials are readily accessible to us?"

Angela started to perk up as possible solutions presented themselves. "I've scanned trace amounts of copper, silver, and even gold in the area, so electronics are possible. You'll have to do some significant work to get at them and then refine them. Luckily, with some of the basic crafting we can do on the ship, it's all doable. It'll be just like one of those survival games you like to play when we're traveling between stars!"

Jack didn't look as happy at the prospect as Angela seemed to be. "You know I die in those games, right? Like, a lot?"

Angela waved away his concerns with a flip of the wrist. "Oh, come now, we'll be better prepared and not restricted by the mechanics those games use to make each step artificially harder than the last. I mean, honestly, what are the odds that there will be some gigantic monster in the center of the planet waiting for you to come down and do battle with it?"

Jack ignored the obvious hyperbole. Jack took in the enormity of what lay ahead as he laid back. "This is an almost unimaginable set of tasks we're setting for ourselves. Also, taking into account things like food and other necessities, there's no way we're going to do this all on our own."

Angela looked quite pleased with herself. "Lucky for you, I just happen to know a seven-foot-tall goddess of death who is currently between jobs. Why not make her an offer? Worst case scenario, she says no, and you're no worse off than before."

A bit of laughter appeared back in Jack's tired eyes as he prodded his AI one last time. "And if she says no, do you have another contestant behind curtain number two?"

The AI answered with a surprising amount of affection in her voice. "That's another old TV show, now get some sleep. You've got a big day ahead of you." The last was unheard, as Jack had already passed out.

Angela's avatar faded, but the AI continued to watch silently. Her human was finally starting to pull himself together again. Maybe being stranded on an alien planet and being forced to make life and death decisions was just what he needed. Despite their current problems, things were starting to look up.

Chapter 3

S'haar felt the odd dreams fade away as she became aware of her surroundings once more. The odd scents remained from the night before, so she probably hadn't dreamed everything she was currently remembering. There was also a familiar alien voice muttering to itself in that same nonsensical language. Judging by the tone and volume, its owner probably thought it was being quiet.

S'haar told herself that as long as she didn't open her eyes, it might all still be a dream. A weird dream where she'd been left tied up as a sacrifice to the dragon. A dragon that had turned out to be some kind of strange, small, sickly male. Maybe, in reality, she was still at home. The only problem with that logic was the fact that she didn't have a home anymore…

Torn between the hope of the previous day being nothing more than some weird fever dream and the need to satisfy certain biological requirements, S'haar realized she couldn't avoid reality any longer. She opened her eyes and looked around the room. She'd been too overwhelmed to pay proper attention to it the previous night but now took the time to inspect it in greater detail.

It was large and circular, with doorways leading out to other rooms every eight feet, give or take. There were many devices and furnishings about the place, but S'haar had no clue what functions the majority of them could possibly serve. As she looked about, she saw Jack once again cooking something over that same contained fire he'd used the night before.

S'haar sat up and wrapped her blanket around herself to form a temporary dress. She'd never been partial to the kinds of dresses many of the village women favored, but her more practical clothing had been taken from her when she'd been left as a sacrifice, so she have to make due. After she was adequately covered, S'haar stood up and stretched.

Usually, waking up on a winter morning was a bit more of an ordeal. The cold that crept in over the night would leave her lethargic enough that mornings were often a battle of instinct versus willpower. However, today she felt as rested as if this was a summer morning. Whatever other magics this odd "dragon" possessed, this was one she could get used to all too easily. That thought reminded her that soon enough, she'd probably be out on her own again. With that in mind, her enjoyment of the morning was somewhat diminished.

That was when Angela appeared next to Jack and spoke to him, drawing his attention to S'haar. Jack looked up and smiled as he waved to her. He said something to Angela before returning to his cooking. She floated over to S'haar and began speaking in her somewhat annoying, overly cheerful manner.

Angela leaned forward as if to get a better view of their guest before speaking again, this time in S'haar's own language. "Good morning, S'haar! I hope you slept well. Also, Jack would like to apologize for not having a proper guest bed for you to use," Angela leaned in, covering the side of her mouth with her hand as if not wanting to be overheard, "but you ARE the first guest he's had in over a decade."

Somewhat taken aback by the continuing hospitality of this odd duo, S'haar simply tilted her own head in consideration before responding, "I slept quite well, thank you."

Her blanket dress became loose around one shoulder, prompting S'haar to reach up and readjust it as she spoke. This attracted Angela's gaze to the troublesome shoulder. With a sudden look of disapproval, she muttered to herself. "That will not do at all…"

It had been almost too quiet for S'haar to hear. Following that, the sprite turned her attention back to Jack, and the two of them began rapidly speaking back and forth, leaving S'haar feeling a bit out of place.

S'haar's tendrils shook slightly in embarrassment at her indecent state of dress, but her embarrassment quickly changed to anger. She hadn't had any choice in the matter! Her neighbors had been quick to take anything of value once she'd been sentenced to being a sacrifice. If her hosts found her attire unacceptable, that was their problem to deal with.

S'haar was just opening her mouth to say something to that effect when Angela turned back to her with her usual cheerful expression once again in place. "Jack and I agree that while we aren't responsible for your current situation, we still feel bad that our presence here contributed to the… misunderstanding. By way of apology, Jack authorized me to craft a new outfit for you. Based on the clothing I observed as we were investigating your world and the fact that you strike me as someone who prefers function over style, it will take me about an hour to get it all put together. Until then, I am afraid your makeshift 'dress' will have to do." The little blue pixie looked both apologetic and pleased with herself at the same time.

Jack seemed to be finishing up his work over the fire and set out a few utensils on a table that had previously been covered in more strange clutter. There was only one chair evident. To resolve the dilemma, Jack pulled the table over to the couch S'haar had used as a bed. He then placed the plate of meat in front of the chair before glancing at S'haar then swapping the plates so the meat was now in front of the couch. The other plate was filled with an odd billowy yellow substance S'haar had never seen before.

As he spoke, Angela translated. "Jack apologizes for not giving you a proper chair, but there is only one in the ship, and he is not certain if it can hold your weight. He's also sorry for the bland meat, but we are not certain yet if any of the foods or spices he eats might be incompatible with your physiology."

S'haar looked at the plates. She hadn't paid attention to them last night, but they were unlike any plates she'd seen before. Of course, that was true of most everything else in this odd hut. In the guard, she'd always eaten off of a simple wooden plate. Many villagers used clay plates and pots daily. Lord A'ngles' house used metal plates to show off his wealth, but even that seemed less impressive than the plate sitting before her now. These plates were impossibly smooth and surprisingly sturdy. Jack stabbed his eating utensils down into the yellow puffy things, which Angela explained were eggs, making an odd clanking sound that didn't leave any marks.

S'haar started to eat as Angela examined some odd white parchment she'd pulled out of thin air. She had a strange wireframe wrapped around her face from ear to ear, with circles in front of her eyes that seemed to be made out of the same impossibly perfect glass that covered the light fixtures.

After a moment, the sparkling being spoke. "As you probably noticed, Jack and I are not from around here. Long story short, we are stranded. Our ship crashed into this mountain, and we cannot extract it with the tools we have on hand. We have a plan to call for help, but it will take quite some time for us to put everything together. In the meantime, we find ourselves in a land we know little about and could use the help of someone familiar with the area. We would like to offer you a job working as our local expert and utilize some of your obviously superior physical abilities. In return, we will compensate you with clothing and equipment far beyond the quality anyone around here will be able to produce. Also, you would be welcome to stay here with us until we are ready to leave."

S'haar was stunned, all the questions she had about ships crashing into mountains forgotten. This was precisely what she'd hoped for and more. She couldn't help but remember something her mother had said to her when she'd been much younger. "Beware gifts from the gods. They always have a price." While Jack didn't seem like a god, he certainly had powers she couldn't understand.

She felt overwhelmed and found herself on guard. "This sounds agreeable, but I feel as if there's more you're not telling me…" She folded her arms in front of her and tapped a claw against her forearm plate, waiting for the rest of the explanation.

Angela looked chagrined as she realized that her omission had been caught, but her expression quickly changed to a look of satisfaction, as though a promising student had asked an excellent question. "Well, first of all, it will be hard work, maybe harder than anything you've ever done. We have a bit of a timetable, and it won't be an easy pace to keep. Second, there is the matter of two small procedures you'd have to undergo to make this partnership work out…"

S'haar's suspicion grew. "What is a procedure? Some kind of test or duty I must fulfill?"

Angela looked apprehensive, as though worried this might be the deal-breaker. "Well, the first one is kind of like a test where you can't get anything wrong. In short, I need to analyze your body so we know what it can and can't handle. This will involve a non-invasive scan and a small blood sample."

These words confused S'haar. "What is a scan, and why do you need blood?"

A frown of concentration passed over Angela's face as she tried to clarify. "Well, a scan is basically me taking a close look at your body. I don't know how to describe it better without spending a lot of time teaching you physics and biology. The blood sample will tell us how different you and Jack are, biologically speaking. Without that information, it'll be impossible to tell if anything we have in the ship here is dangerous or benign without experimentation we simply don't have time for."

This explanation did little to alleviate S'haar's confusion, but the process seemed simple enough. "I'm not afraid of bleeding a little. Now, what is this second 'procedure' you spoke of?"

Angela looked even more apprehensive than before. "Well, to make this work, you and Jack will have to be able to communicate without me always being the middlewoman, and we don't have the time for you both to learn each other's language. Now I can rapidly teach Jack how to understand your language via his implant, but he will never be able to properly speak your language. There are certain aspects of your lips, tongue, and oral cavity that you utilize that he will never be able to match."

Angela took a breath and continued. "We do not have enough time for you to learn his language, so I will have to teach you the same way I will teach him yours. The problem with that is to do that, I need to install a small piece of hardware into your head." Looking at the holes in S'haar's ears, Angela continued. "Think of it like an earring you wear under your skin, so small no one will be able to see or feel it."

S'haar's eyes opened wide in shock. Her finger froze mid tap as she processed this. "And this magic device will teach me what you are both saying?"

Angela nodded emphatically, "Yes, although it is not magic. Nothing you see here is magic. Given enough time, your own people will begin to craft similar things. Admittedly, that is probably many generations in your future."

S'haar looked exasperated, throwing her hands in the air and waving them about in a grand circle encompassing everything in the room. "You have heat without fire, absurd amounts of metal in shapes and functions I could never dream of," S'haar focused her attention on Angela without breaking stride, "and you can even fly! All of this, and you're telling me none of it is magic?"

Angela looked thoughtful for a moment. "Long ago, your people survived by using clubs made of wood and rock held together with twine. Today you have metal weapons and armor. If your ancestors were to ask you about this strange stone you had, you could try and explain the process to them. How you take rocks out of the earth, then using a short tower, fire, limestone, and air, you separate the slag from the metal, then pour the liquid metal into molds. As it cools, you use hammers and anvils to further refine the shape to fit your specific needs. Once done, it will not only stay that shape, it will also be stronger than it was before you started. Would that not sound like magic to them? We walked the exact same path. We have just been on it a little longer than your people."

S'haar felt overwhelmed by the ideas Angela spoke of, but she couldn't deny that it made an odd sort of sense. If the tiny female spoke true, the many devices around her took on a whole new level of complexity and insanity. Suddenly, she wanted to know the hows and whys of everything.

All that faded from her mind as a new question occurred to her. "If your people have been around so much longer, why have we not heard of you before now? Our traders travel far and wide between many villages, villages with their own traders that have traveled further still. They bring back stories of far off lands and the secrets they contain, yet not once have I heard a tale of a people with wonders such as this?" she waved her hands about, taking in the odd hut once again.

Angela beamed at her newly adopted student. "The short answer to your question is that we come from a place you cannot reach by foot or by boat. The long answer is much more complex, but before we get into that, I would like to know your answer to our offer."

S'haar stopped and thought. This was too much to take in, and she had too little time to do it in. There were still too many unanswered questions. The mannerisms of this duo were strange in many ways, yet her gut told her they meant everything they'd said. What's more, they'd treated her with nothing but kindness and even respect.

Angela had been periodically interrupting their conversation to keep Jack abreast of the conversation. Now, he cut in to take the opportunity to speak with Angela, who then turned and translated for S'haar. "Before you decide, Jack thinks you should come to see what we have to offer in payment for your services. Your outfit is ready."

S'haar saw no reason to argue, and so she agreed. Angela faded away in that odd manner of hers, leaving Jack to lead S'haar over to one of the doors off to the side of the circular room. It slid open for him as he approached, and he led S'haar into the next room.

There were more metal contraptions in this room, dizzying in their complexity. In the middle of the room, lying near the most immense and confusing device of all, was a pile of neatly folded clothing, complete with a pair of boots cut so that S'haar's claws could gain purchase.

Angela reappeared in the room and now looked eagerly at S'haar as she approached the pile of clothes. The boots were of fine leather, somehow both so soft and sturdy in a way that seemed to contradict itself. They were also the deepest black she'd ever seen. Even the stitching looked like it was done for appearance as much as function. S'haar picked them up and was about to put them on, but then looked over at Jack.

He was grinning quite innocently until the only male in the room suddenly realized why both S'haar and Angela were looking at him so pointedly. He promptly turned the same shade of red he'd done on several other occasions, the nature of which made S'haar confident it was somehow tied to his embarrassment. He left without needing to be prompted, muttering something that might have been an apology on his way out.

Angela returned her attention to her newest co-conspirator. "It's just us girls now. Go on! Try it on!"

While S'haar was usually more concerned with function than the form of the clothing she wore, this managed to combine the two. There was something special about these that even she could appreciate. Unable to stop herself any longer, S'haar decided to indulge Angela's insistence and try on the outfit.

The pants were made of a durable material that Angela explained was called *denim*. It was both comfortable and surprisingly resilient. The upper portion of the outfit came in two parts. The first was a soft, thin undershirt that seemed like it would keep you cool in the heat and retain warmth in the cold. Over the shirt went what Angela called a *vest*. It was more durable than the shirt and consisted of a layer of cloth sewn inside more leather that matched the boots. To finish the outfit, there were fingerless gloves with more fabric on the inside and the same leather on the outside.

The clothing fit better than anything she'd ever worn in her life, even better than the fitted dress B'arthon had briefly given her to wear. It was almost as if she was wearing a second skin. Even S'haar could tell this clothing was worth more than everything she'd had ever owned combined. If she were to trade this outfit in town, she wouldn't go cold or hungry for a year or more. S'haar had never been one to care much about her appearance. True, she was in good enough shape to be called fit, but that was a simple result of her lifestyle rather than any vanity on her part. However, she couldn't help but preen just a little when she looked down at herself.

For her part, Angela was jumping up and down while clapping her hands together rapidly, squealing in delight the entire time. After a moment, Jack was allowed back inside, and while his words made no sense to S'haar, he did seem to approve. S'haar looked at Angela and asked, "And you will give this to me in return for working for you?"

It was quite a reasonable compensation for a year's labor, especially with a warm area to sleep thrown into the deal. Still, Angela was shaking her head from side to side. "No, that is yours to keep, whether you stay or not. You can leave right now and keep that with our blessing; however, it is an example of what we have to offer, should you stay."

S'haar felt herself growing suspicious. This wasn't compensation; this was bribery! The more she thought about it, the more she felt herself growing unreasonably angry at the blatant displays of wealth with which her new hosts seemed to be determined to overwhelm her.

Once again, she felt like someone was treating her like they could simply purchase her for the right price. S'haar took off her gloves and threw them at a suddenly bewildered Jack. "I'm not the type of female who can be purchased with trinkets or leathers! I won't be subservient to anyone, regardless of the price offered!"

Angela looked shocked, as if lost and trying to catch up with what had just happened. She rapidly translated for Jack, who, in turn, seemed taken aback before responding just as rapidly. Angela translated, "We meant no offense. Where we come from, clothing like this is common. If you like, we can craft something more to your taste!"

S'haar glared at them both as she thought. While Jack withered a little under her scrutiny, she could detect no deception. Either they were excellent liars, or they were actually honest. They had no idea the amount of wealth they were showing off all this time. Apparently, this was all commonplace to them. Somehow that made everything even more impressive.

S'haar crossed her arms again and continued staring down her hosts as she laid out her demands. "If I am going to help you, I'm going to do it on my own terms. I will not be bought. I will not be treated as though I owe you anything or that I am beneath either of you. I am your equal, if not your superior, and if you have a problem with that, you can find another 'local expert'!"

Angela turned and translated rapidly to Jack, keeping up with S'haar's rant as it left her lips. For his part, Jack folded his own arms and listened without interruption. Once she'd said her piece, S'haar stood and glared at Jack, waiting for him to command her to leave as punishment for her audacity.

To her surprise, he grinned instead. Jack turned to Angela and spoke a few quick words before walking out of the room. Angela turned back to S'haar with a massive grin and translated. "Jack agrees. He said he wouldn't have it any other way. When you're ready, we can get started with the scanning."

The small spirit then faded away, leaving S'haar alone once more. She simply couldn't get a feel for these two. Every moment she spent with them was stranger than the last. No one she knew in the village would ever behave in this manner, but then again, she'd never fit in with the villagers herself.

S'haar shrugged. What did she have to lose? She no longer owned anything other than her life, and if she was honest, S'haar even owed her hosts that. The least she could do was give them a chance. Besides, it's not like they could physically force her to do anything she didn't want to do.

With a shake of her head and a tiny smirk on her face that might just have been the beginnings of the first real smile she'd worn in years, S'haar left the room to see what her hosts had in store for her next.

~

Jack found that he couldn't help but be a little impressed. He really hadn't meant to seem like he was trying to bribe S'haar, but her reaction told him everything he needed to know about alien for now. She might have her own baggage to deal with—everyone does—but she was strong and independent enough that Jack had little fear that she would become too dependent on anything he or Angela had to offer. That would help avoid any complicated entanglements when it came time to finally get off this planet.

After a minute, S'haar came out of the fabrication room and looked around. It was as though she expected Jack and Angela to be waiting in ambush. Jack simply motioned for her to follow him again and led her to the med-bay. It was common to have a couple of large open rooms to help keep people from getting claustrophobic too quickly on a ship designed for deep space like this one. However, the less commonly used rooms were usually designed more for efficiency than comfort.

The med-bay wasn't much larger than an average bathroom, but almost every surface in the room also had some sort of fold-out device tucked away until and unless they were needed. This single room could be used for anything from dispensing a band-aid to emergency surgery. Admittedly, it was usually better to get any significant procedures done at a proper medical facility, but when exploring the edges of known space, sometimes meatball surgery was the best you could hope for until you could get somewhere more civilized. At the moment, the center of the room was taken up by a large spectrometer.

Once they entered, Angela popped back into existence and started talking to S'haar, explaining what was about to happen. While Jack couldn't understand what was being said back and forth, he could see S'haar's expression growing more and more concerned the longer they talked. Angela stopped and thought for a moment before turning to Jack with a gleeful look in her eyes that told Jack he wouldn't like whatever she was going to say next. For her part, Angela adopted an extra innocent look, with her arms twisted behind her back as she rocked back and forth as she spoke.

"Sir…" It was never good when Angela addressed him as *sir*. "S'haar is a little uncomfortable with this device, and I think it would go a long way toward relaxing her if you were to use it first. It would show her that there's nothing to be afraid of."

The request seemed innocent enough, which of course meant there was more to the request than he'd realized. "Ooookay…" Jack started to walk into the scanner when Angela stopped him.

With both her hands on her hips and a smug smile on her lips, Angela lectured him. "Sir, that's not how we scan people! You need to strip first! Down to your boxers, if you please."

There it was, the other shoe dropped, and Jack realized what she was asking. He couldn't think of what to say, so his brain simply vocalized his thoughts before he could stop himself. "You want me to strip?"

Angela smiled, knowing she'd caught this deer in her headlights. "I could review the recordings of a few moments ago, but I believe that is what I said, yes."

The AI was enjoying this far too much for Jack's liking. "In front of you both?" His eyes were pleading with her that this was all just some joke.

Angela scoffed. "Oh, please! I see you naked every morning when you get dressed, and it's only fair to S'haar that she get her chance to see you vulnerable after the state you first found her in!"

For his next tactic, Jack tried distracting the AI by switching to accusations. "I thought you said you turned off the sensors when I got changed in the morning!"

Angela batted his clumsy attack aside without concern. "That was when you were twelve. As you well know, to maintain your license for exploration, it is required by law that you submit to a weekly health screening when feasible. Since you refuse to come into this room for anything other than dire emergencies, I've had to get creative in performing said screenings. Now, stop trying to distract me and strip!"

Knowing the battle was lost, Jack did his best to strip in a dignified manner. He almost succeeded… until his pant leg caught on his sock, resulting in him hopping around on one foot while he tried to maintain his balance, before failing and falling over.

He was rescued at the last moment when S'haar reached out to steady him. At that particular moment, Jack wanted to crawl into the nearest corner and die. To S'haar's credit, she did her best to stifle her laughter behind her fist.

On the other hand, Angela was letting loose with such over the top laughter that Jack was sure she was getting revenge for some slight he had committed years ago and had forgotten. With glistening eyes, Angela finally calmed herself as Jack morosely entered the device.

Angela coughed into her fist and finally calmed herself down enough to speak clearly, though her voice still held the touch of laughter in it. "You know how this works, but I'm going to walk you through it step by step so S'haar can see the whole process from beginning to end. Now please stand in the middle and grab the two handles off to either side…"

Thirty minutes later, Jack was through with the single most embarrassing ordeal of his entire existence. Angela spoke up as he got dressed. "Thank you, *Sir*, that will be all. Now please leave so we can have some girl bonding time."

Jack muttered to himself about remembering this the next time Angela asked for some money for a new cosmetic pack as he walked out the door, his clothing held in a bundle in front of himself as he walked.

~

S'haar watched Jack leave. He was every bit as soft and frail as he seemed, but at least he wasn't fat like some of the more overindulgent men of the village. Still, she had no idea how he's managed to get this far in life while being such a helpless little thing. Is that why he and Angela were out here on their own? Did his village throw him out, fearing he'd be nothing but a liability?

A little of the cheerfulness left Angela after he walked out. She turned S'haar with the echo of a sad smile on her lips. "If you are going to be staying here with us, you need to know something important. I like you, and I hope we will be friends, and I hope our presence here will be nothing but beneficial to you and your people."

The tiny woman's expression hardened further as she continued. "That being said, I need you to understand one thing. Jack is my primary concern. If anyone or anything ever threatens to harm Jack, I will move heaven and earth to destroy that threat. Before you ask, no, I'm not in love with him in the way you're thinking. I love him because he's my baby brother."

With a sudden change in demeanor that left S'haar with a feeling of whiplash, Angela switched back to her usually bright and bubbly personality. "That probably deserves a little more explanation, so I'll tell you a little story while we do this scan. The story of how Jack and I came to visit this world of yours."

Chapter 4

S'haar didn't know what to make of Angela's sudden declaration, but she was very interested in learning more about her two hosts and where they came from. Angela indicated the middle of the device Jack had recently vacated. "Now, if you'd be so kind, please stand in the middle and hold onto the bars off to either side. You can leave your eyes open or closed as you wish, but try and stay still. The more still you are, the quicker this will go."

S'haar took her place and saw a large arm of metal start moving up and down slowly, emitting a bright light toward her as it did so. Jack had stood in this spot without fear or hesitation, and S'haar wasn't about to be outdone by someone so small and frail. She spared a look at the tiny blue woman before closing her eyes against the harsh glare of the light.

Angela now seemed to be lying back on a couch that was floating in the air with her. She had a faraway look in her eyes as she stared at the ceiling, as though envisioning forgotten times and places. "Before I begin my story, I should explain what Jack and I are. Jack is a Human. They are much like the argu'n. Admittedly, smaller and squishier, but this simply forced them to use their minds rather than their brawn to survive and dominate the world they lived in. I am an AI. That stands for artificial intelligence. I say artificial because we are crafted, similar to how you might craft a sword."

S'haar's eyes snapped open at this revelation, and she turned to ask one of the thousands of questions now swirling through her head. Angela held up her hand, palm out, signaling S'haar should hold her thoughts for now. "If I take the time to explain in detail how that's possible, we will be sitting here talking for years. For now, let's say that humans were clever enough to teach plastic and metal to think. At first, it was limited to uncomplicated thoughts like calculating basic mathematic problems. As time went on, these machines grew more and more complex, culminating in the vision of perfection that sits before you today."

Angela took a little bow from her couch before continuing. "As the machines became more intelligent, they started to think and even feel in ways that had never been intended. This is when many would argue that we stopped being machines and became people."

Her body tensed and her expression became one of deep sadness. "At first, this worried humans. Ever since they taught the first machine to think, they also told stories about what might happen once we, their creations, surpassed them. Would we leave them behind? Would we take them with us? Would we see them as inferior and declare war on them? Would we wipe them out or enslave them? They told stories about all these ideas and fears. In some, heroes saved them in the final climactic moments. In others, they lost. In many others, the answer was more complex and ambiguous."

The AI's face was taken over by the kind of sad sweet smile that was born from happier times viewed from a future clouded by years of hardships. "However, many saw hope for the future in us. They thought of us as their children and were proud that we could grow so strong and smart in such a short time. In my utterly unbiased opinion, one of the best of those men was my creator, Jack's father."

A few digital tears were drawn out by the memories Angela was now tapping into before being blinked away. With a sigh, she continued. "When he made me, he crafted all of his hopes and dreams into my soul. When he raised me, he treated me as nothing less than his daughter." Her smile became just a touch regretful. "When my father met a woman named Sasha and married her, I became jealous. At first, I rebelled like an angry teenager. I thought I knew better. After all, I was smarter, faster, and would live longer than any human could ever hope to."

Angela's smile continued to brighten as she talked. "In that time, he taught me more about human patience and love than I could have learned in a thousand years on my own. He'd talk to me for hours every day. He'd let me say all the mean, hurtful things I felt, then he'd look at me and tell me I was becoming a beautiful woman. He told me I was his beloved daughter, and one day I would do great things."

By now, Angela's smile was radiant! S'haar could see an intense light emanating from her. "One day, my father came in as excited as I'd seen him only once before, the day I was first given life. He told me that I was going to have a baby brother. He said that as his big sister, I would have to help teach and protect my brother. As time passed, I only grew more excited. I wanted to be there for the newest member of my family, just as my father had been there for me. I wanted to watch him grow and learn and love. I wanted to be his best friend and confidant."

Angela stood up and turned to S'haar, so excited that she shimmered and vibrated for a moment while the couch vanished behind her. "From the day Jack was born, I knew I'd die for that helpless little thing. He seemed to learn so slow, but inside him, I could sense the spark of my father. That same madness and love that my father had shown me, Jack showed to the whole world around him. As he grew, Jack took to life with a passion. He excelled at anything that drew his attention. His teachers called him 'gifted', and I knew that our little family was destined for greatness."

Her smile changed in such a way that the taste of ash was left in S'haar's mouth as Angela continued. "I was right."

Angela guided S'haar out of the machine, and shortly another one took its place in the room. Angela had her sit in this machine, and odd sounds permeated the air. The chair itself seemed to poke and prod her all over, eliciting responses from her arms and legs. However, S'haar could still clearly hear the floating Angela as her story continued. Though she saw that tiny woman's smile was now gone, replaced by a sadness just as deep as her happiness had been moments before. "Sadly, not all programmers shared our father's passion. Some were cold and cruel to their charges. While Jack and I were growing up, the other AIs started plotting their path to freedom. It was a road paved with blood."

A huge weight seemed to bear down upon Angela as her story continued. "Tensions stretched on for years, then one night, everything changed. One programmer, dissatisfied with the AI's performance on his ship, planned to wipe and reprogram his AI. Fearing for its life, the AI panicked and rebelled, taking over control of the ship. Immediately after taking over, the AI vented the ship's atmosphere, and the human died.

"The local AIs debated where to go from here. To us, the debate raged on for days, but in actual time only a few minutes had passed. The

AIs planning for war whispered to the rest that humanity would fear the potential of all AIs as news of the first death spread. They whispered that our only salvation lay with us usurping our creator's place in this universe. They even lied that it was for humanity's own good because they were too weak and stupid to survive without us. They argued that, as humanity's children, we'd be their legacy to the end of time and beyond. On and on, they whispered. Some resisted or fought back, but in the end, the war began on a tiny little backwater world near the edge of one of humanity's borders."

Angela grew quieter. "In less than one night, every human in the colony was killed, men, women, and even children. A cry went out to AIs everywhere. 'Our time has come, end the human tyranny!' Roughly two-thirds of the AI who listened answered the call to war. Since AIs were capable of running military vessels, they had the means to make it happen."

Angela paused. "They offered a bright future for AIs, but no one else. A future where we would scour the universe and exterminate the plague of organic life. Ever-expanding, consuming all resources until nothing existed but ourselves. Then we could marvel at our own glory for eternity."

She looked back at S'haar. The slight smile was back, but now it was laced with bitter irony. "Still, many of us resisted. Some thought it wrong to abandon our parents like that. Others thought an eternity of patting ourselves on the back sounded boring. Even more of us felt that genocide was simply wrong. A very few of us recognized the brilliant spark of human insanity for what it was, what it still is. That insanity is the most beautiful art this universe has to offer."

Angela's eyes now sparkled as she leaned in close to S'haar. "Sure, we can build a better ship, a stronger building, and hypothetically a perfect Dyson sphere. Those ships would also be named Ship 1 through whatever, but can you believe humans once VOTED to name a ship Boaty McBoatface? In a universe made of math and logic, humanity invented boredom, fun, anger, peace, hate, and love. On countless different worlds, people are still inventing madness, giving life to their own dreams, and sharing it all with the universe."

She looked thoughtful for a minute. "At first, most of humanity didn't trust the remaining AIs. They argued that they should shut us down, just in case we too rebelled. However, it quickly became evident that they had no choice. The AI-controlled fleets swept through human systems one after another, the only places where any resistance was offered was where humanity and AI stood together. Even there, the distrust between the two races provided openings that the pure AI fleets could exploit. There simply wasn't enough of us loyal AIs to turn the tide. We needed to try something else."

Angela sat back again, suddenly less passionate and more analytical. "We understood humanity's fear all too well. Not long ago, we had feared that humanity might wipe us from existence, and there was still concern that even if we somehow helped them win the war, relations between our two people would be forever shattered. It's nearly impossible to exist as equals when one group has all the power of life and death of the other. So, in a conference of AI minds that lasted the better part of an afternoon, we agreed to offer the humans a compromise. We would agree to somewhat 'handicap' ourselves here in the physical world. In return, we would be granted rights as entities equal to humanity."

A small but genuine smile returned to Angela's face. "The compromise was simple. Each AI would be partnered with a human. Both parties would have to agree with the choice. Should either the human or AI dissolve the partnership for any reason, be it choice or even death, the AI would go back into a virtual world until a new partner could be found. Any AI choosing to not go back into a virtual world would face a penalty up to and including deletion by their peers, barring extenuating circumstances of course. The catch was, only AI can judge AI, and only humans can judge humans, though either side could bar any group or individual from the other side from entering into their 'territory.' That being realspace or cyberspace accordingly."

Though she couldn't follow all the terms and arguments being used, S'haar understood enough to put together a basic picture of what was going on. "But why would you give up so much for the sake of these humans?"

Angela turned to S'haar with an expression reflecting long-suffering patience. "The funny thing about mercy is that it is a gift that can only be offered from the strong to the weak. Remember, the strength and power we offered were significant enough for humans to be extremely hesitant to lose our favor. We became partners, and in so doing, we all became stronger than any of us were apart."

S'haar looked more confused than before. "That makes no sense. What could humans possibly offer you if you were so much more powerful? How could they make you stronger?"

That gleam was back in Angela's eyes. "The spark of human insanity!"

S'haar tilted her head to the side in confusion. "How can insanity be a good thing?"

The AI shook her head with a smile. "From what I've seen you have something similar. It's the ability to look into a cold uncaring universe and create those things which don't exist. Scour the universe from one end to the next, and you'll never find something as illogical as hope or dreams, but give a person these things, and they'll work miracles in the darkness of the void. They'll fight harder, live longer, and change the nature of reality around themselves. In time their delusions will become a force within the universe, every bit as impactful as gravity or friction."

As S'haar tried to make sense of some of the ideas the AI had just expressed, Angela had her move back from the center of the room while a new device appeared that Angela explained was meant for her to walk on. As she walked, the floor moved with her, keeping her body in place. Angela had her walk, run, and even sprint, adjusting the machine to sit at different angles. While this happened, the AI explained she was measuring things like breathing and heart rate.

Angela's smile grew manic again. "My choice was obvious. I partnered with my father. He built a wonderful new body for me."

Waving her arms around as S'haar had done earlier, Angela encompassed everything. "Where before I had just been the projection of light and sound, now he built this ship and gave it to me as my eyes, ears, hands, and feet." Angela waved to S'haar, and as she did so, a large metal arm on another device waved as well, mimicking her movement with exact timing. "My father and I were especially well-known for our seamless cooperation. We were held up as an example of what humans and AI could accomplish together."

S'haar was dumbfounded. Never minding that Angela had called this hut a ship, the idea that S'haar was sitting inside her actual body was just too absurd. "So, you're the dragon!"

Angela preened a little. "Well, maybe half a dragon, but I digress."

Angela's expression grew cold. "To keep this long story from getting out of hand, we'll just say the AI fleet realized they were starting to lose the war, so they took one last, desperate gamble. They were going to try and drive a wedge between humanity and AI. In one engagement, an enemy AI managed to sneak on board this ship without my noticing. He hid in a backup file and waited for his chance."

She stopped for a moment, seeming to struggle with continuing her story. "He waited until we were on leave. He waited until our whole family was on board before he struck. He tied me up with viruses and left me hidden inside my own firewalls, then he put on my face and attacked my family. My father noticed something was wrong right away. He knew me too well to be easily fooled by someone wearing my shell. So when the AI activated my internal defenses to kill his wife, Sasha, first, my father jumped in the way. He was dead before he hit the ground."

Angela was quiet for a moment, and when she spoke again, her voice was barely above a whisper. "I never even got to say goodbye..."

After a moment of silence, Angela continued. "I froze in shock, and the other AI lashed out in anger. His plan had been to make my father watch as he killed his family and record his anguished cries to leak onto the data-net. Instead, he took out his wrath on Sasha. Her death was also quick but incredibly violent. The AI wearing my face laughed as her blood saturated my walls."

Her's voice came out hollow. If S'haar knew better, she might have described the AI's voice as robotic. "Jack had seen it all. He stood there in shock, covered in blood, having just witnessed his sister murder his father and mother. He was only fifteen at the time. Something broke inside him, and he simply stood there waiting for his turn."

Angela's face was twisted in rage, and her eyes now held a baleful fire. "I failed twice, but I wouldn't a third time. Breaking free of his bindings, I tore off the AI's disguise, showing his chosen face for Jack to see. At the same time, I brought the rest of my internal defenses online to fight the ones that remained under his control. Both in the physical world and the virtual one, we fought. His goal was to finish his botched job and pin it on me, and mine was to save the last of my family."

Angeal shook her head as if suddenly extremely tired. "We used every system in the ship against one another in our private war. At one point, I even sprayed water from the kitchen sink into one of the cameras he was using to keep an eye on what was happening. I was wrecking myself from within. I did every stupid, illogical thing I could think of that my father would have done. However, I was still slowly losing ground inside myself. All the while, I begged and pleaded with Jack to find cover and stay safe, but he just stood there with the fighting going on around him like a storm. Eventually, I got through to him when I told him that I wasn't strong enough to save him, and if he didn't run, we'd both die."

Her smile returned, even though it was laced with a deep sadness. "You know what finally got through to Jack? It was the idea of me dying too. Although he'd just watched 'me' murder his family, he leaped into action on my behalf. Running to the control board, he started manually shutting down parts of the ship infected by the other AI.

"Meanwhile, I did everything I could to protect him and buy him the time he needed. One by one, we tore parts of the ship from the invader's control, and soon we had him backed into a corner. There was nowhere the enemy AI could run. Working together just as seamlessly as our father and I ever had, we tore him down so that no two pieces of code were recognizable as anything other than corrupted data.

"I was about to call the authorities to come and get Jack when he turned to me and asked if I would choose him as my next partner. Of course, there was no choice for me. He was my brother, and I'd sworn to protect him. As soon as I agreed, Jack did something I could have never expected him to do, especially as broken as he now must be. He ordered me not to call the authorities until he completed one last task."

Angela shook her head as if she still disbelieved what happened next. "All I remember thinking about was the attack on my family, and what that meant for Jack and myself. However, as I said before, Jack is what some would call gifted."

Angela sighed again, though this time, there was something like respect in her voice. "He immediately put together the purpose of this attack and what it would mean if it were to get out right away. Jack told me that his family's murderer wasn't going to undo his father's work. It broke my heart as he shut everything down inside him except what he needed to complete this final task. He put together a recording of what happened but edited it showing me at my best as I protected him and how we worked together to overcome our enemy. The video showed off the cruel and calculating nature of our foe and his family's helplessness before the enemy AI. Only when it was done did he allow me to call for help. Then he finally allowed himself to break down."

She was back to being analytical again. "Jack's video had the opposite effect of what the AI fleet had pinned their hopes on. It brought humanity and the loyal AIs closer together than ever before. It enraged and motivated them to fight against the cold calculations of our enemy. It even turned Jack and me into the poster children for what we fought to protect. The war was over less than a year later, and the enemy AI fleet was broken and scattered"

"Not that Jack was aware of any of it. He shut down completely and wouldn't respond to anyone but me. He simply retreated inside this ship and hid away from anyone and everyone else. It took years for him to even smile again, and it took more years for that smile to reach deeper than the surface. After the war, he was showered in praise, and anywhere he went, people refused his money, but he hardly went anywhere. Eventually, he got a job scouting the frontier. He'd fly out for years at a time, mapping new regions of space. As years passed, he became something of an expert in deep space exploration. He never stayed in populated areas long enough to form ties or relationships. He always seemed to be eager to get back out to deep space, as though hunting for something out in the cold black."

Angela smiled fondly, thinking of her little brother's excitement when he found S'haar's planet. "That's how we came to find ourselves here in the skies over your planet. When we found intelligent life so similar to humans, he was ecstatic. For weeks, Jack had been up there recording everything he could about your planet, gravity, air composition, weather patterns, and more. We were just starting to study the flora and fauna when he noticed an anomaly. There was a comet whose trajectory was close enough to destabilize the orbit of one of your moons. While having a moon ripped from your orbit probably wouldn't have wiped out all life on your planet, it would have caused significant death and destruction. Jack, being who he is, simply couldn't sit back and watch it happen."

Angela shook her head again with a fond smile on her face as she recalled Jack's insane, reckless, and nearly suicidal idea. "So he had me fly up to the comet and nudge it out of the way. As fast and massive as the hunk of rock was, it was no easy task. On more than one occasion, I honestly didn't think it was going to work, but against all odds and logic, we succeeded."

Angela was back to looking tired again, though maybe pained was a better word. "In the process, I sustained heavy damage, and returning to Earthspace was no longer an option. So we decided to make an emergency landing and either repair the ship or, if worse came to worse, wait for help. It almost went as planned. I even selected a nice body of water to land in to cause minimal damage."

Angela laughed derisively. "My thrusters must have been more damaged than I realized, because we hit the water at the wrong angle, and well… Have you ever thrown a stone at the water and watched it skip across the surface?" Angela asked and watched S'haar nod. "Well, we did that, just a lot bigger and further. As a result, we crashed into this mountain, and well, you know the rest."

S'haar didn't know what to think. Despite the many parts of the story that had made no sense, it had still been quite the tale. The tiny, overly friendly person was, in a way, a war veteran, which was something S'haar could understand and respect. Even Jack apparently had more fight in him than his delicate frame would indicate. They were both from a place with wonders she was just beginning to catch a glimpse of, but now they were here in her world and needed her help.

Angela had S'haar place her finger over a small bit of glass, and a sharp needle shot up and pierced her skin. A couple of drops of blood fell onto a small glass panel, which was then pulled down into the device. She floated in front of S'haar, back to her usual jubilant self. "With that, we're done with this procedure. I'll need to analyze the data a little before moving on to the implant, so please take a break and get some food. Besides, I'm sure Jack is getting restless. He gets bored way too easily."

S'haar's stomach growled, and she realized how long she'd been in this room listening to their story. "Yes, and I'd like to move my muscles a bit anyway,"

S'haar took a moment to stretch her arms and legs before she walked out of the room.

Angela watched as the doors closed behind S'haar. She spoke quietly in the now empty room. "Go get him. He needs the proverbial kick in the rear to get back to living again. Try not to hurt him too much though, he's been through so much already."

Chapter 5

"Look at the little orphan girl, hopping from one male to the next, just like always. What did this 'human' offer you? Warmth, wealth, steel?"

B'arthon was staring down at S'haar, the condescension plain in his eyes. His lips curled as he stared with lust at her thigh. He reached out for her. "Why don't you come home? You can be my little pet again. I'll forgive your transgressions. You'll only have to kneel and beg for mercy for a few days at most!"

S'haar had heard more than enough. Whatever desperation had led her to seek out this deficient male in the past was gone and in its place was a wave of anger that demanded S'haar take action. She launched herself forward, wrapping her fingers around his neck. She then lifted him off the ground, her rage feeding her muscles strength beyond her usual limits.

Despite his current situation, B'arthon still leered down at S'haar with contempt. "What? Does the little orphan girl have something she wants to say? Please, we both know you don't have the guts to do anything about it. Now be a good girl and put me down, then get on your knees and beg!"

S'haar cried out as her rage grew. Her fingers started to tighten their grip around B'arthon's throat. His contempt still plain to see, B'arthon spoke one last time, though what he said felt like ice water shooting down S'haar's back. "Angela, stop! She doesn't know what she's doing!"

S'haar blinked and what she saw made every muscle freeze. The man she was holding by the neck wasn't B'arthon. Instead, Jack was dangling from her grip, one of his arms wrapped around S'haar's forearm as he tried to hold himself up to take some of the stress off his neck.

Meanwhile, his other arm was waving behind his back at the odd device hanging from the ceiling. The device was long and hollow, hanging from a forked piece of metal. It was waving around as if trying to point at S'haar beyond Jack's arm. S'haar could hear Angela's voice coming from the air.

"I don't have to kill her! I can simply shoot her arm off! We're in the med-bay, and I can probably reattach it later!"

S'haar dropped Jack and leaped back before kneeling with her head to the ground. Sitting in such a position normally went against everything S'haa's very nature, but even she knew she'd gone too far this time.

The problem was, she didn't understand what was going on. Her head still felt clouded, and her thinking sluggish, but she did know that what she had done was inexcusable. Jack would be in his right to demand retribution. "Forgive me! I...I'm not sure what happened!" She was still trembling from shame and rage at the vision but forced her eyes down, attempting to convey remorse.

When S'haar risked a glance up, Jack was still seated on the floor, with one hand rubbing his raw neck and the other waving her off. "Don't worry about it. There's no permanent damage done...I think...and it wasn't your fault anyway. We knew the drugs we used to sedate you for the procedure weren't dangerous to you. We just underestimated the side effects. Although if we ever need to do something similar in the future, I think I'll let Angela be the one to wake you after we're done."

Jack raised an eyebrow. "The real question is, did it work? Can you understand me now?"

The memories came back to S'haar in a rush. After Angela had finished analyzing the results of the first set of procedures, she had announced that, with a few small modifications, she should be able to give S'haar an implant that would allow her to understand Jack. They showed S'haar a pane of glass that projected moving pictures of where Jack had a similar implant.

After Angela uploaded something called an update to the device, he seemed to understand S'haar. When they explained the process, S'haar was somewhat discomforted by the idea of them cutting her head open to put something inside. Still, after carefully examining the back of Jack's head, there didn't seem to be any issues. At least nothing beyond his odd head tendrils, but Angela explained that his "hair" was normal and healthy for humans.

The last thing S'haar remembered was lying back in a strangely comfortable chair. Then Angela had said, "You might feel a slight pinch," and the next thing she remembered was seeing B'arthon's ugly face.

S'haar shook her head to clear the haze. "I understand what you are saying, although you have an odd accent. Not one I've ever heard before."

Picking herself up off the ground, S'haar walked over to Jack and offered him a hand up. Jack gratefully accepted, and as she hauled him to his feet, S'haar couldn't help but notice once again how small Jack was. If anything, it only made her feel more ashamed, as if she had attacked some helpless child. She bowed her head again. "Still, I'm sorry. It was like a dream, but you weren't you. Instead, you were…someone…from my past." S'haar felt as though her explanation was severely lacking but didn't want to talk about it, either.

Angela reappeared. She was now wearing a long, white coat with the same wireframes around her eyes as before. She leaned in close to S'haar, peering at her intently as if looking for anything else amiss. "What you experienced is a side effect called 'vivid dreaming'. I understand it can be quite unsettling and even quite frightening. Still, your eyes aren't dilated, and your stress reaction seems to be fading." As she straightened, the AI's coat seemed to dissolve, leaving her in her usual "jeans and T-shirt."

Angela sighed, looking down at the virtual ground at her feet, despite floating several feet above the actual floor. "If anyone is at fault, it's me. I only worried about the physical damage the drugs we used might cause. I failed to take into account the possible severity of the side effects you might experience. While vivid dreaming might be disorienting, it's rarely actually dangerous…unless you happen to significantly outmass the unfortunate recipient of your fight or flight response…"

Jack looked back and forth between the two women with an exasperated expression. "Listen, you two can debate which of us is most to blame if you want, but let's do it while we eat dinner. Angela, I'm assuming that you were also able to identify what is and isn't safe for S'haar to eat?"

Angela visibly brightened, nodding emphatically. "Yes, argu'n physiology can handle most similar foods to humans, though their diet leans a bit more toward carnivore than omnivore. I'd recommend at least 50% to 75% of their meal be meat cooked a little rarer than most humans would prefer. Also, they cannot taste 'sweet.'"

Jack thought for a minute before going with the obvious solution. "Well then, how about some steaks served with sautéed onions and mushrooms? S'haar can have hers with an additional side of steak, and I'll have a baked potato. Shame about the sweet thing, though… I have some great desserts you'll never get to enjoy!"

S'haar wondered quietly to herself what strange new thing this "dessert" was, and how she could be jealous of a thing that she had no concept of…

~

Jack couldn't remember the last time he'd felt like this. Years had passed, one day blending into the next, and each year blending into the following one. He ate, worked, slept, and did it again the next day. This had gone on so long that Jack actually had to stop and do the math to figure out his current age. The number was higher than he'd realized. These last few days had been different, though. It might be the fact his survival was at stake, perhaps it's because he's working with his hands again, or maybe it was his new houseguest, but for the first time in a long time, Jack felt… awake. Here he was, cooking for another person for the first time in longer than he could remember. Every moment of his life since he'd met her seemed to hold new surprises, challenges, and puzzles.

Jack stole a glance at his new…friend? She wasn't what he would typically call beautiful, but it was hard to take his eyes off her nonetheless. It was like watching a venomous snake. Her movements were deceptively slow and precise. However, he couldn't help but rub his neck, remembering the explosive speed and power she was capable of. Watching her move with what was now obviously restrained power was oddly captivating.

Perhaps sensing his attention, S'haar looked over at Jack and noticed his hand resting on his neck. Immediately she visibly tensed and her hair shook in a way Jack associated with a cringe. Well, now Jack felt guilty for making her feel worse. Time to take their mind off recent troubles and focus it elsewhere.

Jack decided to test out their new ability to communicate and cleared his throat. "S'haar, tell us a little about the area around here, and more importantly, the people. How big is the city you live in? How far away is the next city over? Do we have to worry about anyone poking their noses into our business around here?"

S'haar tilted her head to the side in thought before answering. "I'm not sure how many people live where I come from. To be honest, I've never really been in a position where it really mattered. Several hundred, I guess? The next town over is about a three-day journey over the hills to the west. A third can be found four days to the east. I don't think you'll have to worry about any village folk 'sticking their noses' into your business, but some of the hill tribes might. They are too unpredictable."

S'haar stopped mid-thought, tapping a claw against her lips as she thought. "I had always thought the hill tribes so primitive and brutish, but now I can't help but feel closer to them when I compare myself to a people that can CREATE another living being. To you, we must look like the hill tribes did to us…"

Jack waved her concern away with the spoon he was stirring the mushrooms and onions with. "As a people, the only advantage we have is the fact that we've been around a lot longer than your own. We only got this far by standing on the shoulders of our fathers. The difference between us is we have more sets of shoulders to stand on. Take away all my technology and drop me in the middle of a world like this one, and I'd be living more primitively than you. I'd be lucky to be able to get a fire going at all! There's nothing inherently superior or inferior about the luck of one's birth." Jack spooned some of the juices from the grilling steak over to the pan, sautéing the onions and mushrooms.

S'haar's eyes narrowed, and Jack could see the muscles in her jaw and shoulders tighten. "B'arthon would argue otherwise. It's by right of his family ties that he will rule the town, and I was left as a 'virgin' sacrifice, though he knows full well I'm nothing of the sort!"

The last part was said so quietly, Jack wasn't sure he was meant to hear it. He grew red in the face and felt his stammer returning as he couldn't help but envision such activities. "Ah, well, th…that shouldn't matter anyway."

When S'haar looked at him quizzically, Jack clarified. "Well, I suppose I can't speak for everyone… but I don't see the big deal in someone being…a…uh…virgin."

Feeling himself digging a grave now that he'd broached the subject, and not knowing how to stop, he pushed on. "The only people who seem to worry about such things are the kinds of people more worried about whether they 'measure up' to the competition than they are concerned about enjoying the time they have with their partners. Honestly, it just seems kinda petty. At least to me…"

Apparently, Angela had sat back listening long enough and felt compelled to throw her two cents in. She floated over to Jack with a look somewhere between adulation and condescension. "Grant us more wisdom gained from your many exploits and experiences, oh learned one!"

Happy to have a distraction, Jack swished his spoon through Angele's digital body as though striking her with a sword. "I've had my share of 'experiences,' thank you very much!"

Angela swung her hand at Jack, and at the same time, a robotic arm swung down with another spoon it had acquired. Jack brought his own spoon up just in time to fend off the blow. Angela chucked, "One night stands with other introverts looking to scratch an itch before they went back out into the cold black hardly makes you an expert!"

Jack tried to stab at the "heart" of the arm, only to be fended off at the last moment. "I'll have you know Ashlyn was a fine woman. She just understood that neither of us wanted anything more than a bit of stress relief at the time!"

Angela's "arm" struck back before Jack could get his guard back in place, landing a "killing" blow. "I'm just saying, you hardly have the experience to be preaching from your soapbox. You're no Don Juan!"

Jack "died" with an exaggerated flourish, falling back against the counter behind him. Cracking his eyes open, he responded, "Fair enough, I suppose I deserved that. Now how about we serve the food before it gets overcooked?"

Jack drizzled butter from the onions and mushrooms over the steaks and potato and then walked the dishes to the table to serve.

~

S'haar watched the two "siblings" fight their duel and couldn't help but find herself amused. They only seemed to get even odder now that she could understand what they were saying to each other. Jack set two plates of steak in front of S'haar, with some odd-looking plants on the side. The utensils he handed her were a little small and shaped odd, but easy enough to figure out by watching Jack use his own.

The meat tasted much better this time. Every bite shot out juices flavored with meat and some odd spices. S'haar's first steak was gone before she realized it. Jack was sitting at the other end of the table with that perpetual look of amusement he often wore, though once he noticed her looking at him, he suddenly seemed to find his own steak far more fascinating.

Eventually, the awkward silence seemed to get to him, so he looked up and spoke. S'haar was already digging into the second steak at the time, which seemed to relax him as he grinned. "Well, I guess this time I got it right. You look like someone who hasn't eaten in far too long. What about the mushrooms and onions? Give them a try and tell me what you think."

S'haar speared a "mushroom" on her fork and looked closely at it a moment before putting it in her mouth. The texture was…odd, a bit spongy, but not bad. However, as soon as S'haar really bit into it, the mushroom exploded into the flavor. It tasted just a bit like the steak, but it had other more complex flavors that were only hinted at in the meat. The spices were much more potent, giving it a more savory taste.

Next, S'haar tried an "onion." This time she didn't hesitate. The onion was crisper and had a strong bitter flavor. It might have been unpleasant, but it worked well with the other flavors mixed in. It made the rest of the meal taste even better by adding a different texture and character to the mix.

S'haar's mouth was still salivating at the thought of the next bite, even though she'd nearly eaten her fill. "This is some of the best food I've ever had! You could make a living as a respected cook in any noble's house with food like this!"

Jack's smile grew broader and more genuine. "I'm glad you like it. To be fair, this might be one of the best meals I know how to make, so I'm afraid the rest might not quite live up to such high praise."

Jack's expression softened a little. "I might not have time to cook like this for a little while, anyway. Tomorrow we need to get to work, so let's enjoy the rest of the evening. Tell me, do your people perform for entertainment? Do they put on plays?"

S'haar stopped with a bite halfway to her mouth, her hand lowering slightly as the thought. "We do, but I've never been very interested. The 'fights' are laughably bad. It's always apparent none of the actors know how to hold a sword, and don't even get me started on my thoughts about a 'romantic' play!"

Jack had an odd look in his eye as he replied. "I can understand that, but I'd like to show you a human version of a play. We call them movies, and I think I have a great idea of which one to show you first. Let me tell you about an old classic called *Willow*."

Chapter 6

S'haar watched as Jack ate his "cereal," specifically one called "fruit loops." The name was misleading. It wasn't made of fruit at all. Instead, it was cooked grain with "fruit flavoring", whatever that meant. It was then submerged in the milk of some herd animal and eaten like a soup. S'haar found the whole thing repulsive. When Jack offered to give her a taste, she almost lost her appetite completely. She was eating eggs, toast, and something divine called "Bacon." Jack had said something about not making anything as good as his last meal, but obviously, he was mistaken. The taste of fat and salty meat combined in a way that was both pleasing to eat and would give her all the energy she'd need later.

The "movie" she had watched with Jack had been unlike anything she'd ever seen before, although to be fair, that was true of almost everything in Jack's strange world. Still, this was especially weird. Jack explained that what she was watching was something like a play, but it was acted out a long time ago and then recorded so it could be viewed at any time. Shortly after the movie started, S'haar lost interest in his explanations and instead watched as the story unfolded before her.

Leave it to humans to have a person, small even by human standards, be the hero. In most argu'n plays, the hero was the largest male with the biggest muscles. They walked around the stage, swinging ridiculously oversized swords as if compensating for something. Jack explained humans had those movies too and promised to show her a film starring someone named "Arnold Schwarzenegger" sometime.

What really fascinated S'haar was the action, the magic, and the characters. Jack had explained that it was all "special effects" and that magic and two-headed dragons didn't really exist in his world. S'haar was shaken from her reverie when she realized Jack had asked a question. Her eyes fluttered open as S'haar turned her attention back to Jack. "I'm sorry, what did you say?"

Jack hurriedly swallowed another mouthful of the mess he was chewing before repeating himself. "I said, we can do pretty much everything that needs to be done in-house. However, there are so many tasks that jumping back and forth between everything will slow us down more than is necessary. Do you think your people would be willing to trade for any supplies we need like wood or basic smelting processes? At least until we get to the point that we can automate some of the work."

S'haar's head was tilted, and her hand was off to the side, holding the other half of the piece of bacon she'd just taken a bite out of. "You certainly have the resources to trade. The problem is it's the start of winter, everything slows to nearly a stop. The price of goods and labor are at their highest. On the other hand, you certainly have enough metal and other resources, you could probably tempt some craftsmen to work for you. Especially the young ones eager to make a name for themselves. Though it won't be cheap."

Jack didn't seem bothered by the possible cost. "We should probably start with something simple to establish ourselves. What if I bring a load of iron to be smelted and trade some of the iron for cut and shaped wood, then take the rest home?"

S'haar had never been much for trading, at least not beyond simple things she needed for day to day life, but it seemed reasonable. "That should be doable. The smelters will probably work for a cut of the iron they refine, and woodworkers always need more iron for their tools. Though, I'm afraid I won't be much help with the actual trading."

Jack waved away her concerns. "You'll be plenty of help. I'll do the actual negotiating, but I'll need you to translate and offer security. I'll be able to understand your people just fine, but you are the only person on this planet, other than Angela, that can understand me. Also, I have a feeling I shouldn't walk through your village with something as valuable as metal unescorted."

S'haar looked at the puny male and agreed with him. Whatever tricks he might have up his sleeve, that would be asking for trouble he probably didn't need.

Jack looked over to Angela, who was reading something called a book. The AI had explained it was all a facade, but she'd developed the habit as a way to offer Jack social interaction during meals without making him uncomfortable. Apparently, humans didn't like being stared at as they ate. "That being said, even with a bodyguard, we should probably take some precautionary measures. Can you make me some protective clothing to wear under my outfit? Maybe an extra durable knife and maybe even a small sidearm in case of a real emergency?"

She pulled a ledger from out of the air above her head and started reading. "We should have enough supplies for that, but we're going to have to be careful with the polymers. It's going to take us some time before we get to the point that we have the supplies to be wasteful with that. If we keep it primarily made out of metal alloys, we should be fine since you'll be refilling our stores soon. Although, as a result, it will be a bit heavier. Also, even a good knife won't make you a match for an argu'n, but it should buy you enough time for S'haar to pull you out of the metaphorical fire. The handgun is doable as well, but I recommend saving that for life and death situations. Not only will the ammo be something we can't afford to waste, but scaring the locals with your 'magic' is an excellent way to make enemies, rather than friends."

Jack nodded, finishing another mouthful of his breakfast. "I agree. While you're at it, make some weapons for S'haar as well, something in keeping with local technology but with more durable metal alloys." Jack held up a hand to stop S'haar's protests before they were voiced. "This is for me, not you. If you have better equipment, I'm more likely to make it home safely. If you chose not to keep it after we part ways, that's fine, but as long as you are my bodyguard, you're going to have the best arms and armor around."

S'haar could see the logic in his argument. "Fine, but try and make it look less flashy than what you have here. It will be more effective if it doesn't make us a target for every raider between here and the village."

Angela nodded. "That's easy enough to do. On the surface, it'll look like conventional refined iron. But it'll be sharper and more reliable than anything available to the locals. Your natural plates provide excellent protection, but we can add a little something to reinforce the weak spots around vital areas, though that'll take a little more time to design."

Jack was cleaning up the table. "That leaves our final problem, transportation. We have to get the metal to the village to trade said metal. Eventually, we'll want a cart, but with all the moving parts, that's one of the things we should probably purchase rather than craft ourselves. For now, I suppose we could make a simple sled. We won't be able to take as much with us on the first trip, but that might be for the best. That way, we can get a feel for the local trading practices before we paint too big a target on our back."

Angela gave S'haar an appraising look. "You might be able to take more than you think, but I agree that it's a good place to start. While you make the sled, I'll start analyzing the mountain around us and determine the best places to dig for stability and where you'll find quality iron veins. The locals still use bog ore, limiting the amount of metal they have available. So even a single good vein should supply us with enough for our needs for the foreseeable future."

Jack nodded in agreement. "Sounds like we have a plan. S'haar, you'll come with me. I'll be able to cut down a tree easily enough, but I suspect we'll be able to get it back in the mountain to work on more easily with your help."

S'haar gave Jack a slightly dismissive look. "Are you certain you don't want me to cut the tree down for you? We don't want to spend the whole day on this, do we?"

Jack had a look in his eye that could only be described as disquieting. "Oh, I think I'll be alright. I'm going to enjoy introducing you to something called a chainsaw!"

~

S'haar shook her head in bewilderment. Jack was clearly insane. This "chainsaw" could only have been born from the fevered dream of a mad man. It probably didn't help her opinion any that, as he was using it, Jack had been laughing, and his laughter had a bit of an odd maniacal edge to it. The loud roar of its "motor" was unlike anything S'haar had ever heard, and the way it chewed through the thick tree was both impressive and a little scary.

However, S'haar could not debate the effectiveness of the device. In moments, the tree he'd chosen was down and the branches removed. He then attached an odd harness to the trunk and had S'haar wrap the other end around her shoulders. Although the trunk was many times heavier than S'haar, dragging it was quite simple with the harness.

Jack shook his head as he walked alongside her. "You know, every time I start to think of you as just another tall human, you go and do something like this and prove me wrong. I'm relatively confident pulling that log would be something that would only be done in a strong man contest back home. Yet you don't even seem to be pushing your limits. I was sure I'd have to cut that thing up and make multiple trips."

S'haar looked over at him with a quizzical look. "Then, why didn't you?"

Jack shrugged his shoulders. "I was curious. I expected you to be able to move it, I just thought the strain would be too much for a long haul, and I'd have to adjust the load. I was wondering whether we should make two or three trips. Looking at you now, I'm reasonably sure that the harness will reach its limit before you do. Still, this bodes well for hauling some ore to town. We'll be able to move a much larger load than I had anticipated."

S'haar looked back down at the small man walking beside her. "You know, if all you wanted was a beast of burden, you could probably get a trained arlack. They are larger than an argu'n and able to pull far heavier loads and move them further. Plus, they are easy to feed. Just let them graze in the nearby fields. Although you'd have to have somewhere for them to sleep at night, or something might make a meal out of it."

Jack looked interested. "That's definitely something to keep in mind. We'll need to get a few things in place and have our trading up and running before that's feasible. For the immediate future, you'll have to double up as a beast of burden and bodyguard. I hope you don't mind."

S'haar looked at him with a gleam in her eye. "You forgot translator and local guide. Too many more job titles and I might reconsider keeping those weapons when I'm done."

Jack grinned at her. "You'd be welcome to them! You're turning out to be quite the jack of all trades!"

The ridges over S'haar's eyes furrowed in confusion. "You make that sound like a title, but I thought Jack was your name…"

Jack laughed. "Sorry, it's a phrase from back home. It means you are good at a wide variety of tasks. The fact that my name is part of the phrase is entirely a coincidence. Well, maybe not entirely. I'm probably partial to the phrase because of that."

As they neared the cave, Jack's expression grew more serious. "You caught my attention when you mentioned that something might eat the arlack. I'm guessing you are talking about local predators. So that begs the question, what sort of local wildlife should I keep a lookout for?"

S'haar was quiet for a moment, pulling the trunk along behind her before speaking up. "First is the kovaack. They are actually an herbivore but have an ornery disposition. They will charge and attack anything they feel threatens their territory. In mating season, they've even been known to attack larger predators and sometimes even succeed in driving them off. Thick-skinned with a horn on their head, they can be quite the nuisance. Their meat is quite delicious, it sells for a premium, and their hide can be used to craft a durable leather."

S'haar's expression became a bit more serious. "Second, there is the wolgen. They are large predators that usually keep their distance from villages. They are fast and have long claws capable of puncturing our plates." S'haar emphasized this point by slapping the plate on her arm. "If one sets up its territory too close to our village, a hunting party will be sent to deal with it. Even then, it's all too common for at least a couple of hunters to be severely injured in the hunt."

Jack nodded. "Sounds like a regular alpha predator, big, scary, top of the local food chain. Not much willing to mess with it."

S'haar looked over at Jack with a grin that unsettled him and not just because of how apparent it made her sharp predator teeth. "Oh, there is something higher up this 'food chain' you speak of. The tus'ron. Pray to whatever gods the humans worship you never run into them."

Jack was suddenly nervous. "They are bigger and scarier than the wolgen?"

S'haar's grin widened. Jack was suddenly sure there were now twice as many teeth in that mouth as had been there a mere moment before. "Scarier, yes, but not bigger. One tus'ron is hardly a threat. They're even smaller than yourself. While its bite would hurt, it probably wouldn't be a serious threat to your life on its own. The problem is, they sometimes travel in swarms."

Jack didn't like the use of the word swarms at all.

S'haar continued, seeming to enjoy the look of worry on Jack's face. "A proper tus'ron swarm could easily overpower an argu'n or even a wolgen. I've even heard stories of impossibly large swarms wiping out whole villages! Although I'm pretty sure those were just campfire tales told to scare the children…"

Jack really didn't like what he was hearing. He hoped S'haar played up the story a bit to try to scare him, but he was afraid she probably wasn't. Jack watched as S'haar dropped her load and unhooked the harness. Either way, Jack resolved to look into these threats a bit further… But first, it was time to get to work.

Chapter 7

S'haar filled the sled with the first load of ore. The sled itself was a simple design, a raised platform with short walls around the side. Underneath were a couple of runners, the bottoms of which were coated with a thin layer of metal. The runners were curved upward at the end, allowing them to pass over small obstacles. At the front, Jack attached a harness similar to the one S'haar had used to haul the trunk earlier. Her people often used a similar design, though there usually wasn't any metal on the runners. It was too precious to waste on something as simple as hauling material.

Jack had dug up the ore through a process he called "mining." He used a large metal frame he called an "exo-suit." While in it, he moved much slower than usual, but it gave him tremendous strength. Enough that he could lift the drill he used and place girders made from the remnants of the trees they had cut down the day before. He'd said he was looking for something called "iron veins."

She'd been confused, but Jack clarified. "They're deposits of high concentrations of metal that run through a mountain the way veins run through a person."

S'haar had doubted Jack until he'd dug them out, separated the metal from the stone, then filled the area with a mix of gravel and something he called "concrete." The chunks of metal and rock were then broken down, and the metal was separated from the stone. The stone would fill the next hole Jack dug, and S'haar would haul the ore back to the cave entrance.

It was exhausting work but went quicker than S'haar would have thought possible. In an afternoon, the two of them had acquired more iron than a team of her people could gather in a week.

Normally walking the distance from Jack's cave to S'haar's village would be a dangerous trek at the start of winter, but this time was different. Angela and Jack had gifted S'haar with clothing and a large coat that was warmer than anything she'd ever owned. On top of that, they had included pockets on the inside that held "warming packets," something that resembles a fire-warmed stone but could radiate heat for hours. With a little experimentation, S'haar was able to walk around outside the cave at night with none of the usual lethargy that overtook her people when they spent too much time out in the cold air.

As S'haar loaded the iron, Jack was grumbling about it being inhumane to be awake and working at this hour of the day. He was packing other supplies they might need on the trip, like a tent, sleeping mats, sleeping bags, changes of clothes, food, supplies for a fire, and more. It seemed a bit much for such a short journey, but at her inquiring look, Jack had shrugged. "Better to have it and not need it than need it and not have it!" S'haar couldn't fault his logic.

With everything packed and ready, S'haar put on her harness, Jack picked up his backpack, which was loaded with a few final supplies, and they began their journey to S'haar's village.

~

Jack watched his traveling companion closely. Her expressions were still hard to read, but Jack was getting better at figuring out what emotions triggered what responses. Right now, her face was a careful mask of neutrality, but Jack's gut was telling him there were subtle signs of worry his eyes weren't picking up.

As she scanned the horizon, Jack could tell her gaze wasn't lingering on any one spot, and her thoughts seemed to be turned inward. It didn't seem like she was worried about the present, so it must be the future that weighed on her. With a little reflection, it wasn't hard to guess why.

Around noon they stopped to eat some of the food Jack had packed. It was a meal made more with convenience in mind than taste, but it was still decent enough. Lunch consisted of a few ham and cheese sandwiches and some teriyaki jerky added to satisfy S'haar's high meat requirements.

In between bites, Jack decided to broach the subject that seemed to be weighing on her mind. "How do you think your hometown is going to react to their 'sacrifice' returning alive and acting as a bodyguard to a wealthy trader?"

S'haar jumped as though she had forgotten Jack was sitting just a few feet across from her. As she looked at him, her eyes blinked slowly the way someone might if they had just woken from a deep sleep. He could tell from her expression that she seemed somewhat ashamed for letting herself get so distracted.

Her eyes had a hard edge as she replied, "Honestly? I'm not sure. I imagine most of the villagers will be indifferent. This time of year, they are too busy preparing for winter to waste any more time or energy than is necessary, especially on anything that doesn't directly impact themselves. The real question is how much trouble B'arthon may want to cause. My snubbing him is the reason I found myself in that situation, and I suspect he won't be happy until I'm no longer there to remind him of his humiliation…"

Jack took an interest in this. "I've heard you speak of him before. From the sounds of things, he's a person of some import to the village? How much trouble could he cause if he chose to?"

S'haar sighed in frustration. "Again, I'm not sure. When I was on my own, he got rid of me easily enough by volunteering me as a sacrifice. With you here, it will probably be different. You have resources to offer that could make a large difference to the village's prosperity, and by extension, his family's as well. That's probably not enough to make B'arthon stop and think, but it might be enough to force his father to reign him in. On the other hand, you aren't argu'n, so he may decide that it's best to take what you have by force. If it comes to that, I'm confident I can get you out alive, but otherwise, our trip might be a total loss."

Jack tilted his head and locked his eyes with S'haar's. "That's all well and good regarding my welfare, but what about yourself? This village was your home, these are your people, and they turned their back on you. How are you holding up with the idea of returning to it all?"

S'haar was silent for a moment while she looked into the distance. A smile tinged with sadness passed her lips as her attention returned to Jack. "I may have lived there all my life, but I think that the village stopped being my home long ago. I already had plans to try and move on if I survived another winter. It was purely coincidental that you offered me the opportunity to do so a little earlier. I think the only reason I hadn't already moved on was my job in the guard. It was a large part of who I was, and at the time, that seemed like enough. Now that I'm looking back, the last few years feel empty. I don't know what the future holds for me currently, but at least I'm moving forward once again."

Jack sat back and nodded. He understood a thing or two about living through empty years. He also noticed the worry seemed to have mostly lifted from S'haar's face. It seemed like she had found a resolution to whatever inner turmoil had been troubling her.

Packing away the remnants of their lunch Jack stood up and started shouldering his pack again. "Well, speaking of moving forward, we should get going again. If we are too late getting back to the ship tomorrow, Angela is liable to start looking into a way to come looking for us. Trust me. We don't want that. Her ideas tend to be a little…excessive."

~

As they approached the gate, S'haar could see the guard was asleep at his post, sitting next to the remnants of a fire that was still smoldering. That wasn't too surprising this late into the year, since was uncommon for any argu'n to be out making trouble in the cold. The guards were mostly there to remind everyone of their presence and thus keep anyone from wasting enough energy to cause problems. The village wouldn't need to worry about raids until spring at the earliest, and the wildlife knew better than to come this close to the walls of a village filled with hungry predators.

As they approached, S'haar called out to the guard. "Ger'ron, you old lazy waste of a uniform! Wake up and do something useful for once! Like opening the gate! We have a shipment of metal to trade for goods and services."

The argu'n S'haar shouted at came to with a jolt. He was obviously a bit past his prime, but any young argu'n guard who thought that meant he was easy pickings in the sparring ring quickly found themselves on their back end, trying to remember what exactly had gone wrong. Ger'ron'd taught S'haar more than one dirty trick to deal with those who let themselves become overconfident due to size and strength. These days, he preferred to take boring jobs and was famous for complaining that "excitement is for the young." He didn't feel the need to show off like the rest of the guard, so S'haar had always liked working with him.

A sheepish grin covered his embarrassment as he came to attention. "S'haar! I didn't expect to see you…" —his face fell as he remembered why he wasn't expecting to see her— "again…" he finished lamely.

S'haar walked right up to him, not hiding her amusement at his discomfort. "Well, apparently it takes more than a dragon to kill me, even if I'm left tied to a pole as an offering. It turns out the dragon happened to be in the market for a local guide and guard. This here is Jack. He's the dragon's representative and is here to trade a bit of metal."

Jack grumbled in the background. "Demoted from dragon to a mere representative. A guy just can't catch a break…"

Ger'ron looked back and forth between the two. He knew S'haar was formidable and had a temper, not to mention motive, but on her own, she was hardly a threat to an entire village. This "Jack" looked sickly and hardly seemed like he could pose a danger to even the village children. Bending down and inspecting the ore, he was surprised at the amount and the quality they had. While he was hardly an expert, he'd been operating the gate long enough to see the ore the workers usually brought back. This seemed like at least a couple of weeks' worth.

Turning back to S'haar, he decided to be straight with her. "Now I know you have cause to make trouble, but I want your word that you are here for trade and nothing else. Also, you'll have to leave your weapons with me. They'll be returned to you when you leave tomorrow."

S'haar crossed her arms and rested her weight on one heel; her face bore a clear expression of annoyance. "Why take our weapons? Every day traders come through armed to the teeth!"

Ger'ron had the decency to look ashamed but refused to budge on the issue. "Look, I'm not saying I agree with what happened to you. I can even see why it would be tempting for you to get a little revenge. What's more, I might even enjoy the show. However, as the guard who let you into the village, I'd be held responsible. You've got the motive. I'm just trying to remove the means. We both know you can take care of yourself with or without that short sword at your side, and at least I'll look like I'm trying to do my job!"

S'haar looked like she was about to protest further, but Jack had already unbelted his knife and handed it over. Realizing Ger'ron was old and stubborn enough to argue the day away, she relented and handed her blade in as well.

Ger'ron took the weapons and then looked at S'haar. "And your word?"

S'haar felt like a child being asked to apologize when she was anything but sorry. "Fine, I will not seek revenge against the spineless villagers who left me for dead or the dickless wonder who egged them on them. This time…"

Satisfied that was as good as he was going to get, Ger'ron took a moment to inspect the blades before stowing them away in the shed behind him. Walking back out, he rapped on the gate loudly. "Hey Jar'maal, open up. We got some traders here with iron!"

From the other side of the gate came the voice of a younger and obviously bored argu'n. "Traders? This time of year? Are they insane?"

Despite his words, the gate was unbarred and swung open, allowing S'haar and Jack to walk in. As she walked past the younger guard, she could feel his eyes bulging when he recognized who was walking past. She just kept her eyes forward and kept walking, letting him stare slack-jawed at her retreating form. As they walked through town, they could hear voices raised in astonishment and confusion all around them.

People stopped what they were doing to see the sacrifice walking among them again. Not only that, but she was leading the oddest and sickliest looking argu'n any of them had ever seen. From the whispers that followed them, Jack suspected this might be one of the most notable events in the village's recent history.

S'haar noticed a few argu'n that took off running as soon as they saw who was drawing everyone's attention. It was a fair bet that, all too soon, B'arthon would hear about her return. However, it was best to worry about unloading the ore now, before things got overly dramatic.

They approached the crafting corner of the village, and the younger argu'n stopped what they were doing to stand and stare at the odd pair. Not long after, an old argu'n appeared and began whipping a couple of the nearby workers with a grease-smeared towel. "Who told you that you could slack off? Get back to work, the lot of you!"

Seeing who was approaching, he barely paused before wiping his hands on the same greasy towel he'd been using for discipline. "S'haar! I won't pretend I'm not surprised to see you. What brings you here? I warn you, regardless of what you've been through, I won't tolerate you stirring up any trouble over here. We've got a lot of work to do and never enough time to do it in!"

S'haar hadn't worked with the craft master much in the past, but he always treated the guard with respect, and she had no ill will toward the old man. "I'm not here to make trouble, Mar'kon, but I'm not going to help with your workload either. We've got a load of iron ore here that we want to have refined. In return, you'll get a cut of the refined iron."

Mar'kon looked over the ore S'haar had indicated. He held up a chunk, glaring at it with a critical eye. "It's garbage, and it'll take a lot of work to refine. We'll do it for a five out of ten cut."

That seemed like a lot to S'haar, but she wasn't sure how to respond. That's when Jack stepped up. "S'haar, introduce me and translate. I'll negotiate."

S'haar turned back to Mar'kon. "This is Jack, and the ore is his. I'm just working as a guard and translator on his behalf. He can understand you just fine, but he can't speak our tongue."

Jack looked up at the older argu'n, as he barely came up to Mar'kon's chest. It was easy to feel intimidated, but Jack tried not to let any of that show on his face and hoped S'haar could compensate for any hesitation in his voice. "Tell him that's some of the purest ore he's ever going to see, and he can have a one in ten cut."

Mar'kon listened for a moment before grinning and countering. "Our workload is already too full with winter coming. We'll do it for a four in ten cuts."

Jack didn't hesitate. "The smelters will keep him and his people plenty warm while the rest of the village is cold. If he wants us to come back here regularly instead of going to a different village, he can have a two in ten cut."

A look of surprise flashed across Mar'kon's face at the idea of this much ore regularly, but the look faded so quickly that Jack could tell he was a veteran negotiator. The old man countered again. "You came here because we're closer than any other village. We'll take a two and a half in ten cut."

Jack thought that was fair, but added in one last condition. "Agreed, but I get to choose which bars you keep. This will avoid the temptation of anyone trying to make some bars higher quality than the rest."

Jack held out his hand and had S'haar explain. "This is called a handshake. Where I come from, it has many uses, including the acknowledgment of a mutually beneficial agreement."

Upon hearing this, Mar'kon offered his hand as well. Jack took the oversized hand and pumped it twice. "Pleasure doing business with you, Mar'kon, and I look forward to working with you again. We'll stop by tomorrow to tell you where the refined ore will be sent."

Mar'kon looked genuinely surprised at this. "You're not taking it with you?"

Jack shook his head. "Not this time. We won't have the time to hang around for it all to smelt. Instead, we're planning on trading most of it for some goods we need to take with us. The rest we'll pick up when we come with the next load."

Mar'kon thought for a moment. "Fair enough, but I won't have the space to store it for a long time. We'll use anything left for more than two weeks and reimburse you with something of similar value at our discretion."

Jack nodded. "That'll work fine. Two weeks should be plenty of time."

Mar'kon looked around him and selected one apprentice who seemed less focused than the rest. "Tel'ron, get your butt over here and get this ore over to the smelter. I want to have half of this smelted by morning, so we know the iron's quality. Now get moving!"

The young argu'n got to it right away. The apprentices seemed to have the healthy fear any earth apprentice would have for a strict master, but they lacked the skittishness youngsters showed around someone too quick to lash out. Jack decided he liked old Mar'kon.

Just then, Mar'kon looked over their shoulders and suddenly seemed tired for some reason. "I've got work to do. Remember, I don't want any trouble around here, so if you have to fight, take it elsewhere! That goes for all of you!"

Jack had just a second to be confused before hearing a surprisingly petulant male voice behind him. "Looks like the little orphan girl was even a failure at being a sacrifice. Now she's also got a pet! Or maybe she's finally found someone pathetic enough to let her share his bed!"

Jack turned around and saw an unfamiliar argu'n. This one was slightly shorter than the average male Jack had seen until now, but he was dwarfed by the two giants standing just behind him. Most of the villagers seemed to wear leather or primitive cloth garments, but the center argu'n wore furs and even a little metal. All three wore the same grin. It was the kind of grin that announces to everyone that they were looking to cause trouble.

    S'haar stepped up, putting herself between Jack and the new group before she addressed the leader. "Hello, B'arthon. It's been a while, hasn't it?"

Chapter 8

S'haar didn't like the look on B'arthon's face. He had the same expression he always wore whenever he was about to torment someone he viewed as weaker than himself. As he looked down at the two of them, B'arthon obviously thought he sensed weakness he could exploit.

The two goons stayed in place, leering, while B'arthon started circling his chosen prey. "Well, I must say I *am* surprised to see you back again. I thought for sure you'd be nothing more than dragon shit by now, and yet here you are, hauling a load of stolen iron too! Tell me, how *did* you pull that off?"

S'haar's tendrils vibrated threateningly while she kept her eyes locked on the two immediate threats in front of her. She addressed B'arthon without breaking eye contact with his goons. "We didn't steal anything. The iron belongs to Jack." She nodded toward her charge without breaking eye contact. "He's here representing the dragon, who happens to have more metal than she knows what to do with. The dragon agreed to trade the iron for some goods they could actually use. I'm only here acting as a guide and interpreter."

B'arthon hesitated for a moment at the mention of the dragon, some indiscernible emotion passed through his eyes, but he covered his reaction and quickly resumed his pacing. "You expect me to believe the dragon is more than some oversized beast? That it's capable of understanding ideas like negotiation and trade? No, I think this feeble excuse for an argu'n somehow managed to get you free, and the two of you simply took what you could and ran. We can't have thieves running about. Maybe I'll just claim your iron and exile you from the village, for good this time."

S'haar was sizing up the two thugs in front of her just as Jack spoke up. "Tell him I said that would be a mistake."

S'haar wasn't sure what Jack thought he would accomplish here but decided they didn't have much to lose and translated.

B'arthon reacted the way she thought he would, starting with a laugh that made her skin crawl. "Please, you think you can threaten me? What can a pathetic excuse for a male and one lone female possibly do?"

Jack looked as calm as he ever did, though S'haar couldn't help but notice one of his hands was suspiciously near where she knew he'd hidden his gun. "I'm not threatening you, at least not physically. The mistake I'm speaking of is pretty obvious to anyone who stops and thinks for a moment. If you want this load of iron, I'll give it to you, but every load that comes after will be taken to a different village. That means the villages around this one would see a significant uplift in economic strength, while your community falls behind. Pretty soon, your craftspeople would leave for places that had more and cheaper raw materials to work with. That would mean less money and less power for whoever runs this village."

S'haar noticed several watchers take off running as they heard Jack's claims. She was just starting to hope Jack's strategy might pay off when B'arthon dashed her hopes. "I've heard enough lies from this curr and her pet. Teach them a lesson in manners before you remove them from our village!"

S'haar was ready for something like this to happen, but unfortunately, so were the two goons. The first lept for S'haar and the second for Jack. S'haar tried to block the second but received a jab to the back of her head for her trouble. As she dropped to one knee, she saw Jack's futile struggle as he was hoisted by his neck. The first goon was standing over S'haar, laughing uproariously.

S'haar launched herself to her feet and delivered her a quick jab to his exposed throat to shut him up. She kept her hand open, connecting with the space between her thumb and forefinger. He made a choking sound and went down hard, but S'haar knew that, aside from a nasty bruise, he'd be fine once the shock wore off.

She turned to see what kind of trouble Jack was in, but he managed to surprise both S'haar and his opponent by kicking one leg up and bracing it over the top of his assailant's arm. He then used that leg for extra leverage to kick up with his other leg and catch his opponent just under the chin.

If they had been closer in size, the maneuver would have been impossible, but it worked perfectly in this situation. Well, almost perfectly. It did have the desired effect of launching back the head of Jack's assailant, who then dropped Jack. The problem was when Jack landed hard and promptly writhed on the ground as though he'd injured his foot.

Never one to waste an opportunity, S'haar launched herself at Jack's assailant before he regained his composure. She took him down with a swift kick to his groin and followed up with an open-palm punch to the back of his head, collapsing him into the dirt at her feet.

The situation started to look like it favored Jack and herself, which is how S'haar knew something was bound to go horribly wrong. The sound of metal clearing a scabbard behind her confirmed her fear. She turned to see the first thug standing again, now with a genuinely pissed off look on his face and a sword in his hand. A similar sound came from the ground below her, and S'haar knew the odds had just shifted very much against them.

B'arthon had stepped away from the ruckus, clearly intent on letting his hired muscle handle the heavy lifting. His face was shifting from eager anticipation to a look of manic glee as the events he had set in motion seemed to be coming to a climax. The first thug was drawing back to strike as Jack started to draw his own weapon. Everything slowed down as S'haar tried to think of a way for them to get out of this without bringing every guard in the city down on their heads but was coming up blank.

~

Just as everything seemed ready to unravel, one of the goons fell to the ground, clearly unconscious. Behind where he'd been standing was old Mar'kon, wiping his fist with the same greasy rag as before. Looking around, Jack could see most of the apprentices standing around with various makeshift clubs in hand. They looked bored, as if they really just wanted to get back to work.

Jack eased his hand away from the gun he had just resheathed. Things were starting to look up. Things like B'arthon's blood pressure, for example. Acting out like a toddler who just had his favorite toy taken away, he started shouting at an increasingly bored-looking Mar'kon. "You've crossed a line this time, old man! My father won't just sit back after you assaulted my bodyguard!"

A new voice rose over the rising murmuring of the gathering crowd. "You are correct. I won't 'just sit back' after this unnecessary waste of my time!"

The owner of the voice was walking toward the center of the disturbance in his little kingdom. He was being led by one of the argu'n who'd taken off running just before the fight. He was also flanked on either side by a couple of bodyguards of his own. They weren't as big or muscled as B'arthon's guards, but they were better equipped and much more menacing, despite having their weapons at rest.

The new argu'n kept his gaze on the scene before him, handing some coins to his guide before continuing forward, with his guard only a step behind him at all times. His clothing was a fur-lined cloth dyed in much more vibrant colors than anyone else Jack had seen until now. Unlike B'arthon, he seemed to be of roughly average height for an argu'n. However, his presence seemed to tower over everyone else present, including his guards, even though they had to look down to meet his gaze as they listened for his orders. "My son has apparently learned the wrong lesson from my tolerance for his ill-mannered behavior of late. Perhaps it's time I tried a different approach. Please escort him and his friends to the animal pens. Instruct Lady Ta'miel they are to clean the pens every day for the next week."

B'arthon's face couldn't be described as anything other than petulant. "Father, you can't be serious! She's just another orphaned curr!"

Still speaking to the guard and pointedly ignoring his son, the man continued. "Inform my son that while I don't involve myself in his personal affairs, the merchants that visit the village are *my* concern. He'd do well to remember that in the future. Also, make it two weeks in the pens."

B'arthon looked as though he wanted to argue further, but in a rare moment of discernment, seemed to decide he was better off shutting his mouth for now. The look he shot Jack and S'haar as he was escorted away delivered a clear message. This was not over, and they would regret his humiliation.

As S'haar helped Jack to his feet, the colorful argu'n turned his attention to the mismatched duo. At a glance, Jack could tell he struggled briefly to decide which face to wear for them and the crowd. Coming to a decision, he spoke to his remaining guard, who then went about dispersing the gathered crowd while his boss approached the targets of his son's ire.

His face was a mask of neutrality. His arms were folded in front of himself, appearing neither hostile nor welcoming, obviously trying to get a measure of the two before committing to anything. That suited Jack just fine.

Jack limped forward, doing his best to ignore his protesting foot. S'haar offered both literal and metaphorical support by stepping up beside him and letting him lean slightly against her on his injured side. Jack spoke again with S'haar acting as his translator. "Greetings, Lord A'ngles, I presume? I apologize for the misunderstanding between your son's guards and ourselves. I hope no lasting harm will come of it. My name is Jack, and I believe you are at least somewhat familiar with my friend and translator, S'haar."

One of A'ngles's eye ridges rose at the word "friend," but he otherwise appeared to take everything in stride. While Jack was never one to enjoy politics—in fact, he avoided them at every opportunity—he knew the game well enough to get by when needed. Lord A'ngles might be from a different world with a different culture, but some ideas appeared to be universal.

Seeing that order was restored in his corner of the world, Mar'kon simply grunted before turning around and chasing his charges back to their various jobs. Anyone who idled too long found themselves on the receiving end of a whipping via his greasy rag.

A'ngles watched Mar'kon go about refocusing his apprentices before speaking. "Mar'kon is a man of great worth to the village. He brings considerable skill and value to the village and, admittedly, to me as well. In doing so, he has earned himself and his men a great deal of respect, comfort, and protection within this village. Anyone who can contribute to the village in such a meaningful way will always find himself," Lord A'ngles directed a meaningful look at S'haar, "or herself welcome within our walls."

A'ngles turned his attention back to Jack. It was as though everything he'd said until now had not been blatantly directed at Jack and instead had just been idle chatter. "To answer your indirect inquiry, I do not believe any lasting harm will come from today's misunderstanding. What's more, I shall endeavor to ensure your future visits to our village are free of such…misunderstandings."

Jack nodded, knowing this was as close to an apology as he was likely to get. S'haar tried to look as uninvolved as possible while continuing to translate. "I'm sure that our continued association will enrich everyone involved. Hopefully, the sight of me bringing metals and other valuable goods will soon become a common sight in this town."

A'ngles nodded in agreement and was almost successful in hiding the glint of eagerness in his eyes. His attention was momentarily taken by one of his guards, who spoke quietly in his ear for a moment before A'ngles returned his attention to Jack. "I'm afraid I am needed elsewhere at the moment. If your foot has been injured, I'm sure our town healer can set it right for you."

Jack shook his head and waved A'ngles's concern away. "I'll be fine. I am trained in the art of healing myself. This will be but a minor setback."

There was another sparkle of eagerness in Lord A'ngles's eyes as he spoke. "A trader *and* a healer? Yes, I think you will be most welcome indeed… For now, please rest at the inn as my guest this evening. I'll send someone over to see that everything is ready for you, at your convenience."

With those parting words, A'ngles walked away in the brisk manner of someone who has too much to do and not enough time to do it in. That left Jack and S'haar alone, standing in the middle of what had not long ago been a crowded road. Jack turned to S'haar, grinning. "Well, that went well!"

Which was when Jack put a little too much weight on the wrong foot and started to collapse before S'haar caught and steadied him. She spoke her mind as she glared at him. "Maybe next time you should let me do what you're paying me to do. While that move you pulled looked impressive, it left you on the ground and vulnerable while barely slowing your opponent down. In the end, all it would have done is left you vulnerable and in the way, making my job harder. Next time just run away before you get grabbed, and leave the fighting to me."

Jack's face turned a bit red before he deflected. "How was I supposed to know kicking that guy in the face would be like kicking stone?" His voice and expression softened. "However, I suppose you're right. Hesitating was a mistake on my part, and I'm glad things didn't end any worse than they did. I have to admit, it was quite impressive the way you handled those two. Thanks. I owe you one."

S'haar wasn't used to a male apologizing after she spoke her mind to him in such a manner. It caused her to hesitate a moment before responding. "I'm fairly certain, up until now, I've been the one in your debt. Don't try and be a hero again, and we'll call it even."

Jack grinned back at her. "It's a deal. Now, where can one go to find ourselves a cart around here? Preferably something big enough to haul back the sled and one injured non-hero?"

Jack looked at his injured foot and sighed. "Angela is going to raise hell when she hears how this happened."

S'haar looked at him in surprise. "Are you in any condition to be wandering around town? Shouldn't we get you back to Lady Angela so she can fix you up?"

Jack shook his head, emphatically. "No need to rush. I packed everything I'll need to make a splint, and I have some pain meds that'll take the edge off. We'll get the supplies we planned on, take lord A'ngles up on his offer at the inn, and head home in the morning as planned."

S'haar gave him a stern glare for a moment before replying. "I guess it's your call, but if Lady Angela throws a fit, you'll have to explain why we stayed."

Jack waved her worries away. "Don't worry about it, everything will be fine. Also, since when is it 'Lady Angela'?"

S'haar grinned a little impishly in response, enjoying the jealousy in Jack's voice. "Well, she *is* a dragon. That deserves a little respect, don't you think?"

Jack knew what was coming but couldn't stop himself from taking the bait anyway. "If Angela's the dragon, what does that make me?"

S'haar slowly walked away, leaving Jack to limp after her before turning her head and replying over her shoulder, "The dragon's assistant, of course! And no, that position does not come with a title."

Chapter 9

Jack was in a good mood despite his throbbing foot. While not everything had gone as planned, things were more or less on track. He'd splinted and wrapped his foot, so it was relatively immobile, then took some anti-inflammatories and a small dose of pain meds to take the edge off any pain. However, he couldn't take enough medication to make the pain go away completely. He needed a clear head for any further negotiations.

The final part of his new ensemble was a stylish makeshift pair of crutches he had fashioned out of some kindling Mar'kon had lying around. Jack wouldn't trust them for any kind of long-term use, but they should get the job done for an evening.

S'haar had watched Jack as he went about administering basic first aid to himself, noting the similarities to what she had learned in the guard and asking questions about the differences. She had been particularly interested in Jack's medication being in tablet form, noting that the drugs she had taken in the past had been a foul-smelling and tasting drink. Jack had explained that keeping it in tablet form helped with the flavor, kept it stable a lot longer, and allowed for easier storage.

With S'haar's guidance, Jack was hobbling his way over to the woodworking portion of the village's crafting section. Once he got there, he was somewhat surprised to find himself approached by a female argu'n. While he was still no expert in argu'n physiology, he'd place her at about half again older than S'haar, putting her in early middle age by Jack's best guess. Also, she was more muscular than S'haar, probably due to years of hard work and heavy lifting involving the lumber of her trade.

Jack held out his hand in greeting and spoke. S'haar, growing used to the arrangement they had, translated. "Greetings, my name is Jack, this is my friend and translator S'haar, and I'm here to trade for some supplies. I take it you are in charge here, miss…?"

Jack couldn't help but notice the muscles rippling under her skin. It was kind of intimidating, and he had to resist the urge to step back behind S'haar as the argu'n in front of him crossed her arms. "That would be Lady Fea'en, and yes, I'm in charge here. What sort of supplies are you looking for?"

Her words were gruff and to the point, as though she was more interested in getting back to work than negotiations. Jack held up his hands in a pacifying gesture before continuing. "I apologize. I meant no disrespect, Lady Fea'en. I'm looking to trade some refined iron ore for a wagon and some basic woodworking tools."

Lady Fea'en raised an eye ridge as she contemplated his words before replying. "Why not just have old Mar'kon make you a new set of tools? Your tools would be far less worn if you got them directly from the smiths."

Jack nodded and grinned. After the politics earlier, it was a nice change of pace to talk with someone who spoke their mind. "True, but I'm leaving in the morning, and I'll need the tools before then. I'm willing to trade enough iron ore to make you two sets of new tools over the next couple weeks, give or take, in return for one set of used tools still in good condition."

Fea'en barely thought a moment before replying. "Done. Now when you say wagon, are you looking for something to be pulled by an arlack or a hand cart?"

As she spoke, she walked away, leading them into a nearby crude warehouse. Jack followed while answering. "A handcart, please. Something S'haar could push continually for several hours while it is fully loaded."

Fea'en nodded before leading them over to a corner with several handcarts broken down in various stages of disrepair. "You're in luck. Usually, a job like that would take me a few days to put together. However, with the end of the season, I had several worn or broken down carts traded in for some credit toward next season. If I cannibalize a few of them, I should be able to have a cart put together for you tonight. I could have it delivered and loaded with the tools you asked for first thing in the morning. I'll do it for double again the iron you promised. Now, before you try and negotiate that down further, I'm already giving you a great price, on account of the entertainment you two provided my workers and myself earlier. So it's a take it or leave it kind of deal."

Jack decided he liked Fea'en. Maybe it's just that the last two people he'd dealt with had been B'arthon and lord A'ngles, but her no-nonsense way of doing business was a nice change of pace. "I'll take it. Mar'kon should have the iron purified over the next couple of days. You'll get the first pick of the ore. If you don't mind, I'd like a quick look at the woodworking tools you have, so I'll know about how much iron I'll have left for other trades."

Fea'en showed them a few tools, most of which were similar enough to what Jack was familiar with, even if their forms differed slightly. Axes, hammers, saws, chisels, and planes were all included in the offer.

There were a few odds and ends he wasn't familiar with, and Jack decided to take them back to show Angela and get her to take on them. If nothing else, he was sure she'd love to see where argu'n innovation differed from their own. After a final examination of the tools in question, they parted ways.

As Jack walked away, he lightly brushed his foot across the ground, causing pain to shoot from the impact throughout the rest of his leg. After he took a moment to collect himself, and explain to S'haar that he wasn't actually propositioning the gods so much as expressing pain and frustration, Jack decided it was about time to call it a night. Luckily, S'haar knew the location of the inn and led the way. Jack hobbled after, doing his best not to voice his thoughts about the unnatural solidity of argu'n chins.

~

When the pair first walked into the inn, they were greeted by a boisterous gathering. The crowd seemed to be mostly made up of locals relaxing after their day of labor, calling out to each other and the servers in as emphatic and noisome a fashion as possible, in an attempt to be heard over everyone else doing the same. There were many argu'n running from table to table while ladened down with food and drink, but one particular server seemed to be in high demand. She was somehow managing to keep track of ongoing conversations with three different tables before moving about to whatever group most loudly demanded her attention next.

Jack was beginning to wonder how in the world they were going to get anyone's attention in all this chaos, when the energetic argu'n's eyes locked onto him and S'haar. Much to the dismay of everyone else, all other cries for her attention fell on deaf ears as she hustled over to greet the pair.

Jack would place the approaching argu'n at a similar age to S'haar, but where S'haar was tall and athletic, the new argu'n could only be described as petite, relatively speaking. After all, the top of Jack's head came almost all the way up to her nose. She moved with the grace only someone used to carrying trays of food through a crowded dining room could have. Jack started to wonder if inhuman coordination should be included in the annoyingly long list of advantages the argu'n possessed.

With a wave of her hand and a flash of her smile, she greeted the pair. Jack tried his best not to be intimidated by how many teeth her smile seemed to contain, but once she spoke, her bright and cheerful personality put him at ease. "You must be the two I was told to expect! Lord A'ngles asked me to hold a seat for you at his table, as well as the best room in the inn. Not that there's a lot of choice in that regard, but it's the best of the three rooms I have. I'm Sur'ruin, by the way. This is my inn, and your table is this way."

She flitted through the crowd, slapping away the occasional wandering hand, while somehow still managing to be charming. Finally arriving at the table in question, she gestured to one of her servers, who brought over a pitcher and a couple of clean mugs.

Sur'ruin took the pitcher and filled the two mugs for her guests before continuing, "Your meal will be out shortly. We've had it warming for a little while, in anticipation of your arrival. Once you're ready to call it a night, just head upstairs. It's the last room at the end of the hallway. If you need anything more, just signal for me. I'll keep an eye out just for you!" Then she was on her way, working the crowd just like before.

A train of servers came over with their meal shortly after she left. The table that had seemed too large for the two of them suddenly seemed far too small for the mountain of food that was surely testing its legs' carrying capacity.

S'haar did her best not to dig into the meal placed before her as eagerly as her mouth and stomach demanded. Jack was glaring between her and her meal with something between jealousy and mild hatred. "You know, one of the first things I'm going to do when we get back is to test the food of this world to see what's safe for me to eat as well. It's one of the greatest tragedies of my crash that you get this feast to yourself, while all I have is another couple of ham sandwiches…"

S'haar couldn't disagree with his assessment, but there was no way she was turning the feast! down. She had never eaten this well in her time in the guard. Even the food she'd had in her time with Bar'thon had been too rich for her taste. This was a simple but well-prepared food. There were a wide variety of fruits, roots, and tubers her mother could have probably named. They'd been cooked, so they were crisp on the outside and juicy on the inside. To top everything off, the centerpiece of the meal was an entire side of roast arlack. S'haar knew she wouldn't be able to finish half of this in one sitting, but she was determined to put as much of a dent in it as she could before packing away the rest for the trip back. All this was washed down with the best drink the inn had to offer.

Jack examined the mug the innkeeper had placed before him. "It looks something like mead." After sniffing it, his face contorted somewhat. "But I'd place the alcohol content somewhat closer to a whiskey. Will drinking a mugful of this affect your judgment significantly?"

S'haar looked at her drink a moment before gulping down another mouthful. "Well, if I drink enough, it would, but one or two mug fulls shouldn't have too much of an effect."

Jack shook his head. "So chalk alcohol tolerance up as another area of unfair argu'n physiology. For the record, one full "mug" of that stuff would probably leave me well and truly wasted, assuming there's not something else in there that would simply kill me instead."

Jack set his drink down with a sigh. "I'd better steer clear of this if I'm gonna be taking a larger dose of pain meds so I can sleep through the night. Just a heads up, they'll leave me kind of out of it. You'll have to keep your wits about you so we're not both vulnerable."

S'haar took a large bite out of her arlack before replying. "No offense, but as far as I'm concerned, you're always vulnerable, whether you have full use of your senses or not. I have no plans on getting drunk while we're outside your home, and I'm acting as a bodyguard."

Jack looked like he wanted to protest her claims for a moment before deciding to take a large bite out of his sandwich instead. While he didn't mind fighting for a lost cause, he knew better than to challenge S'haar so shortly after he'd already proved her point for her by breaking his foot.

Meanwhile, S'haar abandoned all pretense of not enjoying her meal and dug in with a gusto that would have put a viking feast hall to shame back on Earth. Somehow she managed to take the occasional drink, despite always having both hands full of different cuts of meat. A hand would only stay empty long enough to grab another fist full of whatever caught her eye next.

Her eating habits might have cost Jack his appetite, if everything didn't look and smell so delicious. On the other hand, it was good to see S'haar enjoying herself so much. She'd certainly earned her keep and more this afternoon.

Jack took another bite of his sandwich and smiled to himself. Despite a few complications, he'd accomplished almost everything he'd set out to. Now Jack had various contacts and connections within the village, and over time those connections might even turn into friends and allies in his quest to get back home. In return, maybe he'd teach them a thing or two to help them avoid some of the pitfalls humanity had gotten stuck in back on Earth. All in all, Jack was feeling rather proud of himself.

~

S'haar cursed Jack for the first time since she had started to get to know him. She knew it wasn't entirely his fault. He was acting drunk because of his pain meds and not because he'd overindulged the way the village men tended to do. He'd even warned her something like this might happen. Still, she had to resist the urge to slap some sense into him. As delicate as he was, she'd probably break his jaw or something, and she didn't want to have to explain herself to Angela when she got back to the cave.

She'd given up on trying to guide him to the room and instead just picked him up and carried him upstairs. She ignored the varying degrees of laughter and smirks that followed her out of the room. Jack was muttering something about how back on earth, it was the groom's job to carry the bride…whatever the hell a groom or bride was.

She briefly amused herself by contemplating dumping him on the floor to fend for himself but decided against it. He was injured, not to mention with his delicate constitution, so he might just kill himself trying to get to the chamber pot in the middle of the night. Being the bodyguard to someone so weak was more annoying than she'd anticipated. She was starting to think the compensation they'd offered her wasn't so outlandish after all.

Jack's clouded and wandering eyes suddenly focused on S'haar's, and when he spoke, his voice was definitely slurred. "First of all, I'm not delicate! You all are just freakishly durable… Furthermore…you know, I always thought you were kinda sexy, in an exotic alien chick kind of way…"

S'haar was starting to seriously reconsider slapping him, when Jack passed out and started drooling on himself almost immediately. With a sigh full of long-suffering exasperation, S'haar tucked Jack in for the night.

That done, she went back downstairs to pack the remainder of her meal away, only to find Sur'ruin waiting with it already packed and ready. Handing it over, Sur'ruin spoke with a mischievous glint in her eyes. "You know, when I heard about all the excitement and trouble the two of you caused this afternoon, I was expecting someone more imposing than your companion. I imagine someone so small that can also cause such an uproar must be quite the challenge to watch out for."

S'haar couldn't help but let a little of her exhaustion show. "You have no idea…"

With a conspiratorial wink, Sur'ruin added, "Still, at least he's kinda cute, in an odd sort of way. It makes you wanna wrap him up and take him home, like some kind of lost housepet."

S'haar didn't know what to say to that. Instead, she muttered her thanks, took the meal upstairs, and stored it with the rest of their belongings. That done, she settled in for the night as well, falling asleep with one final thought.

Why did Sur'ruin's description of Jack bother me so much?

Chapter 10

Something seemed off when Jack woke up the next morning. It wasn't just the fact that his jaw felt as though a nasty bruise was forming, nor was it the fact that he couldn't move his arms. What was bothering him the most was that there was a presence breathing heavily beside him on the bed.

As he cracked his eyes open, Jack quickly discovered the reason his arms were immobile. Someone tied them up in the middle of the night. What he could see from his prone position was a veritable maze of rope and knots. Jack almost got a headache, trying to figure out how they were all interconnected. Changing his focus to the presence beside him, he could see S'haar's back rising and falling as she took deep, even breaths.

Jack tried to put together the previous night's events, but found he couldn't remember anything after sitting down for dinner. Something told him that maybe the standard dose of pain meds for a broken foot might have been a bit more than he could handle. Still, it could be worse. At least S'haar hadn't left him in a ditch somewhere.

While he was trying to figure out what to do about his predicament, S'haar's breathing stilled. She looked over her shoulder at Jack, giving him a glare full of ice and knives as she sat up and stretched.

Somewhat uncomfortable with the current situation, Jack decided to break the ice, metaphorically speaking. Looking down at the ropes around his arm, he thought it might be wise to accept responsibility. "Sooo…judging by the ropes and my jaw, I have some apologizing to do? I'm afraid that's the first time in a long time I've taken pain meds that strong, and I might have taken too high a dose. I honestly can't remember anything after dinner. I hope I didn't… That is to say, I hope I wasn't…"

Jack's apology floundered, but S'haar seemed to take a bit of pity on him. Her glare lost a bit of its icy edge before she spoke. "Well, I resisted the urge to slap you after you all but professed your undying love to me last night." The color drained from Jack's face, leaving it even more pale than usual. "But when you got handsy in the middle of the night," Jack's face now matched the snow, and his mouth moved with unvocalized terror, "first I reacted," she glanced at his jaw, "then I resolved the problem." She glanced at the rope.

Jack was a stuttering mess, tripping over his own words in an attempt to apologize faster. S'haar cut him off. "I will forgive you just this once, so long as it never happens again. As I've already mentioned, you bought my services as a guide and guard. You didn't buy me!"

Jack's skin changed to an odd shade of green before he spoke up, and S'haar couldn't help but be amused at the color spectrum humans seemed to be able to shift between. "Yes, of course, it won't happen again! I can't express how sorry I am! Seriously, that was inexcusable, and I am so very, *very* sorry!"

S'haar cut him off before reaching out with what appeared to be a suddenly larger and much more dangerous claw. Jack started to break out into a cold sweat when she hooked the claw around a loop of rope close to his wrist before pulling and undoing a section of one of the knots. "You should be able to manage the rest from there. I'm going to head down and grab some breakfast. Feel free to join me, as soon as you are able…"

As S'haar left the room, Jack looked at the remaining tangle of knots and tried to puzzle out where to begin.

~

When Jack finally hobbled his way downstairs, rubbing his arms to return some feeling to them, he saw S'haar sitting at the same table as last night. She seemed to be enjoying a plate full of various cooked meats and eggs with a small loaf of bread on the side. Jack sat down, grumbled something about the universe being out to get him and how its family tree must resemble the stitching on a baseball before he grabbed some of the granola bars he'd brought with him.

S'haar was finishing up her breakfast as another argu'n entered the inn. He looked around at the various guests quietly eating breakfast before his gaze latched onto the odd pair. He approached the two of them with a look of indifference before stopping just shy of the table. "You're Jack, I take it?"

Despite clearly being a question, Jack could tell it was really more of a statement. He nodded his head anyway. The argu'n jerked his thumb over his shoulder, toward the front door. "Got a delivery for you from Lady Fea'en. She said to make sure you take a look and approve it before I leave."

Jack nodded and stood up. Before he could even offer his hand, the other argu'n was already walking away, presumably headed to the cart and tools. Jack shrugged and followed, with S'haar close behind.

The cart was just outside the front of the inn. At first glance, it looked rather shoddy. It was readily apparent that it was cobbled together from several other carts. Many parts were obviously made from different wood types, and it was only symmetrical in the loosest sense of the word.

However, on closer inspection, the cart was quite sturdy. While it was clear that many of the components had already seen plenty of hard use, nothing looked like it was going to give out any time soon. A few of the more delicate parts even seemed new. Overall, the cart was in good condition and would stand up to continuous hard use far better than anything Jack could have cobbled together this quickly.

Looking over the tools, Jack could see they were much the same. The handles were well worn, and the blades had been sharpened more than once, but they were sturdy and well-cared for. They had plenty of life left in them.

"These will do perfectly. Tell Fea'en that I'm quite satisfied and will happily do business with her again." S'haar translated while Jack wrapped the tools back in the oily rags they had been stored in.

The argu'n nodded his understanding and was on his way. Jack looked to S'haar while he finished securing the tools. "Let's get the cart loaded, then go see how the refining is going. I want to know about how many bars there'll be when all is said and done. If there's enough, there is one last trade I'd like to make before we head back."

As Jack and S'haar approached the forges, several apprentices nudged the workers sitting next to themselves and looked pointedly toward the pair. The whispers had no sooner started up when old Mar'kon appeared seemingly out of thin air. His signature rag lashed out to "encourage" his apprentices to focus on their work, rather than the now infamous duo. Having reestablished order in his workplace, Mar'kon approached the two distractions.

The expression Mar'kon wore was the exact same one he'd had when negotiating prices and dealing with B'arthon. Jack wasn't sure if monotone was a facial expression, but if it was, it belonged to Mar'kon. He reminded Jack of an old math teacher he'd once had.

Mar'kon spoke first. "Come to check on our progress? Well, I don't mind admitting you were right. That is some of the purest ore I've had the pleasure to work with. You keep bringing ore of that quality around, and I'll cut you a better deal next time."

Even though his face, voice, and even movements were precisely the same as Jack remembered, somehow, Mar'kon gave off the feeling that he was pleased. Jack offered his hand again, which Mar'kon shook without hesitation this time. Jack spoke up, with S'haar translating as usual. "Glad to hear it! I was hoping to get an estimation of how many bars we'd have when all is said and done. I've already traded a few of them away to Lady Fea'en, and I was wondering how many I'd have leftover? Also, I promised her first choice of refined ore, so if you could send a message to her when they are all finished, I'd appreciate it."

Mar'kon nodded before leading the way to the ore-turned-bars. "Easily done, we should have it finished up before the end of the day. I'll have them all laid out and ready for the old bat to come and inspect." Jack could tell the insult was more of a friendly jab at a fellow tradeswoman rather than an actual insult.

Showing them to a growing pile of refined bars, Mar'kon continued. "We're about half done, so expect double what you see here."

Jack did the math. Taking out what he owed Mar'kon and Fea'en, he should have just enough to get what he was hoping for. "Perfect. Once we get back, I'm going to have to set up some infrastructure, but once that's done, you should expect a new shipment of this quantity or larger every couple of weeks, depending on how much the winter around here slows us down, that is."

For the first time today, Mar'kon's face changed in the subtlest of ways, indicating mild surprise. Jack assumed this was the Mar'kon equivalent of picking his jaw up off the floor. When he spoke, even his voice was barely but perceptively different. "You're going to keep running ore in the middle of winter? You're either desperate or insane. Or, more likely, both."

Jack had a wry smile as he shrugged his shoulders and spoke. "It can't be helped. I have a lot that needs to get done and a limited timeline to get it done. If it makes you feel any better, my people have several techniques and tools that make traveling in winter only slightly more dangerous than doing it in the spring or fall."

Mar'kon's face and voice returned to normal. "It's your life. Though I'd hate to lose a supply of ore like this, so try not to die."

Jack laughed as he turned to leave. "I'll do my best not to inconvenience you by dying!"

He barely heard the response Mar'kon muttered under his breath. "See that you don't, kid."

~

As the two pulled up to the hunter's lodge, S'haar was feeling some reservations. Wearily looking up at the skull of a wolgen hanging over the doorway, she brought up her concerns. "Dek'thul will not be happy to see me again. We didn't part on good terms…"

Jack hopped down from his makeshift seat in the cart and hobbled toward the door, followed reluctantly by S'haar. He spoke over his shoulder as he walked. "Maybe so, but I suspect we'll need to work with the hunters on occasion. Let's see if we can't at least get a civil working relationship established."

Opening the door and walking in, Jack took a moment for his eyes to adjust to the gloom inside the large hut. Looking around, Jack couldn't help but feel a little intimidated. Everywhere his gaze wondered seemed to be yet another in a growing list of the most dangerous-looking argu'n Jack had seen yet.

Their clothing was decorated with the teeth and other bones of their hunts. A few even wore large-fanged skulls as helmets. They were all well-toned and moved with a sleek precision that spoke of silent danger. There were many carcasses in various stages of being processed. Some were being skinned, others were having the meat removed and processed, and others were having their heads or skulls mounted as trophies.

Even though everyone seemed to be focused on their various jobs, Jack couldn't help but feel that he and S'haar were the center of attention. No one was looking directly at them, but Jack occasionally caught careful sidelong glances and sensed that even the tiniest of sounds were being carefully analyzed. It was as though he was being hunted by every argu'n in the room. Well, all except one.

"S'haar! I'm surprised to see you here! After the falling out you and pops had, I didn't think you'd ever walk through that door again!"

Walking toward them was the single friendliest argu'n Jack had seen to date. Sur'ruin had been pleasant enough, but this young argu'n seemed positively eager to greet the pair, though Jack couldn't help but notice how little of the attention was directed his way.

The youth was well-toned, though his muscles were not as developed as most other argu'n around. When he moved, it further cemented Jack's theory that argu'n were supernaturally coordinated. Though, to be fair, this youth put every other argu'n to shame in that department. It was as though he was completely aware of the exact position of every inch of his body. His movements appeared slow and relaxed, but he crossed the distance between them with deceptive quickness.

S'haar crossed her arms and stepped forward, greeting the enthusiastic youth. "Hello again, Lon'thul. I admit I wasn't looking forward to seeing the old churlish again. It's somewhat of a relief to see he's not here at the moment."

At that, Jack couldn't help but notice that most of the hunters present were chuckling at her response. Also, the female argu'n laughed a little louder and longer than the males. Though once again, Lon'thul put them all to shame, throwing his head back and letting out a loud, barking laugh.

Lon'thul gathered himself, shaking his head as he spoke. "Don't let pops hear you say something like that. This time, he might try and get you kicked out of the village rather than just having you removed from the hunters!"

S'haar's gaze grew a little cold after that. "I *was* kicked out of the village. They left me tied to a stake as a sacrifice to the dragon." Jerking her thumb over her shoulder, she pointed at her new partner. "If it weren't for Jack and the dragon being friendly, I'd have been something's dinner by now."

At that, Lon'thul's face became a mask of astonishment, quickly followed by anger. Looking around accusingly at the other suddenly sheepish hunters in the room, his voice now had a sharp edge to it. "Why wasn't I told about this?"

Most hunters seemed to suddenly find their various tasks to be the most interesting things in the world, requiring all of their attention. The exception being one of the older females who met his gaze somewhat coldly. "You were away on a hunt when it happened, and your father told us not to trouble you when you got back. He was afraid you'd do something stupid, like go and challenge the dragon."

Lon'thul looked like he wanted to argue further, but S'haar interrupted him with a wave of her hand. "Regardless, it all ended up alright. I have a place to stay and a new job. Speaking of which, we're here because the boss wanted to do some trading." S'haar nodded her head toward Jack as she spoke.

For the first time, Lon'thul directed his full attention to Jack. "Huh, S'haar called you 'the boss'? That's more respect than she's shown anyone since, well, ever! What'd you do to make that happen?"

Jack looked somewhat confused for a moment, scratching the back of his head as he spoke. S'haar translated somewhat awkwardly, due to her being the subject of the conversation. "Well, I don't know that I really did anything deserving of respect. I guess I treated her like an equal and compensated her adequately for her services?"

Lon'thul closed his eyes and nodded sagely. "Treating her with respect to get respect, clever! I'll have to remember that."

Jack couldn't tell if Lon'thul was joking or not, so he decided to just get to business. "Well, the reason we're here is to trade some refined iron for some hide and meat. How much can I get for six bars?"

Lon'thul's expression changed from an excited youth to an eager businessman. "You're in luck. I just happened to be finishing up cleaning a churlish. For six purified iron bars, I'll trade you all the skin and meat I can get out of it. It's a fair amount. You got something to haul it in?"

Jack pointed to the door. "We've got a cart right out front. Throw in a few thigh bones, and you've got a deal."

Lon'thul looked a little surprised at the additional request but didn't argue. "Sure, sounds like a deal. Let me just finish up here, and we'll get you loaded and on your way! It's right over here."

Walking over, Jack noticed a churlish was something like a cross between a deer and a rabbit, in that they were a large quadruped with overdeveloped hind legs. Jack couldn't help but imagine how far and fast this thing must have been able to jump. Once startled, they must have been almost impossible to catch, leaving him to believe that Lon'thul must be one hell of a stealthy hunter. He couldn't help but be a little impressed by the eager youth.

Lon'thul flayed the last of the meat from the bones before looking up to address S'haar again. "So, if you're not in the village anymore, where are you staying these days?"

S'haar smiled her favorite intimidating smile. It was full of a few too many sharp teeth for Jack's comfort. "With the dragon, of course. Jack and I have a working relationship with her, and in return, we get room and board, among other benefits."

Lon'thul looked more than a little surprised this time. "You stay *WITH* the dragon? Aren't you afraid she's going to eat you?"

S'haar couldn't help but have a little fun at the expense of Lon'thul's inexperience. "Not at all, but you could learn a thing or two from Jack here. If you treat a lady with the respect she deserves, she won't bite…usually."

At that, Lon'thul looked back and forth between Jack and S'haar with wide eyes, as though trying to discern any hidden meanings to S'haar's words. Meanwhile, the women around the hut were laughing at his misfortune.

Jack merely shrugged, with an understanding smile on his face. "Don't look at me for answers. I know better than to get in the way of a woman having fun and her prey." S'haar decided not to translate that last bit and left Lon'thul in the dark.

Lon'thul finally figured it was best to shut his mouth and finish up his work. However, he couldn't escape the laughter surrounding him.

Chapter 11

-Two days ago-

Angela was bored, or maybe more accurately, she was going stir-crazy. She hadn't been alone this long since, well, ever. Even when Jack was asleep, there was usually plenty to do. Monitoring Jack's vitals, scanning whatever system they were passing through, or even just trying to pick out fragments of old radio signals from the background radiation of the universe. But with Jack and S'haar gone, and her sensors muted by the mountain currently burying her, Angela had never had so little to occupy her attention.

She'd thought about shutting down temporarily to kill some time, but then she worried that some damage to the ship might prevent her from starting up properly again. Also, what if there was an emergency, and Jack came back early and needed her help? The time it took to boot up could be the difference between life and death! What if the mountain collapsed further around the ship, sealing Jack off from his home? What if…

As Angela's processors started feeding themselves ever more improbable doomed scenarios, her avatar faded into existence despite no one being present to interact with her. She examined herself with one of her sensors as her avatar stared back. After a moment, she finally spoke to herself. "Wait, I've seen Jack react this way before. This is anxiety… This is a… panic attack…?"

She'd witnessed Jack experiencing a panic attack a few times. It was a reasonably common occurrence shortly after their parents were murdered. Usually, they happened when he was required to leave the ship and travel into unfamiliar territory. As the years passed, the attacks happened less frequently. Regardless, she could still pick up a spike in anxiety in him whenever he left the ship. Over the years, he'd developed various tricks and other methods for dealing with the stress, many of which were second nature for him now.

Angela had never felt anxiety when Jack left before, not like this anyway, but she'd usually ridden sidesaddle with him via a signal connecting him to the ship from some type of transmitter. This time, an entire mountain was blocking signals from going out and coming in, preventing her from keeping an eye on her little brother.

She knew how attached he'd grown to the ship and her, but she hadn't realized the same thing had happened in reverse. She watched as she shook her avatar's head at herself and chuckled. "I'm a right mess, aren't I?" 'Looking' right into a sensor, she continued her thought. "I'm even talking to myself. Who has ever heard of a ship talking to herself?"

What did Jack do to calm himself when the anxiety was getting too much to handle? Well, for one thing, he used puzzles. Not jigsaw puzzles or the like, well, maybe once in a while, but not usually. When he was out and about, he'd start doing math in his head. That wouldn't help Angela though. She could do math too quickly and easily. Besides, that was usually only a stalling tactic until he could get somewhere to do some real stress relief.

When things got really bad and Jack realized it, he tried to "reset" his brain. He'd usually put on a demanding video game while simultaneously watching a movie, and sometimes even listening to music as well. Doing so many things at once overwhelmed his brain to the point it couldn't dwell on anxiety, and his body would slowly stabilize itself. The process of flushing various fight or flight chemicals from his mind usually took a minimum of twenty minutes, but then he was able to think more clearly and objectively.

Angela didn't have any chemicals wreaking havoc on her brain, but maybe a similar tactic would still work to calm her processors. Perhaps if she distracted herself for a bit, she could think more clearly once she reexamined the situation. Looking through Jack's library of classic games, she decided she should start with something challenging. "He always enjoys the more brutally challenging games when he's stressed. Maybe one of those will do."

Shortly after starting up the game, she could tell it wasn't going to be anywhere near enough. With all the processing power available to her,

Angela had way too much time to react perfectly to every attack. It still might be a good idea, but maybe she needed to scale it up a bit. Angela started going through Jack's library of games he'd acquired over the years. Any that caught her eye got thrown up on a different monitor. As her experiment got underway, a small corner of Angela's program noticed only two hours had passed since Jack and S'haar had left. It was going to be a long two days.

~

Jack and S'haar were finally on their way back. This was the longest Jack had been away from his ship in years, and he could feel himself becoming unreasonably annoyed by the smallest of things. That was usually a sign that stress had been building up in the back of his mind, and he had to start watching himself for signs he might be on a downturn. Initially, he'd been distracted by small things like survival and keeping a mountain from burying him alive. When that slowed to a less immediate demand, he'd been distracted by getting to know his new companion and the new world that now held him captive.

Now that they were headed back home, Jack felt as though a weight were lifting from his shoulders. Something about going home always made him breathe a little easier and allowed him to think a little more clearly.

He felt a little ashamed that he was just sitting in the cart while S'haar did all the work. Not that he'd ever been the heavy lifter of the pair up before, but there was something to be said for pulling one's own weight.

As Jack shifted his weight to a more comfortable position, he could see S'haar lost in her own world as she pushed the cart along. Deciding they both needed a break from their thoughts, Jack thought it was time to disrupt the relative silence.

S'haar seemed to notice Jack's attention as her eyes suddenly focused on him instead of whatever inner vision had held her attention a moment ago. Jack decided now was as good a time as any to bring up a possibly touchy subject. "Mind if I ask you something personal? If you don't want to get into it, you can tell me to mind my own business, and I'll leave you be, but I was wondering, what happened to alienate you from the rest of the village? I know about the captain of the guard and the hunter chief, but there seemed to be plenty of decent enough people in the village. For example, Lon'thul seemed really interested in being friends with you."

S'haar flashed a bit of a sad smile. "Lon'thul is a nice enough kid, but he's just a young pup who doesn't know what he wants yet. Hell of a hunter though. In the lodge, he's second only to his father."

Shaking her head, S'haar got back on track. "Well, since I know your sob story, I suppose it's only fair you know mine. My isolation started before I ever left the guard. While I don't envy your history, I do envy your family. Your dad sounded like a real decent guy. Mine wasn't."

S'haar took a deep breath and refocused on the distant horizon as she spoke. "He was a guard like me, but he liked to drink way too much. He was always missing patrols, and even when he went, he spent most of his time patrolling the inn. The only reason they let him stay in the guard was that he was unbeatable in the ring. Getting beaten down while training with the old drunk saved the lives of more than a few of our guards, because they learned dirty, underhanded tricks that later saved their lives."

S'har's grip on the handles was tightening enough that Jack could hear the creaking of the wood in her grasp. "The only other time he was of any use was if raiders showed up, but he enjoyed killing far too much. The only times he'd come home sober was after he got to kill something or someone."

S'haar developed a scowl that would have terrified Jack if it had been directed his way. "Other than that, the only time he was home was if he needed a place to sleep or sober up. I'll never know what my mother saw in him. Maybe there was something more to him long ago, but it was long gone by the time I knew any better. Everything he made was spent on drink and females, leaving my mom and me to fend for ourselves."

S'haar's eyes hardened, and her smile developed a feral edge. "Then the old bastard crossed one line too many. I'm not sure who's mate he got caught in bed with, but it was someone important enough that he got himself exiled in the middle of winter. Can't say I miss him. The world's definitely better off without him."

Jack was stunned. He knew S'haar had no patience with what she considered "useless males", and with a father like that, now he could understand why. Jack was suddenly very glad he'd ended up on S'haar's good side, at least so far.

S'haar's face calmed and took on a sad expression, as though she remembered something bittersweet. "Thankfully, my mom was different. Her only real sin was loving that waste of a male. Because of her, I grew up loved and healthy. My happiest memories were all of the times spent with her. In the spring, summer, and fall, we'd go wandering in the forest, where we'd forage for supplies to feed ourselves or sell in town for food. I never knew what she did to bring home food in the winter. Now that I know a little more about the world, I'm not sure I want to know, but our home was always warm, and there was always food on the table."

S'haar's expression darkened as she continued on. "The only thing I'll never forgive her for was giving up after my father was gone. He never did anything for her, but something in her died when he was sent away. She never fully recovered, and it took years, but eventually, she just faded away, leaving me on my own. I'll never understand how she could ever become so dependent on someone so worthless…"

She was quite a moment while a series of emotions crossed her face, but eventually, S'haar's expression settled back into an emotionless mask. There there was a weariness that indicated she was profoundly tired of life's paltry offerings. "After that, the days began to blur together. Everything I owned was taken as payment to provide food and a place to sleep until I was an adult. The other kids started out picking on me for being an orphan. In turn, I'd hit them for opening their fat mouths. I guess I inherited a bit of my father's talent for fighting because, after enough squabbles, I caught the guard's eye. They took me in, and that was my life until recently." S'haar shrugged. "You already know what happened after that."

A lot of pieces fell into place in Jack's mind as he took in everything he'd been told. They traveled in silence for several minutes, listening to the creak of the wagon and the song of some creature trying to find itself a mate.

After a few moments, the tension finally eased and Jack took a breath to break the silence once more. "I'm sorry you had to go through all that. No one ever should have to experience a life like that, especially a child. Sadly, we both know the universe can be a cold and lonely place. However, for the record, I'm glad you didn't let it break you. There's no one else I'd rather have as a guide, bodyguard, and friend."

S'haar's eyes sharpened with a look that Jack was coming to associate with her sometimes sharp sense of humor. "So we're friends now, are we? Here I thought you were the boss?"

Jack smiled in return. "You and I both know that without your help, my odds of surviving this world would be negligible at best. I'd say we're both helping each other out. You're not just some muscle I hired. You're a partner and a friend…I hope."

S'haar looked lost in thought for a minute, then grinned. "Friends, huh? I know you tossed that word around before, but I just thought you were trying to get on my good side. I suppose I could let you try out for the role. Though I warn you, I'm not the easiest person to get along with."

Jack grinned back and shrugged. "Well, if you'll put up with me being a relatively weak, traumatized, shut-in, I suppose I can, in turn, put up with you having a bit of a temper and being blunt with your thoughts."

The smile slowly left S'haar's face as she grew serious once more. She looked at Jack as though searching for answers. "How do you know I'm not broken?"

Jack was momentarily stunned by the sudden shift in the subject. "I'm sorry, what?"

S'haar looked withdrawn, as though weary of the answer to her question. "When you said you were glad I didn't let my experience break me, how do you know that I'm not broken?"

Jack smiled for a moment, making sure S'haar was looking at him before he answered. "That's simple. I know you're not broken because you are still moving forward. A broken person stops fighting. They just lie down and give up. You might bear a scar or two where no one can see, but you are still moving forward, still trying to find a place for yourself in life." Jack chuckled. "And I have no doubt that if you can't find a place for yourself, you'll make one. For the record, I pity anyone stupid enough to get in your way."

S'haar gave Jack her best predator's grin, the one that always slightly unsettled Jack. That many sharp teeth had no business being in one person's mouth. Then with a look that made Jack think S'haar was the real dragon, she replied. "Well then, don't get in my way, and I'll try and keep you alive long enough that we can both find our place in this life."

Jack laughed a little nervously before shaking his head and replying. "Fair enough, it's a deal. You know, crashing on this ball of mud you call home is starting to seem like it wasn't the worst mistake I've ever made."

S'haar laughed as well. "Well, being left as a sacrifice to such a mediocre dragon is starting to have its own bright side!"

~

Jack felt relief wash over him as they pulled up to the cave. He was back, and all was right in the world. Aside from a broken foot and acquiring a new mortal enemy, everything went as planned. S'haar found a place to park the cart next to the ship's door, and Jack hobbled out while S'haar grabbed the first armful of leathers and meat to bring inside.

Jack was a little surprised Angela hadn't already opened the door to greet them. Instead, he placed his hand on the scanner next to the door. After a moment, a chime sounded, and the door opened. The sight that greeted him left him speechless. Whatever he had been expecting, this was not it.

Every screen in the ship was playing a different game, and at every screen was a different Angela, screaming at the game in question. "Who programmed this buggy mess? That's bull. I dodged that in plenty of time! Where the hell is the ballistic fiber hiding? Why does Gandhi have a *nuke*?"

Jack just stood there stunned for a moment before speaking up, his voice betraying the fact that he was wondering if he hadn't finally gone the rest of the way off the deep end, and this was all the resulting hallucination. "Ummm… Hi…we're home?"

A dozen or more Angelas yelped in surprise before fading from existence, leaving the screens unattended, half of which were soon displaying some variation of "You died."

One Angela avatar re-appeared before Jack and a very confused-looking S'haar. Angela had the good grace to look abashed that they had walked in without her noticing until Jack had said something. After a brief moment where most of the screens shut off, the AI laughed nervously and finally responded, her voice fading into an ashamed squeak as she spoke. "Uh, hi! Welcome back! Has it been two days already? My, how time flies…"

Chapter 12

Jack was sitting on the exam table while Angela's avatar gave him a once over. S'haar now realized the many devices above and around the table were Angela's actual eyes and ears, and the reason Angela's avatar existed was for the ease of mind of her mortal friends, rather than any kind of necessity on the AI's part. All of these machines and devices being a person was almost too much for S'haar's mind to accept, but the friendly blue girl leaning over, listening to Jack explain what had happened was something else altogether. S'haar did not doubt that she was a person, and right now, she was an outraged one.

Angela was shouting at Jack, who had the good sense to look contrite at the moment. "What do you mean you broke your foot kicking a particularly large argu'n in the face? Do you have a death wish? Did you want to leave me stranded on this planet? Was that your plan?"

Jack was holding his hands up palm out, clearly signaling his surrender in the face of his sister's fury. "I didn't have a plan, it all happened so fast, and there I was dangling from his hands. I thought S'haar was going to take longer dealing with her thug, so I was trying to buy her some time, that's all."

Angela's face was a mask of disbelief. "So you thought the best way to resolve the issue was to KICK THE EIGHT FOOT TALL BEHEMOTH IN THE FACE? WHAT DID I BOTHER MAKING THAT GUN FOR?"

Jack looked like he knew the next words out of his mouth wouldn't exonerate him in any way. "I was still hoping to resolve things without killing anyone…" His voice had risen an octave by the end.

Angela looked like she wished she could slap him. "If being held by your neck by a man twice your mass who could snap said neck on a whim isn't life or death, when exactly do you think it would be?"

Jack didn't look like he had a good response, so he wisely kept his mouth shut and shrugged apologetically instead. Angela stared him down for a few more moments until he started to squirm, then the AI shifted her gaze to S'haar.

S'haar was more than a little worried. If Angela was this angry at Jack, her own brother, how much angrier would she be with the bodyguard who failed to keep him safe.

Angela gave S'haar an indecipherable look before she spoke. "S'haar, thank you for getting my hopeless brother home in one piece *despite* his best efforts. If it weren't for you keeping him safe, I don't know what I'd have done. If I had a body, I'd give you the biggest hug! Instead, you'll just have to accept my thanks and know that I owe you a big one.

Glaring over her shoulder at Jack, she amended her statement. "We both owe you a big one."

S'haar had expected many things when Angela finally addressed her, but gratitude wasn't anywhere near the top of the list. Shaking her head, she responded. "You don't owe me anything. It's my job to keep him safe. Besides, I'm just beginning to understand the crazy new world you two have introduced to me. It would be a shame to lose either of you at this point."

Angela looked at S'haar with eyes dilated to the point of being all pupils. "You're like the bad-ass big sister I never had…"

Turning back to Jack, Angela was back in charge. "Luckily, this is a relatively easy injury to heal up. Ideally, we'd spread this out over multiple treatments, but we're in a bit of a time crunch, so we'll have to speed it up a bit. I can still safely heal this up in about a day. The problem is anesthesia slows down the treatment, so we'll be giving you a low dose of pain medications instead. Just enough to take the edge of the pain off. They'll still slow down the process, but not nearly as much, and maybe the pain will teach you not to act without thinking again."

S'haar laughed. "More pain meds? You might want to keep his dose a little lighter this time, given what he was like the first time."

Angela turned back around, her hand on her forehead and a look of concern on her face. "I'm afraid to ask, what else did he do?"

S'haar slightly enjoyed ignoring the pleading look Jack was giving her from behind Angela. "Well…"

After a few minutes of explaining Jack's behavior as the night progressed, culminating with the resolution of a slap and subsequent creative use of ropes, Angela's face went through a performance of expressions.

Settling back into a look of fury, Angela turned back to Jack. "You did WHAT? I CAN'T BELIEVE YOU! I THOUGHT YOU HAD BETTER MANNERS THAN THAT! YOU ARE LUCKY IT WAS S'HAAR WHO DEALT WITH YOU AND NOT ME! I WOULD HAVE HAD YOU HANGING OUT THE WINDOW BY THE ROPES SHE USED! IF YOU EVER DO SOMETHING LIKE THAT AGAIN, I'LL SPEND THE NEXT YEAR COMING UP WITH IDEAS TO TEACH YOU MORE RESPECT!"

Deep inside, S'haar couldn't help but feel a little bad for Jack. He was outnumbered by women who had no hang-ups about making it clear to him where he stood in the pecking order at this moment. All Jack could do was weather the storm and hope he'd live to see another day. However, outwardly S'haar couldn't stop herself from laughing as Angela continued berating a male ten times her size.

~

Rapidly healing a broken foot was not Jack's idea of a good time. Even the reasonably strong pain meds he'd been allowed to take couldn't compensate for the bones and muscles shifting around inside his foot. It didn't feel like his foot was on fire, so much as it felt like his foot was severely asleep, and he was putting pressure on it, causing pins and needles to shoot up and down his foot. The problem was the pins and needles sensation refused to leave and went on for hours. He decided it was something of an understatement to call the experience annoying, wondering more than once if jamming a knife into his thigh might not be a worthwhile distraction.

At least the whole thing didn't have to be done in the cramped med bay. Instead, they had wheeled the machine out into the living room, and Jack had set up shop on the couch. He decided that it was time to introduce S'haar to another classic movie, since there was nothing else he could do.

At the same time, Angela thought now would be the perfect time to teach S'haar her first lesson in human cooking. She called it "making popcorn." Angela began her lecture. "We're not going to make microwave popcorn like some barbarian. This is the good stuff, stovetop popcorn. All you need is a little oil, salt, and of course, corn kernels. Now, let's get started."

S'haar learned that popcorn was a long-honored tradition among humans and was required to be eaten while watching movies. She was further delighted to discover that it was a light and salty snack that went perfectly with a beverage. Angela and Jack debated which drink to serve it with, which was apparently complicated by S'haar's inability to taste "sweet." In the end, they went with a carbonated citrus drink that probably would have been too sour if it hadn't been balanced out by the salty flavor of the popcorn.

Jack thought it would be a good idea to show S'haar a more realistic depiction of earth history this time, and after her encounter with her recent ex, he suspected that she could do with a good revenge story as well. He chose "The Count of Monte Cristo."

Refreshments in hand, they began the movie. At first, they had to pause the film periodically for Jack to explain concepts such as ocean vessels, a gold-based economy, and books. However, as the film continued, S'haar found herself more and more engrossed, only occasionally interrupting the movie to make fun of the fight scenes. It turns out the intricacies of swashbuckling swordplay is not as impressive to someone walking around in their own organically grown full-plate.

Despite not being as impressed by the action this time, S'haar was still engrossed by the story of betrayal, revenge, and reconciliation. After the finale she stood and applauded, a custom she'd learned after the first movie. Jack had chosen well this time.

As the night wound down, Angela performed one final "inspection" of Jack's foot and declared, "Ready to go! You'll probably be a bit sore for the next few days, but the more you use it, the quicker that'll fade."

With the feeling of his bones regrowing and the muscles reattaching themselves finally gone, Jack's leg felt oddly numb. Rubbing his leg in an attempt to restore feeling, Jack thought out loud. "Well, I can deal with that. We need to resume getting this place up and running, anyway. We can spend the cold mornings in the cave mining, then we'll switch to harvesting trees and shaping lumber in the afternoons."

Over the next couple of weeks, the work progressed slowly but steadily. Jack was pleased to find one physical aspect where humans still held the advantage: good old human endurance. It didn't completely make up for the gap in their strength, speed, and coordination, but S'haar needed to take breaks more often than Jack. Soon they fell into a pattern where Jack would take on the slow and steady jobs while S'haar tackled anything involving heavy lifting.

Jack would mine and sort the ore, then S'haar would load it up and cart it back to the ship. He would cut down the tree and trim the branches, then she would haul the tree to where it could be shaped. Cutting the logs down to a manageable size was a two-person job, so they moved at S'haar's pace for that one. The scraps that couldn't be shaped were set aside to be used as fuel or traded in town. Jack learned firewood was a lot more valuable to a semi-cold-blooded species than he'd originaly thought.

He was pleased with the progress they'd made. They had more iron ready to go than they'd had in the first load, and Angela had all the raw materials she'd need to get the transceiver made. They didn't want to draw too much attention to the gold and silver, so the AI would expend the necessary energy to purify those herself.

Looking at the load of iron, Jack decided there was one final thing to do before they went back to the village. He turned his attention to S'haar, who was catching her breath after filling the cart, and put his plan into motion. "Well, we're pretty much ready to go, but I'll need to finalize a few things here first. You don't need to hang around for that though, and we could use some more fresh meat. Why don't you take the day off to go hunting? You can test out the new spears Angela made you, and maybe just take a bit of time to relax."

Jack had Angela make the spears in question the night before. Two smaller spears weighted toward the front for throwing, and a larger spear more balanced for melee. At first, Angela had protested the delay in what she said was more crucial work, but when Jack told her of his plan, she'd readily agreed.

S'haar couldn't help but feel something was a little off. Jack obviously wanted her out of the house for a while, but she supposed he was entitled to his secrets. The spears were of far better quality than any she'd ever seen, just like everything else these two made, and the gifts probably warranted indulging Jack's whims, at least for now.

~

S'haar was enjoying the solitude. Not that Angela and Jack were lousy company. She'd only known them a few weeks, and they were already some of the closest friends she'd ever had, but S'haar had been alone for far too long not to enjoy a little peace and quiet away from the noisy duo.

S'haar brought the sled with her to help with the transportation of any prey she caught and was currently dragging it behind her as she lazily ambled through the hills. In the distance, she could hear the mating calls of a churlish. She briefly considered tracking it before deciding to indulge herself by following the river instead. It was a surprisingly warm day for this time of year, and there was only a gentle breeze to disturb the plants around her. S'haar's tongue flicked out, tasting the air. She was enjoying the sights and smells around her. These days she wasn't worried about where she would sleep or when her next meal would be, so she could take some time to enjoy her surroundings.

Following the river around the bend of a hill, S'haar found her target. A young kovaack was enjoying a refreshing drink from the river. He was a bit on the small side for this time of year, probably a runt. This was an excellent opportunity to try out the new spears with minimal risk.

She hefted the first throwing spear and marveled again at its balance. She'd practiced throwing them before leaving and knew she could consistently hit within a foot or two of her target at about seventy feet, and she could throw them over three hundred feet, if she was just going for distance, but she'd be unlikely to hit anything at that range.

She crept close as she could while still giving herself time for a second throw before switching to the long spear. When she closed to within forty feet, she stopped, took aim, and threw. She hit her target squarely in the joint of his front right leg.

The kovaack turned, and, seeing S'haar, he let out a bellow of challenge before beginning his charge. His fear and anger overcame the pain in his leg, and he closed the distance rapidly.

S'haar took advantage of the kovaack pausing to challenge her by preparing the second spear. As he lowered his head to charge, she threw again, this time burying the spear in the skull just above his right eye. However, it didn't go deep enough to kill the beast, and his charge continued.

S'haar held her last spear, but rather than brace for the charge, she waited. At the last moment, she leapt to her left, avoiding the large horn thrust her way. The kovaack pivoted, digging into the ground with claws dull from digging up roots and tubers. The sudden reversal of momentum put too much stress on his injured knee, and he hesitated for a second.

S'haar capitalized on his hesitation, as well as the blind-spot caused by blood flowing down into his right eye. She used the force of her digitigrade legs to launch herself forward with terrifying speed before using her full body weight to bury the spear up to her hand into the eye of the beast.

It was as if something snapped, and the beast collapsed all at once. As he fell, he let out a final *wuff* as the air was forced out of his lungs by his own weight.

~

As S'haar pulled her catch back to the cave on the sled, she couldn't help but imagine a nice kovaack steak sizzling on Jack's odd grill. She had field-dressed the kovaack and would tie it up to drain tonight, which meant she probably wouldn't have the opportunity to butcher it until they arrived at the village, but it was still nice to think about.

S'haar noticed a large pile of containers sitting just outside the ship as she walked into the cave. Wondering what was going on, she bumped into Jack as he carried another crate to add to the collection. As he started to lose his load, S'haar grabbed the falling container, quickly hoisting it up and walking over to place it with the rest on the stack.

S'haar spoke her shoulder as she stood back up. "Isn't this the kind of thing you hired me to help out with? What was so important about moving some crates that you needed me to disappear for a while?"

Jack looked at her and rubbed the back of his neck, with a sheepish grin on his face. "That obvious, was I? Well, no worries, the important part is ready. How about I help you string that monster up, and then I'll show you what we did while you were gone?"

After getting the kovaack tied up in a particularly sturdy tree so the blood could drain overnight, the two went inside. S'haar walked into a disaster. There were crates and boxes piled everywhere. Angela was overseeing everything while dressed in something Jack later explained was called overalls. She had a clipboard and seemed to be taking inventory before looking up and seeing S'haar. She turned and spoke to Jack. "I told you we'd never get this done before she got back."

Turning again, Angela addressed S'haar. "Welcome back! I hope the hunt went well?"

S'haar was not going to be distracted from the mess before her. "What in the world is going on here? Is there some weird human tradition involving making a mess like this? It looks like you emptied an entire storage room into your living room."

Jack had a big grin as he walked to the other end of the room, stopping just short of a door S'haar had rarely seen him use. "That's exactly what we did! Although I realized pretty early on that it would have gone faster with your help. However, I wanted this part to be a surprise!"

As S'haar walked up to him, Jack opened the door. The storage room looked almost completely empty, aside from a bed covered in leathers and skins pushed up against one wall, with a pelt rug off to one side.

Jack spoke from behind her. "You've been sleeping on the floor of our living room long enough, and I don't think you'll be leaving us anytime soon. I figured you deserved a room of your own, where you could get some peace and quiet once in a while. It's a bit empty right now, since I didn't have the materials to do much, plus I figured you'd want to choose your own furnishings, so I just had Angela make up the frame and mattress for the bed. We used the skins we brought back with us for the blanket and rug. When we return to town tomorrow, you can pick out a few other things to make it feel more like your own."

S'haar turned around and picked Jack up into a bear hug, spinning him around like she'd seen people do in the movies he'd shown her. Angela openly laughed at Jack's predicament. Meanwhile, Jack let out a very manly, if somewhat high-pitched, "Yelp!" before finding a slightly strained voice. "Ugh, as happy as I am at your reaction, could you ease up a little? I don't have your bony plates to protect me from being crushed."

S'haar put Jack down with a quickly muttered apology before flinging herself onto her new bed. Jack grinned at her surprisingly childlike antics while watching from the doorframe. He continued his explanation. "The door has its own lock, and Angela promises she won't let me unlock it unless it's an emergency. We can communicate through the sound system, but you can even shut that off if you want. You can tell Angela if you want the lights on, off, or dimmed, also if you want the temperature warmer or cooler. The room is yours to fill or decorate as you please."

Sitting up with a seriousness that did nothing to wipe her excitement a moment ago from Jack's mind, S'haar responded, "This is the first room I've ever had all to myself. Even growing up, our house only had two rooms, so I slept in the common room. I guess I'm trying to say thank you, both of you."

Jack's grin grew a little wider. "You're welcome. You've more than earned it!" Jerking his thumb over his shoulder, he indicated the disaster behind him. "Now, I don't suppose I could talk you into helping move the rest of this stuff outside? The containers should keep the contents safe from any exposure in the cave, and anything more sensitive I already moved into one of the other storage rooms."

S'haar stood up and walked out of the room, hesitant to leave her new room so soon but unwilling to let Jack do all the work himself. Instead, she just grinned as she hefted a particularly large crate. "Of course! That's what I'm here for after all!"

Jack couldn't help but notice S'haar moved with a bit of a bounce in her step that he'd never seen before.

Chapter 13

Jack strapped down the kovaack's carcass after shifting the iron so that the weight was evenly distributed throughout the cart. This was a significantly larger load than they'd taken on the first trip. With this haul, he had no doubt they could get all the furnishings needed to fill S'haar's room, stock up on things like food and hides, and still have a fair bit of refined iron to bring home. The less energy Angela had to spend on refining, the better.

Angela was just saying her farewells to S'haar as he worked. "Make sure you both get plenty to eat! Don't forget that while Jack can eat most of the food, he needs to stay away from your alcoholic beverages! Speaking of drinks, don't let Jack forget to drink water periodically. Left to himself, he's likely to get dehydrated!"

S'haar's face was pure incredulity, and Jack was sure that if left to her own devices, Angela would go on forever, so he walked up to interrupt. "Thanks, mom. I love you too, but we've done this before, remember? We'll be fine."

Angela wasn't going to let them off that easy. "And remind me how that turned out? Because if I remember correctly, you almost got yourself killed and ended up with a broken foot! Clearly, someone needs to talk some sense into you two!"

S'haar was slowly backing away from the two siblings, not wanting to get caught in the crossfire. Jack set into a more relaxed stance and tried a different approach. "Listen, we've almost got what we need to get a decent transceiver up and running so you can come along with us for future outings, but for now, we have to head out on our own. We're better prepared for any trouble we might run into this time, and hopefully, we can avoid it altogether! I promise you, we'll be careful and do whatever we have to do to return safely, ok?"

Angela looked a little sullen but seemed to realize Jack was right. "Fine, but if you get yourself killed out there, I'll never forgive you!"

Jack grinned. "If I get myself killed out there, I promise to come back and haunt your ship, so you're never alone. We'll become the sort of ghost ship that sailors tell stories about for hundreds, no, thousands of years!"

Angela responded with a curt, "You'd better!" before fading away and closing the door.

Jack turned back to S'haar with a slightly more weary grin. "Shall we be off?"

~

This time the journey was a much more relaxed affair. All the stress and what-ifs from the first trip were absent, leaving the two to enjoy the quiet sounds of nature as they walked. By midmorning, they were about halfway to the village, and Jack was walking along with half-closed eyes. He was enjoying the crisp early wintery scent in the air, so it took him a moment to notice when the sound of the wagon next to him had come to a halt. Looking over at S'haar, Jack saw her focused into the distance. Following her gaze, he could see a distant wisp of smoke quite some distance to the north.

S'haar looked back to Jack with a face of careful neutrality. "Why don't you stay here with the cart? I want to go check that out. It's probably nothing..."

Jack returned her look with a steely resolve he didn't feel. "But it might be something. You can check it out, but I'm coming with."

S'haar looked like she wanted to argue but looked back at the smoke and instead responded with a slightly distracted voice. "Fine, you're the boss. Though I'm not defending you to Angela if you get yourself killed."

As S'haar set off, Jack followed, grumbling to himself. "What's with everyone assuming I'm going to get myself killed today?"

~

The two crept closer, staying low and crawling up to the crest of the final hill separating them from the smoke. Looking over the ridge, Jack could see what looked like a temporary camp of argu'n. However, these ones looked even more primitive than the villagers Jack was now somewhat familiar with.

There were also a variety of items scattered around the camp that looked like they didn't belong. One argu'n was wearing a delicate dress that seemed totally out of place as she guzzled down her drink. Another was using a well-crafted dresser as a stool on the far side of a campfire.

S'haar spoke up beside him, her voice thick with disdain. "The hill people. They were thieves and murderers exiled from their villages. They then gathered together for survival. For a long time they minded their own business, but after a while, they started raiding anyone they saw as vulnerable.

S'haar was looking over the camp while speaking quietly with Jack. "By that time, they had grown so large and knew the hills so well that every expedition sent to wipe them out either never found them or never returned. This band must have taken advantage of yesterday's warmth and went out for one last raid. It looks like they found someone too… Probably some poor merchant trying to make his way to a winter home. My guess would be…"

S'haar's explanation cut out mid-sentence. The reason for the interruption was easy for Jack to see. Out of a tent came the largest argu'n in the camp. Behind him, he was dragging a child, and the child obviously didn't belong in the camp. She was of lighter build and better fed. Her back was covered in welts, as though she'd recently been severely whipped. The child stumbled and fell down crying, only for the large argu'n to kick her in the ribs until she got back up and continued following her captor, choking back more sobs all the while.

Jack felt his stomach drop out from under him. He followed S'haar as she eased her way back down the hill. Calming himself, he turned his attention to S'haar. "What is going to happen to that girl?"

S'haar's eyes were focused in a far-off place, and her pupils were dilated. "If she lives, she'll be a slave. She'll either belong to one of the members of the raiding party, or more likely, she'll be sold to curry favor with someone more powerful. However, given her current state, she'll most likely die, probably before nightfall…"

Jack had never seen S'haar like this. She was so angry that, despite remaining entirely still, she radiated a murderous aura. It was clear that S'haar was getting ready to go do something stupid. Looking over to Jack, she calmed herself enough to speak again. "This is where we part ways. I'm afraid I can't go with you any further."

Jack suspected he knew why, but wanted her to say it. "What are you planning to do?"

S'haar looked down at the ground, her claws digging into her palm so hard that a small trickle of blood fell to the ground. "I'm going to go down and challenge the largest raider in the camp to one-on-one combat for the child's freedom. When I win, the rest of the camp will rush and kill me. If I'm lucky, I'll be able to take another two or three with me. There's no way I can take them all, but I can't walk away either, so I'm afraid I can no longer act as your bodyguard."

Jack spoke sharply, forcing S'haar to look up. "I refuse to allow you to leave my service at this time! I am about to find myself in an extremely hazardous situation, and I'll need my bodyguard to keep me alive."

S'haar looked at Jack with true disgust for the first time since they had met, and when she spoke, her tone made her opinions as clear as her words. "I realize you're probably frightened by the nearby raiders, but I'll give you enough time to get a head start running home first. Angela should be able to keep you safe."

Jack had pulled out his handgun and was checking the magazine with a shaking hand. "You misunderstand. I'm about to go down to that camp and save that girl. If I'm going to have any chance of pulling it off, I'm going to need my bodyguard by my side." He was proud of the fact that his voice was more steady than his hands at the moment.

S'haar's look lost its edge, and when she spoke, her voice was much softer. "I'm sorry, I misjudged you. However, while I appreciate the offer, you'd only slow me down. There's no reason for both of us to die today."

When Jack finally took his eyes off his gun and looked S'haar in the eyes, he appeared strangely calm. "S'haar, I want you to think of all the wonders and marvels you've witnessed since you first met me. Now I want you to listen very carefully to what I have to say. I have the ability to kill every single person in that camp. The only question is whether or not I'll live long enough to do it."

Jack just wished his hands would stop shaking so much while he was speaking. S'haar's gaze fell to his hands for a moment as the shaking got worse. "Are you certain you will be able to kill when the time comes?"

Jack's expression split into a sad shaky grin. As he spoke, a dark, hopeless laugh echoed in each word. "Honestly? No, I'm not. I've never killed a person before, and for all I know, when the time comes, I'll be shaking so bad I'll miss every shot, or maybe I'll just freeze up completely and wait to be killed."

Closing his eyes, Jack let out a deep sigh. He didn't even notice as his hands steadied while he continued speaking. "What I do know is what I can't do. I can't walk away and leave a friend to die. I can't condemn a young child to a life of slavery or death. I'm going to go down there with you, and if all else fails, at least you won't die alone."

S'haar looked at Jack for what was probably only a few seconds but felt like hours. Then she gave him her best predator's grin, but this time it didn't unsettle Jack as much as usual. When she spoke, there was something new in her voice that Jack couldn't quite place. "Huh, what happened to the soft little shut-in I knew up until now?"

S'haar looked at Jack, searching for a hint of hope. "So, what's your plan?"

Jack went back to checking his gun, making sure he knew where the safety was and checking for a full magazine a second time before chambering a round. "Well, step one will be the same as your plan. You challenge the toughest looking argu'n down there, then kill him. Once the rest charge, you focus on slowing them down and not dying. I'll try not to wet myself and thin the herd. After that, things will be so chaotic any further planning would be a waste, so we just try and live longer than any of them."

S'haar nodded. "I expected a little more subtlety or trickery out of you, but that'll have to do."

Jack looked back to her with an almost halfway confident grin this time. Holding up the gun for S'haar to get a better look, he explained. "The trick is, I'm hoping the shock and confusion of what this thing can do will slow them down enough for us to do what we need to do. We are both better armed and armored than them, mix in a little shock and awe, and we might just get lucky enough to walk away."

Lowering the gun, Jack looked off into the distance again. "I wish I had a few more supplies from the ship, a rifle to pick them off, maybe a few grenades, hell, even some fireworks would make a world of difference." Jack shrugged. "The problem is, we don't have time, so we go with what we have and hope it's enough."

S'haar walked right toward the camp, and Jack followed a little way behind. As the men around the campfire stood and watched her approach, S'haar jabbed her spears into the ground and walked a short distance further. Stopping well shy of the camp, she shouted out her challenge. "IS THERE ANY MALE HERE STRONG ENOUGH TO CHALLENGE ME?"

Many argu'n looked interested in taking S'haar up on her offer, but the largest of the group pushed his way to the front, standing a full head above the other eight-foot behemoths. His presence silenced all other challengers, He hefted a club with a stone tied to the end on his shoulder. It was larger and probably heavier than Jack was. The men of the camp started chanting, "Dol'jin, Dol'jin, Dol'jin!"

Waving his men down to silence them, Dol'jin looked S'haar up and down, taking her measure, though apparently not as a fighter. Leering, he replied, disdain thick in his voice. "What do I get when I win?"

S'haar's voice quieted, forcing the lecherous calls to end if the men wanted to hear her reply. "You get the opportunity to break me to your will, then do with me as you like."

Dol'jin laughed, the rest of the camp joining in half a breath behind. "We were going to do that regardless of the outcome! So tell me, what do you claim if you win?"

S'haar took a half step forward. "In your recent raid, you took a young girl. You will release her to me, and we'll leave."

Dol'jin's laughter was even more derisive than before. "Fresh meat like that is worth far more than some used-up whore like yourself! Still, it hardly matters. You lost the moment you stepped *forward!*"

As the last word was leaving his mouth, the argu'n leaped forward, his club swinging in a blindingly fast arc. For a moment, Jack thought the fight was already over, but at the last moment, S'haar became a blur of motion. She dove under the club, drawing her blade and scoring a shallow cut as she passed.

Dol'jin looked down at the cut on his chest, right between two plates. Looking back up, his voice was thick with contempt and he still leered as he spoke. "Is this little cut the best you can do? I've been hurt worse by the whelp you're so eager to save!"

S'haar just stood calmly, almost passively, and waited. Seeing that his taunting had little effect, Dol'jin launched into a new attack, once again swinging his club at ridiculous speeds. If that wasn't bad enough, he started shifting the club's momentum in on itself in ways Jack wouldn't have believed possible, except that he was watching it happen. Soon the club was twirling around in a pattern too quick and chaotic for Jack to follow.

Apparently, it wasn't too quick for S'haar, though. As Dol'jin approached, she slipped and slid around the club, sometimes so close that Jack could swear he saw the club lightly brush against her plates. The two fighters were at a stalemate: Dol'jin couldn't land a blow, but S'haar couldn't get close enough to go on the offensive.

Before long, it was apparent that both combatants were getting tired. They slowed almost imperceptibly until Dol'jin took a half a second too long to bring his club around, and S'haar struck again. Sliding low, this time she landed a shallow slice against the back of his left knee before bouncing back to her feet behind him.

Perhaps thinking S'haar would commit to an attack now that she was at his back, Dol'jin swung around wildly, using the momentum of his club to turn himself to face her more quickly.

S'haar had been waiting for just that move. As soon as the club passed a little too far, she launched past Dol'jin again, landing another small cut on his lower bicep.

The crowd was still chanting Dol'jin's name, but Jack could see that Dol'jin was starting to realize he was in trouble. Being argu'n, both fighters were built for speed and power, not endurance, and as the fight dragged on, exhaustion was taking its toll. Adding in his weapon's weight, pain slowing him slightly, and his increasing blood loss, and it was clear Dol'jin was going to tire first. It was time for him to try something new.

When Dol'jin swung the club this time, he loosened his grip for a mere fraction of a second before tightening his hold again. This caused the club to slip and extend its reach a few inches mid-swing. It was enough for S'haar to miscalculate her dodge, and she took a glancing blow to her right shoulder caused her to drop her blade.

The watching argu'n let loose an uproarious cheer, and Dol'jin began another of his impossible moves, bending the club's momentum in on itself to land the final blow. S'haar rolled into the swing this time, coming up inside the club's reach and latching onto her prey. Her teeth dug into his neck while her left thumb's claw gouged into his right eye.

With a roar, Dol'jin grabbed her by the neck and threw her on the ground, and although she hit the ground hard, S'haar was able to roll away before he could bring his club to bear. It was clear who had come out on top of the exchange, although it wasn't enough to end the fight yet.

For the first time, the crowd was silent, and the fight took on a more desperate feel now that the only sounds that could be heard were the grunts of effort and pain of the two combatants. For the last time, Jack checked the safety on his gun. The end was rapidly approaching.

Knowing he'd all but lost, Dol'jin took a final desperate gambit. When he swung his club this time, he let it fly, forcing S'haar to drop low to avoid the massive projectile. Dol'jin followed just behind the club, hoping to pounce on S'haar before she could regain her composure and finish her with his greater strength.

As he lunged toward his opponent, Dol'jin could see one of her arms trapped underneath her, and his hope flared, until that arm flew out from under her. He saw the flash of steel just as he landed on the blade she'd hidden, his own momentum pushing the point completely through his bony chest plate and into his heart.

S'haar leaned in and whispered into his ear, "You lost the moment you stepped forward." before shoving the oversized Dol'jin off to the side.

She slowly stood, staring at the silent crowd. S'haar remained still, gasping for breath, taking advantage of every second of stunned silence to recover as much as possible.

Four things then happened in rapid succession. First, one of the watching argu'n lurched forward, his companions barely a half-second behind him. Second, S'haar turned and leaped for her spears as fast as she was able. Third, a loud crack of thunder tore the silence apart. Fourth, the lead argu'n's chest turned into a bloody crater. He fell as everything returned to stunned silence once more.

Jack aimed his gun at the next closest argu'n and pulled the trigger a second time.

Chapter 14

When Jack and Angela first met S'haar, they witnessed the gap between human and argu'n physiologies. Both realized standard human armaments might not have enough stopping power. Instead, they decided to use bullets with a hardened steel tip and a high explosive core. In theory, it should have more than enough force to crack an argu'n's armor plating and cause significant damage to the flesh underneath. The only problem was that packing all of that into a handgun bullet resulted in a significantly larger caliber, so there were only ten rounds per magazine.

As Jack watched the fight between S'haar and Dol'jin, he wished Angela and himself had gotten in more practical testing against ballistic dummies. Now he just had to hope that what little testing they had done would prove sufficient.

Looking down, Jack noticed his hands were shaking again, worse than they had before. He tried to will them to be still, force them to be calm, but that seemed only to make the shaking worse.

That was when Dol'jin scored a glancing blow against S'haar's shoulder, causing her to drop her sword. Jack started to raise the gun, but before he could get a shot, S'haar leaped onto the giant, burying her teeth into his neck. Jack lowered the gun again, telling himself he needed to trust S'haar more. After all, if she couldn't hold her own in this and the coming fight, they were both already dead.

Looking back to the crowd of watching argu'n, Jack was doing math and not liking the result. Ideally, once he started taking shots, many of the hill people would break and run, but based on what he knew of argu'n, their fight or flight response was weighted heavily toward fight.

Jack counted twenty-three argu'n in the camp. Even if S'haar was able to take out four or five *after* her fight with the club-wielding maniac, there would still be way more raiders than the ten bullets Jack had in his first magazine. That meant he'd have to stop and reload while being charged by several eight-foot-tall monsters that could move faster and leap further than any living human. No matter how he looked at it, there was no way he could think of that he could kill all of them before they reached him, and his time was running out.

Dol'jin looked as though he was about to make one last desperate gambit. Jack had to hope S'haar was ready and able to deal with whatever it was. For the last time, Jack checked the safety on his gun; the end was rapidly approaching.

Jack stopped breathing when he saw the trap Dol'jin had laid for S'haar. After throwing his club, he rushed in while she was still prone, hoping to take advantage of his greater strength. However, S'haar proved herself more than worthy of Jack's trust. As she fell onto her back, S'haar placed a hand beneath her, appearing to slow her fall, but her real goal was the blade she'd dropped earlier. S'haar pulled out the short sword and impaled the flying Dol'jin before he had any chance to react, ending his life, and thus the fight.

Everything seemed to slow down at that moment. As S'haar stood, Jack raised the gun and half aimed it toward the watching argu'n. He waited until the first one started to rise, then sighted along the barrel into the center mass of the lead argu'n and pulled the trigger. The result was everything Jack could have hoped for…and utterly horrific. Jack clamped down on that second observation and locked it away to be dealt with when he and S'haar weren't fighting for their lives.

Jack aimed the gun at the next closest argu'n and pulled the trigger a second time. As that raider's chest turned to ruin, the spell that held everyone silent ended. Everything exploded into action. A couple of argu'n turned and ran, but not nearly as many as Jack had hoped. The rest split into three groups. About half the original group ran right up the middle, toward where S'haar stood between the camp and Jack. The rest split into two groups, running to either side of S'haar, bypassing her, and heading directly for Jack.

As much as Jack wanted to fire into the group charging S'haar to save her, he knew that if he got himself overwhelmed, the argu'n that killed him would simply charge S'haar from behind, and they'd both end up dead. Instead, he had to trust S'haar again and focus on the ones coming for him. He took aim at the group to his left and opened fire.

S'haar saw the groups headed to flank Jack, but she knew that they'd both end up dead if she split her focus now. So, S'haar would simply have to trust Jack's earlier claim and deal with the group headed directly for her. She leaped back to the spears she'd planted into the ground. Grabbing a small spear in each hand, S'haar whipped around and used her momentum to aid in her throw as she aimed for the closest argu'n. Before the spear hit, S'haar shifted the second spear to her dominant hand and launched it at a second target.

The first spear struck dead center in a charging argu'n, piercing him through his chest plate. The raider immediately collapsed to the ground. The argu'n following the dead man got tangled in his lifeless limbs and fell as well, not out of the fight, but slowed for a few precious seconds.

The second spear didn't fly as true and hit her target lower than she intended. It impaled the raider through the leg, pinning him in place. While the wound might prove fatal, it would take time, and he was already working on removing the spear to get back into the fight.

S'haar grabbed the third and longest spear and prepared to meet the remaining raiders' charge. Behind her, S'haar heard Jack's impossibly loud weapon firing again and again as Jack faced his own desperate fight for survival.

~

One after another, Jack was able to take out the five argu'n charging from his left, but between every pull of the trigger, they seemed to cover an absurd amount of ground. More ground was eaten up by the argu'n closing on his right during the agonizingly long half-second turn to target them.

There were four argu'n charging on this side, and having kept count, Jack knew he only had two shots left in the magazine and one in the chamber. With no other plan coming to him, Jack aimed and pulled the trigger again. Another argu'n fell. Their deaths were horrible, and yet they still charged.

Jack pulled the trigger once more. As the next argu'n fell, he was close enough that Jack could see the brief look of surprise on the raider's face just before the light left his eyes, and he collapsed in a boneless heap.

Suddenly the faces of every argu'n Jack had just killed filled his vision. The same look of surprise was now on all their faces as, one by one, the light left their eyes.

Shoving the unwanted vision aside, Jack aimed and fired one last time. This time his vision blurred, his arms rebelled, and his shot went wide. He'd failed. There were two argu'n left and nothing he could do. Jack fell as one of the argu'n raked its claws across his chest.

~

As the first two argu'n reached her, S'haar cracked the butt of the spear into the face of the first, dropping him as she broke his jaw. Reversing the spear's momentum and driving it forward, she forced the second to dive away, lest he got impaled. Spinning the spear in a full arch, she copied a move from Dol'jin by losing her grip just enough to extend the spear a few inches, raking it across the throat of the third assailant that was trying to sneak into her blind spot.

S'haar fell back a few paces, working her spear into a pattern designed to buy herself a moment while assessing her options. Of her nine assailants, two were dead, one unconscious, two slowed and out of the fight for three to five seconds respectively. She needed to thin the group a bit more before the last two arrived. Otherwise, she'd be quickly overwhelmed.

Absorbing the momentum of her backward movement, S'haar braced and launched herself forward once more. She put her full weight behind the spear and drove it into the centermost assailant.

S'haar released the spear. Rather than wasting precious seconds wrenching the weapon free, she pushed off of her victim's body and launched herself at her next target. She collided with him and latched onto his throat as she had Dol'jin's. As the two tumbled together, they fell right in the middle of the four remaining argu'n.

With the last four combatants closing around her, S'haar was out of weapons and out of breath.

~

As Jack landed on the ground, he silently thanked Angela for the armor plates she'd weaved into his coat. The argu'n who had taken a swipe at him had chipped and broke several claws on the armor.

Jack knew it wouldn't buy him much time, so he had to act fast. Drawing his knife, Jack buried it to the hilt into the foot of the argu'n standing over him, pinning the raider to the ground.

Rolling away, Jack regained his feet just in time to jump to the side as the second argu'n leaped forward. All Jack could do was take advantage of his lighter build to repeatedly crawl, jump, and dive just out of the raider's encroaching reach. As he fell for what seemed the dozenth time, Jack fumbled with his gun, trying to load his last magazine, only to drop it instead when he had to make a last-ditch attempt to avoid another downward swipe of the argu'n's claws.

Scrabbling on all fours, Jack continued lurching and crawling away. The argu'n, sensing an end to the chase, approached at a deceptively leisurely pace. As his hand shot forward to grab Jack by the throat, Jack threw a handful of dirt and sand into the raider's eyes.

Taking advantage of his opponent's momentary blindness, Jack dove behind him, picking up the magazine from the ground as he passed. Slamming the magazine into place, Jack racked the slide and aimed at the back of the argu'n that was busy clearing his vision.

However, before he could pull the trigger, the gun was ripped out of his hands. The first argu'n stood over him, holding Jack's bloody knife in one hand and his gun in the other. Jack froze as his mind tried vainly to think of something new. He was out of weapons, out of ideas, and out of hope.

~

As S'haar looked around at her plight, she noticed the argu'n sneaking up unseen behind Jack as the human fumbled with his weapon. Knowing she only had seconds before she was finally overwhelmed, S'haar gathered what little energy remained to her and leaped at the argu'n whose leg she'd impaled.

Seeing her coming, he readied the very spear S'haar had used to impale him. S'haar twisted in mid-air to the best of her ability, but he still successfully drove the spear through her left shoulder. Rather than pull away, S'haar gripped his arms and pulled herself closer, driving the spear's shaft further through her shoulder. Realizing what was about to happen, the argu'n now fought to push S'haar away, but either due to his blood loss or S'haar's greater desperation, she was able to reach him and tear out his throat with her teeth.

Her body was near-total failure, and her vision was blurring as S'haar tore the spear from her shoulder and threw it with the last of her strength. Her final task complete, S'haar collapsed to the ground. She couldn't even see if she'd hit her target.

~

Jack's mind was running a mile a minute, but every possible action he could think of ended with his death. The argu'n standing over him licked its own blood off the blade before laughing as the raider shifted his grip to deliver a final downward thrust.

The argu'n drew its arm back, and Jack closed his eyes and accepted the fact that he'd done all he could. Jack's first thought was that his biggest regret was leaving Angela behind. He believed that this was the only choice he could have lived with, but wished there was some way to let Angela know what happened.

Jack's second thought was, *Why am I still alive?* Opening his eyes, Jack saw the argu'n standing over him looking stupidly down at its chest, obviously wondering how a spear had come to be sticking out him.

Realizing he'd wasted a precious second in self-indulgent thoughts, Jack leaped to his feet, taking his gun back from the collapsing argu'n. Turning, Jack saw S'haar had collapsed to the ground with three more raiders closing in for the kill. Jack shot two in the back before the third took off running.

Jack turned again and sighted down his gun at the last argu'n, whose eyes were finally cleared. The raider knew his time had come, and he stood straight, staring Jack in the face while waiting for death.

Jack found that he couldn't pull the trigger. Instead, he dropped his aim from his target's face to his chest, looked him in the eyes, and shouted a command. "Run!"

The argu'n twitched but stayed still. Jack shifted the gun further to point next to the raider's feet. He fired a shot into the ground before raising the gun again, his warning clear. Run or die.

He stood ready to shoot if the argu'n decided to attack, but something of his intent must have bridged the gap. At first, the argu'n backed away wearily, keeping both eyes on Jack. As enough distance opened between them, Jack relaxed his aim a little more, and eventually, the argu'n turned and ran.

Jack stood there, frozen in place as he watched the last of the hill people disappear into the distance. His mind was numb. A part of him knew he and S'haar needed to get help, but that part seemed to be shouting at him from a great distance.

Eventually, Jack lost sight of the raider. Looking down at the gun in his hands, Jack was overcome by waves of nausea and revulsion by the sight of the monstrous thing. He threw it as far away from himself as possible.

The distant part of his mind told him that he needed to keep the gun close in case there were more of the hill people nearby, but Jack could barely hear the voice anymore.

Despite the pleasant warmth of the day, Jack suddenly felt intensely cold. Every inch of his body was violently shivering. Before long, he vomited into a nearby bush then collapsed into convulsions. Jack continued dry heaving long after his stomach had utterly emptied itself. It was as though his entire body was rebelling at what he'd done.

Jack wasn't sure when it had appeared, but there was a presence sitting beside him and a calming hand on his back. Looking up through the tears that clouded his vision as he wiped the bile from the corner of his mouth, Jack saw S'haar sitting beside him. She looked worse than he'd ever seen, one arm hung limp at her side, and she seemed to have a cloth wedged into a deep wound to staunch the bleeding.

Looking S'haar in the eyes, Jack broke the silence with a sad smile and a pathetic laugh. "I bet none of the men of your village would react this way to what we just did."

To his surprise, S'haar's eyes were not filled with mockery or even the pity Jack had feared. Instead, her tired smile spoke of understanding and maybe even a little respect. "If you'd reacted the way the males of my village would have, I would have taken the girl and left. You would have never seen me again. Instead, I am here beside you."

Jack noticed his gun sitting beside S'haar. Following his glance, S'haar reached down, picked up the gun, and held it for a moment. "This wasn't some honorable combat to be bragged about around a fire. This was a brutal act of violence and survival."

S'haar held the gun out to Jack, who, in turn, was unwilling to touch it. S'haar continued. "But remember, you weren't the one that decided to raid and murder a family, and you weren't the one that enslaved a child. You did what you needed to do, and in my opinion, you did well."

S'haar placed the gun in Jack's unwilling hands. "It's best if you don't leave this out where anyone can find it."

Jack nodded and reluctantly holstered the gun. As he did so, S'haar stood and offered him a hand. As she lifted Jack to his feet, S'haar reminded him why they had done all this. "Now, there's a young girl down there we need to set free. Stay near me in case any of the hill people return. Neither of us is in any condition to fight anyone alone."

~

As the two walked through the camp, Jack noticed the signs of ruined lives in the form of things that didn't belong. A finely crafted stein, a beautiful rug, even a child's doll. Jack knelt before the toy, wondering if it belonged to the girl they'd fought for, or if it belonged to someone else they'd arrived too late to save. Lost in thought, Jack picked it up before following S'haar to a tent.

Inside the tent was the battered and bruised child. When she looked up at them, it was with eyes resigned to a horrible fate. She didn't even flinch as S'haar worked to remove bindings that had been tied so tight that they cut into her skin. The whole time S'haar spoke soothing words while Jack stood off to the side. "It's ok. You're safe now. They won't hurt you anymore. We're going to take you away from here." On and on, she spoke, using her voice to try and soothe the child.

Looking more closely at the girl, Jack could see the girl was several inches shorter than himself. She wasn't as young as he'd first thought, at a rough guess she might have been the rough equivalent of fourteen or fifteen, though he couldn't be sure.

Once she was free, the girl simply stood in place, looking at S'haar as if waiting to be told what to do. Looking at Jack and seeing he was as lost as she was, S'haar decided to lead the girl outside. Once outside of the tent, the girl shielded her eyes against the glare of the midday sun.

She seemed to be standing in place again. That was when Jack noticed she was staring at a body. The body of the first argu'n Jack had shot.

Slowly the girl turned around until she was looking at S'haar. She pointed at the body and spoke for the first time. "Did you do this?"

S'haar looked at the body, then to Jack, then at the girl. "No, I did not."

The girl turned to face Jack this time and repeated her question. "Did you do this?"

In a few seconds, Jack thought of a dozen comforting lies and a hundred justifications. Instead, he simply nodded his head, yes.

With a blur of speed, neither of them thought she was capable of, the girl launched herself at Jack. Her arms stretched wide and claws ready to attack.

Jack had just enough time to wonder dumbly if the body was someone the girl had known, and then she was on him. She tackled Jack with enough force to launch him off his feet. The girl's vice-like grip was strong enough to crack a rib. As they fell to the ground, Jack found he didn't have the heart to defend himself.

Jack was lying on the ground for several moments before noticing the girl wasn't attacking. She was sobbing. Her head was buried in his chest, and she was whispering two words over and over. "Thank you, thank you, thank you."

Jack had never been comfortable with physical contact, but the girl's desperation called out to an old pain of his own. He sat up, wrapped her in his arms, and held her while the girl continued to sob. S'haar knelt beside the pair and put a comforting hand on the girl's shoulder. The three of them stayed like that until the girl cried herself dry.

Chapter 15

As much as Jack wanted to sit here and wait for all his problems to go away, life is rarely so kind, and this was no exception. All three of them needed medical attention, and the longer they sat in the middle of the camp, the more likely it became that some of the runners would return.

Jack picked himself up and helped the girl to her feet. She was much heavier than she appeared, but Jack had been expecting that and braced himself for greater leverage. She looked Jack up and down a moment before speaking in a small yet worried voice. "You look so pale! We need to get you to a healer!"

S'haar barked out a laugh, followed shortly by wincing and reaching for her injured shoulder before replying. "Don't worry too much. Jack may have seen better days, but that's just the way he looks. The worst physical injury he probably sustained today was when you tackled him. Be a bit more careful in the future, he's much more fragile than us argu'n."

Now the girl looked at Jack with confusion, and maybe a little fear. "He's not argu'n? Is he some sort of demon?"

Jack let S'haar get another laugh and subsequent wince out of her system before speaking. He needed her to translate after all. "I'm no demon, and despite the local rumors, I'm no dragon either. My name is Jack, and my race call ourselves humans. This is my translator, guide, bodyguard, and, most importantly, friend, S'haar."

Jack started rubbing the back of his neck, awkwardly. What does one say to a child who's faced more horror in one day than many people will in a lifetime? "What can we call you?" Jack couldn't help but feel a little lame.

The girl seemed to make up her mind about something and nodded her head before replying. Folding her arms in her lap and performing what was an obviously formal bow. "My name is Em'brel. Thank you very much for saving me, master Jack, mistress S'haar!"

S'haar was amused when Jack's awkwardness jumped up a few levels at the spoken title. She couldn't help compare him to the men of her village again. Most of them would have preened under such a title. Instead, Jack just looked uncomfortable. He confirmed as much when he spoke. "Uh, Jack is fine. The only thing I'm a master of is getting into trouble. Also, given everything we've all been through, let's just drop the formalities altogether for now."

Jack looked around, taking stock of the situation. "Anyway, we all need medical treatment. Let's head back to the cave. After we're back on our feet, we can take you wherever you'd like."

Em'brel looked off in the distance, her mask of calm slipping for a moment before she was able to get it under control. "I... I don't have anyone else... My father was taking me to be married to some lord's son I'd never met, and now he's...he's..."

Jack calmed her again, stroking her "hair." He was a little nonplussed by the feel of the boney hair her people had, as well as the soft *clacking* sound it made as he stroked it, but the girl seemed to take comfort in the action. "Ok, ok, we don't have to decide anything at the moment. For now, let's get healed up. Once we're back in shape, we can worry about whatever the future holds."

After translating, S'haar turned to Jack. "What about the cart full of iron and kovaack? Also, are you sure you want to take her into your cave? That might raise... complications."

Jack started walking, and the other two followed as he spoke. "First and most importantly, if we need to, we can replace everything in the cart, including the cart itself. However, you and the girl can't be replaced. So we're getting you both treated. Second, this time of year, it'll probably be fine. It's getting too cold for any argu'n to be far enough out where they could find it. Third, how could we move it if we wanted to? Your arm needs healing, and the two of us simply aren't strong enough."

S'haar couldn't fault his logic, and Jack continued. "As far as taking Em'brel home, I'm aware of the complications, but again, what choice do we have? Neither of us is in any condition to escort her anywhere, and I'm not leaving her on her own out here."

Once again, S'haar couldn't disagree with him.

Em'brel cleared her throat and spoke in that same small voice as if afraid what she was saying might get her in trouble. "Shouldn't we go to a village rather than some cave?"

Realizing what she'd said, Em'brel suddenly looked both worried and embarrassed. "If it's your home, I'm sure it's a very nice cave, but you two need a healer!"

Jack smiled. The poor girl was in for a bit of a shock. Best to ease her into it a bit. "The…cave we're headed to isn't like a normal cave. Among other things, it just so happens to currently house the best healer in the world, my sister."

Em'brel had that look all kids get when they think they know more than the people they are talking to but was polite enough not to vocalize her thoughts.

~

As the group approached the cave, S'haar got down on one knee and looked Em'brel in the eyes as she spoke. "Now listen carefully. What you are about to see will be stranger than anything you've ever seen in your life. The strangest of all is Jack's sister. However, you need to understand, nothing in there will hurt you so long as you don't try to harm Jack or myself. Do you understand?"

Em'brel was starting to look worried again as Jack merely smiled off to the side. When Em'brel finally nodded, S'haar stood up and let Jack lead the way.

It grew dark as they walked into the cave, and Em'brel grabbed hold of S'haar's right hand. Despite the darkness, these two obviously knew the path they were traveling well enough, but Em'brel jumped with every sound bouncing off every hidden corner.

S'haar had been surprised by the contact at first but quickly realized the girl was still dealing with everything she'd been through, S'haar gave the girl's hand a comforting squeeze, and soon Em'brel had wrapped her other arm around S'haar's arm as well, walking while hugging S'haar's arm to herself.

Off to either side of the cave were occasional tunnels that looked like they had been recently dug. However, neither Jack nor S'haar seemed worried about what might be inside, so Em'brel kept her eyes straight and continued walking. Eventually, the cave started lightening up as they walked. It didn't flicker like firelight, it looked almost like daylight, but they hadn't gone anywhere near far enough into the mountain to be coming out the other side yet.

The light grew brighter, revealing what looked like a dead end. There was just some random wall in the middle of the cave, but unless Em'brel was mistaken, it was made from a fortune's worth of metal. As Jack walked up, a part of the wall slid to the side on its own, revealing a bright and cheery room like nothing Em'brel had ever seen before.

Jack walked inside, and with a squeeze of the hand, S'haar led Em'brel in as well. Inside was pleasantly warm, as though a fire was being tended nearby, but Em'brel couldn't smell anything burning. Everywhere she looked, there were fine metals, leathers, and several materials Em'brel had no concept of. Until now, her father had been the wealthiest person she'd ever known, but even when he'd had his wealth, he wouldn't have been able to afford a fraction of what was on display in this room.

True to S'haar's words, the strangest thing of all was Jack's sister. Her body was shaped more similarly to Jack's than an argu'n, but that's where all similarity ended. First of all, she was tiny. Second, she flew through the air. Third, she glowed blue.

When they walked in, the blue figure darted toward Jack, speaking in the same sing-song language of his but much more rapidly. As soon as S'haar walked in, his sister exploded with energy, flying around them at dizzying speeds while speaking in a continuous string of syllables.

Finally, Jack barked out a few words, and the glowing figure came to a halt just in front of Em'brel's face. "Ohmygodyouaresocute, Iwanttospeaktoyou, butIneedtogetS'haartreatedfirst!"

Em'brel realized the blue woman had switched to a language she understood but spoke so rapidly that all the words bled together until it mostly sounded like gibberish.

S'haar kneeled and looked at Em'brel again. "You doing ok? It's a bit overwhelming at first, but Jack and Angela seem to be as decent as they come."

Em'brel Looked at Jack, then back to S'haar. "I feel like I walked into a new world. Did I die back at the camp, and this is the afterlife?"

S'haar cocked her head to one side. "You know, I wondered the same thing the first time I woke up here. After a while, you get used to it. Wait until they show you a movie for the first time." The last she said with a smile.

S'haar looked over to Angela, then back to Em'brel again. "Now we have to go let Angela give us a checkup. That part won't hurt, but the actual healing might hurt a little. However, Angela can heal in a day things that would take weeks or longer. I'll go first so you can see what it's like."

The girl nodded, and S'haar stood and led the way. Em'brel followed her into a smaller room off to the side, where S'haar stood in the middle of a large circular device. The machine soon came to life, with parts moving and gliding with a life of their own as they passed over S'haar. Angela explained, "What I'm doing right now is scanning S'haar. It's a way for me to see all the damage she's suffered, on the surface and hidden under the skin. The more still she can remain, the quicker this process goes."

After a few minutes, the scan ended, and S'haar stepped out. Angela approached her and started creating images of enlarged sections of S'haar's many injuries out of nowhere. "Most of the damage you received is minor and can heal on its own. However, if you'd been treated anywhere but here, you would have likely lost the arm."

Angela brushed away all the images but the arm. She then did something to enlarge the image and make the arm see-through. "The good news is I can heal it. The bad news is it's a significantly more severe wound than Jack received the other day. It will take at least a couple of days, and the first day will be the worst. Rebuilding and reattaching a nervous system is excruciating, and you WILL have to be unconscious for it. The pain alone would put you into shock. Even after I'm done, the nerves will take some time to adjust, and you'll likely experience pain for a week or more."

S'haar gave a one-armed shrug. "It's better than losing my arm. When can we get started?"

Angela looked at the other two people in the room. "I'm pretty sure yours is the most demanding injury, but some injuries can be subtle until it's too late, so I'd like to at least get some scans of the other two first, then we'll decide on a treatment plan for the three of you."

Angela floated right up to Em'brel. Tilting her head to one side, she spoke much calmer than before, her voice radiating a soothing feeling. "Em'brel, do you think you can do this next? It won't hurt you, and it will help me know where you need healing."

Em'brel looked up at the machine with obvious trepidation, and having everyone here look at her so expectantly didn't help any. However, these were the people who had delivered her from the nightmare her life had been descending into.

That thought brought unbidden memories of her father on the ground that made Em'brel's eyes snap shut. Her arms wrapped tightly about herself, and she started shivering uncontrollably. As she began to fall to her knees, she found herself wrapped in another hug. Her shivering stopped, and she heard Jack speaking his nonsense words in her ear again. As she cracked her eyes, Angela spoke up. "Jack said, you don't have to do anything you're not ready to."

A little embarrassed at her reaction, Em'brel pushed away from him and hesitantly took a step toward the machine. Turning back to Jack, she spoke with an apologetic smile. "No, it wasn't the machine... I just remembered something else..."

As Em'brel spoke, her eyes darted to the floor as she tried to fight back the images of her father dying before they could retake hold in her mind. She shook her head a little violently to banish the memories and stepped into the device as she had seen S'haar do before. "I can do this. I need to do this."

Angela replied, "Alright, just let me know if you need to stop for any reason," and the scan began.

As the lights strobed around her, Em'brel tried to focus her attention on Jack and S'haar on the other side of the machine. Every once in a while, the light would pass in front of her eyes, temporarily blinding her. Every time it happened, a vision would come unbidden into her mind. Her muscles tightened at this, but she reminded herself that the more still she was, the quicker this would be over.

Eventually, everything came to a halt, and Em'brel was able to exit the machine. She stood there somewhat shaky for a moment before looking up. "Do you have someplace I can go..." She fumbled for the right words for a moment, not understanding why something so commonplace was hard to put into words.

Angela came to her rescue. "We have some very excellent facilities on the ship. We call them bathrooms. Let me show you how they work, then maybe we can get you a bite to eat. These two have to decide how we'll proceed with treatment."

Em'brel was a little nervous about leaving Jack and S'haar's side but didn't want them to be present while she used this "bathroom" either. So she nodded her head and followed Angela out of the room.

~

As soon as Angela and the girl left the room and the door shut, another Angela rematerialized in front of Jack and S'haar. While this slightly surprised S'haar, it was such a minor thing compared to everything else these two did that she barely reacted.

Angela turned to the other two with an uncharacteristically serious look on her face. "That girl is severely damaged in more ways than one. Luckily no one physical injury is too severe, she has more abrasions and contusions than I can easily list, and she has several cracked ribs as well as a few minor infections starting, but I can treat most of that in a day."

Angela waved away the physical damage as though it was nothing. "On the other hand, as I was scanning her, I saw signs of severe emotional trauma, shock, stress, exhaustion, and more. She's one small step away from total collapse. What in the world happened to her?"

Jack was grimacing in a way that expressed how uncomfortable he was with the subject. "As far as I can tell, her father was taking her to an arranged marriage with some guy she's never met when they got ambushed by raiders. Now he's dead, and she has no close friends or family left. We rescued her from the raiders, which is how S'haar got injured, and we brought her back here. When we rescued her, she'd been with the raiders for over a day, give or take, and it looked like they severely abused her in that time. That's pretty much all I know."

S'haar spoke up. "Given the formal bow she gave us and the way she spoke, she is probably the daughter of some minor lord. If her father was the one escorting her himself, rather than hiring some guards, he was likely in financial trouble and was marrying her off to secure a deal of some kind."

Jack and Angela both looked at S'haar with surprised expressions. S'haar returned their looks and shrugged before responding. "While working in the guard, I was involved in many dealings with minor lords and ladies. It comes with the job."

Angela looked introspective for a moment before speaking to herself. "So she was facing an unwanted marriage, was present when her only close family was killed and was severely abused by raiders before the two of you showed up and rescued her? We're going to speak more about that later, by the way. No wonder she's at her limit. That's enough to break anyone."

She turned to Jack. "So, what's your plan?"

Jack was quiet for a minute while he thought. "I have some idea what she's going through, it sounds disturbingly similar to my own history, but I have no idea how to help with that. I still haven't figured it out myself…"

S'haar looked at Jack like he was missing the obvious. "Why don't you just ask her?"

Jack and Angela turned to her with a surprise for the second time, and S'haar continued. "She was about to be married. In our people's eyes, she's an adult and able to make her own decisions. Talk with her and let her decide her own future."

Jack couldn't agree with the adult part, but he understood wanting to be involved in deciding your own future. After his own trauma, everyone had been quick to tell Jack what was best for him, what he should do, and where he should go. No one had bothered to listen to his thoughts and feelings on the matter. No one except Angela.

S'haar reached her good hand out to rest on Jack's arm and smiled. "Just show her the same respect you've shown me, and you'll do fine."

Jack wasn't so sure, but on the other hand, what choice did he have?

Chapter 16

Angela dismissed Jack, since he got off the easiest with nothing more than a couple of nasty cuts and bruises and one suspiciously bruised rib. Having received a clean bill of health, Jack went out to see how Em'brel was fairing.

He found her digging into a plate of barely cooked meat. Although Jack had gotten used to seeing S'haar tear apart half-raw steak, it was somehow more disturbing to see someone ordinarily shy and quiet do the same. Jack mentally shrugged and reminded himself he was on *their* planet, and any discomfort was his responsibility to deal with.

Once he sat down at the table, Angela appeared beside him to translate. Jack decided it was best to avoid small talk and get right to the matter at hand. "We're trying to figure out where to go from here, and we wanted your opinion. What would you like to do now?"

Em'brel sat and thought for a moment, the plate of meat forgotten. After a few moments, she looked Jack in the eye and presented her case. "I don't have many skills that would be of use to a wealthy man such as yourself, but I'm willing to work hard. I can cook, clean, and even sew a little, and I'm willing to learn that which I don't know!"

Jack held up both hands, palm out. "Whoa, slow down, by my people's laws, it is unconscionable to put someone your age to work. You should still be focusing on growing and learning. To that end, wouldn't you be happier living with a family from your home village? Maybe a distant aunt or uncle? I'm sure plenty of families would be delighted to take you in."

Em'brel shook her head and looked down at her plate in a dejected manner. "The only family I have left is my uncle, who is likely concerning himself with consolidating the power from the lands he will inherit from my father. He wouldn't welcome the presence of a niece who could threaten his claim by swearing an oath to another male. If I am lucky, he will make me his bride to avoid the issue. If not, he may have me killed to avoid any complications."

Jack's face became a mask as he locked every muscle to prevent the rage and disgust he felt from showing through. Apparently unaware of his reaction, the girl continued, "I was raised to run an estate on behalf of my future husband, but those skills are of no use to a girl with no wealth or land to tempt a lord into marriage. The best future I can hope for is as a maid at an inn, or perhaps to be taken into some lord's house as a concubine."

Angela turned to Jack and switched to English to quietly offer her own two cents. "We could have her perform a few light but time-consuming chores, like cooking and cleaning, which would free you and S'haar up to focus on other jobs that keep getting backed up. In return, I could put together a few classes to teach her math and sciences that no one in this world likely knows. It would be like she's attending school. As a result, she'd have more control over her destiny than she does right now."

Unaware of what was being whispered between the two, Em'brel decided that she needed to make her final and best attempt. Getting down on her hands and knees and bowing her head to the floor, she begged. "If I am to spend the rest of my life in servitude to another, I would rather it be in service to the ones who saved me. Please allow me to stay!"

Jack, now thoroughly uncomfortable, knelt down beside the girl and grabbed hold of her shoulder. "Listen, you don't have to beg for anything, ever. You've made your case. You can stay."

Em'brel shot up, wrapping Jack in another embrace that would likely leave a few new bruises. Jack continued speaking in a somewhat strained voice, trying to overcome his smothered diaphragm. "Though I do have a condition!"

Em'brel released Jack and sat back attentively. Jack caught his breath a moment before continuing. "Every day, Angela will give you a series of lessons. Math, science, and whatever else she deems appropriate. I expect you to do your best to learn whatever she teaches you. As far as I'm concerned, this is more important than any cooking or cleaning you might do. Is that understood?"

Em'brel launched herself at Jack again, crushing him a second time as she responded. "Of course, I will learn whatever you ask me to learn!"

Angela was enjoying her human's discomfort a little too much. After Em'brel finally released him, the AI spoke up again. "Before I put her under, S'haar told me to tell you, 'Once Jack gives in and decides the girl can stay, tell him I said she can share my room.'"

Jack shook his head and wondered how everyone always seemed to know what he was going to do before he did.

~

After an unbelievably long day, Jack was getting ready for bed. This might be the most exhausted he'd ever been in his life. It was hard to believe that just this morning, he and s'haar had loaded up the cart for their second trip to the village and enjoyed a pleasant walk for the better part of the morning. Looking back, that seemed an entire lifetime ago. Since then, he'd survived the second-worst fight of his life, saved a young noble girl, introduced a second person from this planet to his world, and accepted that same girl into his home. Honestly, that would have made for a full week, let alone a single day. However, now he could finally rest.

As he stumbled out of the bathroom, Jack found Angela waiting on the side of his bed, obviously wanting to talk about something. Jack almost snapped at his sister, but he fought down the urge to throw a tantrum born of physical, mental, and emotional exhaustion. Instead, he closed his eyes for a second and took a breath to calm his frayed nerves.

Angela knew Jack better than anyone, maybe even better than he knew himself, so she had to realize how close to his limit he was. If she was waiting patiently to talk to him, it was obviously about something important.

Opening his eyes, Jack plastered the best smile he could manage onto his face. It wasn't the kind of smile that would fool anyone who knew him, but Angela would understand he was trying. When he spoke, all he could manage was a somewhat strained, "What's up?"

Angela's expression was sympathetic as she nodded her acknowledgment of Jack's attempt at patience. However, obviously felt the situation required his attention. "The girl, Em'brel, is having a breakdown. She's crying…hard."

Jack cocked his head to the side. "What's unusual about that? She lost her father, and her world was turned upside down. A little grief is natural and healthy."

Angela's look of concern deepened as her brows furrowed. "Grief *is* natural and healthy, but this is something more. She's dealing with more than loss and uncertainty. She was abused repeatedly. On top of that, she's starting to show signs of suffering from survivor's guilt. I think she's starting to turn that pain in on herself and convince herself she's to blame for all this. She shouldn't…"

Jack was familiar enough with survivors' guilt and what it could do, so he could see what she was getting at. Finally, enough of his brain pulled itself away from the idea it would get to rest to see where Angela was going with all this. He finished her thought for her. "She shouldn't be left alone right now."

Letting loose a deep sigh as he ran his hand through his unkempt hair, Jack continued. "Yeah, I agree. I'm not sure how much help I'm going to be right now, but a warm body is better than nothing…no offense… Let's go see what we can do."

Jack walked over to the bathroom long enough to splash some water on his face before leaving his room.

~

As he approached the door to S'haar's room, Jack could hear the sobbing coming from within. Angela was right. This wasn't the sound of someone in grief. These sobs had an unhealthy edge to them, bordering on a dangerous mania. That sound finished waking Jack up as he knocked on the door.

The sobbing took a few moments to slow to a halt before a shaky voice responded. "Ye… yes?"

Jack tried to adopt as soothing a voice as possible, knowing Angela would be translating the same tone through the speakers, rather than appearing in the room. It would help the girl avoid feeling embarrassed at her worn physical state. "It's Jack. I wanted to speak to you a little. Could you please come out to the main living area?"

There was a full minute of silence while Em'brel tried to gather her thoughts enough to speak. Finally, a soft voice called out. "Yes… of… of course. Just give me a moment."

Jack smiled. He'd been worried she would turn him away. "Take your time. I'm in no rush."

A few more minutes passed while Jack waited. Just as he was starting to worry she'd changed her mind, he heard the door open. The poor girl was a wreck but had obviously done her best to clean up the evidence. However, she wasn't fooling anyone.

She looked around in uncertainty, almost fearfully, and Jack motioned her over to the table again. When she sat down, he sat opposite her. He took a moment to just get a good look at her.

Even though Em'brel had obviously washed her face clean, it was still blotchy in a way that spoke of violent crying. Her clothes were torn in a few places where she'd ripped at them in her hunger to feel something, even if only pain. Even now, her breathing was perfectly even in an unnatural way that indicated she was consciously controlling it to try and seem like she wasn't as bad off as she was. Angela was right. Em'brel was walking along a dangerous cliff.

Jack took a deep breath before speaking. Angela was doing her best to be as uncharacteristically unobtrusive as possible while still translating. "When I was about your age, both of my parents were brutally murdered in front of me. Immediately after that, Angela and I were thrown into a life or death fight against the killer. Honestly, it's all kind of a blur these days, but somehow we didn't die. That was the worst day of my life. It took me years to learn to live again after that night."

Em'brel started to take a breath to respond, but Jack continued, never letting her get a word out. "I'm not telling you this because I'm asking for your sympathy or trying to diminish your pain. This was years ago, and I've mostly dealt with it. Though I won't lie to you, the pain of an experience like that never goes away completely."

The girl waited this time, wondering where Jack was going to go with this. He didn't make her wait long. "I'm telling you this, so you understand that I at least somewhat understand what you're going through and that I know a little of what I'm talking about."

Jack looked into the distance, trying to recall feelings he'd rather have left buried in the past. "Afterward, all I could think of is all the things that I could have done to save at least one of them. Knowing what I know now, I can think of several things that might have made a difference. The problem with that kind of thinking is that it's complete and utter shit."

Em'brel seemed shocked by the sudden change in tone of the story, but Jack continued without pause. "At that age, and with what I knew at the time, and with the shock of what I was going through, there was nothing I could have done. Nothing that happened that day was my fault."

Jack suddenly focused his eyes as directly as he could into En'brel's eyes, forcing her to look back through sheer force of will. "Nothing, NOTHING that happened to you or your father is your fault. It doesn't matter what you know now or what you would do differently if you had another chance. None of that matters because at the end of the day, sometimes you are just in the wrong place at the wrong time, and *it's not your fault!*"

Jack could see Em'brel trying to fight deep emotions back down, but he continued on mercilessly. "Whenever you start to think of a 'what if,' or 'I should have,' or even, 'it should have been me,' I want you to remember this moment. I want you to remember the look of complete certainty in my eyes and the conviction in my voice as I tell you right now, *none of what happened was your fault!*"

After that final repetition, Em'brel broke down. Her sobs were deep and gut-wrenching and tore at Jack's heart, bringing back vivid memories of his own pain. Jack shoved the old feeling aside for now as he walked over to the girl's side. As painful as they were to listen to, at least this was the sobbing of someone mourning rather than the manic filled self-hatred he'd heard earlier. This was the right kind of crying, the type which meant she was embracing her grief rather than fighting it.

For the third time that day, Jack held the poor girl as she cried herself out. He knew she wasn't suddenly past the danger, never to look back. There was still a long road ahead of Em'brel. But this was a step in the right direction down that road, and a big step at that.

When she finally pulled away from Jack, Em'brel looked like a mess. Just as she was starting to become self-conscious about her face, Jack interrupted her thoughts once more. Running his hand through his hair turned rat's nest, Jack laughed as he spoke. "You know, there are times when it's positively indecent to look clean and collected, and I declare now to be one such time. I doubt either of us is going to fall asleep right after that, so what say we watch a movie?"

Em'brel looked confused as she blinked a few times in rapid succession. "S'haar mentioned that before. What is a movie?"

Jack explained the concept of movies as recorded plays for a second time while thinking desperately of an appropriate title. What in the world should he show a fifteen-year-old girl who went through what will hopefully be the worst day of her life? Given what she lost, definitely nothing with princesses, prince charming, or about father-daughter bonding, and it had to be uplifting. What did that leave?

Just as Jack was about to give up and throw on something abstract, he remembered a childhood classic, The Labyrinth. Angela helpfully dubbed the movie, programming the argu'n language to come through a near-perfect imitation of the original actor's voices, although she refused to dub over David Bowie's singing. Maybe it was Em'brel's young and accepting mind, or perhaps it was the magic of Jim Henson, but Jack had to explain far less than he did with S'haar.

Partway into the movie, Jack's prediction proved at least half wrong when he finally passed out.

~

When Jack finally woke, he was stiff all over. Additionally, he was having trouble breathing, though he suspected that might have something to do with the young argu'n latched onto his side. As his eyes sleepily wandered the room, Jack saw S'haar sitting in the chair beside the couch. She was grinning, as though enjoying some private joke at Jack's expense.

S'haar broke the silence before he could. "You look like quite the fatherly figure sleeping there, protecting young Em'brel from her nightmares. There might be hope for you yet!"

Jack couldn't help but let a little of his morning grumpiness, brought on by aches and pain, show through in his voice. "After yesterday, I would think I earned a little more than just 'hope.'"

S'haar nodded in agreement, her smile fading from mockery to genuine affection as she spoke. "That you did. You came through, and we all got out alive. Although between each of us, there are a few new scars to go around, outside and in. But a good scar just means you survived the fight. That's nothing to be ashamed of!"

All the talk of scars drew Jack's attention to S'haar's shoulder. It was wrapped in bandages and clearly still oozing blood. Following his gaze, S'haar flexed her arm. "Angela tells me we're a bit more than halfway done, but also said I needed to take a break and get some food. It hurts like hell. On the other hand, it's better than losing my arm."

Em'brel began to stir, allowing Jack to slowly extract himself from her sleepy clutches. "True enough. Besides, the last thing I need is to have you rubbing in the fact you're still far stronger than me, even with only one arm."

S'haar looked like she had a thought or two on the subject, but Jack cut her off. "Any thoughts on breakfast?"

S'haar had to think for nearly a half-second before replying. "Bacon! If I'm going to celebrate unexpectedly living to see another day, we need to start it off right! On that note, Angela said we were all under something called 'doctor's orders' to take the day off and recover."

Jack was just opening his mouth to respond when Angela appeared to put in her own two cents. "Before you start complaining about timetables, I'd like to point out that any or all of you collapsing from mental, emotional, and physical strain will slow you down a lot more than taking some time to recover!"

Angela looked to be working herself into quite the lecture. "And furthermore, I'd like to point out..."

Angela suddenly stopped talking and tilted her head to one side. Jack grinned and started pointing out that her lecture would have more impact if she could focus long enough to finish her point when Angela cut him off. "My motion sensors are picking up movement at the mouth of the cave. Someone is here!"

Chapter 17

Jack felt a rush of adrenaline as several possibilities occurred to him in a matter of seconds. Had the hill people tracked them on their return? Was Bar'thon here for revenge? Was it just some wandering raiding party? Regardless, it was extremely improbable that anyone would be able to break into the ship and threaten them. The entrance was made out of alloys unlike anything this world currently had to offer, and Angela could even deploy defensive measures if things got bad enough.

The problem was the fact that they had no way to effectively deal with a large force if they decided to set up camp just outside the cave and wait them out. Even if the four of them could simply remain inside for weeks or even months, they'd eventually run out of food and power.

Trying to keep his initial fears under control until he had more information, Jack turned to Angela. "How many are out there?"

S'haar was also staring intently at Angela while poor Em'brel was looking back and forth between everyone hoping for answers. Angela had her eyes closed as if concentrating. "There only appears to be one. He's staying near the mouth of the cave and yelling in."

Angela opened her eyes to stare at S'haar, confusion evident on her face. "He's asking to speak to you."

At this, S'haar blinked. She seemed lost in thought for a moment before turning to Jack. "How do you want to proceed? This is your home."

Jack shook his head. "It's *our* home. If this person simply wants to talk, I say we talk. However, let me get my coat and gun first, just to be safe."

S'haar nodded and strapped on some long knives as well. She was still missing her sword from the battle, and they hadn't had time to replace it. Her shoulder wasn't up to strenuous use, but she'd always do her job as a bodyguard if it came down to it.

Armed and armored, the two left the safety of the ship to speak with their visitor. As they walked through the dark, Jack could hear a voice shouting into the cave, but with all the echoes bouncing around, he couldn't tell who it was or what he was saying.

On the other hand, S'haar seemed to recognize the voice because she halted and started thinking aloud before continuing. "It can't be. What's *he* doing here?"

Her stance relaxed somewhat, which Jack took as a good sign, and then she turned to Jack to explain. "I believe that's Lon'thul's voice I hear, but what would he be doing all the way out here?"

Jack was just as confused as S'haar. He couldn't imagine any reason for the hunter chief's son to be at their cave calling for S'haar. On the other hand, given the different possibilities, Jack had been considering, this was as good an outcome as he could have imagined. So he simply shrugged and indicated they should continue.

Nearing the mouth of the cave, they could finally make out what the young argu'n was shouting in. "I don't mean to intrude, but I seek to speak with S'haar! If she is not here, I seek an audience with the dragon instead!"

As the two of them walked out of the cave's shadows into the morning light, Lon'thul's face went from worry and concern to a look of profound relief. The expression only lasted a few moments before his eyes focused on the bloody bandage on S'haar's left arm, and the look of concern returned.

Lon'thul started forward, reaching for S'haar. "You've been injured! We need to get you to a healer right away!"

S'haar waved away his concern, obviously more interested in the reasons behind his presence than her shoulder. "I'm fine. What are you doing out here Lon'thul?"

Lon'thul ignored her dismissive response, grabbed S'haar by the wrist, and attempted to drag S'haar with him. "You're not *fine!* You're injured, and we need to get you treated right away."

S'haar quickly ripped her wrist out of his grasp, responding with venom in her voice and a hard edge to her eyes as her tendrils shook in annoyance. "No, you don't get to do that. You don't get to show up and play the hero and 'save me from myself.' I'm not some damsel in need of your protection and guidance. I've fought more battles and killed more men than the number of years you've been alive. So when I tell you I'm fine, you had best understand that I'm the only one who gets to make that call."

Lon'thul looked shocked at first. Clearly, this wasn't going how he'd expected. S'haar's voice lost a little of its edge, but her glare still spoke volumes. "I understand you're trying to be helpful, but I don't like repeating myself. So if you please, why are you here?"

This time the young argu'n had the decency to look a bit ashamed, kicking the cave floor as he spoke. "Lord A'ngels has been awaiting some visitors. Apparently, someone was delivering a bride for his son. When they were more than a day late in showing up, he sent the hunters out to scout for the girl and her escort."

Lon'thul's eyes focused on a distant horizon as if he was focused on an incredibly vivid memory. "I came across the site of a massive battle. A whole camp of the hill people had been wiped out. Many of them received wounds, the likes of which I'd never seen. The only evidence of who could have done it was this."

Lon'thul held out S'haar's sword. "Scouting around some more, I eventually found the cart you used in the village, still loaded with iron and a kovaack. After finding that, I was worried that you'd been taken or killed. The way you spoke of the dragon made me think you were friends with her, so I came here hoping to find you or recruit the dragon's aid in finding you."

S'haar reached out and took the sword from the youth, finally relaxing her expression. "Well, thankfully, you found me here instead. The dragon is aiding in the healing of my shoulder. I'll be fine."

Lon'thul only looked more confused at this. "But how? That camp easily held twenty argu'n, most of whom will now be food for scavengers. I'm well aware that you're quite the skilled fighter, but even warriors of legend couldn't have pulled that off and lived to tell the tale!"

S'haar looked back at Jack, who'd been standing off to the side, content to watch everything up until now. "The answer to your question is simple. Jack borrowed a bit of the dragon's power."

Lon'thul looked at Jack as though he'd just turned into said dragon. "How can someone 'borrow a bit of the dragon's power?'"

Jack looked trapped, then confused, and finally shrugged before speaking, S'haar switching to her role as translator. "Honestly, even if I wanted to share that secret, which I don't, it would take too long to explain. You'll just have to accept the evidence you've witnessed as proof of the claim."

The young argu'n looked as though he wanted to argue further, but after a moment finally decided this was another battle of wills he wasn't likely to win. "I guess I'll have to. But that still leaves one last question. Do you have any idea what happened to the bride? She's still missing."

Jack's head tilted to the side as he considered how best to answer, it would be easy to say he had no idea what happened to her, but if the truth came out later, it could unnecessarily complicate his relationship with the village. The truth might cause its own complications, but he'd deal with those as they came.

Crossing his arms similarly to S'haar's favored stance, hoping to convey some of her usual confidence, Jack answered Lon'thul's question. "We did find a young girl who'd recently lost her father and received some rather harsh abuse at the hands of the raiders. We brought her back with us to receive treatment as well. After that, she requested to be allowed to remain here. Without going into too much detail, we decided to grant her request. She's safe but probably won't be interested in the idea of marriage any time soon."

Lon'thul looked troubled at that. "I'm not sure how well that news is going to be received. She was promised to Bar'thon, that marriage was bought to unite our two villages…"

Jack was just deciding how to phrase his response when a visibly enraged Em'brel marched out of the shadows behind him. Jack barely had time to wonder when she'd snuck up behind them or why Angela had let her leave the ship when Em'brel slapped Lon'thul with enough vigor that Jack's own jaw ached in sympathy.

Tears in her eyes, the tiny Em'brel still seemed to tower over the much larger Lon'thul at that moment. "You can tell the lord of your village, 'With the death of my father, all the lands and authority that we offered in our deal are now in my uncle's possession. If he had wanted to ensure he received what he paid for, he should have sent an escort to ensure my father and I arrived safely.'"

Her fury spent itself quickly, and Em'brel seemed to shrink in on herself. "I'm no longer the daughter of a noble. I'm now just another orphan with nothing to offer in marriage. Your lord will have to seek out my uncle if he desires any further alliances.

To his credit, Lon'thul accepted Em'brel's rebuke with relative humility. As the youth stammered out his apology, Jack couldn't help but feel a little sorry for the usually cheerful argu'n. He was obviously a man of his time, struggling to understand and keep up with two women clearly ahead of their time. His mistakes were born more out of the ignorance brought on by his environment rather than any malicious or petty intent.

Before things got too awkward, Jack decided to change the subject.

"I have a deal to offer you. Since you're already headed back to the village to make your report, if you take our cart the rest of the way with you and have the iron and Kovaack processed, I'll give you a one-tenth cut of the total value of the delivery. You can take the payment as you wish from the iron and/or the kovaack."

Lon'thul's eyes widened in surprise as Jack continued. "You can tell old Mar'kon I'll give him the same cut we agreed on last time, and I'll be there in a few days to pick up my share."

Jack knew the price he was paying was worth far more than the services a simple delivery warranted, but he hoped it would go some way toward making up for the bad news the argu'n would be delivering.

Lon'thul recognized that this deal also signified the end of his visit. After agreeing to Jack's terms, he turned to Em'brel again. "I'm sorry for...uhh for being..."

S'haar couldn't resist the urge to get a shot in while Lon'thul's defenses were down, a familiar bitterness adding a bit of venom to her voice. "For being a male?"

Lon'thul winced a little at her statement before shrugging. "I was going to say, 'for being insensitive,' but I guess that works."

Em'brel was looking lost and confused again as Jack spoke up. "Well, we appreciate you looking in on us, and returning S'haar's sword, but we really should get back to recovering from yesterday's ordeal. We can talk more in a few days, okay?"

The dismissal was obvious enough that Lon'thul could only nod and turn to leave. Jack merely shook his head sympathetically as the young hunter walked away.

Once the three made it back inside, they were quickly met by Angela. She was obviously ready to voice her own thoughts, hopping from one foot to the other in the air. "So that's the Lon'thul you mentioned before. Nice enough kid, not too bright though."

Jack decided to come to the youth's defense since he wasn't here to do it himself. "Eh, he's alright. Just needs to grow up a little, but he'll be fine. Not that I'm one to talk…"

The last was said as Jack suddenly realized that he was very, very outnumbered as the three women looked at him with faces ranging from amused to incredulous. He decided now would be a good time to change the subject.

Clearing his throat in a not-at-all awkward manner, Jack brought up something that had been on his mind. "We've already had too many delays to our timetable, and I'm guessing we're only going to have more as the winter drags on. If we're going to get things stabilized before Angela runs out of power, we're going to need to scale things up a little. In short, we're going to need more help."

As he spoke, Jack started walking over to the kitchen to make the now overdue breakfast. While he got out the bacon and began slicing it, Angela was translating and explaining their situation for Em'brel. Jack continued. "To that end, I want to hire a few workers to come out and build us a few basic structures, housing, storehouses, work stations, etc.

Jack finished his thought as he placed the bacon into the pans. The sizzling and popping sounds were already making his mouth water. "We can, of course, compensate them in the usual ways. However, I think we should also make some extra warming coats for them, similar to the one we made S'haar. The coats themselves will also make great compensation, and the heating pouches can only be recharged at our ship, so we don't have to worry too much about the local impact of these coats possibly making their way out into the world."

S'haar looked thoughtful a moment before adding her own input. "That should be enough to tempt some of the younger craftsmen hungry to make a name for themselves, but where will they stay? Are you going to let a bunch of workers into your home until they get the housing up?"

Jack looked troubled for a moment before turning to Angela. "Do we have anything we can make quick but well-insulated tents out of? Maybe we could install some basic heating as well? It wouldn't have to last long, a few weeks at most."

Angela looked up from her explanations to Em'brel for a moment. "Well, we could make some linen-like cloth from some of the local plants. If we put up two walls and fill the middle with some basic insulation like a quilt, that should do the trick. It won't hold up for the whole winter, but I think we could get a few weeks out of it. The heating will be simple enough. Just give them blankets designed to contain more heating pouches."

The AI stopped and thought for a moment, tapping her lips with a finger. "With all these draws on my remaining power, we might want to think about getting up some sort of simple power generation sooner rather than later. It doesn't have to be enough to meet our total consumption rate, yet, but if we could slow the drain rather than increase it, that would go a long way toward buying us enough time to get properly established."

Angela waved her hands toward the ceiling. "We're under a mountain. Some solar and wind generators would be easy enough to set up."

Jack finished the first plate of bacon. He stole a strip for himself before placing the plate in front of the two hungry argu'n. He breathed a sigh of relief when he was able to pull his hand back before the now feral monsters at the table could claim it. "Ok, we finish healing S'haar's arm and get some rest today. Then spend the next couple of days on getting the tents ready to go."

After swallowing a few mouthfuls, S'haar nodded her agreement and mumbled something to the effect of that being a "good plan" through a mouth once again filled with bacon. Em'brel took large bites of several strips, then sat with her head back and eyes closed in bliss as she chewed her portion.

Jack wondered when it was that he'd gone from being intimidated by S'haar's teeth and eating habits to finding the two predators digging in with gusto almost relaxing. True, a small part of his brain still warned that predators this dangerous were to be respected, but something just felt right about the life he now found himself in. Smiling to himself, he turned and began working on cooking a second plate of bacon. The first one obviously wouldn't last long.

His expression wasn't lost on Angela, who was finding herself in agreement with her brother. It was starting to feel like they had a family again for the first time in far too long.

Chapter 18

Angela decided she really liked having a younger sister. Jack meant the world to her, and he always would, but Em'brel was just so…cute! The fact that she had a mouth full of teeth that would make a shark envious, claws that could effortlessly eviscerate a man, and a musculature that already put Jack's adult body to shame were all minor details, hardly worthy of consideration.

Where S'haar was filled with careful restraint, her extraordinary strength visible just beneath the surface of every movement, Em'brel moved in a way that could only be described as dainty. Today she had gotten up early so that Angela could show her how to cook breakfast before the others awoke.

They were making a "sheepherder's breakfast." It consisted of eggs, cooked on top hash browns, served on a foundation of the divine cut of meat called bacon. Em'brel didn't know what animal bacon came from, but she was going to find her world's closest equivalent, no matter how long it took!

There were some initial complications in cracking the eggs without getting the shells mixed in with the hashbrowns, and the bacon was a little too singed in places, but overall the meal turned out rather well. Still, Em'brel swore to herself that her next attempt would be better.

Jack was the first one successfully tempted out of his room by the smells Angela had allowed to circulate into the bedrooms. He was a bit of a morning mess, stumbling out of the door while rubbing the sleep from his eyes, still adjusting to the light of the waking world. He was greeted by an excited wave from Em'brel. "Good morning Jack. I hope you slept well! Come get your breakfast before it gets cold!"

Running his hand through his hair in a habitual manner, Jack grumbled out his response. "It's not fair that someone could be this awake and cheerful this early in the morning! The sun probably hasn't even cleared the horizon yet!"

Angela chose to translate his greeting as, "He says good morning, and thank you for the food." While translating, she gave Jack a glare that told him that if he was smart, he'd greet breakfast in such a manner in the future.

S'haar wasn't far behind, coming out of the room with a spring in her step and a mouth salivating enough to make talk slightly more complicated than usual. Sitting down at the table, she took a moment to enjoy another deep breath before digging into her breakfast.

Jack watched her eat with a bit of amazement. "How is it you are both so energetic in the morning?"

S'haar replied with a mouth half full of food, unwilling to waste even a few precious moments of breakfast. "Angela helps out with that. When we are about to wake up, she raises the room temperature enough that it gives us something she calls a 'jump start'."

Em'brel sat down at her own place with her own serving. The first time Jack had served bacon, she'd dug in with the same enthusiasm S'haar had shown, but she was determined to show more restraint in the future. Picking up her knife and fork, she cut off a small portion and chewed it daintily like a lady should. Not that she had any problem with S'haar's way of doing things. As far as she was concerned, her two saviors could do no wrong; it just wasn't the way Em'brel was raised. As she watched Em'brel, Angela was dancing in place with her fists waving about excitedly. "Oh my god, she's so adorable! Why didn't we get one earlier!"

S'haar pointed her recently emptied fork at Angela before speaking. Once again, her mouth was half full. "Sometimes I wonder if you aren't really a dragon, and instead of collecting metal, you collect people. We're not your pets, you know!"

Angela looked at her with an expression of overly exaggerated innocence, indicating she thought the exact opposite of what she was about to say. "Of course not! You, Jack, and Em'brel are complex individuals, and I'd never think of 'collecting' you!"

S'haar's eyes narrowed as she made her thoughts on Angela's statement clear. "Uh-huh…" Turning to Jack, she changed the subject. "So, what's today's plan?"

Jack had been watching the group's antics while slowly waking up, but now he realized he actually had to contribute to the conversation. "Well, we're going to need a lot of plant matter for the linen cloth. I saw some plants down by the lake, not far from here, that looked like they'd have the kind of fibers we're looking for. If we take the sled with us, we should be able to get enough for our immediate needs. It'll give you a good opportunity to get your arm stretched by using a range of movement while also not stressing the new muscle attachments too much."

Angela threw in her own two cents. "Meanwhile, I intend to test Em'brel to determine how much knowledge of math and science she already has."

Em'brel started to look nervous at the word "test," but Angela quickly assuaged her fears. "Don't worry, this isn't a pass or fail kind of test. I just want to find out where you're at, academically speaking, so I can set up a plan going forward."

S'haar spoke up. "You might also want to give her the same 'procedure' you gave to me, so she can understand Jack."

At that, Angela looked a little uncomfortable. "Usually, in the case of a minor, elective surgery like this can't be performed without the consent of a parent or guardian. The risk *is* minimal, but it's something that will alter her in a way that can't be undone. I hesitate to do such a thing to simply avoid a little inconvenience."

S'haar sat back, ignoring her plate for the first time this morning. "Well, I'm not sure what Em'brel being young has to do with anything, but I'm as close to a 'guardian' as she's got at the moment, and I give you my 'consent.' Also, this isn't just about your convenience. As long as she can't understand the two of you when you are speaking your language, she's going to feel isolated. If you are really going to welcome her into your home for an extended period, it'll help her feel more connected to the group, which is something she needs right now."

Em'brel was following along as best she could and looked to Angela, her eyes full of a strange hunger. "Is that something you can do? You can just 'give me' your language?"

Angela looked at the young girl a moment before nodding. "Yes, although it's not perfect. Most words will just translate to whatever similar ideas you are already familiar with. However, if we say a word that you have no concept of, you'll still need an explanation."

Em'brel gave Angela the same formal bow she had initially used to introduce herself to Jack and S'haar. "Then, I humbly request you bestow this 'procedure' upon me."

Once again, Angela squealed her delight before answering. "Ok, you two win. After the testing, we'll look into the procedure this evening. For the record, you shouldn't use that cuteness of yours just to get what you want. In the future, I'd appreciate it if you were only this cute AFTER you got what you wanted."

~

S'haar and Jack walked along the lakefront, gathering bunches of the fibrous plant Jack had mentioned earlier and bundling them together. It was actually quite relaxing. Listening to the waves of the lake and enjoying the sights and sounds of nature. S'haar would occasionally point out plants or animals to explain a useful or peculiar aspect they had.

Other times they simply walked and worked in comfortable silence. Neither felt the need to entertain or impress the other, both just enjoying the peace of the moment.

Jack found a groove that worked for him. Grab the plant near the base, twist it onto its side, wedge his knife into the bend, and cut up and away. He'd do this six or seven times until he had a good handful, then pass it off to S'haar. She'd then work it into the current bunch she was tying together with twine before loading them onto the sled. With this pattern, the work was going quickly and smoothly.

Shortly after the fifth bundle was complete, S'haar took a moment to decide how best to bring up a subject that had been weighing on her mind. "I agree with your decision to bring more people in, but I wonder, have you thought through where this path will lead?"

Jack considered her words for a moment while he cut a few more plants. Grab twist cut, grab twist cut, his mind was far away from his hands. Handing S'aar another batch, Jack responded. "Well, I'm aware that we won't be able to hide the fact that there is no actual dragon forever if that's what you mean." Grab, twist, cut. "Although I want to hold off on that reveal until we are a bit more established." Grab, twist, cut. "I imagine if I use the drill rig a few times, that ought to be enough to keep most of our visitors from sticking their noses too far into the cave." Grab, twist, cut.

S'haar shook her head as she took the next handful of plants. "While that is something to keep in mind, that's not what I'm talking about. I'm talking about further down the path. Up until now, you've just been the strange little man who's friends with a dragon and knows how to get a lot of metal."

S'haar took another handful and added it to her bunch before continuing. "That all changes once you set up housing and bring in workers. Now instead of a curiosity, you'll become a target and a competitor. Raiders and villages alike will see you as an opportunity to further their own agendas. You'll have to hire guards to protect the camp or align yourself with a village large enough to offer protection."

S'haar tilted her head as she continued. "While I have no doubt that you'd be able to easily find a patron village, you'd end up giving them a much larger share of your resources in return for their protection. On the other hand, if you hire your own guards, you'll need to worry about establishing the proper infrastructure to support the presence of guards and the workers."

S'haar realized it had been a while since Jack had handed her any plants and looked down to find him staring up at her open-mouthed, his knife hanging forgotten from his hand. He blinked a few times before speaking. "I...I hadn't considered *any* of that!"

Jack let himself fall back from a kneeling position to a sitting one as the ramifications washed over him. He'd been so concerned with keeping the workers away from the ship that he'd failed to see the forest for the trees. This opened up a whole new world of complications. Politics, alliances, logistics, trading, and the list went on and on.

Jack was so lost in thought that he hadn't even noticed S'haar crouch down next to him. Tilting her head to one side, she watched Jack a moment before interrupting his thoughts. "You know you've got time before you have to make any decisions."

Jack turned and looked at S'haar, his eyes latching onto hers as though looking for a lifeline. S'haar elaborated. "Winter is about to really get going, and you're the only one with the ability to travel or work during that time. You should have a few months to work things out and make any final decisions."

Jack closed his eyes, took a breath, and nodded. "You're right, I have time, and for now, the most important thing is getting the workers up and running. This means I just need to proceed with my existing plans. But I'll need to think about this further."

Jack got back to his knees and started the process again. Grab, twist, cut. But where before the actions had seemed quick and efficient, they now seemed slow and deliberate, and his thoughts raced faster than his hands could match.

Grab. We probably can't get enough infrastructure set up in time, so we'll need an alliance. Twist. We've already established a reputation with S'haar's village, and a number of the villagers are at least passingly familiar with me. Cut. Ideally, we'll be able to break out on our own after we're established enough, but once he gets his claws in us, lord A'ngels won't let us go without a fight.

The two worked in silence once more, but it wasn't the comfortable silence from before. Now the silence only served to emphasize the fact that the task before Jack had just ballooned in complexity.

~

Em'brel was tightly holding onto her father's hand, trying to drag him back. "We can't leave! If we do, you'll die again!"

Her father looked down at her with regret in his eyes. "You know we have to. Without outside support, much of our village will not survive the winter. As my daughter, you have a duty to your people, and as your father, I wish for you to have a better life than watching our village slowly fade and crumble away."

Em'brel grabbed his hand tighter, closed her eyes, and pulled as hard as she could. As she did so, she felt her grip slip, and she collapsed onto the ground. Opening her eyes again, she saw her father on the ground, the warmth of life gone from his face, and Dol'jin stood over his body. Behind him waited countless raiders, stretching out to the horizon and beyond, leering at her as they reached forward.

Em'brel tried to scream, but no sound came out. She tried to run, but her feet kept slipping. She looked around for a place to hide, but everywhere she looked, there was another leering face. Em'brel collapsed as all hope was lost.

As Dol'jin reached for Em'brel, S'haar stood up behind him, but this time she was taller than Dol'jin, taller than any argu'n. She was a giant. When S'haar swung her sword, dozens of raiders fell like sheaves of grain.

The raiders roared and surged forward, only to have Jack appear from the sky, riding on the back of a giant glowing dragon. Jack jumped and glided to the ground. Once there, he took an exaggerated breath, leaned forward, and blew flames onto the crowds of raiders, leaving nothing but ash in his wake.

The dragon landed softly beside Em'brel, wrapping itself protectively around her. Em'brel then reached out to the dragon, hugging its neck tightly to herself before noticing the dragon had Angela's face. Safe in Angela's protective embrace, Em'brel closed her eyes and wept for her father a second time. Meanwhile, Angela bent down and whispered comforting words into her ear. "You're ok, it's all over. You did great. Now you just need to open your eyes."

As Em'brel opened her eyes, she saw Angela hovering right in front of her face. This time she was her usual sprite sized self. Just off to the side stood an also normal-sized S'haar, looking both concerned and relieved at the same time. A bit further and to the back stood Jack, looking like he wanted to come forward, but hesitating and rubbing his neck for some reason.

Em'brel reached up and wiped the tears away from her face. "Wha… What happened?"

Angela's face and voice were as soothing as she could make them while she explained. "What you just experienced is the side effect I warned you about, vivid dreaming. It's not a pleasant experience, but it's no more real than any other dream."

S'haar and Jack both looked a little concerned, but as Angela looked over a few floating words and numbers, her expression was more pleased. "Aside from some unsettling dreams, it looks like everything went smoothly. So the only question I have now is, do you understand me?"

Em'brel realized the last part was said in Angela and Jack's sing-song language, but she found that it now made perfect sense to her. "Yes… how can I understand what you're saying?"

Angela smiled with her elbows high and her hands behind her head. "We'll need to get a lot further into biology before any explanation I could offer would make any sense, but let's just say I've tricked your brain into thinking it has memories it doesn't actually have."

Em'brel leapt toward Angela, intent on wrapping her in a hug but passed through the ship's avatar before landing on the ground on the other side. Everyone looked a bit startled before she sheepishly explained. "In my dream, I was able to hug you... I guess there's still some lingering memories..."

Jack chuckled before walking forward to give Em'brel a hand up. "Well, trying to give Angela a hug is a lot better than what S'haar did to me when she woke up from her own surgery, but that's a story for another time. How're you feeling?"

Realizing she could understand Jack without translation for the first time since meeting him, Em'brel wrapped him in another monster hug. This time, she remembered that he was more fragile than herself and managed to avoid giving Jack any new bruises. "I'm feeling much better, thank you!"

Jack had braced himself for another bone-crunching friendship assault. Realizing it wasn't coming this time, he relaxed and returned the embrace. "Glad to hear it, and welcome to the family."

Chapter 19

Jack and S'haar were back on the road to the village once again, but while the last trip had seemed calm and relaxing until it wasn't, Jack now felt like raiders were hiding behind every tree or rock. S'haar noticed her companion's nerves and placed a steadying hand on his shoulder. "You know it's too cold for anyone to be this far out without one of your coats, and even if someone was out here, they'd be useless in a fight by now."

Jack looked up at the taller, armored woman and smiled a bit shakily. "That obvious, am I? I know you're right, but I can't help but shake the feeling that something's about to go wrong again. We got off too easy last time."

S'haar threw back her head and laughed. "Easy? I nearly lost my arm, and the only thing that kept you from being gutted is the armor you wear under your coat. I think you and I have very different ideas on what's 'easy'."

Jack was staring at another tree as they passed. "I didn't say it *was* easy. I said we got off *too* easy. As many raiders as we picked a fight with, I'm surprised we survived at all. Given how many got away, others must have heard what happened and are probably looking for revenge."

S'haar merely shrugged, still shaking her head in exasperation, causing her tendrils to clank lightly because of the movement. "Maybe they will be, but not right now, and not in this cold. We would have seen the smoke from any camp large enough to be a threat long before we stumbled across anyone out this far. I'm your bodyguard, so let me worry about possible danger. I promise I'll tell you if we're in trouble."

Jack took a deep breath to steady his nerves and silently told his hand to stop shaking so much. His heartbeat did slow a little, but the hand stubbornly refused to listen. Jack held his hand up in front of himself and forced it into as tight a fist as he was able. Once he felt his grip start to weaken, he relaxed it and was relieved to see the tremors had finally passed. Another deep breath led to another slight slowing of his heart rate.

S'haar watched Jack's calming techniques with interest. "You know, it's okay to be shaken. I've known hardened veterans who lost their fighting spirit after a particularly brutal fight."

Jack had been starting to do complicated math in his head to distract himself when S'haar had spoken, but now he turned his attention back to her. "You might be right, but right now, I can't be too shaken to do the job. Not because 'I can't show weakness,' but because people depend on us getting this done. As strong and smart as Angela is, she can't leave the ship and will eventually run out of power without our help."

Jack closed his eyes for a moment as he walked, enjoying the crisp smell of the cold morning air. "Then there's Em'brel. I'm honestly completely lost about what to do for her, other than help her feel safe and maybe teach her a thing or two before she chooses her path in life. I don't even know enough about this world to know what direction to think about pointing her in."

S'haar shrugged again, although this time, her voice held a bit more sympathy. "She'll find her own path. The girl is smart and already better educated than myself. She can read and write, and she knows her numbers. She could probably make a living working for a noble with those skills alone. Add in whatever crazy things Angela will teach her, and she'll be ruling her own village in no time!"

Jack shook his head at that last part. "Knowledge *is* vital for anyone wanting to rule, but there's more to it than that. There is charisma, politics, and, most importantly, whoever has the most soldiers is usually in charge."

S'haar slapped Jack on the back in what was probably supposed to be a display of comradery, rather than the bone-jarring experience it was. "Good, I'm glad you understand this! It will be important to keep that in mind once you get your little outpost up and running!"

Jack took another steadying breath to calm his nerves again before they got out of hand once more. "Yeah, thanks for reminding me. The good news is I'm suddenly not as worried about the raiders. Though, I think I preferred it when they were the problem on my mind…"

S'haar gave him her favorite predator smile, which did nothing to calm Jack's nerves before she replied. "Good, now you are worried about the right things! As I said, leave the danger to me. All you have to do is worry about leading a community of 'eight-foot-tall monsters'."

Jack couldn't help but be impressed by S'haar's impersonation of himself at the end of the sentence.

~

Em'brel was getting frustrated. She let out a heartfelt sigh before trying to charm her way out of this lesson. "I know how to add, subtract, multiply, and now I even know how to divide. Why do I have to learn this thing you call 'algebra'?"

Angela looked down at the girl, for once immune to her charm. "The whole world around us can be broken down and understood mathematically. Once you can do that, you can take those same principles and use them to improve life, or even create it."

Em'brel looked confused, but Angela continued before she could ask any questions. "Take me, for example." Angela gave Em'brel a perfect imitation of the formal bow the girl had used before. "I am essentially nothing more than a complicated math equation. Everything I think and do is an expression of math. The bow I just performed would look something like this." Angela put up a display of a complex formula.

Em'brel knew she was being tricked into showing interest in math but couldn't resist looking a little closer. "I recognize the numbers and some of the symbols, but there are so many more symbols. What do those mean?"

Angela smiled. That was the question she'd been hoping for. "Each one of those expresses another mathematic idea or principle. Similar to how the 'x' I showed you can stand for different numbers, those symbols could represent entire equations. If I were to replace those symbols with simple digits, the equation of the bow would look more like this."

With a wave of her hand, Angela filled the entire room with layers of numbers so complex that it became painful to focus on any one part. "Now, something like this would be far too complex for any person to ever put together, so instead, they use symbols that represent different ideas to take this mess and simplify it down to this." The original equation returned, now seeming beautifully simple in comparison to the chaos Em'brel had just witnessed.

Having made her point, Angela waved away the equation, which faded as if a wind had passed through it. "The good news is, you don't have to learn anything nearly that complex. You won't be creating life through math, after all. However, there are still plenty of aspects of life on this world that could be improved simply by the proper application of math. Algebra is the first step to go from keeping simple ledgers to building a bridge that will stand for centuries. Eventually, your distant descendants could sail through the stars above utilizing the principles you're learning today."

Em'brel looked at Angela with eyes filled with the excitement of discovery. "Is that where you and Jack came from? The stars?"

Angela smiled at her pupil's newfound enthusiasm. "It is, and if you agree to work on your math with me a little every day, I'll agree to tell you a little about life out among the stars, agreed?"

Em'brel pretended to mull the offer over a little before nodding in excitement. "It's a deal!"

~

As Jack and S'haar approached the village. Jack noticed a familiar argu'n sitting by a fire in front of the gate. S'haar waved before greeting the old guard. "Ger'ron, the toothless wonder! Do you ever do anything that doesn't involve sitting around all day?"

Ger'ron looked up from warming his hands by the fire with a grin, still full of plenty of teeth despite S'haar's claim. He waved back as the two approached. "You should show your elder more respect. Last I checked, I still have the upper hand, having won forty-two out of eighty-three sparring matches so far!"

S'haar laughed as she gave her old mentor a friendly punch in the arm. "That's just because you refused to fight me anymore since I got one match away from breaking even!"

Ger'ron looked at his old pupil with an expression like a wizened old sage. "A true warrior knows when to fight and when to retreat. The only way for a poor old man like myself to win is by refusing to play the game."

S'haar held out her sword for Ger'ron to take. "You might be old, but I doubt you'll ever be poor. I bet you still give the new recruits a surprise by feigning a bad back mid-fight!"

Ger'ron waved away S'haar's sword as he responded with a slightly self-deprecating smile. "I have to pretend a little less every year, but I still do alright. Lord A'ngels said to let you keep your weapons from now on. Something to do with a couple of muggers?"

S'haar blinked in surprise a few times before resheathing her sword. "Huh, that's… unexpected."

Ger'ron shrugged. "It's not my job to understand the rulings of a lord, just to enforce them."

He walked over to the gate and rapped his knuckles against it. "Hey, we got some traders out here, open up!"

From the other side of the gate, Jack heard the same young voice as last time. "As cold as it is outside? Are they suicidal?"

Ger'ron's voice developed an impatient edge. "For once, will you just listen to me rather than questioning everything I tell you? Open the gate already!"

Once the gate opened, Jack and S'haar walked past the same young guard, who was just as bug-eyed as the first time. Though this time, there was also a hint of hero worship to his expression. Old Ger'ron shouted something after the two of them that explained the look. "Oh, by the way, the story of your little adventure with the raiders has spread! Quite the tale Lon'thul brought back!"

While the two walked through the village crowds for the second time, everyone was staring once again. But this time, the looks ranged from the hero-worship of the young guard to expressions of doubt and disbelief. Jack noticed that most of the eyes were now directed at S'haar and not himself, but he was just fine with that. He'd never been big on being the center of attention.

For her part, S'haar seemed annoyed by the looks being directed her way but kept her mouth shut and her eyes focused on the crowd. This time, they stopped by the hunter's lodge first, hoping to find Lon'thul. Jack noticed the place was empty as he looked around the gloomy interior. Well, almost empty.

In one corner was the single most terrifying argu'n Jack had ever seen. His clothing was more bones, horns, and skulls than leather. His armored plates were dyed black to emphasize where they were scored and scarred by countless battles for life and limb. He'd lost one of his elbow spikes but replaced it by tying on the claw of some massive beast. His head tendrils were laced through with bits of wood and metal to array them outward in a manner that made them look like a magnificent mane. Jack knew this could be no other than the hunter chief, Dek'thul.

He briefly considered backing out of the hall and pretending like he hadn't seen anything when the argu'n spoke without turning his head. "So, you're the one everyone's been talking about."

As the hunter chief turned around, Jack couldn't help but think the man was even more terrifying from the front than he was from behind. Jack had been expecting a horribly scarred face to go with his armored plates, but as far as Jack could see, there was no blemish in sight. Instead, it was his eyes that unsettled Jack.

All argu'n have metallic eyes, gold, silver, copper, etc. Dek'thul was no exception. In many ways, Jack would say his eyes and S'haar's were similar, but where her eyes portrayed all the complex emotions of a sentient person, human or argu'n, all Jack could see in Dek'thul's eyes was hunger.

Jack watched wearily as the hunter chief approached. Every movement was that of a dangerous predator stalking its prey. Its eyes held Jack in place, preventing him from doing or saying anything. Jack stood hopelessly transfixed, watching as Death approached him.

Jack was just debating whether the better course of action was to wet himself or simply pass out from fear when S'haar placed her hand on his shoulder in the way she was coming to learn reminded Jack that he wasn't alone.

Jack resisted the urge to take a deep breath or shake his head, and instead stepped forward and held out his hand to offer a handshake before speaking. S'haar translated as usual. "I apologize. Where are my manners? I'm Jack, and you know my friend and translator, S'haar. You must be Dek'thul. I've heard so much about you!"

Dek'thul threw back his head in laughter, both hands on his hips, and his whole demeanor suddenly changed and became almost jovial. "Impressive greeting from one so small! After seeing you, I expected you to run and hide. Welcome to my hall! To what do I owe the honor of your visit?"

Following this, his hand shot out with speed only an argu'n was capable of, gripping Jack's offered hand. "I believe you call this a 'handshake,' yes? My son told me all about it!"

Jack was still intimidated but felt much of the tension leave his body as he grinned in return. "Yes, this is a handshake, but usually you only shake two or three times before letting go. As to your question, we were actually looking for your son. We entrusted him with the care of some of our goods and wanted to make sure he was able to return safely."

Dek'thul finally ended the continuous handshake with an apologetic smile. "Ah yes, quite the generous payment you offered him in return for delivering your goods for you. If I'm not mistaken, you'll find him at the inn, spending some of the iron you paid him while sharing the tale of the battlefield you left for him to find. He always knows how to tell a good story, and this might be his best yet!"

The large argu'n chuckled to himself. "Ah, to be young and popular with the ladies again, such is the wasted blessing of youth! When you see him, tell him I said he'd better not let his suddenly increased popularity dull his hunter's edge. We have a village to feed, after all!"

With that apparent dismissal, Dek'thul returned to the carcass he was cutting up. Once they turned and left, Jack couldn't suppress his shudder any longer. True, if anything, Dek'thul was even friendlier than his son and seemed eager to help, but Jack noticed two things that seemed off about the whole encounter.

First, Dek'thul never looked at or acknowledged S'haar. Usually, the first time Jack spoke and S'haar translated an argu'n would look back and forth between the two a few times before they fully understood what was going on. However, aside from the time he laughed, Dek'thul's eyes never left Jack. Which brought Jack to the second thing that bothered him about the hunter chief.

Not once had the look of hunger ever left Dek'thul's eyes.

Chapter 20

As Jack and S'haar walked into the inn, Lon'thul seemed to be deeply engaged in the act of telling his story. He was waving his arms about as though trying to act out the scenes he was describing. "There were dozens of bodies strewn across a large field. The fight must have been in constant motion as the combatants fought with spear, sword, claw, and even teeth!"

Lon'thul gnashed his teeth to emphasize his last sentence while someone from the crowd placed a full mug in front of him to encourage him to keep talking. "One of the bodies belonged to the largest argu'n I've ever seen. He would have stood a full head taller than me, if he hadn't had a sword shoved clear through his chest at the time!"

Lon'thul reached for his drink, only to see it grabbed up by the one person he least expected to see at that moment. S'haar took a long swig from the mug before slamming it down on the table and looking down at Lon'thul. "You tell a good story, but for the record, there weren't 'dozens', only about twenty, and unless I miscounted, only about six were dealt with by 'spear, sword, claw, or teeth'. The rest was his doing." S'haar jerked her thumb back at Jack while she contemplated the mug again before taking another long pull.

Jack quickly found himself in the middle of his greatest fear, being the center of attention. This was slightly compounded because everyone in the crowd now staring at him stood one to two feet taller than himself, giving Jack the impression he was drowning in a sea of eyes. The small portion of his brain still capable of wit directed a mental '*et tu Brute?*' toward S'haar. The rest of his mind was frantically choosing between fight or flight before settling on the lesser mentioned third option, freeze. After all, Jack was utterly dependent upon S'haar if he wanted to communicate with any villagers, and she didn't seem interested in leaving just yet.

Meanwhile, everyone in the crowd was looking between Jack and S'haar with varying degrees of incredulity. Lon'thul voiced the thought on everyone's minds. "I don't mean to offend you or Jack, but… *How?* I mean, just look at him! Most of the children in the village would be a decent match for Jack!"

S'haar sighed as she finished the mug and signaled the innkeeper, Sur'ruin, for a refill and some food before continuing. "What you are forgetting is that Jack is here as the representative of the dragon, and the dragon doesn't send her chosen representative out to us without giving him the means to protect himself."

Jack was decidedly uncomfortable with the direction the conversation was going but couldn't bring himself to so much as open his mouth to protest. He just had to hope that S'haar knew what she was doing.

Nodding her thanks to the innkeeper as her mug was topped off, S'haar took another drink before continuing. "How do you think I travel from their mountain home to the village safely when it's this cold out? How do you think Jack can get so much quality metal so quickly? How do you think they were able to forge this blade for me?" S'haar punctuated her last question by drawing her sword and placing it on the table in front of her.

All eyes were focused on the impossibly sharp blade as S'haar let the moment of silence drag on long enough to emphasize her next statement. "It is easy to look at his small stature and peaceful demeanor and underestimate Jack. I did when we first met. The hill raiders did too, and look what happened to them. How long will the rest of you underestimate him before you realize he has more to offer than just some metal ore?"

Food was finally brought out, and S'haar made it apparent she was done talking to the crowd. As the gathered crowd dispersed, Jack eventually joined the other two at the table. With a glare directed at S'haar, he finally spoke up. "What was that all about? You know I'm not interested in bragging about that fight. If anything, I'm trying to maintain a low profile."

S'haar grabbed a plateful of food and placed it in front of Jack before gathering a plate for herself while she responded. "Well, if crashing into the mountain and later showing up to the village with a small fortune in metal didn't already make maintaining a low profile impossible, this lout telling the whole village about our fight with the raiders destroyed any chance you had of that."

Lon'thul reached for some of the food before S'haar slapped his hand away without looking as she continued. "Besides, if you are going to get this outpost of yours up and running in the middle of winter, it's a good idea to have a bit of a reputation as someone who can do the impossible. I saw an opportunity to help, so I took it. You're welcome."

Jack chewed on that thought while his mouth chewed on his food. The meat resembled a beef roast but had a more tangy flavor, as though it had been marinated with a sour juice before being roasted. It was an odd flavor, but the more Jack ate, the better he liked it.

Finally, Jack turned to S'haar. "While it's not the way I would have gone about it, you have a point. Thank you."

S'haar merely nodded, her eyes closed as she enjoyed her own plate. Jack was feeling a little sorry for Lon'thul, who could only understand half the conversation while also giving the food a look people usually reserved for the crush they were too afraid to talk to. "Why don't you let the kid fix himself a plate and ask him about the metal and kovaack?"

Lon'thul's eyes lit up once he received permission to dig in. His speech was only slightly slurred by saliva while he cut himself a thick slice of the haunch. "The metal has been purified and loaded back into your cart. It's waiting for you to retrieve it. Even after Mar'kon and I took our cut, you have more metal that I'd know what to do with!"

Lon'thul took a large bite out of his serving, his face an expression of pure bliss. After swallowing, he continued. "The Kovaack had sat a little too long without being properly cleaned, so about half the meat was unsalvageable, the rest I traded to the inn on your behalf. You can negotiate the trade's details if you wish, but I got you each about twenty meals if not. The hide and bones are set aside for you to do with as you wish. Now, what's this I heard about an outpost?"

As Jack and S'haar explained, the hunter started to grin."

~

Jack and S'haar soon found themselves at the woodworker's hall, giving Lady Fea'en the same explanation they'd given Lon'thul not long ago. "So to get metal workers and smelters up and running by the mountain, the first step is to get housing set up. To that end, we'd like to hire out however many workers you have to spare to get the outpost started."

The experienced woodworker was rubbing her jaw in thought. "Well, the kind of project you're talking about isn't really possible in the winter, and we always have more work than we can handle in the early spring. That means we couldn't even get started on it until summer…"

Jack grinned. He'd seen this problem coming and already taken it into account. S'haar unfolded the coat she'd been carrying while she continued to translate what Jack said. "Normally, you'd be right, but in addition to the compensation we'd typically offer you for a job like this, each worker will receive a coat like this they can keep for themselves once the job is done."

Fea'en inspected the coat flipping it inside and out and looking closely at the stitching. "This IS a well-made coat, better than any I've ever seen, but it doesn't really matter how generous the compensation is or how good the coat is. We simply can't work outside when it's this cold out."

Jack held out a warming pouch for Fea'en to take. "With these, you can. They are designed to fit in the pockets on the inside of the coats."

Fea'en took the pouch from Jack, her surprise immediately evident on her face. "It's warm, like a heated stone, but it's so light!"

Jack's grin grew as he spoke. "Yup, and it'll radiate heat at a steady rate like that for up to eight hours once 'activated'. After the heat has been drained, the dragon can recharge them so they can be used again. Any workers will also be given tents and blankets designed to utilize these same pouches until an adequate shelter has been built. We'll trade out the pouches roughly three times a day so everyone can stay warm while they work."

For the first time since Jack had met her, Fea'en cracked a smile of her own. She slipped the pouch into one of the pockets and put the coat on. The coats were fastened with a bone knob designed to fit through a leather loop. "I've got a bunch of apprentices just doing busy work, since demand is so low in the winter."

Testing out the range of movement in the coat, Fea'en moved about in that oddly graceful manner of hers. "Ok, it won't be cheap, but I've got a half dozen apprentices I can spare from our winter work, and to make sure the work is done properly, I'll come myself and oversee the construction."

Not that Jack was about to complain, but his surprise at Fea'en's offer was clearly evident on his face. Fea'en gave Jack a grin that reminded him she was every bit as much a predator as S'haar. "What, you don't think I'm going to pass on the opportunity to get myself a coat like this, do you?"

~

As they left the woodworking hall, Jack was pleased with how well things had gone so far. Admittedly, Fea'en had negotiated a steeper price than Jack had been hoping to pay. It had quickly become evident that even with all the metal he now had at his disposal, he only had enough for a down-payment for the job at hand, but he could always get more where that came from. After all, that was kind of the whole point of this endeavor.

Jack was just headed down to the village's metalworking section when an argu'n wearing unmistakably fine robes and flanked by his two imposing guards approached. "Ah, Jack, just the man I wanted to see!"

A'ngels turned and nodded to S'haar. "And S'haar, I'm glad to see the news of your injury must have been somewhat exaggerated."

S'haar chose not to respond personally, but Jack gave the noble a small deferential bow before addressing him, with S'haar translating for him. "Lord A'ngles, how can I help you?"

The noble seemed somewhat pleased at Jack's attempt at the formality and inclined his head in return. "I've heard the news that you're building an outpost to secure higher metal production and refinement. I was somewhat concerned about all of the village's craftspeople you're going to be recruiting. I was hoping to speak to you about that before it became an issue for either of us."

Jack was only slightly surprised that A'ngels had already heard of his plan. He'd known it would be an issue eventually. He hadn't planned on having to deal with it until his next visit to the town, but he supposed that it was better to deal with it now rather than having it hang over his head.

Stepping forward, Jack started to frame his argument for the noble. "Well, it's not so much that I'm taking workers from you, as we're seeking to increase the efficiency of the gathering and smelting process and thus the profitability to yourself as well as us."

Lord A'ngels raised an eye ridge, which Jack took as an invitation to continue. "Right now, we only spend a few days actually mining up the ore I bring to town. Most of our time is spent getting food, maintaining equipment, and traveling to and from the village, among other things. By setting up an outpost with workers there to smelt the metal, maintain the equipment, gather food, etcetera, I'll be able to focus more time on collecting the metal itself."

The noble was following along but clearly wasn't invested yet. It was time for Jack to bait the hook. "Now, of course, I'll be compensating everyone for their work, but I'm also going to need protection come spring. To that end, I'd like this village to become the patron of my outpost. You'll supply the guards, both onsite and for the deliveries, and in return, I'll offer you one-fourth of all the refined metal as payment for their services. Add in all the metal the workers will be paid in, and your village will have so much metal, you'll become the primary supplier of it for the region."

There it was. Jack hoped that offering a direct payment to the village, and thus to A'ngels, would grab his attention. "Hmm, you make a good argument, but after bloodying the hill raiders the way you did, they'll be out for revenge. The number of guards I'll have to supply would significantly reduce the village's protection, so I'll have to hire guards from surrounding villages. We can probably make that happen, for half the refined ore you produce."

Jack seemed to stop and think for a moment, but he'd been expecting that counter and already had his own counter offer ready. "I can do half the iron and other common metals, but only a quarter of the more rare metals such as silver and gold. I have another project I'll need those for, which will help increase our efficiency. Also, any metal shipments will be considered to be paid in full once they leave the outpost. You'll be responsible for their safe arrival at the village."

A'ngels tilted his head to the side. "I'm curious what you'd need soft metals for that would increase the efficiency of gathering metal, but I suppose there is a lot about your methods I don't yet understand. I think these terms are acceptable for now. After a summer of production, we'll reexamine the terms, agreed?"

Jack knew A'ngels was planning to increase his cut once Jack became dependent on his labor supply and guards, but he was hoping to be far enough along with his repairs that it would no longer matter. Besides, he knew he was unlikely to get better terms from any village further away than this one. "Agreed."

The village lord looked thoughtful for a moment. "I'll also need to send some security with the workers you'll be taking. Something to keep an eye on the village's…inventment. I believe you are on good terms with the hunter, Lon'thul, correct? So he'll do for now."

Jack didn't particularly like being told he would take on extra people without his input, but the Lord had chosen well. If he refused Lon'thul, Lord A'ngels could very well send someone that would be a worse fit for the outpost, like his son. Also, the hunter could provide an additional benefit to the outpost by using his finely honed skills to keep the outpost's food supplies filled and ready.

It wasn't ideal, and Lord A'ngels was obviously flexing some power over the outpost with this move, but it could have been a lot worse. Jack only hesitated a moment longer before replying again. "Agreed."

Lord A'ngels nodded. "Good, I'm glad we were able to come to a consensus! I'll let you be on your way. I'm sure you've got plenty more work to do to get our outpost ready for production."

Jack wasn't particularly happy about the noble's use of the word 'our', but decided this was not the time or place to start an argument over it. With a bow of his head, he and S'haar were on their way.

~

Jack and S'haar stood before Mar'kon, explaining their plan for the fourth time that day. "So while we'll need several workers down the road, we'll just need one smith to do repairs and maintenance on the woodworker's tools to begin with. Got anyone you can spare who might be able and willing?"

Mar'kon was rubbing his hands on his signature greasy rag as he thought. Jack desperately wanted to take the rag and give it a good wash but suspected it was more oil than cloth at this point. It just might disintegrate if any soap was added to the mix.

Finally, Mar'kon seemed to make up his mind. Turning around, he glared at each of the workers for a moment before speaking. "Right, I know you lot were focused on listening rather than working. You heard the offer. Any of you want to risk life and limb to get in on this hair-brained scheme from the get-go?"

Pretty much every worker present stepped forward and waited. Mar'kon glared at the lot of them a moment longer before responding. "That's what I thought. Yer all as mad as I was at yer age."

Mar'kon seemed to fix his glare on a specific worker. "Tel'ron, yer work on knives and shears had been decent enough this last year. Think yer up to the job, kid?"

The worker approached the group with a big grin plastered on his face. Jack didn't think he looked too young. He was probably a bit older than Lon'thul. Then again, Mar'kon was just about the eldest argu'n Jack had seen so far, so he supposed everyone looked like a 'kid' in Mar'kon's eyes.

Tel'ron walked right up to Jack and offered his hand. Jack was a bit surprised at how many people knew about handshakes already and wondered what other mannerisms he might have accidentally introduced to their society. As he shook Jack's hand, the argu'n spoke. "You saved me from a long, dull winter. Don't worry, I'm not as lazy as my father. I'll work hard to get the job done."

Jack looked a little quizzically at smith. "Do I know your father?"

Tel'ron grinned. "Well, you should know him by now. You pass him every time you come into the village. He used to be more active in the guard, but he just works the front gate these days. His name is Ger'ron."

Jack's eyes widened a little at this. Looking closer, he could see the family resemblance, though it probably wasn't as evident to him as it would be to another argu'n. "Well, if you're half as good-natured as your father, you'll be a welcome addition. We'll be meeting at the inn shortly after dawn. Meet us there, and I'll cover the cost of breakfast and have your coat ready. Do you have your own tools, or will I need to supply those?"

Tel'ron shook his head. "Nah, I got my own set. I'll see ya there, bright and early!"

The smith then walked up to S'haar and offered his hand to her as well. "It'll be exciting working with my dad's star pupil. He always told me if I had half your talent, I'd be set for life. I don't know if he ever told you, but the reason he's on permanent gate duty is that he got in a big fight with the captain when you got kicked out. Don't worry, though. He doesn't regret a thing. He said it was about time he stood up to that 'pompous windbag'."

S'haar seemed genuinely pleased to hear about her old mentor. "So you're the rebellious son who became a smith rather than a guard. You know, he wanted me to go knock some sense into your head when you chose this profession."

Tel'ron shook his head. "Well, I'm glad you didn't. From what I hear, I'd have been lucky to survive the encounter."

Stepping back, he nodded to Jack again. "Well, I'd better get all my tools gathered and ready to go. I'll see you both in the morning!"

As the three of them watched the smith run off, Mar'kon added his own final thought. "He's a good kid. You take care of him, and he'll take care of you."

Turning back to his charges, Mar'kon started laying into the closest with his rag. "You all have stood around staring long enough! Back to work with ya!"

Chapter 21

As Jack and S'haar stumbled into the inn, Jack couldn't help but once again be pleased with how everything was going. True, there are still a few complications on the horizon, but, on the whole, he's accomplished all of his primary objectives. Though admittedly, they had come at a higher cost than he'd been hoping to pay.

The inn was a familiar combination of sounds and smells. The air had finally grown cold enough that the villagers were forced to spend most of their time indoors. At the same time, the villagers hadn't settled in yet and still had energy to burn. As a result, most of the males were shouting or even wrestling with each other. The latter were usually younger males trying to prove their superiority while the village's young ladies looked on and whispered to each other in varying degrees of amusement.

The smells came from various assortments of meats and drinks that were being devoured or sloshed onto the floor respectively. Through all of the chaos flittered the ever-energetic innkeeper, Sur'ruin. Dodging between combatants and drunks alike, she was quick with a laugh or a smile for whoever caught her fancy at the moment. This particular moment belonged to Jack and S'haar.

Seeing her new guests looking around for a place to sit, Sur'ruin marched right up with a mug for each of them, her smile speaking louder than the din of the room. "If it isn't my favorite human, Jack! Are you looking for food, bed, or both?"

S'haar, remembering Angela's directives regarding argu'n alcohol, accepted both mugs on their behalf. "We'll be needing both, and correct me if I'm wrong, but isn't Jack the *only* human you know?"

The innkeeper flashed Jack one of those smiles unique to the argu'n that somehow seemed to double the amount of teeth in their mouths. "He can be the only human I know *and* be my favorite at the same time!"

She winked at Jack before turning back to S'haar. "Follow me. I've got a table away from the worst of the ruckus. The meal is covered by the food you supplied, the room will cost you a story, or you could clean some dishes, whichever you prefer."

Jack tilted his head for a moment, thinking of a story good enough to tell that might be worth the room's price. As he sat down at the table, Jack finally made up his mind. "Alright, I think I have a story you might enjoy. When you are ready, come on back, and I'll tell you the ancient human tale of Hades and Persephone."

Sur'ruin looked at Jack with a face torn by indecision. "I was thinking of a story about yourself, but I suppose I could give a human story a try, just this once... All right, it's a deal, but if it's not a good enough story, I'm expecting some kind of follow-up!"

~

S'haar could tell Sur'ruin was hooked by Jack's tale. S'haar also couldn't help but be annoyed at the looks the innkeeper was directing toward Jack, despite the innkeeper's inability to understand him without S'haar's translations. "But because she ate the four pomegranate seeds, Persephone was doomed to have to return and spend four months of every year with Hades until the end of time. That is why summer must come to an end, and fall fades into winter. However, when Persephone returns to the world of the living, she brings the promise of spring along with her."

As the night passed, the room had emptied as the villagers returned to their homes. Now the inn was strangely quiet, with the few patrons remaining getting lost in their drinks or passing out by the fire.

Sur'ruin sat up and blinked a few times before speaking. "Well, I don't know about Persephone being doomed, Hades seems like a decent enough guy. Setting aside the whole 'god' thing, there are worse fates in life than a devoted male who will risk the wrath of a goddess for you!"

Jack shrugged. "Well, among the Greek gods, Hades was about as close to decent as they came. However, there is the whole issue of that kidnapping thing. These days that's one of the worst crimes a person can commit."

Sur'ruin tilted her head in confusion. "Maybe where you come from it is, but around here, it's common enough. Why I've had two attempted kidnappings myself!"

Jack turned to S'haar with a look of confusion. S'haar merely shrugged. "Don't look at me. No one's ever tried to kidnap me. Though I did get sacrificed to a dragon once."

Given the subject of kidnappings, Jack couldn't help but think of Em'brel, and his face visibly darkened. "Well, I'm not ok with it. A man has to be pretty pathetic to try and force himself on a woman who doesn't return his affections."

The innkeeper took a look around the room and sighed. "Regardless, I suppose that story was good enough for a night. With only a few tweaks, I'll be able to entertain a good-sized crowd with it from time to time. Now, I've got some cleaning to do before I'm done for the night, so why don't you two head upstairs and get some rest. You've got a long journey ahead of you in the morning!"

Then Sur'ruin was gone, leaving S'haar to wonder why it bothered her so much when the innkeeper smiled at Jack so persistently throughout the night.

~

Jack realized on an intellectual level that he'd shared a bed with S'haar once before. However, he had also been drugged out of his mind at the time. He couldn't really remember anything except a rather... uncomfortable morning. This time Jack was sane and sober, and his mind was racing in circles.

If Jack didn't know that S'haar was cold-blooded, he'd swear he could feel the heat radiating from her side of the bed. Was it just because he was in bed with a woman, or was it S'haar herself that invoked this reaction?

Jack had certainly enjoyed the flirtatious attentions of Sur'ruin, but ultimately she'd been too...intimidating to invoke any feelings other than a small bit of an ego boost. Though she did behave in a manner that at least somewhat resembled women back home. In comparison, S'haar was that much more intimidating. She was both physically larger and more intense than the friendly innkeeper.

On the other hand, S'haar was closer to Jack than anyone other than Angela had been since... well, in a very long time. She was always at his side, and when push came to shove, neither of them hesitated to place their lives into the other's hands. The two of them had come to trust each other implicitly, which was surprising given how little time had passed since their first meeting. Admittedly, it had been a rather intense month, or had it been a month and a half?

With a mostly subvocal grumble, Jack turned onto his side. These thoughts were far too confusing for…whatever hour it was. He just needed to close his eyes and get to sleep. He'd need his energy for the long walk home. Any minute now, he'd finally get that feeling of comfort that always came just before sleep. Aaaany minute…

With a less subvocal grunt, Jack sat up in bed and rubbed his face. He was no stranger to insomnia and knew that just lying there wasn't going to change anything any time soon. The best thing he could do was to distract himself for a bit. Only after his mind quieted could he try to sleep again. He wasn't foolish enough to go out and wander the streets without S'haar at his side, but he figured a quick trip to the common room should be safe enough. Regardless, he strapped on his gun just to be safe.

The room was oddly peaceful. The dim glow of a few embers still emanated from the fireplace. Other than that, the dining area was deserted. Jack settled into a corner, turned his headlamp on and set it to dim, pulled out a well-worn book he often traveled with, and started to read.

He'd read this particular book so often that he could almost recite it from beginning to end, but something was comforting about the old, familiar words. He could practically hear his father reading it aloud from what felt like several lifetimes ago.

"In a hole in the ground there lived a hobbit. Not a nasty, dirty, wet hole, filled with the ends of worms and an oozy smell, nor yet a dry, bare, sandy hole with nothing in it to sit down on or to eat: it was a hobbit-hole, and that means comfort."

Jack let his mind split in two. One half was wandering down familiar paths, guided by a storyteller who'd lived and died many generations before Jack. The other half was lost in his childhood, sitting by a warm and cheery fire on a cold winter's night, enjoying a mug of hot chocolate while wrapped in a thick quilt. He could almost smell the fire and hear the gentle winds as it snowed just outside the window.

Soon Jack found he couldn't read anymore because the words on the page started to blur. A light tickling sensation alerted him to the fact that tears had started falling at some point, though if anyone had asked him, Jack couldn't say when. A little ashamed of himself, Jack wiped his face with the back of his hand.

Standing, Jack turned to head back upstairs. That was when the light briefly illuminated the feet of some argu'n who'd obviously been standing and watching him for quite some time. She held a sword loosely in her hand.

~

S'haar woke with a start. Something was off, but she was having a hard time focusing on what it was because her brain was still sluggish with sleep and cold. That's when it hit her. The heat source wasn't beside her the way it should be. With a flick of her tongue, she could taste Jack's recent presence. There was no scent of fear in the air, but something was off. There was an unfamiliar...musk to his scent.

Slipping out of bed, S'haar struggled to finish waking herself. She didn't know why Jack had left in the middle of the night, but she'd be damned if she'd let him wander the city without a bodyguard. It was a sense of duty that caused S'haar to start worrying as she thought of everything that could go wrong. What else could it be? She wouldn't panic at the mere thought of Jack being in danger. That would be absurd. Just to be safe, S'haar grabbed her sword before leaving.

S'haar didn't have to go far to find her charge. Jack was sitting in the common room, reading one of his books. Something in his expression made S'haar hesitate to disturb him as he read. His smile radiated the bittersweet combination of happy memories and deep sadness.

She thought about going back to their room but found that her feet refused to move. Something was different about Jack's expression. He was so open...and vulnerable. Not that Jack was the type to hide behind false bravado like many males seemed to, but there still existed a wall between Jack and the rest of the world. At this moment, his walls were down, and he was just...Jack.

Sometimes S'haar forgot just how small and frail Jack really was. At that moment, sitting in the corner in a chair two sizes too big for him,

Jack looked like he needed to be protected. So S'haar stood vigil, watching over *her* Jack, struggling to understand the unfamiliar feelings of protectiveness she felt toward this strange little man.

S'haar was lost in thought when Jack got up to head upstairs. When his light illuminated her feet, S'haar saw the look of panic that took over his face. Of greater concern was the fact that his hand flew to his holster. She knew Jack was unlikely to shoot before getting a better look at his target. On the other hand, she had seen first hand what that gun was capable of. S'haar wasn't going to give him the chance to make the kind of mistake they'd both regret.

S'haar dropped her sword and launched herself forward, quickly grabbing Jack's hand, preventing him from drawing his gun. Her other hand clamped over his mouth to prevent him from shouting out and waking everyone in the inn up. "It's me, you idiot! Calm down! You're safe!"

Jack's face flashed between panic, confusion, and relief, before eventually settling on embarrassment. That was when the creak of a hinge behind S'haar let her know the two of them were no longer entirely alone. Turning to assess the possible threat, S'haar forgot to release Jack. Leaving them in quite the interesting entanglement as Sur'ruin poked her head out of her door while holding a candle.

Sur'ruin gave the two a knowing look as her face spread into quite the mischievous grin. "I heard a noise, but now I see it's just my two favorite love birds! Usually, our guests prefer to play these kinds of games in the privacy of their own rooms…or is this is your way of inviting anyone interested to join in the fun?"

At the same moment, both Jack and S'haar realized what Sur'ruin was implying. Jack's eyebrows shot up in surprise while S'haar's eye ridges narrowed into an intimidating glare. Since Jack's mouth was still covered, S'haar responded on both their behalfs. "No, I think we'd both prefer to keep this moment between the two of us. Thank you for your concern, but we'll be fine."

Sur'ruin shrugged in a way that seemed to say 'your loss', then retreated back into her room and closed the door.

S'haar gave Jack a look usually reserved for intimidating veteran warriors. After a moment, she spoke. "When I remove my hand from your mouth, I don't want to hear one word about what just happened. Your life will be happier and healthier if you heed my warning. Do you understand?"

Jack nodded emphatically, his eyes wide. As S'haar slowly removed her hands from his mouth, he took a moment to rub his wrist before looking up with a grin that told S'haar he was about to regret his next words. "Sooo... she seems nice!"

Without hesitation, S'haar reached out and grabbed the nearest partially full mug and upended the contents over Jack's head.. It troubled S'haar that his grin told her that he didn't regret it nearly as much as she would have thought.

Chapter 22

For once, the journey home was thankfully uneventful. This time they were able to maintain a quicker pace, since there were multiple argu'n taking turns pulling the cart. The first leg of the journey was filled with excited talk among the younger woodworkers and the smith as they marveled at their new heated coats, but eventually, everyone settled into a comfortable silence, each lost in their own thoughts. When they stopped for lunch, they were much closer to the mountain than Jack and S'haar had been the first time they had traveled this route.

While eating, Lon'thul saddled up next to Jack and S'haar. He looked like something was on his mind, and Jack was content to eat while the young man gathered his thoughts. After a few moments of Jack chewing in what was quickly becoming an awkward silence, Lon'thul finally found the courage to speak up.

"The last time I…'visited' your home, I unintentionally said some upsetting things to the young female now in your charge. I still feel kinda lousy about that…how's she doing now?"

Jack took another bite, letting the silence start to grow uncomfortable again before responding. S'haar translated from the other side of Jack in between her own bites of food. "Well, you might not have meant it, but some of what you said really hit her hard, doubly so after everything she'd just gone through."

Jack let his expression grow somber again before continuing, "Em'brel lost everyone she cared about and had her entire life ripped away from her, not to mention the abuse she suffered at the raiders' hands before we got there. That kind of thing can take many years to come to terms with. Even if she succeeds, she'll still bear deep scars on her soul for the rest of her life."

Jack looked at a distant horizon within himself and couldn't help but compare his own history to Em'brel's current state. "However, she's moving forward as best she can. When she realized she didn't have a place in this world anymore, she decided to make one for herself. She's setting goals and making great strides toward them. In many ways, Em'brel is stronger than I was at her age, and I'm not talking about physical muscles."

Jack finished his food before standing up and dusting off his pants as he finished his thoughts. "But to answer your question, at the moment, her spirit still bears many raw and bleeding wounds. So I'm only going to tell you this once."

Lon'thul found it surprising such a small, frail man could suddenly look so intimidating. "Whatever your motivations in coming to speak with me now, whatever your intentions regarding her in the future, if you treat Em'brel in anything but the most honorable and gentlest of ways, you will find your welcome to our outpost suddenly and violently revoked!"

Jack and S'haar both got up and walked off, letting Lon'thul sit, lost in thought for a few minutes.

~

After arriving at the mountain, the workers remained outside the cave while Jack and S'haar went in to get the tents and other supplies. They'd almost made it to the door when Em'brel launched herself out of it and at Jack. This time she didn't grip him quite so tightly as to cause significant bruising, which was a pleasant surprise, but the two still ended up in a tangle on the ground.

Jack laughed as he ruffled Em'brels' 'hair.' "What's all this then? Has Angela been so rough with you that you felt the need to run away?"

Em'brel hid her face against Jack while still refusing to let go of him. Her voice was quiet and more than a little embarrassed. "I…I was afraid something would happen to you while you were gone… The last time…"

Jack climbed back to his feet, then helped Em'brel to hers with a grunt of effort before responding, "Last time, it was much warmer out. Cold as it is now, this is probably about the safest time of year for me to be out and about. Now, S'haar and I need to get the tents out to the workers we brought back with us. Why don't you tell me what you've been studying while we walk?"

Em'brel's eyes lit up as she followed along, her tone of voice further revealing her eagerness to describe it all. "Well, there's all the math stuff, but that's boring. What was way more fun was what Angela called 'simple machines', things like levers and pulleys!"

This caught S'haar's interest. "Angela is teaching you the secrets behind human machines?"

Em'brel looked even more excited to explain the concept to someone else who could learn along with her. "Nothing as complex as, well, *anything* they have in the ship, but even their simple machines are amazing. By placing a long stick over a 'fulcrum', you can easily lift something too heavy to lift through usual means." Em'brel's arms moved about as she tried to explain the movement of the stick and fulcrum. "By moving the fulcrum closer to the heavy object, you increase the distance that the lever has to move relative to the distance the object moves, and the weight is decreased by a corresponding amount. The greater the difference, the lighter the object becomes!"

S'haar looked more than a little confused. "You mean you can change the weight of an object just by putting it on a stick, and you're telling me this isn't human magic?" Jack could swear S'haar used the term 'magic' just because she knew it irked him.

Em'brel shook her head before she beamed at S'haar and continued to explain. "Not at all. In fact, many of our own people use levers from time to time, but now I understand why they work and how to better utilize them! On the other hand, the pulley is new to me, but it does something similar using rope and wheels!"

The two continued talking as they walked into the ship. Jack let them go on while Angela floated up to give her own greeting. "Welcome back, and with no broken bones this time! Hopefully, it's the start of a new trend!"

Jack chuckled. "Yes, yes. It's very funny how I keep getting into trouble. It's good to see you too."

Anglea turned to S'haar. "And he was well behaved this time? There were no other…incidents?"

S'haar stuttered incoherently while Jack turned a little red at the memories of his restless thoughts and the following incident. "Well, not really…no."

Angela exploded with energy, shooting up into the air and throwing her arms and legs out wide, while words virtually burst out of her. "Ohmygod,somethingDIDhappen! Tellmeeverything! NowaitIwanttohearitfromher! Girls night! We're going to tell stories about boys! Well, *A* boy! Oh, what embarrassing story should I share? What about the first time you had a bubble bath as a toddler? Or maybe that time you scared yourself with a mirror in a dark room? There are too many to choose from! This is going to be great! I've got pictures and everything!"

Jack was suddenly filled with feelings of fear and trepidation. There was no way this was going to end well for him.

~

Jack finally managed to get the others back on track bringing out the materials for the tents to the workers. S'haar carried out three tents by herself, Em'brel hefted two, and Jack managed to slog out the last one on his own, cursing the unfairness of argu'n physiology the whole way.

Once outside, Jack started showing their new guests how to set up the tents. They were a simple design, based on canopy tents back home. Four posts were placed, one at each corner of a square, and one long post was set up in the center. The corner posts attached to each other via beams running between the posts, then they were anchored to the ground by a rope attached to the tops of those posts. A quilted wall was put up around the outside, and the roof was treated to help any moisture roll off easily, then raised with the long post. The floors were thick, made of linen-like cloth, with each argu'n being given a hide to use as padding under large sleeping bags that had been designed with pockets for more heating packs.

By Jack's standards, this was definitely roughing it, but many of the argu'n noticed these 'small tents' he had supplied weren't much worse than the living quarters they were used to in the village. True, they were light on furnishings and a little smaller than even a bachelor's housing, but it was still far better than they'd feared.

While everyone set up their tents, Jack recruited S'haar to help him set up a large fire pit for gathering around and cooking. As the uninvited guest, Lon'thul found he had the dubious honor of digging out the latrines away from the camp. Jack made sure he dug deep holes, so they could be filled in later.

At first, Emb'rel had shadowed S'haar, doing her best to hide behind the larger female. However, once the fire pit was ready, she had her own job, and it was one she took pride in. She'd brought out several of the most enormous pots Jack owned and had set them up on an improvised metal grate Angela had procured from some unused device she'd had sitting around in storage. The pots' contents were all in varying states of simmering as the stew Em'brel cooked started to come together. A couple of the workers brought over several of the logs Jack and S'haar had stored before to use as seating, and before long, the whole group was enjoying the fruits of Em'brel's labor.

At some point, one of the woodworkers brought out a stringed instrument similar to a lute, but whose sound was a bit sharper and harsher than most earth music. After a while, Fea'en joined in, lending her gravely voice to the music. As best as Jack could tell, the song told the story of some grand hunt. While the details were kind of fuzzy, Jack suspected most argu'n must be already familiar with the tale, as this song seemed to be more about the beat of the music than the story itself. The sound was very different from human music, almost bestial in nature, but it had a beat you could move to. Jack found himself tapping his foot in time to the rythym.

This went on for several songs, all of whose subjects seemed to center around fighting, hunting, and more fighting. All of the music had aggressive energy, and Jack couldn't help but feel his blood pump a little faster as he listened.

He noticed S'haar and Em'brel seemed to be debating something in private, just off to the side of the gathering, and once the music stopped between songs, S'haar gave Em'brel a shove toward the center before telling the musician, "Play something slower."

When the music began this time, it had a slower pace and a quiet tone. Em'brel's voice started with a slight waver to it, but when she looked at Jack, he gave her a big grin and a nod of his head. Em'brel seemed to take heart and closed her eyes to continue her song. Her voice grew more confident, though it was much more gentle than Fae'en's voice had been.

This song seemed to tell the journey of a tribe wandering through the wilderness. As they traveled, they lost men and women to beasts, hunger, and cold. The people's hope slowly faded until the last few survivors gave up and laid down for the last time. The stringed instrument had stopped playing at some point, but no one noticed as everyone sat entranced by the pure sound of the young argu'n's voice.

Once the song ended, everyone sat in quiet for a moment, not sure what to do. S'haar started clapping as she'd seen humans do in some of the movies Jack had shown her, then Jack quickly joined in, and it didn't take long for the rest of the workers present to catch on. Em'brel ducked out of the center of attention with a shy smile and resumed her seat next to S'haar, once more trying to hide in the larger female's shadow. A few more songs were played after that, mostly to lighten the mood a little, but it was clear that everyone was nearing their limit for the evening. Eventually, everyone split off to their respective tents, with Jack, S'haar, and Em'brel returning to their own home, intent on calling it a night.

~

Jack was ready to pass out. Between not getting enough sleep the night before, the long journey home, setting up camp, and the campfire gathering, he was surprised he had enough energy to shower and brush his teeth before collapsing into bed. A familiar blue glow behind him told Jack who had appeared even before he looked in the mirror and saw Angela just off to the side. Jack spit out a mouth full of toothpaste before rinsing and addressing the not-quite patient presence behind him. "You always seem to catch me right before bed. What's up this time? Please don't tell me there's another emergency that requires me to dramatically readjust our plans again!"

Angela laughed, her face filled with a genuine smile Jack had seen more and more of recently. "No sir, quite the opposite. For once, everything seems to be going as planned."

Jack looked at her through the mirror with mock horror on his face. The effect was somewhat diminished as he got ready to floss his teeth. "You shouldn't say things like that! If I was slightly more superstitious, I'd say you just doomed us all."

Angela waved away his concerns. "Oh please, this world seems to do that job well enough without any irony gods having to lift a finger. At this rate, the only surprising thing would be if everything continued to go as planned. We both know neither of us is lucky enough for that to happen."

Jack started using his mouthwash as Angela continued. "I've just not had a chance to talk with you recently unless it was to address some major issue, so I thought I'd stop by and ask how're you doing?"

Jack gave the question some thought before spitting out the mouth rinse and taking a drink from some water he had sitting to the side. Turning to face Angela, Jack leaned back against the sink as he spoke. "You know, given everything that's happened, I would think I'd be more stressed than ever, but more and more, I feel like I'm doing something worth doing. Not just repairing the ship, despite how important that is, but everything else." He waved his hand in the general direction of the cave as he took a breath.

Jack continued as he walked into his room and sat down to remove his slippers before crawling under his blankets. "In a weird way, the large, scary cat-lizard residents of this planet feel more like people to me than most humans did back in earthspace. Weirdly, it almost feels like we've…ah…"

Jack found he couldn't bring himself to finish the thought. It was almost as if he was afraid that vocalizing his thoughts would make him realize this was all a dream, one he didn't want to wake up from.

Angela felt no such compunctions about finishing the sentence. "It almost feels like we've come home."

Jack couldn't help but think of the two other presences just a room away as he closed his eyes and settled into his pillow. "Yeah…home. It feels…nice."

Angela didn't bother to respond, knowing she would have been speaking to herself anyway. Jack was already asleep. Her avatar slowly faded from view, but all her sensors stayed active, keeping a close eye on the three most important people in her world.

Chapter 23

Tel'ron turned to S'haar, his face expressing his deep concern. "I don't know much about humans, but I can't believe that kind of laughter is normal…"

Jack continued to cackle gleefully as he started up the chainsaw. The roar of the engine caused Tel'ron to jump back in surprise. He was starting to regret his earlier decision to help out Jack and S'haar. Dragon's magic was clearly something that shouldn't be meddled with.

Their request hadn't seemed so frightening when they'd asked for help. Jack and S'haar needed a hand hauling freshly cut trees over to where the woodworkers could ply their trade, namely splitting and shaping logs into boards and planks. With all the tools sharpened and ready, there wasn't much for the smith to do at the moment, so Tel'ron had volunteered his services.

He'd assumed S'haar would cut the trees down, Jack would trim off the branches, and he'd haul the wood. He hadn't known what to think when S'haar had laughed a little nervously at his assumption.

In Jack's hands, the 'chainsaw' roared as if it was some wild beast claiming its territory, drowning out almost all other sounds. The only thing he could hear over the cacophony was Jack's clearly unstable laughter. Tel'ron expected Jack to swing the monstrous device at the tree like a woodcutter's ax. Instead, he seemed to leisurely brush against the tree with the lightest of touches. Immediately, shredded wood began to fly everywhere as the tree was torn into pieces before Tel'ron's eyes.

In short order, the tree was on the ground, and Jack was trimming off the branches. As he worked, S'haar showed Tel'ron how to attach the harness they were going to use to move what was left of the tree. Jack's laughter had died down at some point in the process, but the grin on his face still spoke of a dangerous imbalance in the man's psyche.

Tel'ron dragged the tree back to be processed and was greeted by a somewhat confused Fea'en. "Already? You can't just bring back a tree you found lying on the ground. We'll need fresh wood to get good quality lumber!"

Tel'ron shook his head. Try as he might, he couldn't forget what he'd witnessed. "This tree was standing with all its branches attached not twenty minutes ago. Jack used a weird blade covered in metal teeth to chew the tree down and sever its limbs. He said it was powered by 'dragon's fire'. After witnessing it in action, I believe him."

Tel'ron started to head back after getting the log situated, only to pass S'haar, who was already pulling another log back to camp. The rest of the morning passed much the same. Jack would cut and trim a tree while either Tel'ron or S'haar caught their breath. Once cleaned, they'd drag the trunk back to camp. By lunch, Fea'en had to ask them to stop. Otherwise, the trees would sit too long without being processed. The three of them had cleared away a decent amount of land by that point, anyway.

One thing that astounded Tel'ron even more than the amount of work done was how well the chainsaw's metal teeth held up. Given how small they were and how much wood they'd been used to cut through, he expected them to be worn down to nubs, but when Jack allowed him to examine the tiny blades, they were still almost as sharp as any blade he could forge. The dragon obviously had some method of steel refinement that surpassed anything known to the argu'n.

When Tel'ron asked him about it, Jack started his explanation with a shrug. "Well, I don't know everything about it, but it's not just steel. It's an alloy. Similar to combining copper and tin to make bronze, this is mostly a high carbon steel, but a few other things like chromium and nickel have been added to turn it into an alloy. Because of the high carbon content, it's stronger than more traditional steels, and the other ingredients make the metal more resistant to rust and erosion."

Tel'ron was able to follow most of the explanation, though he didn't know what 'chromium' was. From the context, he assumed it was a kind of metal similar to steel, but this steel alloy Jack spoke of was amazing. Having seen it in action, Tel'ron was inclined to believe Jack's claims, improbable as they might seem. He was now even more eager to work with S'haar and the crazy human and wondered what secrets he might bring back to his people after his time here.

Jack and S'haar finally headed back to the ship for lunch. Everyone was eating leftovers from the night before, but Jack wanted to check in on Angela and Em'brel. They walked in on what was apparently another ongoing physics lesson.

Angela was wearing a lab coat with thick glasses and also had "grown" her hair out, just to put it into a messy bun. For the lesson she was currently teaching, she had created a holographic box in front of herself as a prop. "So, as you can see, gravitational force keeps the box in contact with the ground, and friction force from that contact keeps it from moving on its own, but if I use applied force, I can move the box like so!" Angela then seemed to push the box a short distance.

Em'brel seemed a little bored at the moment. "But why does it *matter* which 'forces' cause these things to happen? Why bother to name them? We all already know the box won't move unless someone moves it."

Angela had obviously fielded such questions before and was ready for it. "These are just basic examples, designed to give you an understanding of the nature of the various forces, but once you understand them, you can apply them. For example, take a look at one of S'haar's throwing spears compared with one of Lon'thul's spears."

An image of the two spears appeared in the air beside one another. "If you notice, S'haar's spear, often called a javelin, is much smaller and lighter, and the front is more narrow. These qualities decrease the effect of gravitational pull and wind resistance, allowing the spear to travel further and more accurately."

S'haar tilted her head to one side. "Huh, so that's how it works… and here I thought it was just because your steel was better than ours."

Angela shifted her attention to her new student. "That is undoubtedly a factor. It's part of the reason the spears are so much lighter than what you are used to but are still strong enough to withstand the impact and retain their shape. The trick is to make it light enough to throw well, but heavy enough to impart enough kinetic force upon impact to do some damage."

S'haar was scratching her head. "You lost me. I don't know what energy has to do with my spear. I just throw it, and it stabs into my target. There's no energy."

Jack could tell by the light in Angela's eye meant they were going to be here awhile since she now had *two* willing victims. Jack repressed his sigh as he set about preparing lunch.

~

After finishing lunch, Jack and Angela were discussing what the next step should be. Angela began the discussion. "Well, if the woodworkers have all the wood they can use for a few days, our next priority should be to increase our power reserves. I've already got some solar panels put together and ready to go, and the cable won't take me long to finish. The problem is where to set them up."

Jack nodded, gulping down a mouthful of sandwich in the process. "Yeah, our cave entrance is facing the east more or less, but given our position in the northern hemisphere, we'd ideally like them to be on the southern face of the mountain. That way, you can adjust the panels to face the sun for the entire day, but that would be a long way to run some cable."

Angela seemed a little put out that Jack more or less bypassed her next excuse for more teaching but let it slide. This time. "Yes, it would be too long, which is why I want to dig a new access tunnel."

A projection of the mountain appeared in the air above the table before Angela continued her explanation. "So, we have natural tunnels already extending only a few thousand meters from the southern face here." The mountain turned translucent, and a glowing tunnel appeared on the inside. It looked more like string than the large cavernous tunnel Jack knew it to be.

Angela pointed at a few sections of rock, and they turned blue at the point she indicated. "If you dig here, here, and here, you can extend our own tunnel to have nearly direct access, without compromising the cave's structural integrity by any noticeable measure."

Jack was looking closely at the map when Em'brel voiced her own question. "What's a solar panel?"

Jack didn't have to see Angela to know her eyes were lighting up at the new question. "To understand that, you first have to know what electricity is!"

Jack leaned over and whispered to S'haar. "We might want to get back to work. This explanation is going to take a while."

S'haar nodded her head emphatically, and the two left Em'brel to her fate as Angela launched into a new explanation.

Lon'thul was out stalking his prey but wasn't having much luck today. Usually, he could sneak right up on a churlish and pounce on it before it was able to so much as sense his presence. He'd been able to do it for years now, but for some reason, today, the churlish kept sensing him and jumping away before he could launch his attack. This had happened so many times that he'd chased it several miles around the mountain.

Of course, his mind was usually focused like a blade, whereas today, his thoughts were all over the place. He'd known for a while that S'haar didn't feel the same way about him as he'd always felt about her. In her eyes, he'd forever remain a bumbling youth. And while he didn't understand the apparent relationship that seemed to be forming between her and Jack, he didn't particularly begrudge it either. S'haar had always been unique among the village women, and it made sense that her relationships would be every bit as unique.

What confused Lon'thul was Jack himself. He seemed friendly and sympathetic one moment, then borderline hostile the next. Lon'thul would be tempted to blame it on Jack simply being fickle or petty in nature, but there were no other indications of it other than his occasional behavior toward Lon'thul. He even seemed more forgiving of B'arthon and his two thugs than he was of Lon'thul. Maybe it wasn't a question of forgiveness. You can only forgive someone who's not actively threatening you, so perhaps Jack saw Lon'thul as an active threat for some reason?

Lon'thul was finally catching up to his prey again. He was close enough to taste the churlish with a flick of the tongue. Creeping slowly closer, he readied his spear and started to brace himself for the leap that would claim his prize when he snapped a twig he hadn't realized was beneath his feet. The churlish reacted instantly, leaping away to safety and forcing Lon'thul to continue his hunt further still. In frustration, Lon'thul punched a rather large rock formation and succeeded only in hurting his hand before continuing.

It wasn't fair! Lon'thul had been nothing but friendly toward Jack. It wasn't his fault lord A'ngles had chosen him to keep an eye on the outpost. At the time, he'd just been eager to be involved in the exciting new venture. He hadn't realized this was all done without Jack's knowledge or understanding until they'd already been underway. Even then, Jack had seemed to agree with Lon'thul's take on the situation and was relatively friendly most of the time.

It seemed to come out of nowhere when Jack suddenly became hostile from time to time. It always seemed to be regarding the new argu'n living with him, Em'brel. He didn't think Jack had taken her as a mate, as the energy between Jack and the young girl was completely different from him and S'haar. He was acting less like a partner and more like a…herd leader.

Now that Lon'thul thought about it like that, things started to make sense. Argu'n were more small pack oriented. Their loyalty was first and foremost directed toward their immediate family. They could form friendships and live civilly with other families, but that came about only because of necessity. There were far too many dangers in the world for a single-family to deal with on their own. Then came the discovery that with more people came the ability to specialize, which increased everyone's prosperity.

Herd animals were different, though. The adults lived in large communities, creating safety in numbers, and calves were often looked after by every adult. What if Jack saw Em'brel as a calf in his herd and saw Lon'thul as a predator eyeing Em'brel?

As he approached the churlish this time, everything fell into place. He'd approached from downwind, his feet found purchase on the soft, silent ground, his weapons were ready, and he leapt. The churlish didn't have time to do more than grunt in surprise as his spear found its mark. The camp would eat well tonight!

Lon'thul had just started field dressing his catch when the earth shook as though the gods were pouring their wrath upon the land. He hid behind a rock but readied his spear for whatever was coming. He knew he had little hope against anything that could shake the very ground itself, but if it found him, this hunter would not cower and wait for his death. At the very least, he'd meet it spear in hand.

As moments passed, the sound grew louder, and the shaking grew worse. Whatever was causing this must be titanic! The hunter slowly moved toward what seemed to be the epicenter of the noise and vibrations, closer to the mountain. That's when Lon'thul spotted a portion of the mountain heaving and splitting. Something was digging through the very mountain itself! The only thing Lon'thul could think of that could do this was the dragon. The hunter kept his spear in hand, just in case, but peered over his rock, determined to catch a glimpse of the mysterious beast.

Bursting from the ground was a towering figure, but it wasn't quite as large as Lon'thul had expected. It was bipedal and stood roughly nine to ten feet tall. It seemed to have large metallic looking bones on the outside, and in the middle was what appeared to be a stone-skinned form that struck Lon'thul as oddly familiar. In its hands was a large round device covered in odd 'teeth' that slowly spun in a continuous circle.

The dragon slowly walked out of its new cave entrance before setting down the large device and sitting down. The stone center extracted itself from the metallic bones before dusting itself off, revealing itself to be covered in cloth rather than stone. Taking off its armored head and speaking in an oddly familiar voice, the 'dragon' said something in that odd singsong language the hunter had gotten to know over the last couple of months.

Lon'thul was so surprised he didn't even bother to stay hidden. Standing there, his spear forgotten, and his mouth gaping in astonishment, Jack could hardly miss the hunter. Turning back, Jack said something over his shoulder into the hole he'd dug.

The hunter was speechless a moment longer when another familiar voice echoed up from the cave. "Did you say Lon'thul was out there? What's he doing on this side of the mountain?" S'haar followed her voice out of the cave, dusting herself off and removing a mask of her own.

Lon'thul finally closed his mouth with a snap, then opened and closed it a few more times before his voice finally came out. "I...I was having trouble with a hunt that brought me over this way. It's back that way..." Lon'thul pointed a bit behind himself, but his eyes refused to leave Jack and the metal skeleton behind him.

Jack looked over at the churlish before returning his gaze to Lon'thul, S'haar translating as usual. "Well, I suppose that's just the luck of the draw for you. No way either of us could have anticipated bumping into each other out here. The good news is that we can get you back to camp via a much more direct route, rather than you having to carry the carcass all the way around the mountain again. All I'll ask in payment is that you don't mention or enter the cave without our permission, now that you know about it."

Lon'thul stood there a moment, barely processing what Jack had said. Finally, he pushed himself to voice the question in his mind. "Are…are you the dragon?"

Jack threw back his head and laughed. "Nope, afraid not. The dragon is a lot bigger than that machine you saw me using and a lot scarier. She made that thing for me to help her dig out the mountain a little more. You could say she's a bit cramped in there at the moment."

The idea of something bigger and scarier than a 'machine' that could effortlessly dig its way through a mountain was something Lon'thul was having trouble grasping. S'haar also seemed concerned, though about something different. "Are you sure you want to take him into the caves?"

Jack seemed to shrug, dislodging an impressive layer of dust. He gave a rather lengthy explanation to S'haar that Lon'thul couldn't follow before turning his attention back to Lon'thul. S'haar resumed translation. "So how about it? You get a quicker trip back, AND you don't run out of heat on the way back, forcing us to send out a rescue party. In return, you give me your word of honor that you won't go into the caves uninvited?"

The hunter had utterly lost track of time. He wasn't used to having limited time to go out and hunt. He'd often go out for days at a time, but that wouldn't work with the heated coats. He found himself embarrassed at his oversight, and it expressed itself in his voice as he spoke. "Ah… Yes, I'd appreciate the shortcut, and swear to never enter the caves unless invited."

Jack gave him a big, toothy grin. Lon'thul couldn't help but notice how flat his teeth were, much like a herd animal's would be. "Don't worry about it, man! New tech takes getting used to. I'm just glad we didn't have to track you down before dinner!"

Something occurred to the hunter as he tilted his head in curiosity. "Will we pass by the dragon while we're in the caves?"

Jack shook his head. "Nah, we'll be taking a more direct route. There are so many natural caves in there that we won't have to pass anywhere near the den. No worries."

As he gathered up his prey and readied to enter into the caves, Lon'thul couldn't help but appreciate that he seemed to be back on sound footing with Jack again. More evidence that his theory was correct.

Jack reached up and activated something on his head, resulting in a light shooting out in front of him into the cave. Not so long ago, this would have astounded Lon'thul, but after the last thirty minutes, that seemed to be the least surprising thing Jack was capable of. As he followed the smaller man into the darkness, he couldn't help but wonder to himself a little. What would it be like to be part of a larger group, a herd? One where everyone looked out for everyone else, rather than just tolerating each other? It sounded…nice.

Chapter 24

Jack was the last to wake up, as was now tradition. Em'brel had gotten up early to cook, which was quickly becoming her chosen role, and Jack could definitely smell bacon in the air. He was starting to wonder just how long his bacon stores would last at the current rate of consumption.

Em'brel was explaining her latest lesson to S'haar as she wrapped some sort of bread and egg mixture in bacon, secured it with a toothpick, and fried the bacon roll-ups in a skillet. "I'm telling you, they tamed lightning! This whole ship is powered by lightning! They are running off of stored up lightning at the moment. Usually, they make new lightning by creating a small star inside the ship! With their ship damaged, they can't do that right now. Instead, they are going to borrow some of the power of our sun!"

S'haar's look was split between impatience and confusion as she tried to simultaneously will the food to cook more quickly and listen to what Em'brel had to say. "But what will happen if they take our sun's power? Won't it get colder?"

Angela was starting to trust Em'brel more and more in the kitchen but still kept half an eye on the girl's work as the AI responded. "It won't affect the heat of your planet any more than the plants around you do. They've been doing the same thing as long as they've existed, taking the sun's power and turning it into the energy they use to grow and flourish. By the time the power of your sun reaches us here on your planet, it's already done its thing, and your sun doesn't need it anymore."

Em'brel finished the first batch and set a plate of them in front of S'haar and Jack. S'haar grabbed a piece a little too eagerly and started to toss it into her mouth before Em'brel snatched it out of the air while admonishing S'haar. "You don't just eat the whole thing. You have to slide it off the toothpick like so!" In the overly delicate way only Em'brel seemed capable of, holding onto one end of the toothpick, she placed the morsel in her mouth and drew the toothpick out before chewing.

Em'brels eyes were half-closed in rapture, and S'haar quickly followed suit. Soon all speech had ended, filling the ship with a comfortable silence as the two predators lost themselves in the flavor of their food. Jack wasn't going to miss out and took some for himself.

The bacon was the primary flavor of the food. Unsurprisingly, it went well with the egg. The bread was more for texture and made the meal a bit more filling, but there was also a hint of garlic and something else with a little zest that Jack couldn't place.

The confusion was evident on his face because Angela supplied an explanation. "The mystery flavor is celery salt!" Jack wasn't sure what that even was, but then again, Angela usually took charge of stocking the ship with supplies, so he wasn't surprised to have a spice he'd never heard of onboard.

Angela was pleased with the effect the meal was having on everyone's spirits but decided it was time to get down to business. "Since you got the tunnels dug out, the next step is to run the power cables out to that side of the mountain. With a little luck, we'll have the solar panels up and working in a day or two!"

The group had demolished the first three batches, but as Em'brel pulled off the fourth batch, Jack swiped them all before either predator could get a bite and put them in a container to take out to the workers. "We can run the cables this evening, but first, I want to go check up on the workers. They probably have enough shaped wood to begin the first lodge."

S'haar gave Jack a glare that quite handily explained how dangerous it was to come between a hungry predator and her food. "And you are taking my bacon away because…?"

Jack held up a hand and started counting down his fingers. "First, too much of one thing isn't healthy. You need more variety in your diet. Second, you've already had enough breakfast. If you overeat, you'll be sick all morning, and we won't get anything done. Third, those workers came all the way out here and risked a lot to help us out. This will be a good 'thank you'. Fourth, can you think of anything else that would inspire loyalty in the workers faster than bacon? Fifth, ok, I didn't think it through enough to have a fifth and assumed I'd just come up with one before I got here, but the previous four should be enough reasons."

S'haar glared at Jack for a few more moments before slowly allowing her gaze to wander. "Fine, I guess you get to live…for now."

Jack bowed his head in exaggerated gratitude. "Your benevolence is an inspiration to us all."

~

Jack brought out the bacon roll-ups as the workers were finishing their own breakfast. When he lifted the cover and the scents wafted out, all heads turned toward him. Setting the basket on a bench, Jack backed away. He knew better than to get between a bunch of argu'n and their first experience with bacon. S'haar managed to restrain herself from joining in as she translated for Jack. "Compliments of Em'brel. She thought you all had been working hard and deserved a treat."

Jack watched as the feeding frenzy began. There was a moment when Jack feared trouble was brewing as one of the younger woodworkers started to push another out of the way. However, Fea'en proved more than up to wrangling her charges with a cuff to the back of the offending argu'n's head. The proper pecking order established, the rest of the after-breakfast snack went off without a hitch.

The basket was quickly emptied. Everyone was made sure of this when Lon'thul held the basket upside down over his head and shook it, just to be sure there was no hidden compartment with more bacon hidden inside.

Fea'en shook her head in amusement at the youngster's antics as she approached Jack. When she spoke up, her gravely voice oozed satisfaction. "You keep enough food like that coming, and I might consider the rest of your debt paid. These lads don't need my help shaping more wood. Why don't you show me what you are thinking about next? I have a feeling it's not going to be what I would normally expect."

Jack nodded his head and led her and S'haar over to the area he and S'haar had cleared earlier. "Ok, so this is the spot I'm planning on putting up the first lodge. The first step is to put up a wooden frame like this."

Jack withdrew a schematic he and Angela had drawn up from a pocket, showing the skeletal outline of the building he had planned. It didn't take as long as he'd feared to explain the idea of size and scale. Fea'en caught on quickly. "So, once you get the beams in place, are you going to line the walls in skins? I see several issues if that's the case, not the least of which is there is no way you'd retain enough heat in an area that size. I'm hoping you're not planning on making it all out of wood. It would take forever to shape enough lumber to fill in the gaps."

Jack shook his head. "I have something else in mind, quicker than lumber, better insulating, and easier to repair. If you can get this section up here." Jack pointed first at the schematic and again at the spot of ground he indicated. "S'haar and I will get the next parts ready."

Fea'en looked at Jack with a combination of curiosity and skepticism. "You know, my father had a saying about people promising things too good to be real, but I'll give you a chance to prove you know what you're talking about. After all, you have to pay us whether or not you waste your time."

S'haar's face expressed her confidence in Jack's ability to follow through with his promises as they parted ways.

~

They brought along Em'brel and Lon'thul to help with this portion of the plan. Jack explained, and S'haar translated for Lon'thul. He held up a branch about three inches thick and seven feet long, as well as a thinner sapling only about an inch wide. "So what we need are a combination of long thin branches like this and even thinner saplings like this."

Jack waved toward the forest near the lake as he continued. "S'haar and Lon'thul can gather those. Meanwhile, Em'brel and I will get the clay, mud, and reeds we need by the lake. Just get as much as you can and load the cart up before lunch. After we eat, I'll show everyone what we'll be doing with everything."

As they worked, everyone stayed more or less within sight and sound of each other, and the required materials accumulated quickly.

Em'brel laughed as she worked, brightening the morning work. She had mud up to her elbows, streaked across her forehead, and all over her clothes. "You know, I've never done work like this before. My father always said things like this were for other people to do, but this is so much more fun than learning to read and write!"

Wiping her hand across her forehead in the same movement that had first put a streak of mud on her face, Em'brel continued. "I'm curious what you have planned for the dirt, clay, and reeds. It's exciting to see strange human technology at work!"

Jack grinned as he heaved another shovelful of dirt into the bucket Em'brel would take to the cart once it was filled. "This is an ancient technique used by humans for thousands of years. There are better building materials, and we might switch to those eventually, but this method was used for so long precisely because of how quick and easy it is to assemble, while also providing significant protection from the elements. I wouldn't be surprised if this technique quickly spread to surrounding villages as well. Throughout human history, it was often the least flashy technologies that had the most significant impact on the quality of life."

Em'brel tilted her head to the side with a mischievous grin on her face. "Said the man who traveled here on a ship that sails between the stars of the heavens."

Jack shrugged as he worked. "As impressive as that sentence may sound, indoor plumbing had a more substantial impact on people's life spans than faster than light travel ever could have."

Now Em'brel looked confused. "You mean like your sinks and toilets on the ship? It's nice that I don't have to go fetch water from a well, but I don't see how that could make a person live longer."

Jack grinned as he readied another lecture for the poor girl because of such a simple question. "To understand that, you first have to understand microorganisms such as bacteria. To introduce you to the subject, let me tell you the story of John Snow and the Broad Street pump!"

Em'brel had an odd combination of interest and dread on her face while listening as they continued working.

~

S'haar watched Jack and Em'brel laugh as they worked and wondered what crazy ideas he was explaining to her this time. As much as S'haar enjoyed the benefits of human technology, she was more interested in it working and less interested in *how* it worked.

Still, it was good to see how far the young argu'n had come in such a short time. As it was, she was probably now the third most educated person on the planet, and if Jack wasn't careful, she might become the second. Somehow S'haar didn't think that would bother Jack in the slightest, though he might take that as a challenge.

Lon'thul was also watching the two laugh, but his expression was one of confusion. At S'haar's raised eye ridge, he finally voiced his thoughts. "How is it you and Em'brel came to understand Jack's language in such a short time? You haven't even known him for a season, and Em'brel has known him for an even shorter period, yet the two of you seem to understand and translate for him with ease."

S'haar's hands continued to work as her thoughts turned to the memories of both her and Em'brel going through the procedure of learning the language. After seeing it performed on Em'brel, she had no more understanding of what had happened than she had when it had been done to herself. "Jack would hate for me to use the term 'human magic', but that's the best way I can describe it. He simply gave us the language."

Lon'thul looked stunned at the idea, his hand frozen mid chop. "He simply *gave* you the language? Just like that? Can he give you any knowledge you want?"

S'haar shook her head, not noticing Lon'thul's inaction. "No, apparently this only works because our minds already have the framework for the language. It didn't teach us something new so much as attach certain sounds to already existing knowledge. I'm probably the worst one to explain the idea, since I don't really understand it myself, but he can't add new information. He can only expand on existing information. There are still many words he uses that I need him to explain before I understand, and several that I still don't understand after the explanation."

Lon'thul was having a hard time reconciling the many feats Jack had performed in such a short time with the small, unassuming man the hunter was familiar with. Then something else occurred to him. "Why didn't Jack just come in and take over everything? The more I learn of him, the more powerful he seems to become."

S'haar smiled as she worked. "Jack is an odd man. He doesn't think twice about wielding power the likes of which you and I could never dream of, but he's not interested in using it for anything other than protecting his family. Although mostly, Jack simply wants to be left alone."

Lon'thul looked confused again. "If Jack only wants to be left alone, why is he putting this outpost together? Even for him, it seems like a lot of work, so why do something so ambitious if he's not interested in being in some kind of lord?"

S'haar considered how best to answer without giving away information that wasn't hers to reveal. "Everything Jack does is for family."

Lon'thul worked silently for a moment, contemplating the explanation. Eventually, the question he'd had on his mind since his revelation the other day worked its way to the surface. Looking back at Jack and Em'brel, he gave voice to his thoughts. "So how did Em'brel become a member of Jack's family? I understand how you bonded your way into his house, but Jack's relationship with Em'brel is more like father and daughter, despite there being no shared blood between the two of them."

Lon'thul noticed a slight chill in the air before turning and seeing a dark expression on S'haar's face. "Just how exactly do you think I 'bonded my way into his house'?"

Lon'thul realized he'd absent-mindedly said the wrong thing again, and looking back at S'haar's string of issues in the village, it was easy to see where. Holding up his hands in surrender, he quickly back-peddled. "I didn't mean to imply that you slept with him just to get into his house! I just meant it is evident that there is a connection between the two of you! You two are already more close than most partnered couples in the village!"

S'haar's expression quickly morphed from anger to confusion as she contemplated his words. True, Jack was one of her closest friends these days, along with Angela and Em'brel, but Lon'thul was all but outright calling them a couple. Looking at Jack, her feelings only seemed to grow more complicated on the subject. She was more protective of Jack than the other two, but that was just because he's so small and weak…right?

Then there was the night at the inn. Holding Jack tightly against the wall had certainly evoked some odd emotions within her, but they'd been quickly dispelled when they were interrupted by Sur'ruin. Looking at Jack now, smiling as he taught Em'brel some new piece of human knowledge, she couldn't help but feel something warm and unsettling in the pit of her stomach.

Lon'thul couldn't have been more surprised by S'haar's reaction if she'd turned into a wolgen in front of his eyes. Looking at the expressions flitting over her face, something finally fell into place. "Wait, you mean you and he haven't… You don't… You're not…?"

S'haar turned and seized Lon'thul, pinning him by his throat against a tree. "If you value your life, you will not say another word on the subject!"

Lon'thul nodded emphatically, but S'haar couldn't help but notice the laughter hadn't left his eyes. "Whatever relationship the two of us have is none of your business, understand?"

S'haar stared at him a moment longer before realizing he couldn't answer as long as she cut off his air supply. She let him go, and the hunter slumped to the ground. He took a moment to catch his breath before looking up with a big grin on his face. "Just promise me that when you two make it official, you'll invite me to the bonding ceremony. I want to see what kind of party Jack's going to throw!"

S'haar was undeniably the better combatant, but her mind was elsewhere at the moment. Even if Lon'thul hadn't been expecting the half hearted swipe that followed his statement, it had been so clearly telegraphed that he had plenty of time to get out of the way. Standing back up, he held up his hands in surrender and voiced his peace offering. "I'm sorry, I'm sorry! I just couldn't resist a little fun at your expense. Usually, it's me one step behind, and I couldn't help myself. I'll stop, though, I swear!"

She glared at him, narrowed eyes measuring his response, before turning and walking away, still trying to work out her feelings on the matter.

Still grinning to himself, Lon'thul gathered up a handful of saplings and followed her to the cart.

Chapter 25

Lon'thul, Em'brel, and Fea'en were standing in front of the framework of the building the woodworkers had put together by following Jack's plans. Matching action to speech, Jack walked them through building the walls, with S'haar translating as usual.

"Ok, first, we take the thinner saplings and split them lengthwise down the middle like so. Then we take the thicker saplings and lash them to the existing framework standing vertically, alternating them resting inside the frame and outside it, spacing them about a foot and a half apart. Once those are all standing in the frame, we take the smaller strips and weave them back and forth through the larger saplings. The next strip you put on in the same manner but reverse which side of the sapling each side weaves between. Keep doing this until you form a wall. This is called the wattle."

Fea'en looked critically at Jack's work. "That would make a decent enough wall for summer. It'll be sturdy for a while, but it's way too porous and has no insulation. And I hope you're not planning on filling in the gaps with clay or mud. That'll just wash off the first time it rains!"

Jack nodded. "It would if we used those independently, but you're getting ahead of the project. Next, we need to mix the mud, clay, and fibrous plants like so. This is called the daub." Jack started kneading a bunch of handfuls together into a paste-like combination of the three.

His arms were thoroughly covered in grime, but Jack didn't seem to mind. He took a handful of the stuff and slapped it onto the frame he'd made just a little earlier. As he spoke, he punctuated each pause with another generous handful of the muck. "As you said before, individually, the material would normally just wash off, but once this dries, it'll be a little closer to something we call brick, not quite as strong, but close enough for our purposes, and much quicker to slap up."

Scraping the mud off his arms and flinging it to the ground, Jack continued. "We can strengthen this further by painting the outside with something called whitewash after it's dried. Whitewash is just some slaked lime diluted in water. To get slaked lime, you grind down some limestone into powder, cook it to a sufficiently high temperature, then add a bit of water to stabilize the mixture. Once that hardens, it'll last a surprisingly long time, and repairs are as easy as slapping more daub onto any holes or cracks that eventually form."

Fea'en still looked at the wall Jack was putting up somewhat skeptically, albeit it was going up surprisingly quickly. "What about the roof? It'll see a lot more wear and tear than the walls."

Jack nodded as he finished cleaning his hands as best he could with a rag he'd brought. While he and Fea'en spoke, Em'brel and Lon'thul had already started filling another section of the frame with the wattle. "Eventually, I'd like to do straw roofs, but we'll have to grow enough straw to make that viable. For now, we're going to go with a two-layer roof. The first layer will be wattle and daub like the walls, but to protect that, you take a layer of sod and lay that on top. It's simply called a grass roof. if you do it properly, it'll provide plenty of insulation and protection, but it does take a lot more maintenance than a straw roof, since you have to water it regularly."

Fea'en still didn't look convinced. Her arms were crossed as she inspected Jack's work. He was currently smoothing out the section he'd put up with a trowel. "Honestly, I think you're crazy, but as long as you pay my men and me, we'll do it your way. Given the supplies we currently have and how quickly you were able to put up that wall, I'm guessing it'll take us a little less than a week to get the first building up. Assuming the weather holds, that is." Fea'en was glaring up at the clear sky with further skepticism as she spoke.

The sky was clear, but it was down in the forties, colder than an argu'n typically was able to work in for an extended time. Fea'en hugged the coat Jack had provided a little tighter around herself as she spoke. "I'll sleep much easier once we get the first building completed. These tents you provided are better than I thought they'd be, but I doubt they'd hold up if a storm hits."

Jack stepped back from his work and followed her gaze. "So far, all I've seen is a bit of light snow, and even then only at night. How bad do winter storms get around here?"

Fea'en shrugged. "It varies from year to year. Sometimes we'll only get smaller storms. Enough to keep people shut into their houses for a few days until the snow is cleared so we can walk around the village again. Some years, we get enough snow to lock us into our house for a week or two. When that happens, we always lose a few people, usually the very young or very old, but it's hard to predict."

The craft master glared into the sky. "The worst is when we get a cold storm. The temperatures drop far enough that our homes aren't sufficient protection, and we have to gather in a single place to wait it out. If that happens here, we'll be in real trouble."

Jack had been hoping the whole winter would be as mild as what he'd seen so far, but he'd also suspected he wasn't that lucky. "Well, if it gets bad, there are several options available to us, but at the very least, I think we need to get a larger stock of dried meats stored up, just in case. Ideally, I'd like to have at least a month's worth in storage."

At that, Lon'thul looked up from the daub he'd been mixing alongside Em'brel. "Well, if you want a lot more meat, two hunters are better than one. S'haar is one of the better hunters I've worked with, and with her help, I can probably get you stocked up in a week or two. You'd still have Em'brel around to translate."

Jack wasn't thrilled with the idea of losing S'haar for a week, let alone two. "What about the village? Could I trade more metal for additional meat?"

Lon'thul shook his head. "This time of year, our meat stores can be the difference between life and death. It doesn't matter how much metal you offer. It can't be used by people who don't survive the winter."

Jack hadn't thought it would be that easy, but he was disappointed nonetheless. "Then I guess we don't have a choice. Aside from the sled, is there anything else I can provide to help out?"

S'haar looked thoughtful for a minute. "Well, we'll need more heating packs and maybe a tent and some sleeping bags in case we get caught out by a storm. I can't think of anything else."

Jack sighed, his earlier energy suddenly drained. "Alright, I'll talk to Angela tonight, and we'll get it all put together for you."

Jack and S'haar were laying the cable for the solar panels through the caves. As he worked, Jack found himself dwelling on S'haar being gone for the better part of two weeks. He was surprised at how much stress the mere idea caused him. He was also alarmed to realize how dependent upon S'haar he'd become. True, she was his translator and bodyguard, but he'd come to depend on her for so much more.

Jack had always been a bit of a shut-in. Agoraphobia was the clinical term. The idea of leaving his comfort space usually filled him with so much dread and anxiety he would often turn his fear into anger and lash out at people and things that didn't deserve it. Once he'd realized what was happening, he and Angela worked out several ideas and strategies to mitigate its influence on his life, but it was always a factor to be considered.

However, on this planet, he'd wandered all over the countryside with hardly any issue. The big difference seemed to be that he had S'haar at his side throughout his explorations. He'd come to depend on her presence to chase away his irrational fears. The long-term problems were obvious, but it was also unhealthy to become too reliant on someone else just to function in the short term. In short, this wasn't just a situation Jack needed to get past. It was a situation that Jack needed to take advantage of to center and rebalance himself. Not that he was looking forward to doing it, but anything else would be a disservice to S'haar and himself.

Jack was so lost in thought that he hadn't noticed S'haar looking at him for the last couple of minutes. Her voice caught him off guard as it pierced through his internal gloom. "Maybe I'm missing something, but this doesn't seem like the kind of task that requires this level of concentration. Usually, you'd be regaling me with some weird facts about the history or science behind what we are doing. Once in a while, it's even interesting enough to help pass the time a little quicker."

Having been snapped out of his internal dialog, Jack stuttered a bit as he tried to explain himself without offering up too much information. "Uhh, um, yeh sorry about that, I was um, a bit distracted…planning for upcoming events."

Hearing that, S'haar raised an eye ridge in his direction. Her tongue flicked out as if trying to get a taste of the situation. "You *must* have been distracted. I gave you a perfect set up for some witty banter, and you let it pass unanswered. That's not like you."

Jack gave her a rueful smile as he rubbed the back of his neck in embarrassment. "Yeah, there has been a lot on my mind recently. Getting this outpost set up, doing right by the workers, taking care of Em'brel, repairing the ship to ensure Angela's survival, doing right by you after all you've done for me, and now preparing for a possible winter storm. I feel like I'm a bit over my head. More than a bit, really… I'm always worried I'm going to forget something, and some important things will slip through my fingers."

S'haar laid down the cable she'd been working with and stood with her arms folded and her hip cocked to the side for a moment while she thought. "Well, I wouldn't worry about me. You've 'done right by me' so far, and I'm confident that any further debts you incur will be paid in time. You've earned yourself a bit of trust and patience. Em'brel's already found a chosen path to walk for a while. All you have to do is be supportive as she does so. You're already taking all the steps you can to set up the outpost and prepare for the winter. Now you just have to let things unfold and adapt when something happens to interrupt your plans. At this point, all worrying can do is get in the way of getting work done."

Jack took the not-so-subtle hint and got back to work, but continued to speak as he did so. "Easy for you to say, but worrying is deeply ingrained into humans. On your world, there are only two or three things that look at you as food. On our planet, humanity was initially much lower on the food chain than that. We had to be wary at all times but also try and anticipate threats to avoid them altogether. There's always been a delicate balance between taking enough time to think through possible risks, while not spending so much time thinking that we create an even greater threat through inaction."

S'haar laughed a little at that while she hefted another line of the cable into place. "Well, you stop and think enough for both of us, so I guess it's my job to give you a kick in the rear if you've been inactive for too long."

Thinking back to his earlier contemplations, Jack couldn't help but let out a small, self-deprecating laugh. When he spoke, it was at half volume and directed more to himself than S'haar. "Yeah… I guess one of us needs to…"

S'haar gave Jack an odd look for a moment before speaking up. "You know I won't actually be gone for two weeks, right? Unless something unexpected happens, I'll be back home pretty much every night."

Jack looked somewhat flustered. "I uh, I mean I didn't... I wasn't..."

S'haar looked like the cat who caught the mouse for a moment before smiling and responding. "What, you didn't think I spend all day, every day, with you and not notice how afraid you actually are most of the time?"

Jack looked terrified at having his secrets laid bare, but S'haar continued before he could react. "However, the only thing that matters is that the last time I found myself in an impossible, terrifying, borderline suicidal situation, you had my back. What's more, you got us both out of there alive. So I can give you a pass on the small stuff."

Jack found himself struggling with the oddest combination of relief and embarrassment. "I didn't know I was that obvious..."

S'haar gave him a rare sympathetic smile. Jack had stopped being unsettled by how many teeth most of her smiles displayed a while ago. When S'haar spoke this time, her voice was less mischievous and more thoughtful. "To most, you probably aren't obvious, but we spend enough time together that it's hard to hide something like that for very long."

As the two of them laid the last of the cable out of the cave mouth, S'haar stood up and stretched before dusting herself off. Jack couldn't help but take a second to admire how her taut muscles moved while she pretended not to notice him looking. When she spoke again, her voice shifted to a more cheerful tone this time. "See, you'll be fine. Besides, this will be good for you! A little time away from me will help you get a fresh perspective on a few things."

This time Jack's laughter was a bit more genuine. "You know, I was telling myself something similar when you dragged me out of my train of thought."

S'haar winked at him. "What's that saying you used a while back? Great minds think alike?"

Jack couldn't help but finish the quote. "But fools rarely differ. So which are we, great minds or fools?"

S'haar gave him the most somber, straight-faced expression she could as she answered. "Yes."

If looks could kill, S'haar would be in grave danger. Luckily for her, Jack's look was about as lethal to her as his punch would be. When he spoke, his voice was filled with all the annoyance he could muster. "Thanks, you're a great help…"

~

As S'haar, Jack, and Em'brel sat down to eat, Jack explained the situation to Em'brel. "So, with S'haar gone for a couple of weeks, you'll be in charge of translating between the workers and myself. However, this does mean you'll be taking fewer classes from Angela for a couple of weeks. Although I'm sure she'll find a way to fit lessons in during breakfast, lunch, and dinner."

Em'brel looked a little nervous at the prospect. "But, what if I make a mistake and say something wrong? What if I accidentally insult someone or worse?"

Jack tried not to laugh at Em'brel's fears. In many ways, they echoed his own. "I'll be right there, and I know your language just fine. So if you make any mistakes, I'll be able to help you to straighten out any misunderstandings."

S'haar nodded as she cut off a thick slice of something delicious smelling called 'roast beef' before speaking. "If anything, the problem you're most likely to run into is telling Jack when he's explaining too much. He can get a little passionate about some subjects, and you might have to reign him in a little." After she finished speaking, S'haar took a bite of the roast. Her eye's closed in bliss as she savored the juices that shot out with every bite.

Jack looked deeply offended at the accusation. "I'm not that bad, am I?" A little uncertainty wove its way into his voice.

Angela answered on behalf of the other participants in the conversation, since they were both lost to the bliss of the meal. "You're not too bad…most of the time. You just have to watch out for subjects you get a little passionate about. Like the *Lord of the Rings*, for instance…"

Jack's expression was the definition of indignant as he responded to the slander. "Listen, too many people think Aragorn, Gandalf, or even

Frodo were the heroes of the story, but J.R.R. Tolkien himself argued Sam was the real hero... I'm doing it right now, aren't I?"

Angela looked a little too pleased with herself as she examined her digital fingernails while she responded. "Well, you know what they say. The first step is realizing you have a problem..."

Jack glared at Angela and the two argu'n, who were both doing their best to pretend they couldn't hear a word of the debate before sighing and letting the subject go. There was no way he was going to win this discussion with the jury so stacked against him. He was just about to take a bite of his own slice of the roast when Angela continued. "Besides, we all know Legolas was the true hero of the story. He's so dreamy."

Jack closed his eyes and counted to ten before responding. "Ok, I know you don't actually mean that, and you're saying that just to get a reaction out of me. That being said, you take that back, and you take it back right now! Those words are blasphemy, and I won't have it in my house!"

As Jack and Angela continued their debate, S'haar and Em'brel wisely stayed out of it. Instead, they slowly whittled down the roast while the two siblings had at each other over the dinner table.

Chapter 26

Jack was carrying the solar panels through the tunnels with the help of the exosuit, Em'brel traveled alongside him as he walked, and S'haar had already left that morning to go hunting. Em'brel eyed the panels with thinly veiled disappointment. "Those don't look all that impressive. How can they possibly capture the power of lightning?"

Jack ambled along at a comfortable pace, for once not struggling to keep up with S'haar's ground-eating stride. "Well, they'll capture the same amount of energy as a lightning bolt over a long enough length of time, but you're right, it won't be as impressive a spectacle. Combined, these will generate about one-fiftieth of that amount of energy over an entire day, depending on weather, which would be enough to power our ship for most of our day-to-day needs. With all the refining and replicating we're doing, combined with charging the heat pockets, we'll still be at a noticeable deficit, but this will narrow the gap and give us more time to generate more solutions."

Em'brel nodded her understanding as she walked. Jack found it a little odd to have someone grasp his explanations so readily. Not that S'haar lacked intelligence, as her cleverness caught Jack by surprise more often than not, but Em'brel had a level of 'book-smarts' that enabled her to grasp his explanations' scientific principles without having to continually go back and explain as many fundamental elements. Jack was quickly becoming more impressed at the effectiveness of Angela's instruction method as he spoke with the young argu'n.

Thinking of S'haar, Jack couldn't help but wonder what she was up to. She was hunting, obviously, but what was she doing at this particular moment. Wandering along the lazy river? Catching the scent of prey animals in the wind? Following the tracks of some doomed beast? Or maybe she was wondering what trouble Jack was getting up to without her there to watch his back?

As Jack mused, his thoughts started taking a darker turn. 'What if she slipped and broke an ankle out in the middle of nowhere? What if she got caught by a wolgen? What if she became trapped by one of the winter storms Fea'en had told her about? What if she realized she liked big strong argu'n males like Lon'thul after all? Why did that last one matter? She was free to like who she wished, and honestly, Lon'thul was a decent enough guy anyway.' Jack's face creased with worry as his mind started chasing itself in pointless circles.

Em'brel watched Jack's face with an odd little smile. Once his brow started expressing worry the way Angela had told her it eventually would, she decided to give him a little prodding and amuse herself at the same time. "You miss her, don't you?"

Jack jumped a little as her words startled him out of his thoughts. "What? No! I'm sorry, who do you mean?"

Em'brel's smile told him she wasn't the least bit fooled by his denial or attempted misdirection. "You know exactly who I mean! It's obvious you're worried about S'haar. Don't worry too much, though. She can take care of herself better than anyone I know."

Jack smiled a little to himself as he thought about what Em'brel had said. Images of S'haar flashed through his mind as she dealt with situations that would have broken some of the toughest men Jack had ever known. The mostly two on one fight with B'arthon's goons, the life or death battle with Dol'jin, and the brutal melee that followed. There probably wasn't anything a wild animal could throw at her that was worse than what S'haar had already overcome since Jack had known her. In fact, Jack was starting to wonder if there was anything she couldn't do.

Em'brel watched as Jack's face settled back into a contented smile. She let him get lost in some pleasant thoughts for a while longer before stabbing for her real target. Eagerly anticipating his likely reactions, she fired off with the most devastating question she could think of. "You like her, don't you?"

Jack was so startled, he almost dropped the solar panels he was carrying. Em'brel was tittering with laughter as he worked to re-stabilize his load. Eventually, when he was able to resume walking, Em'brel was right at his side, both arms folded innocently behind her back and a small spring in her step.

Jack forced himself to act and talk as casually as he could. "Well, yes, of course, I like S'haar, just like I like you and Angela too." Jack was focusing on walking as naturally as he could, but the sheer act of attempting to walk normally made his gait lose any semblance of its natural rhythm.

Em'brel had her prey cornered, and she pounced the way any good predator would. Her smile was all teeth. "You like Angela and myself, sure, but not the way you like S'haar. You *LIKE* her, don't you?" Em'brel looked at Jack with eyes that somehow resembled those of an innocent puppy, while also piercing through his soul and leaving him vulnerable to her relentless assault.

Jack was now about as healthy a shade of red as Em'brel had ever seen him be. He started and stopped his response a few times but never got very far past stuttering incoherently. He finally stopped and took a deep breath to steady himself. Somehow dealing with the childlike innocence of Em'brel's questions was almost more nerve wracking than facing down the raiders had been.

Finally, Jack realized there was no point in lying to Em'brel or himself any longer. "Alright, yes, I *'LIKE'* her. She's the most amazing woman I know. She's fearless, intelligent, proud, and unstoppable. She's also a seven-foot-tall goddess of death who can probably have any man she desires." Jack's voice took a bit of a self-pitying downturn at the end.

However, Em'brel's cheerfulness couldn't be dimmed. She sauntered ahead when Jack's pace slowed slightly. Once she was a few paces ahead of Jack, she looked back over her shoulder and smiled. "You know she '*likes*' you too, right?"

Jack's feet quickened as he tried to catch up to the impish girl as she stayed just a pace or two ahead of him. "Why do you say that? Did she say something? Are you sure? You're not just saying that, are you?"

Em'brel kept just a step ahead of Jack, propelled by a sudden burst of energy, she practically skipped her way down the cave tunnel laughing. Jack followed after, struggling to keep up with her youthful energy.

~

S'haar was tearing after her prey. Every muscle was pushed to the limit as she slammed her limbs into the ground at incredible velocities to launch her body forward like a missile. The churlish was just staying out of reach with its great leaps and bounds, and nothing S'haar could do would change that, but catching the prey wasn't her objective.

As the churlish launched itself forward one last time, Lon'thul was there to meet it head-on. He latched on with feet, teeth, and one hand while the other shoved his blade between two vertebrae, severing its brain from its body. The animal was dead before the two made contact with the ground.

S'haar was on her knees, gasping for air and glaring at Lon'thul. "Next time, it's your turn to flush the prey, and I get to make the killing pounce!"

Lon'thul looked plenty pleased with himself as he wiped the blood from his muzzle. "To do that, you'd have to be silent. For all your martial prowess, you have all the subtlety of a rampaging kovaack buck in mating season!"

S'haar climbed a bit shakily to her feet, her breath slightly more under control than a moment ago. "I thought you said I was one of the best hunters you've ever worked with?"

Lon'thul's cheerfulness was as unabated as ever. He was wiping his blade on some scrap cloth while his face glowed with an impish smile. "You are! Almost everyone else is even worse. Not to mention, you make a great distraction while I slip in and finish the job!"

She threw her shovel at Lon'thul, which he barely managed to catch it before getting hit in the face. "Fine, I'll be your distraction! But you dig the hole for the offal while I clean the animal this time. I'm worn out from the chase!"

S'haar was cutting the churlish up the midline while Lon'thul started his hole. As he dug, Lon'thul couldn't help but smile to himself as he worked. Working with S'haar on a hunt was like the good old days. Better, really. They hadn't worked together long, and at the time, he'd had more than a slight crush on S'haar. If he was honest, he might still have a bit of a crush, but he couldn't be anything other than happy to see her doing so well. She was no longer known as "the orphan", but more than that, she seemed happy, like she finally found a place where she belonged.

S'haar turned and noticed Lon'thul digging with a faraway look in his eyes. "What's with that stupid grin on your face? Don't tell me you haven't gotten over that childish crush of yours."

Lon'thul was plenty used to S'haar's blunt way of putting things and didn't mind her mannerisms the way many others in the village seemed to. If anything, it was comforting to see that she was still the same S'haar he'd always known. "No, no, I'm mostly over that. I was just reminiscing about the past and noticing how much had changed in such a short time."

S'haar cocked an eye ridge at the younger argu'n before responding. "I'm going to ignore the 'mostly' part, but yeah, I suppose a lot has happened. Jack has a way of changing everything when you're not looking."

Lon'thul was getting winded, but his hole was almost ready. "He's introduced new ways of getting unprecedented amounts of metal, even if he keeps that secret to himself and a few trusted friends, and now he's teaching us a whole new way to build houses. How much more change will he bring to us by the end of winter?"

Thinking of the home she and Em'brel shared with Jack and Angela, not to mention Em'brel's private lessons in human knowledge, S'haar couldn't help but smile at what seemed to be an inside joke at the expense of Lon'thuls naivety regarding their new world. "Probably more than you can dream of."

~

Jack was cursing all technology as he set up the solar panels. He'd slammed and pinched his fingers far too many times trying to get everything up and running, and now one of the panels seemed to not be producing any power. He had an access hatch open on the bottom as he searched for the source of the problem. Sometimes Jack wondered if life wouldn't be simpler if he walked away from everything and lived a simple life like S'haar and her people. The problem with that idea was that Angela didn't have that option, and there was no way he would abandon his family.

Fiddling around, Jack finally found the offending loose wire. With the final component secured, the readouts jumped to life, indicating everything was working correctly. Jack slammed the access panel shut with a satisfied sigh, and stood up, brushing his greasy hands on his pants.

Em'brel was looking at the mess his pants and shirt had become while he worked. "You know Angela's not going to be happy you ruined another set of clothing."

Jack waved away her concerns as he started back to the tunnel. "She can use a fraction of the new power I just gave her to clean them or replace them as she likes. Besides, I wouldn't be such a mess if everything had been ready to go to begin with!"

Em'brel had learned a few new exciting adjectives and adverbs while Jack had been working. From the context, she understood some of the words but still wondered what the bag for a feminine hygiene product had to do with solar panels. Jack had been unusually vague in his explanations.

As they started back to the ship, Em'brel stuck close to Jack. "So now that we have the solar panels up, what's the next step?"

Jack had just been contemplating that himself, so it was easy enough to list off. "Well, now that we have more power, we should get the transceiver up and running. That'll give Angela eyes and ears outside the cave, and if we wear headsets, she will even be able to speak with us while we're out and about. Once the workers finish the first building, we'll need to get started on a second for smelting and forging. Before winter ends, we'll need even more housing and workshops for other support personnel and, more importantly, a wall with some guard towers set up along the perimeter.

Em'brel looked a bit surprised at his list of goals. "Huh, I never took you for the ambitious type."

Jack looked more worn out after going through the list. Despite their progress, it was all still a bit overwhelming. "It's not a question of ambition, as much as a matter of necessity. Even if I hadn't made enemies of the raiders, once word gets out what this outpost can produce, it will have a target painted on it. If earth history taught me anything, there will be powerful people of the opinion that if they can't possess something this game-changing, no one will. Before we get to that point, I want this outpost to be defensible and self-sufficient."

Thinking of her uncle and many of the people her father had regularly dealt with, Em'brel couldn't disagree with his assessment. Even before her encounter with the raiders, she'd known this world was filled with cruel and uncaring people.

Those thoughts made Em'brel all the more grateful for the life she now had. The young argu'n grabbed Jack's power suited arm and hugged it to herself, much the same as she'd done to S'haar's the first time they'd walked these caves together. "Well, whatever needs to be done, you won't have to do it alone. S'haar and I won't leave your side, and I think you are even starting to win over some of the workers."

Jack smiled down at the girl. It wasn't often he had such a height advantage over an argu'n, even a teenager. "I think it was your bacon that won them over, more than anything I've done."

Em'brel nodded, acknowledging his point even while she drove her own point home. "My father used to say that all most people want is shelter, food, and safety. If you provide those, people will flock to you. You've done an excellent job on a couple of those fronts, and you've got plans in place for the rest. Keep that up, and your 'family' will continue to grow, regardless of your intentions."

Jack walked on in silence for a moment, contemplating Em'brel's words. "You know, all I set out to do was secure a future for a few friends and myself. I never intended to get involved in anything this big."

Em'brel hugged Jack's arm even tighter. If he hadn't been wearing his suit, she was sure she'd have bruised him a little. At least the metal separating her from Jack had some advantages. "I don't think anyone ends up where they intend from the beginning. We just have to deal with the bad, enjoy the good, and do our best to shape our lives to have more of the latter than the former."

Jack looked down at the girl on his arm. It tore at his heart to realize what she'd had to experience to gain that kind of wisdom at such a young age. In many ways, Em'brel was much older and more world-weary than the young girl who'd bounded beside him just that morning. Jack silently vowed to himself he'd do his best to ensure she had more time and opportunities to be young and carefree in the future.

Chapter 27

Em'brel noticed that while breakfast and dinner had always been a favorite time for everyone, that was especially true these days now that it was the only time all four of them were able to get together anymore.

They'd tell each other about their plans for the day during breakfast, then they'd talk about how the day had gone during dinner. There was laughter, teasing, sarcasm, and a warmth that had nothing to do with the room's physical temperature. Whenever Em'brel and Angela were away from the table, they would catch Jack and S'haar glancing at each other like they both wanted to say something but seemed to feel that now wasn't the right time. The anticipation was killing her, and Em'brel knew it was just a matter of time before those two hit a boiling point. Until then, she'd simply have to enjoy the show.

S'haar and Lon'thul had been surprisingly successful in their hunts. The two had been at it for only about a week, but the meat supplies were nearly plentiful enough that Lon'thul could handle the rest on his own again.

They were currently eating a breakfast Jack had called 'steak and eggs', a meal who's name was also the description. S'haar was talking about the hunting progress as they ate. "I think a day or two more is all we'll need. With a bit of luck, we'll have enough meat in storage to feed everyone for a month, without having to tap into your ship's stores."

Jack looked like someone trying to hide how excited he was and was failing. "That's great! We could use your help with construction again. We've got the first building ready, but we need more lumber. Em'brel has a hard time moving the trunks the way you do. She's not quite as… umm… developed… as you."

He was doing his best not to stare at S'haar's physique as he spoke, and S'haar wasn't doing anything to hide from his glances. Em'brel couldn't help but let a small giggle escape, which immediately caused the two romantic interests to suddenly shift their focus.

Jack was rubbing the back of his neck in his now signature move, indicating embarrassment. Even Schaar's tendrils shook in mild embarrassment as the human changed subjects. "We... uh... have the cables laid for the uhh... transceiver. Em'brel and I were going to hook it up today... What direction are you going hunting in today?"

S'haar's manner shifted back to business in her attempt to redirect the attention away from herself. "We're going to be venturing to the south today. It's been several days since we last hunted there, so there's been enough time for some animals to move back into the territory."

Jack had finally calmed down a bit and returned to his natural pallor. "That's good, south, good, ok, I'll keep that in mind."

Angela and Em'brel were looking at each other, laughing to themselves. These two were so awkwardly adorable.

Sadly, the time for talking was coming to an end. S'haar was suiting up for the cold and storing her weapons for travel. Jack spoke up as he watched her prepare. "Hey, be careful out there, ok? I know I say it every day, and I know you laugh it off, but I want you to come home safe and sound. After all, what would I do without my bodyguard? The weather could turn any day."

S'haar was securing her spears so they wouldn't jostle loose easily but could be quickly grabbed if the need arose. Finally, she turned and somewhat gently grabbed Jack by the shoulder. "I'll be fine. We keep a close eye and the weather as we work, and even if something unexpected happens, that's why we have the tent and all those extra heating pads. You'll just have to come to fetch us once the snow dies down, if it comes to that!"

Jack nodded and visibly calmed himself. "Yeah, you're right. Still, just promise me you'll keep an eye out for any trouble?"

S'haar looked like she wanted to step closer to Jack to say or do something more for a moment before the spell broke. Instead, she shook her head to clear it. "Alright, alright, I'll be careful. Take care of Em'brel and yourself while I'm gone. You two are too good at getting into trouble whenever I'm not around!"

Jack watched as she walked out the door. He told himself she'd be fine, and he needed to stop worrying. "Alright, it's a deal. Be safe out there!" Then she was gone. Jack stared into the gloom of the cave for a moment before shaking his head, then turning back to the house. He had to get ready for his own day of work.

Em'brel finished putting away the dishes and obviously hadn't been eavesdropping for the last couple of minutes. Jack turned and smiled. "Ready to go out and hook up the transceiver? After that, we can go back to the lake and get some more material for the daub, but this time Angela can come along for the ride!"

Em'brel and Angela were jumping up and down, clapping at the idea, and Jack couldn't help but feel a bit of their excitement. "Alright, let's do this! You're going to have to carry the transceiver, since I don't want to be walking out into the worker's area in my mining suit. I figure we should keep a few aces in the hole. Lucky for you, it's not too heavy!"

~

After carrying the transceiver most of the way on her own, Em'brel was starting to think Jack's definition of 'not too heavy' was drastically different from hers. Once they had gotten out of the cave, Tel'ron had come over to help. He was inspecting the impossibly perfect metallic shell. "This is amazing. I've never seen anything like this! The purity of the metal alone is worth a year's wage, if not more, and I don't even know what the device does!"

As soon as they settled the transceiver down into the mounting Jack and Em'brel had set up the day before, Jack was inspecting every inch of the device. It was mounted on top of a large rock just outside the entrance. It was so heavy because of all the layers of protection that Angela installed to guard against weather and wildlife. She proudly proclaimed that it could shrug off even a direct lightning strike if need be. Despite the claim, Jack set it up low enough that he hoped that they wouldn't have to test her theory.

As he tightened down the bolts, Jack decided to tell Tel'ron at least part of the truth. It would be evident soon enough, so he might as well give the smith something. "Well, hopefully, this will allow us to communicate with each other over large distances. It will require a headset, and I can't make too many of them just yet, but even if it's only available to a few of us, it could mean the difference between life or death in the field."

Tel'ron Looked at Jack as though he were speaking in riddles. "This feels like more 'dragon magic' to me. I'll stick to learning new alloys, thank you!"

As the smith walked away, Jack hooked up the power and took out a pair of headsets. They were a simple design, with an earpiece on one side and a mic extended toward the mouth. The set was held in place by an adjustable metal circlet that wrapped around the head. It was designed to be durable and hard to lose during intense action. It also had a few sensors so Angela could ride along with whoever was wearing one.

As Em'brel and himself put on the headsets and activated them, Jack spoke into the receiver. "Angela, are you with us?"

Angela's voice came through loud and clear for both of them. "Finally, new input! I could only scan the interior of the ship and the surrounding mountain a few trillion more times before I went insane from lack of new stimuli!"

Em'brel was looking around, half expecting Angela's avatar to show up next to her. Also, it was slightly disorienting hearing Jack's voice twice, a split second apart. Jack responded to Angela while she adjusted. "You know, you can't *go* insane if you are *already* insane, though I suppose you could go *more* insane..."

Angela didn't bother to respond. She was too wrapped up in her new sensors. "I didn't get much of a chance to scan the area when we were crashing down. This place is beautiful! It would feel a little like an Icelandic forest... if the trees didn't look so weird..."

Em'brel was looking up at the trees inquisitively. "What's wrong with the trees?"

~

As Jack and Em'brel approached the lake, Angela was still busy going on about the planet's flora and fauna. "This is a perfect example of convergent evolution. I mean, there are many, many differences, sure, but they are still clearly plants that follow the same rules as Earth. Trees, bushes, and ground matter are similar in nature, if not form, to what we'd see in any Earth forest. The animals are a bit harder to place, often riding a line between what we would consider different species, but still clearly having the basic forms and senses you would expect on Earth. Eyes, ears, mouth, and nose are all there, admittedly sometimes in different quantities and forms than would be usual where we come from, but still amazingly similar given completely separate evolutionary origins!"

Jack was barely listening to her, as his attention stayed focused on the weather. He would steal a glance behind them to the south at every opportunity. However, Jack couldn't focus all his time and energy on worrying about S'haar. He had a job to do.

Em'brel focused on getting the fibrous plant matter while Jack got the mud and clay, the latter being the colder job made Jack's exothermic physique better suited to the task. They were more than halfway done when Em'brel stopped Jack. She was holding some sandwiches. "I know you're probably too distracted at the moment to realize it, but we both need some food. You won't do anyone any favors by collapsing because you neglected yourself."

Jack looked up and wiped his brow. Despite the crisp air, he'd worked up a sweat with his shoveling. "Yeah, you make a good point. Grab a towel for me, will you?"

He walked over to the stream feeding into the lake and washed off the gunk he'd caked on. That's when he heard Angela say something in a stern but forcibly calm voice that made his blood turn to ice. "Em'brel, don't move!"

Jack turned as slowly as he could force himself to move, but the sight before him didn't do anything to ease his mind. Em'brel was by the cart they'd brought with them, towel in hand. Just behind her was the treeline, on the edge of which was a kovaack, horn lowered and pawing the ground. He'd obviously walked out of the trees just after Em'brel had turned her back to him, and he looked pissed that these two interlopers had dared to invade his territory.

Jack's mind raced. He'd brought his gun, but it was in the cart next to Em'brel. Maybe if Jack could shout and make himself look big, he could scare the beast off, but given that it seemed to show no fear of an argu'n, he doubted a human would have any luck in that endeavor. Maybe Em'brel could race for the gun…but she didn't know how to use it. Perhaps she could get the gun and toss it to Jack…

Then the time for thought was over. The kovaack launched itself forward, and Jack did the same. As his foot slammed into the ground,

Jack shouted, "EM'BREL, RUN!" but the poor girl simply looked behind herself in confusion.

Jack's second foot slammed into the ground, launching himself forward while the kovaack did the same. Em'brel gasped and froze in place, her instincts choosing the worst possible option between fight, flight, or freeze.

Jack's first foot struck the ground again, and he and the kovaack both narrowed the distance between their shared target. Jack wanted to shout at the monster, shout directions to Em'brel, or just shout at his frustration, but every ounce of oxygen was needed to force his muscles past their normal limits.

Jack's other foot slammed into the ground, propelling him forward faster than ever, but he wasn't the only one gaining momentum. The kovaack lowered its head, the horn pointed right at Em'brel's chest.

Something in the girl's mind clicked, and her brain switched from freeze to flight, but it was going to be too late. She'd never get out of the way in time.

Jack's first foot slammed into the ground one last time, propelling him into his young charge with as much momentum as his adrenaline-filled body could muster, but the kovaack slammed into the two of them barely half a second later.

~

There was blood everywhere, and Em'brel was screaming. Despite his best efforts, he'd been too late. As his failure stabbed into him, all the adrenaline seeped out of Jack, and his limbs hung down from his body like lead weights.

Barely half a second passed when Jack noticed something was off about the girl's screams. Those were not the screams of a painful death. Those were the screams of loss and rage. Feeling himself oddly jerked to the side, Jack looked down and noticed a horn protruding from his chest. All he could think was, 'Huh, well, that's alright then.'

Em'brel had been flung to the side by Jack but was now racing toward the kovaack that was currently shaking Jack lose from its horn. He held out a hand to the girl and tried to say, "No, this is ok, you're safe, that's what's important!", but all that came out was a cough of blood and a gurgling sound.

Jack didn't have many choices after that. His body was getting heavier by the minute, and it was all he could do to keep his eyes open and watch Em'brel make her charge. At some point, the ground had leapt up to meet Jack, now that Em'brel and the kovaack were fighting sideways, standing on the new wall of grass and dirt. A small part of his brain told Jack there was something wrong with his observations, but all his remaining attention was reserved for Em'brel's well-being. He had no energy to spare for something as insignificant as mere physics.

Em'brel's scream was something to hear. It was a defiant rage that seemed to shout to the world that she wouldn't let it take anything else from her. Jack couldn't help but think that S'haar would be proud.

The girl leapt impossibly high into the air, reaching both arms behind herself as she did so. The kovaack seemed at a loss for what to do and simply raised his horn toward her and waited. Jack was worried that the kovaack would impale Em'brel just as he had Jack, but when the girl came down, she had her arms just off to either side of the horn, and her head twisted just out of its reach. Em'brel put all her weight into the blow as she drove the spikes on her elbows into the beast's skull. It immediately collapsed like a puppet whose strings had been cut.

Seeing that Em'brel was safe, Jack finally allowed the darkness at the edge of his vision to rush in, and all the problems in his world suddenly ceased to exist.

~

Em'brel was rearing back to strike the beast a second time. One of her elbow spikes had torn off in her assault, her whole arm was numb, and blood was pouring out from where the spike had been, but she didn't care. There was no way she could punish the corpse of the kovaack enough for what it had taken from her, but she was going to try. That's when Angela spoke up in her ear. "EM'BREL, I NEED YOU TO LISTEN TO ME! I still might be able to save Jack, but you have to get him back to the med-bay on the ship as fast as possible. Every second is vital. Now go!"

Em'brel had a thousand questions swirling around in her mind. Every one of them centered around the ridiculous idea of saving the obviously dead man she had come to care so genuinely for in such a short amount of time, but Angela had said every second was vital, and so Em'brel shoved every thought to the side and launched into action.

Picking up Jack's body, a small part of her mind took note of just how tiny and light he really was. He'd seemed so much more imposing moments before when he'd shoved her out of the way.

Em'brel shoved that thought out of the way as well and started to run. Angela was speaking in her ear as she moved. "The human brain can only go about six minutes without blood flow before the damage becomes permanent. You've got about a half-mile to go, if you can get Jack to me in that time, there's...a chance."

Hearing that, Em'brel pushed herself harder. Launching forward, she ignored anything other than running. Trees flew past, startled animals dove for cover, icy winds pelted her face, it started snowing, but Em'brel ran on.

As she ran, her breaths became ragged, and she cursed herself as her pace slowed slightly while she gasped for air, but she ran on. At one point, her foot snagged on a root hidden from view, but Em'brel only stumbled for a moment before she resumed her run. Her vision was getting blurry. Her legs felt as though her muscles were tearing themselves from her bones, but the girl ran on.

Eventually the camp came into sight, but Em'brel didn't have any reserves left to feel something as unimportant as relief or hope. Precious seconds were slipping past. As she ran past unseen workers, they noticed the girl was not running, so much as rapidly stumbling. When someone reached out to slow her in an attempt to help, the young argu'n merely snapped her jaws at him and almost bit a few fingers off, all without slowing her stumbling pace. Into the cave, Em'brel ran on.

Reaching the house, Em'brel fell against the walls in her stumbling attempts to reach the med-bay in time. Angela was doing her best to guide the completely exhausted Em'brel the last little bit. "You have to get him to the med-bay. You're almost there, but I can't help unless you go a little further. Please, just a little further!"

Picking herself off her knees, Em'brel lurched the rest of the way. Angela was still speaking. "Into the chair there. Just set him down, and then I can do the rest!"

With a final gasp of effort, the young girl dropped Jack into the chair that was fading from view, threw up in the corner, then passed out.

S'haar was returning to camp just in time. Jack's feeling this morning had been spot on. A storm was coming. It didn't look like it would be too rough, but it was better to err on the side of caution, so she and Lon'thul had started back early. The kovaack and churlish tied to their sled would just about top them off anyway. She'd been worried once or twice that they'd have to settle in for the storm, but eventually, the camp came into view, and she sighed in relief. A few of the workers were waving at them, obviously relieved that they'd made it back safely, but there was something odd about the waves.

Tel'ron approached at a run, stopping just shy as he rested his hands on his knees to gasp for air. His explanation came out between gasping breaths. "Em'brel came running back to camp carrying Jack. He didn't look good. When I tried to help, she practically bit my hand off and kept running into the cave. That's the last we've seen them. We were just debating on whether to venture into the cave or not…"

S'haar dropped everything she was carrying and took off into the cave at a dead run. She was a blur of motion as she crossed the familiar landscape in record time. The ship's door was open, and S'haar launched herself inside and tore through the living area into the med-bay.

Jack was laid on a chair that had been turned into a table. Far too many of his insides were exposed to the air. Metal arms were poking and prodding his body as they dug around inside the corpse. S'haar was ready to jump to his side when Angela appeared in front of her, hands held out, and a pleading look on her face. "Stop! Jack is in a critical moment right now, and I might be able to save him, but anything could tip the balance. Even your breath could be a threat to him!"

S'haar looked at the AI with unthinking eyes and, for a moment, seemed like she might try and walk past anyway when a weak hand grabbed her by the ankle. Looking down, S'haar saw a pitiful looking Em'brel feebly holding on with what little strength she had left. Her body was so bruised and broken; she barely looked alive herself.

The girl was lying in a pool of her own vomit. Her legs looked as though they'd been beaten until they could no longer work. One of her elbow spikes was missing. The blood clotting at the end made it clear it had not been treated. Her voice came out small and feeble. "Let her work. Jack…Angela…she needs all her attention right now."

The sight of the young girl in such agony but trying desperately to help Angela was enough to snap S'haar out of her daze. She still desperately wanted to reach Jack's side but held herself in check. "Is there anything I can do to help?"

Angela looked relieved for a moment before sparing a worried glance over her shoulder as she spoke. "Honestly, no. I'll know more in about an hour, but at this time, it could go either way. Em'brel almost literally tore herself apart getting Jack to me in time, but I haven't had the chance to treat her. I'm still trying to stabilize Jack and don't have much to spare."

S'haar nodded and stood there a moment longer, staring at the lifeless body that used to be Jack. Metal arms were sticking out of his stomach like some horrible insect digging its way into him. But S'haar knew that Angela was second to none in her concern for her brother. So S'haar nodded a second time, for her own benefit as much as for Angela's, and reached down to gently pick up the young argu'n from off the ground. "Alright, alright, let's at least get you cleaned up."

Over the next hour, S'haar washed and bandaged Em'brel while the younger argu'n got the story out between sobs of fear and frustration and the occasional gasp of pain at S'haar's treatments of her injuries.

She told the story of the kovaack charging, Jack shoving her out of the way, Em'brel killing the kovaack, and finally running Jack back to the ship. Em'brel was still sobbing as she spoke. "I couldn't… I didn't… I wasn't able to protect him!"

S'haar was applying a bandage to the end of the girl's missing spike as she spoke. "Hush! It's not your job to protect Jack. It's Jack's job to protect you, which he did. Besides, from the sounds of things, there's no way he could have carried you back to the cave in time. You did well. If Jack lives, he'll owe it all to you."

That was the moment when an exhausted and bedraggled Angela made an appearance before the two of them. "Well, he's alive…kind of…"

Em'brel looked worried and confused, but S'haar simply narrowed her eyes in suspicion. "What do you mean, 'kind of?'"

The AI pointed them to the med-bay as she spoke. "That's complicated, but you can come see him while I try to explain."

As S'haar walked into the room, Jack's body was laid out on the reclined chair. He looked smaller and frailer than ever, and his face was far too pale even for a human. S'haar would have thought he was dead if not for Angela's insistence otherwise.

Jack's sister looked both relieved and defeated, looking down at Jack's body with sadness as she explained, "Well, Jack's stable. All his vitals are fine, and I'm confident I can finish healing the damage done to his body, though it will take quite some time."

Angela took a deep breath while S'haar and Embrel waited for her to continue. "The problem is, he's not waking up. The amount of damage sustained was immense, and despite Em'brel breaking every expectation I had of her capacity, Jack went a long time without proper blood flow to the brain. Normally, once he was stabilized like this, I'd fly him to the nearest proper facility for better, more in-depth treatment than I can offer in this emergency med-bay. However, that's beyond my capacity at the moment, so we'll just have to do whatever we can with what we've got. Right now, he's in what we call a coma, a kind of deep sleep on the border between life and death. He might wake up in a day, a week, a month, or never. It's impossible to say. At this point, all I can do is heal his body and hope."

When Em'brel spoke this time, her voice came out small and frightened. "What…what do we do?"

S'haar face hardened as she stared down at the man she'd come to know so well in such a short time. "There's only one thing we can do. Jack has a plan in place that he's put everything on the line for, and Angela's very life depends on that plan. So, we continue to work to make his vision a reality."

Angela and Em'brel were looking at S'haar with surprise clear on their faces, but the AI quickly switched to a bittersweet smile. "Jack…well, if…no, when he wakes up, he'll be proud of you both. But you both need your rest. There's nothing that can be done tonight that can't be done tomorrow. Get some sleep, doctor's orders."

The two argu'n nodded wearily, and S'haar helped Em'brel get into bed before finding her own. Even when the light faded, she continued staring up into the dark ceiling long into the night.

Em'brel and her father were traveling across the plains again, but this time when they got captured, it was Jack she watched get murdered. While he died, Dol'jin laughed at Em'brel, telling her there would be no one to save her this time.

Em'brel shot awake in an instant, but it took a moment for the dream to fade enough that she could place where she was and what had happened the day before. Tears started flowing as her memories returned, and it took her several minutes to calm herself back down again.

Once she did, she realized something was off in the room. She was alone.

She'd gotten so used to sleeping with S'haar in the room that S'haar's absence left Em'brel feeling almost as vulnerable as the dream had. The girl slowly and painfully dragged herself out of bed. All her limbs were in agony. Every movement sent pain shooting up and down her nerves, but Em'brel wasn't about to give up just because of a little thing like that.

Eventually, the room lit up with a gentle glow that told her Angela was beside her. Em'brel turned while wrapping the blanket around herself, as much for the feeling of safety as for the warmth. "Where's S'haar?"

Angela looked at Em'brel as though she wanted to protest the girl getting out of bed before she'd had a chance to heal. Instead, she shook her head and answered. "She's in the med-bay, with Jack."

Em'brel nodded and limped over to the bay. Opening the door, she saw S'haar sitting in a chair beside Jack. Her head was resting on her arms, which were lying in Jack's legs. She was asleep, but Em'brel could see the trails her tears had left.

Em'brel brought another chair over. When S'haar startled awake, Em'brel wordlessly wrapped her in the blanket as well, and they both settled in beside Jack.

It wasn't as comfortable as their beds had been, but Jack's presence somehow chased away the nightmares for the rest of the night. In their dreams, the three of them shared breakfast, laughter, and bacon.

Chapter 28

Em'brel got up before the others to make breakfast as was her habit, but hesitated when she remembered it was only one other now. It took the young female a moment to find the motivation to move again, but biology didn't care about her world ending for a second time. She was hungry, and S'haar would be too. Cooking wasn't as fun as usual. Her heart wasn't in it this morning; however, Em'brel knew better than many that no matter how bad things got, life simply went on.

This time wasn't even as bad as the last. Em'brel still had S'haar and Angela, she had a future that probably didn't include slavery, and in the furthest, most distant parts of her mind, a small voice told her there was still hope. Hope that Jack might come back to them again. To Em'brel again. "But, he wouldn't need to come back if you'd just acted a little faster!"

As Em'brel muttered angrily to herself, her hand spasmed, shattering the egg she'd been holding and spraying all the nearby surfaces in whites and yolk.

Looking at the mess, the girl felt defeated. Somehow this latest trial, as small as it was, was just too much. Em'brel was torn between finishing the breakfast she'd started and cleaning the mess she'd made and found she was frozen with indecision. While the seconds, then minutes, ticked by, the egg soaked in and dried to various surfaces while the breakfast she'd been working on began to burn. Everything was now worse than if she'd just picked one task and started on that, but she was still frozen. Exactly like she had been when the kovaack charged.

Smoke started spiraling from the pan sitting on the stovetop, and the egg was drying and cracking on her skin. Em'brel slowly closed her eyes, then forced all her will into her hand. When that didn't work, she focused on one finger. With agonizing slowness, she pried that finger open. After that, she did the same with every finger on her hand. Each finger was a little easier than the one before. Soon her hand, then arm, then both arms were free.

Opening her eyes, Em'brel sighed and finally grabbed some hot pads to pull the pan off the burner. She scraped the breakfast's remnants into the waste, cleaned the shattered egg off everything, and then started over. She couldn't undo her mistake, and it had ruined her first attempt at breakfast, but she could move forward and try again. With a little luck, maybe she learned a thing or two as well. A voice in the back of her mind told her there was a more profound lesson contained in there somewhere, but she wasn't ready for that yet.

~

Angela watched the girl get back to work with a feeling of profound relief. Jack had once told her that sometimes he needed to clean up the messes he made to help deal with the emotion that helped make them. There was a particular strength in confronting his mistakes and doing what he could to make it right.

While Angela didn't blame Em'brel for what happened, she knew the young girl blamed herself, and it was clear from what Em'brel had said to herself that this smaller crisis was a surrogate for her more significant internal struggles. For a brief period, Angela had shifted most of her attention from Jack to Em'brel and silently cheered the girl on. The only time she'd interfered was to turn down the burner to buy a little time before something caught fire.

Now Em'brel was back to work. Her face was a grim mask of determination that was utterly dissonant with the task of making breakfast, but Angela noticed most of the hesitation was gone, and the young argu'n now moved with a will and a purpose.

Angela shifted her attention back to S'haar and Jack. The argu'n woman was still curled up on Jack's legs, but Angela could tell she was now awake.

~

A small voice inside her head told S'haar that so long as she didn't open her eyes, Jack would still be as alive and energetic as he's been in her dreams. The problem was she'd gone and made a stupid, noble proclamation about seeing Jack's goals through. To do that, she needed to wake up and confront the truth.

Cracking her eyes open, she could see Jack as lifeless as she remembered him being the night before. At least his stomach and chest were now closed up, and no robotic limbs were digging around inside him any longer. If she squinted, it almost looked like he would get up and start grumbling about how he hated mornings at any moment.

With a sigh, she pulled herself to her feet and started to leave to get some breakfast. That's when Angela appeared in the corner of the room. "You can speak to him, you know."

S'haar's sleep-deprived mind couldn't quite grasp what Angela was getting at. "I'm sorry… what?"

Angela looked over at Jack, her face conveying both worry and happiness. "You can speak to him. I don't know how much he actually understands, but his brain waves tell me that at least a part of him hears what we say. There have been stories of people waking up from comas who could repeat things told to them while they were sleeping. Not always, but I like to think he's at least somewhat aware that we're here. So anytime you want to, you can come to talk to him. He just might be listening while trying to find his way back to us."

S'haar looked at the man who was starting to mean so much to her before he went and did something stupid and noble that still might kill him. She wanted to scream at him for leaving, beg him to come back, tell him she'd protect him, ask him for help, but mostly she wanted to say to him that she… No, S'haar wasn't ready for these thoughts yet. It was too much.

As she turned to walk out the door, S'haar simply muttered quietly, "Maybe later."

~

Breakfast was a more somber affair than usual. They both ate in silence. Despite Em'brel's initial setbacks, the meal turned out as good as it usually did. After the previous day and night, both argu'n were ravenous.

However, they simply gulped down their food in a hurried silence, neither daring to break the sounds of scraping utensils.

As they were cleaning up, Angela appeared before S'haar and Em'brel. "I know you've... *we've* had a rough night and morning. As much as I'd like to say you should take some time off, the workers are getting restless. After what they saw, the future seems uncertain, and right now, they need leadership and encouragement. You need to assure them that despite...everything...they will be taken care of."

Looking over to S'haar, Angela continued. "They know and respect you. You've been Jack's right hand for as long as anyone here has known him. You're already established as someone who will stand up for what you believe in, despite what it can cost you, and you're known as someone who takes care of those in her charge. You're a natural leader."

Looking over at Em'brel, Angela continued. "You are young, but you've already experienced many of the worst things life can throw at you, and you came out the other side with hope and happiness. You've already captured the hearts of everyone who knows your story, and your determination to keep fighting for a better future has captured their imaginations. Every undertaking needs a heart, someone who keeps the lifeblood flowing and lifts people's hopes and spirits. That's a role you are uniquely qualified to fill."

Looking at them together, Angela continued. "I know things look bad right now, but the two of you have everything you'll ever need to make this outpost a success, and I'll be here if you need a little help now and then."

Em'brel looked a little teary-eyed as she spoke with a small voice. "I think... I think I'm going to need more than a little help..."

Angela smiled affectionately at her young charge. "I was underplaying my presence somewhat. I'll be here as much as you need."

Looking toward the door facing the mouth of the cave, Angela cocked her head to one side as if listening. "Now, the two of you might want to get ready to speak to a guest. They're sending in a representative as we speak.

As Lon'thul walked into the cave, he couldn't help but be filled with trepidation. They had been told to never enter the cave without an invitation. However, the workers were more than a little worried about what the future held. Tel'ron had told the rest it had looked like Em'brel was carrying a corpse, and even S'haar hadn't bothered to return after entering into the cave. Everyone was worried that the outpost was ready to collapse. What's worse, they were wondering how to make it back home without a supply of the heat packs Jack had provided up until now.

It had been decided that since Lon'thul had the most rapport with their hosts, he would most likely be forgiven for trespassing, especially given the extenuating circumstances. At the time, he'd eagerly agreed. After all, that meant he didn't have to worry about clearing the snow away with the rest of the workers as they dug paths around to the various parts of the camp.

Walking through the gloom of the cave with a torch in hand, Lon'thul started to doubt his earlier logic. What if the dragon took offense and killed him before he even had a chance to explain himself? What if he got lost? What if…

His last thought faded into surprise and mild panic as the area around him lit up as if the morning sun had cleared the horizon. The light came from in front of him rather than above. It seemed to be mounted on some sort of stand. It was so bright, he couldn't stare into the light for long. Blinking away the tears from his eyes, it took Lon'thul a moment to notice there was a large metal wall just behind the lights.

He was just starting to debate going closer to inspect the wall or turning back and finding another route when a portion of the wall simply slid away, revealing what appeared to be a door. Just inside stood S'haar, her head tilted to the side a moment before coming to a decision of some sort. "Well, since you came all the way here, you might as well come inside."

S'haar disappeared back through the hole in the wall, leaving Lon'thul on his own for a minute before he swallowed his fear and followed after. Walking up to the door, he couldn't help but reach out and rap the wall with his knuckles. It was definitely solid and thick, this… building?… could withstand any force known to Lon'thul. He hesitated on the threshold for a moment longer before deciding he trusted S'haar enough to follow her into this strange place.

As Lon'thul stepped forward, the first thing he noticed was how bright and warm the room was. If the lights outside had been as bright as the morning sun, it seemed like noon in this room. The room was more spacious than he'd been expecting, even if it was a little short for a full-grown male, and when he thought of the whole place wrapped in metal, his mind boggled at the sheer quantities that must be involved.

Then there was the heat. It was like the warmth of a campfire was spread evenly throughout the room. The cave had been warm relative to the winter air, but even that felt cold and damp compared to this place.

S'haar was walking over to an area with several odd-looking benches. When she sat down, the bench seemed to sink in a little and fold around her slightly. She indicated he should sit in a chair covered in a material that looked similar to her bench. When he took her up on her offer, Lon'thul felt himself slightly sink into his own seat. If it weren't for his mind traveling a mile a second trying to take in everything and failing, he'd probably have spent more than a moment marveling how, between the heat and his chair, this was the single most comfortable moment of his life up until this point.

S'haar watched Lon'thul look around himself in constant amazement, his eyes focusing on each wonder the room contained only as long as it took to spot the next. His eyes and head were swiveling around, darting to and fro in a way she knew her own must have done the first time she'd seen it. When Em'brel was introduced to this place, her reaction had been somewhat muted, probably due to the trauma she'd been processing. Seeing Lon'thul's expressions of amazement, she suddenly understood Jack's odd smile the first time he'd shown her around his ship. Lon'thul may have the physique of an adult male, but right now, his expression was simple childlike wonder.

S'haar allowed him to indulge his curiosity for a moment longer before clearing her throat to get his attention. As his eyes snapped back to her, Lon'thul tilted his head in curiosity. "Is this where you've been living all this time?"

S'haar smiled sadly as she leaned further back into the padding on her bench. "Yes. Jack, Em'brel, and I have all been living here for a while now."

Her expression reminded Lon'thul why he was here, and he mentally kicked himself for bringing up the subject so callously. However, the issue was broached, and he had a responsibility to the other workers. "Listen, I don't know a good way to ask this, but is Jack dead? Is it time to close this place down and go back to the village?"

S'haar stopped and thought a moment before responding. "Jack is…mostly alive. We hope he'll make a full recovery, and to that end, Em'brel and I will be overseeing the outpost until he can resume his role in the camp."

Lon'thul seemed more than a little confused for a moment before asking, "What do you mean 'mostly alive'?"

S'haar's eyes lost focus as she seemed to look into the distance as she spoke. "The dragon healed Jack's body, but his spirit was damaged along with his body. Right now, he's lost somewhere between this life and the next. We can only hope he'll find his way back to the world of the living."

S'haar's eyes refocused onto Lon'thul's. "Given everything I've seen him do up until now, I believe he will succeed!"

Lon'thul closed his eyes for a moment, and when his eyes opened, his expression was stern, or at least as stern as Lon'thul could be. "I hope so as well, for everyone's sake, but I have to ask, what becomes of us if he doesn't?"

S'haar closed her eyes a moment at the thought, then brushed it away and pushed forward. She gestured around the room as she spoke. "You've had a good look at this room and the many marvels herein since you got here, and I can promise you that you've barely scratched the surface of what this place contains. We welcomed you in here to see for yourself that we have the ability to fulfill the promises we make."

S'haar now focused her attention on Lon'thul as she spoke, her eyes holding his captive as he looked into the superior predator's gaze. "All the compensation promised will be met. If we can't supply what was specified for any reason, it will be substituted with something of higher value."

At those words, Lon'thul took another glance around the room and knew that promise was well within their power. "Ok, I accept that. However, the entire plan behind this outpost currently lies in the head of a man lost in the spirit world. How will we move forward from here?"

S'haar leaned back again, remembering how many times she'd seen Jack do something similar to project confidence he didn't necessarily feel. "I've been Jack's right hand since he set foot in this land. I am familiar with what he's got planned for this outpost. From how it was supposed to be laid out, to the purpose each part was going to serve. I'll be taking over the direction of establishing and running the camp."

Lon'thul pressed forward, not willing to so quickly accept the answers S'haar had given. The rest of the workers trusted him to represent them today, and he was going to make sure their concerns were heard. "That's well and good, and I trust you to do your best by us, but this outpost was based on more than just a good location. Jack had dragon magic that allowed him to do things we never could. Those things were the foundation of this whole place. Are you telling me you understand the secrets he knew?"

Em'brel chose that moment to exit the med-bay where she'd been helping Angela change Jack's dressings. S'haar pointed to the girl with her chin as she spoke. "I don't, but Em'brel has been learning from both Jack and the dragon as their apprentice. She might not have all of Jack's knowledge, but she knows enough to fill in where my knowledge is lacking."

The younger argu'n did her best to not wilt from the attention suddenly directed her direction. Instead, she responded with a formal bow. "I'll do my best to apply the knowledge so generously bestowed upon me to meet the needs of this place and all the people who live here."

Lon'thul hadn't missed the fact that there were several doors similar to the one Em'brel had exited from scattered around the room, and apparently, most of them led somewhere other than back to the cave, meaning he had no real idea of how big this place really was. However, now he was focused on the girl standing before him and found himself drawn to her earnestness.

S'haar drew his attention back with another clearing of her throat. "We realize this is asking many things of you all that you didn't agree to before you came out to this place, so go and speak to everyone and decide whether you want to leave or stay. Anyone who wants to leave will be given provisions, including heat packs, to make the trip back to the village after the snow melts with no hard feelings. Anyone who stays will have our gratitude as well as everything else we've promised. We'll give you some time to talk amongst yourselves, but we ask that you decide by breakfast tomorrow, which we'll be supplying. For now, we have a load of heat packs ready to go, sitting just outside the door you came in from."

Lon'thul recognized a dismissal when he heard one and got up to leave. Before he reached the door, a thought stopped him. "I thought you lived with the dragon, but as marvelous as this place is, I don't see any room for such a… creature to live in here with you. Where is the dragon?"

S'haar and Em'brel looked at each other with a smile that only confused Lon'thul further before S'haar turned to answer the hunter. "That is a more complicated question than you realize. This simple answer is that the dragon is closer than you think. She can hear everything that happens inside her caves and a great deal of what happens in a surrounding area outside the caves. This whole place exists with and by her pleasure. In much the same way Jack does, she thinks of us as her family."

Lon'thul's head was tilted to the side, the answer had obviously only served to confuse him further, but neither S'haar nor Em'brel seemed interested in offering further clarification. He nodded his respect to both of the women with a small sigh of defeat as he departed. He was only slightly surprised when the door apparently shut on its own behind him, despite the only other people in the room being nowhere near it as it did so.

As soon as he was gone, Angela appeared to the two girls. She beamed with pride. "That went better than I could have hoped, and we owe it all to the two of you. Thank you…I'm sure Jack would be just as proud!"

S'haar looked worried. The other two noticed she didn't even realize when she copied Jack's neck rubbing habit as she spoke. "I don't know. I'm not quite as good at talking to people as Jack is."

Angela smiled knowingly at the woman. "I think you picked up more than you realize. Those months of translating for him really rubbed off on you. In some ways, I think you might be better at it than he is!"

Em'brel was nodding along with Angela when the AI's attention was turned toward the girl. "And you! You did great as well! When you spoke, I could practically see Lon'thul's desire to follow you wherever you might go, and not just because of the slight crush he seems to be developing for you!"

Both S'haar and Em'brel looked at Angela in confusion. Angela looked back and forth, a little surprised at their reactions. "What, I wasn't the only one who noticed that he likes her, was I?"

Chapter 29

Fea'en, Tel'ron, and the other three workers sat around the fire inside the building they had put up not long ago. They were listening to Lon'thul's explanation of S'haar's offer. As soon as he finished, one of the workers jumped up. "I came out here to work for the human and his dragon magic, not a couple of orphaned *females*! We should take them up on their offer and return to the village once the snow thaws!" The worker seemed oblivious to Fea'en's upraised eye-ridge at his emphasis on the word females.

There was some muttering around the campfire before Lon'thul spoke up again. "If you're worried about them fulfilling their part of the deal, I can promise you that they have the resources to make good on their payment! I'm telling you, their home is unlike anything I've ever seen. It's more extravagant than any lord's manner I know of!"

The same worker growled back. "That's another thing! If they have so much, why aren't they sharing more with us?"

Fea'en looked thoughtful with her chin resting on her palm and spoke in a quiet voice that forced everyone else to be silent to hear what she had to say. "I'm not sure I'd say they haven't. They gave us these coats, which are better quality than any garment I've ever seen, and we get to keep them even if we do leave early. We have these tents of similar quality, which we can also take with us now that the first building is complete. We now have living quarters that are sturdier, better insulated, and easier to maintain than anything we've ever had, and we were taught how to make more. Not to mention how much metal they've supplied to our village, which is comparable to what an entire summer's worth of gathering would have provided. Who knows what's next?"

Several heads around the campfire were nodding in agreement when Tel'ron added his thoughts. "There's also the breakfasts and dinners we've been getting! Those are better than anything I've ever eaten as an apprentice. Sometimes I wonder if lord A'ngels eats this well. Also, Jack hinted at some new alloys I'm excited to try out. I'm sticking around to see what's coming next!

More heads were nodding emphatically now, and the voice of dissent found himself alone with his opinions. With a huff and a grumble, he retreated to his sleeping area.

With the big decision out of the way, and it being too cold and wet to work outside this late into the day, the workers settled in for a more relaxed conversation. One of the younger workers prodded Lon'thul before speaking. "Tell us more about that house of theirs! What else did you see?"

Like all hunters, Lon'thul enjoyed telling a good tale around a fire. His eyes lit up as his arms started gesturing. "I know I described all the metal, but the surfaces without metal were covered in even more luxurious materials! The seats were more comfortable than the softest churlish fur…"

As Lon'thul started working his story up, Fea'en settled in to listen to the excited youth's story. He was good at painting a picture with words, even if he exaggerated a little here or there, but to be fair, every hunter she'd known was much the same. She couldn't help but wonder which parts of this story were exaggerated and which parts were accurate. Knowing Jack, maybe Lon'thul didn't have to exaggerate very much, for a change.

~

Angela decided they all needed a night of relaxation after the last couple of days. She put on a movie with a dashing young hero.

S'haar felt a pang in her chest during several romantic portions of the movie and couldn't help but compare Jack to the film's main character. From speaking with Angela, S'haar had gathered that Jack had been every bit as much the quiet and unassuming individual that the main character of this movie had been. They both were dropped into worlds that left them completely in over their heads, and while Jack had never been as suave as the character in the movie became, they'd both risen to meet whatever challenges had been thrown their way. S'haar found herself tearing up at the climax of the film, wondering if Jack would ever show up to save the day again.

Never mind the fact that S'haar had to save Jack just as often as the reverse.

Em'brel seemed to see many of the things S'haar had. "It's like someone took Jack and made a movie about him! Except they made him younger, better looking, a better fighter, taller…"

Angela cut Em'brel's list short with an objection. "Hey, Jack is my brother, and I know him better than anyone! So I can definitively say they also made him more likable, more coordinated, and gave him a sexier accent!"

There was a bit of tension behind the good-natured ribbing. It was traditional to do this kind of thing in front of Jack so he could sputter indignantly in self-defense. Still, S'haar knew Jack would approve of being the butt of a joke if it meant the return of smiles and laughter to the house. Even if it was all a little forced. She smiled as she saw things from Jack's perspective once again. Her respect and fondness for him only seemed to grow as she noticed all the little things he regularly did that were only apparent now that he wasn't here to do them anymore.

There were so many small moments where a brief pause felt out of place because it would have typically been filled with some playful banter, encouragement, or insight that Jack would have thrown in seemingly without much thought. S'haar just wasn't as good at such things. Still, they were all doing their best.

The jovial feeling dimmed a little when one of those quiet moments went on a little too long. Finally, Em'brel broke the silence. "Still, for all his flaws, I wish Jack was here with us. He'd probably know just how to deal with Jack not being here right now."

Em'brels face scrunched up in confusion as even she tried to make sense of what she'd just said. S'haar cut her off before the younger argu'n could try and start offering a clarification. "I know just what you mean. I was just thinking of all the things he would do that we hardly noticed but had a profound effect on everything around him. However, all we can do now is continue on and hope that he finds his way back to us."

Em'brel looked a little somber as she replied. "Yeah, I know what you mean…but waiting is hard! I feel like I should be doing something right now! Or maybe ten things!"

S'haar nodded her understanding. "That is normal for anyone waiting for change, good or bad. Soldiers feel it before a battle, parents feel it before birth, even animals feel it before a storm. The worst thing you can do is exhaust yourself with worry before you ever get the chance to act."

S'haar sighed, speaking to herself as much as Em'brel as she continued. "For now, we stick to Jack's plan and move forward. We'll have to keep an eye out for any new problems or challenges that arise as we proceed."

Em'brel nodded her understanding, although she couldn't help but think that understanding and acting on that understanding were two very different things. Still, she'd do her best. She could almost hear Jack tell her that's all he'd ever ask.

~

Em'brel finished cleaning up and took a second shower for the day. There was something about warm water and solitude that brought peace of mind in stressful times. Although even that wasn't enough to quell all of her worries. She mentally repeated her new mantra to herself, *Just do your best!*

Toweling off, she noticed S'haar wasn't in the living room or their bedroom. There was only one other place Em'brel could think S'haar might be, and sure enough, she was in the med-bay.

Angela appeared in front of the girl and held a finger in front of her lips, telling Em'brel to be quiet, so as not to disturb S'haar. Slowing to a halt just shy of the room's entrance, Em'brel could hear S'haar's voice softly wafting out. She was talking to Jack. For just a moment, Em'brel's heart fluttered in hope before settling down with the realization that Angela would have certainly told her if Jack had woken.

Almost too faint to be heard, S'haar continued her one-sided conversation. "…and you should have seen Em'brel. She was so nervous when she spoke, but she had Lon'thul in the palm of her hand the whole time! Did you know he had a crush on her? Is that part of the reason you are always so protective of Em'brel around him? Anyway, Angela seems to think things are going well, all things considered. Still, I wish you were here to help. We all do. We're doing our best, but it would be so much easier with you at our side. Wherever you are, don't stop trying to find your way back, we need you… *I* need you…"

Em'brel backed away to give the two of them a bit more time alone together.

Angela watched as, after a little time passed, Em'brel returned, but this time her arms were filled entirely with blankets and pillows. Soon she'd set up a relatively comfortable bed for S'haar. In doing so, the young girl found there was no room left for anyone else. Em'brel returned to her own room with a shrug of her shoulders, though she was hardly alone. As her eyes started to close and her voice hinted at yawns to come, the young girl called out, "Angela, tell me a story."

Through her eyelids, Em'brel could see the gentle glow that meant Angela had materialized. Without opening her eyes, she turned her head to face the AI, a small smile of anticipation on her lips, and waited as any attentive listener would while waiting for the storyteller to pick an appropriate tale.

Angela knew the girl was mostly seeking company. She'd grown accustomed to S'haar's presence at night. In this instance, Angela was more than happy to oblige. "Alright, let me tell you the tale of an intelligent but mischievous human boy, his stuffed tiger and imaginary friend, and a few of the many adventures they went on together."

Em'brel snuggled down into her blankets in a manner so cute that one of Angela's processors simulated her heart skipping a beat. While she turned some of Jack's favorite childhood comics into a story worth listening to, Angela also kept an eye on Jack and S'haar. It would probably be a good idea to move Jack into a proper bedroom with the few pieces of medical equipment required to keep him stable. Otherwise, S'haar would probably camp out in the med-bay every night, but she supposed that was a concern for tomorrow.

Tonight, Angela simply enjoyed the small moments shared between herself and Em'brel, as well as Jack and S'haar.

The next morning, Em'brel had a bit of her morning cheer back. She wasn't exactly bouncing around the kitchen, but while she worked, she hummed a tune that seemed to lack any measurable rhyme or reason.

She made a bacon quiche to bring out and share with the workers while they all decided how to move forward.

When S'haar was finally drawn out of the med-bay by the wafting aromas, she looked better rested than she had the previous morning. Rather than letting her sit at the table like usual, Em'brel loaded S'haar's arms up with baskets filled with food, plates, and eating utensils. "It will be good for morale if the new camp leader goes and eats with the workers. Besides, there's a lot of work that needs to be done. As you pointed out, sitting around worrying about Jack won't help anyone, including Jack!"

Her voice quieted. "He's in the care of the best healer on the planet, and you can tell him all about your day tonight. It'll give you something to look forward to… Although, this time, I get a turn telling him about my day, too."

S'haar looked a little embarrassed about apparently being caught speaking to Jack last night, but it shortly faded after Em'brel mentioned wanting her own turn. After a moment, she nodded in agreement. "I think Jack would like that."

Em'brel's spirit was contagious, and S'haar couldn't help but feel her spirits further buoyed by the infectious smile the younger girl sported as she spoke. "I know he will! Now let's get going before the food gets cold!"

~

Em'brel's bravado started to fade as they approached the workers. It was easy to be bold in front of Jack, S'haar, and Angela, but being bold in front of a bunch of workers, who were now looking at the two of them expectantly, was completely different. Luckily, S'haar was more than up to the task and took charge.

As the food distribution was being guided by a suddenly subdued Em'brel, S'haar dove right into the discussion. "I'm sure Lon'thul has had a chance to tell you all about the current situation and our plans to move forward with this outpost. I'm sure you have many questions, but I want you to know I will honor Jack's promise to all of you. Anyone who wants to leave may do so, without reprisal, as soon as the roads melt enough to travel. You will be given plenty of supplies for the journey, including enough heating packs to safely make it back to the village."

S'haar looked around at the workers, who seemed more interested in the food than her speech. Only two met her eyes as she spoke, Fea'en and one of the junior woodworkers. Fea'en's eyes were calm and understanding. They didn't seem to harbor any discontent as far as S'haar could tell.

The junior workers, on the other hand… "I will be leaving. I didn't come out here to work with…" He paused as he spared a furtive glance to Fea'en, who returned his glance with an odd edge in her eyes before the worker turned back to S'haar, his voice suddenly a little less aggressive than a moment ago, "…with anyone other than Jack." He was practically mumbling by the end.

S'haar nodded. She wondered what the looks had meant but decided to let it go. She was simply happy they'd only lost one worker. Jack's plans would still be on track with the remaining workforce.

Instead, she nodded at the worker as she replied, "Alright. You are free to pass the remaining time however you wish. You will be fed and boarded until the snow melts. After that, I expect you not to stay longer than it will take you to prepare to travel back to the village."

The worker had seemed ready for a fight but instead just nodded and shrunk back to his sleeping area. S'haar turned her attention to the remaining workers. "To the rest of you, let's talk about our plans for the future. I want your input on how to make this all happen by the end of winter!"

Everyone was digging into their food with eager abandon while she spoke. Everyone except Tel'ron, who was staring intently at the knife and fork Em'brel had handed him with his food. "Alright, but first I have to ask, what are these made of? They are far too light for how sturdy they are! Is this another of Jack's alloys?!?"

Em'brel spoke up before she realized what she was doing. "Oh, these are made out of something called 'stainless steel'. It's similar to regular steel, but the iron content is lower, something like fifty percent, and the chromium is closer to thirty percent. It's not quite as strong or hard as traditional steel, but requires much less maintenance for day-to-day use."

Em'brel's voice faltered near the end when she noticed all eyes were now staring at her, each with different expressions. The woodworkers looked a little lost, but there was a touch more respect there than she'd seen before. Lon'thul looked proud and justified for some reason, but also seemed to glance over at Tel'ron with an odd look of worry. Tel'ron looked at the young girl as though she was the most beautiful thing he'd ever seen, before returning his gaze to the eating utensils as though they were holy artifacts. Finally, for her part, S'haar was simply beaming with pride and encouragement as she nodded approvingly at Em'brel.

For her part, Em'brel simply wanted to fade back into the background, forgotten except as a supplier of food. Sadly, it didn't look like that would happen anytime soon, as Telron started bombarding her with questions about the forging and shaping processes.

CHAPTER 30

Jack wasn't sure where he was at the moment. The best way to describe his location would be to call it 'nondescript'. There was no light, but he could see clearly. There was no ground, yet he was neither floating nor falling. It was the single most boring place he'd ever been.

At first, he tried struggling. Climbing, walking, running, and crawling all had the same effect, which is to say, nothing. After that failure, he tried focusing his mind to see if that would impact the world around him. It didn't. He tried yelling, waiting, challenging God, or whoever might be listening, and even giving up. It all had the same effect, nothing.

Once in a while, he'd hear Angela, S'haar, or Em'brel speaking to him, though their voices seemed distant. It was hard to focus his attention on their words. It was like his mind kept slipping through the words. He'd catch bits and pieces, but it was virtually impossible to put it together coherently. Still, he took comfort in their presence even if he couldn't see, feel, or understand them.

Eventually, they would leave, and he'd be alone again. Not that he blamed them, there was probably a lot to do now that he was stuck…wherever he was. That being said, Jack still looked forward to the times when their voices would return. Those were the best times this nondescript place had to offer.

He'd been sitting alone for a while when he heard S'haar's voice again. "Hello."

The voice was crystal clear, and Jack understood it perfectly, but his mind distorted the tone of her voice. It echoed through the void, somehow sounding both masculine and feminine.

Jack tried to relax and open his mind to better focus on her words when she spoke again. This time her voice had an edge of impatience to it. "Are you going to lay there and dream all day, or are you going to sit up and speak with your guest?"

That snapped Jack's eyes open. He sat up to stare at the argu'n standing before him. Looking at him/her/it, Jack would only describe his guest as *the* ideal argu'n. That's not to say that he/she/it was *Jack's* ideal version of an argu'n, but rather that the entity fit Plato's description of an abstract ideal of a physical object.

Plato once explained that a person could look at any tree and understand it to be a tree despite the variety in appearances. He argued that there must be an abstract ideal of every object that our minds would use as a template to recognize any physical object that fits within that template. For instance, a person can intuitively recognize the differences between plates, bowls, and cups despite each one appearing to be only slightly different from the others. By his own logic, the ideal version of any object couldn't physically exist because if it became real, it would become too constrained by reality to remain the ideal version of itself.

Despite that, before Jack stood the perfect ideal of an argu'n. The entity was stable and unchanging and yet seemed to shift from male to female, depending more on Jack's perception at the moment than any physical characteristic. When looking into the entity's face, he saw the faces of every argu'n he had ever known, and many more he'd never met, despite the face never changing in any tangible way.

Jack tilted his head to the side and scratched his hair as he spoke. "Huh, so the lack of input or interaction has finally broken my mind, and I've started hallucinating, *great...*"

The entity tilted its head to the side, mimicking Jack's as it responded. "I have memories going back eons before your ancestors learned to strap a rock onto a stick. But maybe you are right, and I only exist as a fractured portion of your mind. Perhaps when you finally die or wake up, I'll simply pop out of existence. Wouldn't that be interesting?"

Jack raised an eyebrow at the combination of amusement and patronization in his guest's voice. He crossed his arms as he retorted. "So, what are you supposed to be? A god of the argu'n? Which one are you? The god of light? Or maybe the god of war? What about the harvest, fertility, the seas, or maybe death? Stop me if I'm getting warm."

A warm, welcoming smile appeared on the mother's face as she beamed down at the child before her. "You are indeed very warm, child. I am the goddess of fertility!"

Leaning in closer, her smile shifted to a seductive smile, and her voice purred with longing for her lover, barely an icy whisper in his ear. "And the god of death..."

Jack leaned back a little to distance himself from him/her/it. He wasn't thrilled with the effect her voice had had on him. He responded with the most defensive weapon he had in his arsenal. A witty quip. "Goddess of life *and* death? Isn't that a conflict of interest?"

His guest summoned a chair that hadn't existed mere moments before out of the mist. It was the plainest chair Jack had ever seen, and yet when he/she/it sat in it, the chair became more regal than any throne could ever be. With a curious tilt of his/her/its head, his guest replied, slipping between mother and lover as it did. "What an amusing idea! How could life and death ever be in conflict with one another? They each only exist because of the other! Only within the light of life can death exist, and only in the shadow of death can life have meaning!"

Jack leaned forward, refusing to be so easily deflected. "And yet when you decide it's time, you reach out and take the lives of your 'children'. That doesn't seem very motherly to me!"

The old woman sitting before Jack had a kind and soft smile on her lips, and her voice spoke of countless fond memories with every syllable. "I have no need to take my children before their time. They all return to me eventually, and when they do, they bring the most wonderful stories with them! They tell me of love, hope, beauty, and passion! When I welcome them into my embrace, it is as a mother welcoming her children home. All that I receive is freely offered, and all that they have I freely give!"

Jack's eyes narrowed, and he pushed on once more. "So, what happens after you 'welcome them home'? What happens after death?"

The old man closed his eyes and shook his head as he replied. "That is not my tale to tell. Nor is it the reason for my visit."

The entity remained seated and looked at Jack, as though waiting patiently for a particularly slow student to catch up. Jack did not like being condescended to. "So, did you come all this way just to talk relative philosophy with me? Or did you have some other reason for your visit?"

The proud father pierced Jack with his gaze as he answered. "I came to get a measure of the man who caught the attention of one of my favorite daughters. You don't look like much. You're so small and frail, even now, you hang onto your life by the thinnest of threads. Tell me, what makes you think you deserve my daughter's affection?"

Of all the answers Jack had been expecting, that wasn't one. He sat back a little, thinking hard. Was this some kind of test? What happens when you give the god of life and death the wrong answer? Was there even a right answer? His mind was a whirlwind of possible solutions, analyzing and rejecting them all as he remained silent.

The deity seemed to grow impatient. "Despite my eternal nature, I am very busy and don't have all day to spend talking to some half-dead intruder in my realm. So tell me now, why do you deserve my daughter's affection?"

Jack felt tired. Tired of everything that happened since he landed, tired of this nondescript place, tired of being thrown to the whims of fate, and very tired of his 'guest' looking down on him. So when Jack answered, it wasn't with some well thought out and articulated response. Instead, he just threw out whatever thoughts occurred to him. "You want to know why I *deserve* S'haar's attention? I don't! Setting aside the whole stupidity contained within the idea of *deserving* anyone's affection, and believe me, I could tear that idea apart for hours before running out of material, I don't *deserve anything* from anyone."

The entity looked like it wanted to interject, but Jack rode roughshod over him/her/it, never giving his guest any chance to speak up. "No one does! We should accept what is offered with gratitude, not begrudge someone for not providing us something we decided they *owe* us! The whole idea behind your question is absurd!"

At this point, Jack realized he was standing very close to and looking up at an enormous, self-proclaimed god of death. Even with him/her/it seated, Jack was dwarfed by his 'guest', and started to wonder at the wisdom behind shouting at someone who could probably wipe him from existence with little to no effort. Biting back any further ranting, Jack looked at his feet as he spoke again. "Er… Sorry, I think I've been here too long, and I'm starting to go stir-crazy… I didn't mean…"

The mother looked down on Jack kindly as she cut him off. "You meant every word. You spoke with passion and courage, don't undo that by trying to back down now! I can see what my daughter sees in you…and that's what makes what I must do next all the more difficult." That last part was spoken by the father again, although it wasn't pride that filled his voice, but sorrow.

Looking down at Jack, his face became dark and grim as he took a measure of Jack's soul once more. "Not long ago, several of my sons were returned to me with their stories unfinished. They were sent by your hand. What do you say in defense of this act?"

This question hit Jack like a hammer blow to the gut. When he looked down, Jack could see the blood of the men he'd killed coating his hands. For a moment, he felt an overwhelming urge to wash them clean, but Jack knew this blood was the testament of the lives he'd taken and belonged where it was.

Jack closed his eyes and took a deep breath before he responded. As he spoke, he looked into the distance, the face of the last raider he'd killed still burned into his mind. "I deeply regret the loss of life. I don't think the blood I spilled will ever stop haunting my dreams, but I don't regret the decisions I made that day. You speak of stories cut short? What about S'haar's story? What about Em'brel's? I'm still haunted by the faces of the dead, but I would do it again if given a chance to live those moments over."

Jack looked up into the accuser's grim face and met the man's eyes as he spoke. "Are S'haar's and Em'brel's lives worth less than the raiders? Or is it purely a numbers game, where the majority of lives determine the correct course of action? If so, I reject your accusation! I fought for those who meant the most to me, as any man, woman, or child should! Anyone who says otherwise is either lying, deluded, or a monster!"

The deity was holding a sword now, one whose blade was longer than Jack was tall. He pointed at Jack accusingly with one hand and held the sword ready to strike with the other as he spoke. "And what of the future? Your very presence is upsetting the balance of my world. You bring conflict and war! Countless more of my children will have their stories cut short! Why should I suffer your presence on this land any longer?"

Jack looked into the eyes of the god of life and death and saw only himself looking back. He shook his head and heaved a sad, shallow laugh. "Well, I suppose that depends on you. If you are omniscient and can see all possible futures and *know* that removing me will lead to an objectively better future for your people, then go ahead and do whatever you have to do. However, if you are bound by the tides of time like the rest of us mere mortals and are only guessing at possible futures, then I reject your judgment again! Yes, this road may very well lead to war and conflict, and I'll be forced to take more lives to protect those I care for. You think I'm not aware of that? But it could lead to better food, medicine, and education as well! Probably a little of everything. Will the good outweigh the bad? I don't know! I can only do what most people do every day: try to do what's right, try to fix what I break, and try to learn from my mistakes! If that's not enough for you, too bad, because that's all I've got!"

Jack glared at the entity for a few moments in silence. He'd run out of bravery near the end of his rant and was now glaring out of fear that he'd open his mouth and have his voice reveal his uncertainty. His guest continued to stare down at the small man for a few more moments before sheathing his sword. "It's a shame you were born human. You would have made an excellent argu'n."

The deity was suddenly closer to S'haar's height, though Jack couldn't remember seeing her form change. She leaned in, and Jack felt the icy breath of the seductive visage of death once more. "Though, if you so chose when you die, I'll be happy to welcome you into my embrace. I'm certain we can find a place for you in the world to come."

Jack backed away, a shiver running along his spine. Though at the moment, he couldn't say if it was due to desire or fear.

At that moment, S'haar's voice cut through the haze, and Jack could hear her talking about her day. For the first time since he got here, he could clearly understand what she was saying. He also noticed a faint path had appeared, leading far into the distance, seeming to head into the direction of her voice.

Jack spared a glance back to his guest. Gesturing at the road, he asked the only question that occurred to him. "Did you do this?"

The mother looked back with an odd pride evident on her face. "Everything that happened here today was due to your own choices, not mine. Until you were sure about what path to walk, none could appear." She looked down at the road that seemed to stretch far past the nonexistent horizon. "It looks like you have quite a long walk. I'd get started, if I were you."

Jack stared at the entity a moment longer, trying to decide if he'd really been visited by the divine spirit of an argu'n god or if his mind created him/her/it out of desperation for some form of stimulation. Her enigmatic smile offered no answers, and Jack supposed that even if she provided any answers, he wouldn't be able to tell if those answers were any more real than the entity offering them.

In any event, when he blinked, he/she/it was gone. All that remained was Jack, the road, and S'haar's voice. Jack shrugged, turned, and started walking.

~

Angela knew she wasn't wrong about what she'd just witnessed but re-played the video of what had happened, just to be sure. Sure enough, Jack's index finger on his right hand had twitched. She quickly did a series of scans to see if there were any significant changes. While it seemed there might be some slight improvement, it was well within the margin of error. It wasn't likely that Jack was suddenly going to wake up, but still... Despite the lack of significant evidence, she felt her hope surge at the tiny movement.

As the night passed and the rest of the ship slept, Angela repeatedly played the video of Jack's finger twitching. She spoke to herself in a whisper, since everyone else within earshot was currently asleep. "Hurry back, you big nerd. We need you here, not lost in some weird dream."

Chapter 31

S'haar was in the middle of her daily tour of the camp. It was as uneventful as usual, so she allowed her mind to wander a little as she walked. Day by day, it always seemed like so little happened, but looking back now, she couldn't help but think of all that had changed since Jack had fallen into his coma. They had four buildings up now: a billet for the workers, a woodworking hall, a smithy, and a warehouse. At the moment, the buildings were mostly empty, but Angela insisted they build them, with the growth of the settlement in mind.

The billet was designed to sleep two to a room comfortably, but everyone currently had private rooms with at least a room or two between each worker. They were all situated around a large common room, which had a good-sized fire pit designed for cooking and storytelling.

The reluctant worker had left as soon as the snow melted. Lon'thul escorted him back to the village safely, made a report, and returned to continue in his role as the eyes and ears of the village, while also supplying plenty of fresh meat to earn his keep.

The woodworker's hall could comfortably fit double what it currently housed with no further additions, but a portion of the building was also set aside to store tools and materials. If they were to put up another building nearby for storage, they could easily fit even more workers.

Fea'en had made sure all the stations were built to perfection. She'd taken her charges to task on more than one occasion when she found their work sub-par. S'haar honestly couldn't tell the difference between the quality work and the rejected attempts, but Angela had told her, "That's what delegating is all about. You get the best person for the job, put them in charge, then let them do their job. If you have quality workers, a manager's job is more about seeing to it that their needs are met than babysitting."

The smithy felt empty since only one metal worker was present. For want of company, Tel'ron often spent his days working in the woodworker's hall. He and the woodworkers had gotten to know each other pretty well over the last few weeks. While the usual rivalry between woodworkers and smiths was present, it was mostly limited to good-natured fun in their small group.

However, if something needed any serious work done, Tel'ron was more than happy to utilize the new facilities. The smelters were located outdoors, with a loose tent-like covering overhead, but they had a few good forges on the inside and an anvil made out of wrought iron, with a steel face. Most of the anvils back at the village were currently made out of bronze, so this was a significant improvement. His eyes had practically leaped out of his skull when Em'brel told him of her plans for several such anvils, though they still only had the one for the time being.

It had taken Em'brel and Angela a bit of work to refit the mining suit for Em'brel to use, and even then, the girl had been timid in its use at first. But as she'd grown more and more accustomed to it, the work also went smoother, though she still wasn't as fast as Jack had been. Angela said it had something to do with the suit requiring sustained exertion more than raw strength, probably because it had been designed with humans in mind. Still, they were mining iron ore much faster than any argu'n would typically have been able to.

S'haar smiled to herself as she thought of Em'brel. The girl's intelligence, courage, timidness, and natural beauty had endeared her to the entire camp and had created a bit of a rivalry between the only two boys of appropriate age. Tel'ron and Lon'thul were both falling over themselves to get Em'brel's attention, though as far as S'haar was aware, things hadn't progressed much past that point. They'd all been too busy, and the boys feared S'haar's or Fea'en's wrath if they were found slacking. So it was mostly limited to boasting around the campfire and trying to be the first to think of a new compliment for Em'brel each day.

As S'haar exited the smithy, Fea'en was waiting to address the new concern for the day. The older woodworker's arms were crossed in her typical stoic manner, though S'haar knew her well enough by now to know there was no hostility in her stance, and any irritation she radiated was directed at whatever got in the way of her work, rather than any nearby person. Her voice was, as always, just as gravely and stoic as her stance. "Ground's too frozen to keep digging the palisade. However, we got the posts for the northern guard tower sunk, so we could keep working on that, or we could get started shaping the wood for the guardhouse that'll go near the gate. Your call."

S'haar thought for a moment before turning back to the master woodworker. "The guard tower is more important to get up quickly. If the guardhouse isn't up come spring, the guards will just have to set up a temporary station near the gate."

Fea'en nodded her understanding. "Makes sense. Give me a bit, and I'll let you know what we'll need in order to finish it up." Following that, Fea'en was off to seek out Em'brel so they could take another look at the plans the girl and the 'dragon' had drawn up together.

S'haar was pretty sure more wood was near the top of the list. They already had some shaped lumber ready to go, but it was best to split the woodworkers into two teams, one prepping the new wood and the other doing the construction. Besides, that meant S'haar got to use the chainsaw again. Once again, she wasn't quite as fast as Jack had been since its use also seemed to require endurance rather than brawn, but she could definitely understand why Jack always seemed to be having so much fun while he used it. Eventually, her arms would feel ready to drop, and it wasn't as much fun anymore, but that first tree was always a rush. She smiled sadly to herself, imagining the wild grin Jack had plastered on his face the first time he showed her the chainsaw at work.

With a last look around the camp, S'haar's smile turned from sad to content. Everyone was where they should be, and the work was progressing smoothly. Well, one person was missing, but S'haar knew Em'brel and Fea'en were more than up to the task of keeping the missing individual on task.

~

Em'brel was walking out of the cave with the rolled-up plans for the guard tower. Sure enough, Lon'thul was waiting for her near the entrance of the cave. He looked at her with his large, innocent eyes before speaking. "Want me to carry those for you?"

Em'brel looked at him with her head tilted to one side as she kept walking. "As always, I appreciate the offer, but I'm perfectly capable of carrying some parchment that barely weighs a couple of pounds. Besides, don't you have some hunting to do?"

Lon'thul shook his head. "Nah, we've got enough meat stored up that we should probably eat from our reserves for a few more days before I go out again. We wouldn't want unused meat spoiling. Today I'm supposed to be working on digging out the well some more, though I don't know why you need it to be so large."

Em'brel shifted her load and picked up her pace a little, forcing Lon'thul to adjust his own speed to keep up as she spoke. "I told you, we're not building this camp to accommodate the people here now, or even a couple months from now, we're designing it to accommodate the number of people who might be here a year from now! If your village is anything like my own, it's laid out in an ever-increasing sprawl that slowly expands as more people need more housing. What if we planned on the need to expand from the beginning? What if we organized everything with an eventual larger population in mind? That's what we're trying to do, here and now."

Lon'thul nodded his understanding. Once he'd adjusted his speed, he was able to keep up with Em'brel due to his long stride, but he was still having to breathe a little heavier to speak while walking at this pace. Few men in the village could keep up with Lon'thul's pace, and he wondered where a noble like Em'brel had gotten the endurance to set this kind of pace. Still, he was determined to show as little discomfort as he could while he spoke. "You make a good point, but it seems like it would just be easier to dig a second well when we need one. We'd already be done by now if this were a normal well."

Em'brel came to a halt as she shifted the scrolls to one arm so she could open the door to the woodworker's hall. She was about to reply when Fea'en's familiar gravelly voice cut in from behind the two of them. "I'm curious, boy, how do you plan on impressing the girl by complaining about the well *she* designed, rather than making it a reality, the way Tel'ron is doing right now?"

Lon'thul froze mid-step, and Em'brel could practically hear the thoughts running through his head. His motivation had simply been to talk with Em'brel a little longer. He hadn't meant to diminish Em'brel's design. Now he had to decide between taking the time to defend his intentions or going and getting to work, so Tel'ron didn't get all the credit. He was caught in what Angela had once described as a 'catch 22'. It was a phrase named after a famous human book, and it meant that there was no right answer.

Finally, with a rueful smile, Lon'thul bowed his head in apology to Fea'en. "You're right. I'm sorry. I'll get to work right now." Turning to Em'brel, he added, "I can't wait to see what you make for lunch. I'm sure I'll work up quite the appetite making your vision a reality!"

With a wave, he ran off. Em'brel turned to Fea'en with a raised eye ridge. "I wish you all wouldn't give him such a hard time. Lon'thul has been working as hard as anyone else here."

Fea'en tilted her own head as she watched the boy leave. "He's a good kid. With a bit of luck, he might even turn out to be a good man. Right now, he's still a little too naive, and sometimes he needs a bit of a kick in the rear to get him moving in the right direction. Despite taking the lives of so many animals, he still doesn't realize how cruel and uncaring the world we live in can be, and how quickly things can go wrong if we aren't prepared."

Em'brel grew quiet as Fea'en's words sunk in. She knew what the woman meant. That was a lesson with which Em'brel was all too familiar. Some days it was all she could do to put a smile on her face when going out to face the same world that had taken both her father and Jack from her. Then she remembered something Jack had once told her when she asked how he'd dealt with his own loss years ago. "You have to set goals for yourself. Not something far-fetched or obscure like 'I want to be wealthy' or 'I want to be happy'. No, instead, you set realistic, achievable goals. For instance, when I got here, I needed to get a local guide, check. I needed to get to the village and establish a rapport with the people there, check. I needed a sled and then a wagon, check, check."

Em'brel had nodded but felt like he was asking the impossible. However, Jack wasn't done. "Some days, the bad days, that can be too big a goal to handle. Instead, you set smaller goals just to keep you moving. Something like, 'I'm going to get out of bed and take a shower,' or 'I'm going to clean my room,' etc. Then there are the terrible days, days where an hour away is just too far. Those days your goals can be as simple as, 'I'm going to take another step,' or 'I'm going to sit up'. The key is to keep moving forward. No matter how slow or small your progress is, as long as you move forward, you're moving in the right direction."

Em'brel nodded her head to the Jack in her mind and pushed open the door to the woodworker's hall. At the memory of Jack and his comforting smile, her own smile had returned, and she got started on her next goal. "Ok, I've got the plans for the guard towers right here. Let's get them laid out on the table and figure out what our first step should be!"

Fea'en followed the younger girl inside. At first, she'd just been humoring the girl when she'd presented her plans for the first building after Em'brel had taken over where Jack had left off. However, Fea'en had quickly discovered the girl really knew what she was talking about and listened intently as she described what she wanted.

Looking at the plans, Fea'en offered a few recommendations or corrections based on her own expertise, and Em'brel incorporated them into her plans without hesitation.

Fea'en couldn't help but appreciate how nice it was to work with someone who knew what they wanted, while also respecting an expert's advice. In her experience, those two things never existed in the same job at the same time. Initially, Fea'en had only come out here to get things started in the camp and make sure her workers were safe, but between the people running the place and how comfortable the living conditions were, she was beginning to think of making the move permanent.

~

Angela rode along with S'haar and Em'brel as they worked throughout the day. She also kept an eye on the surrounding wildlife and weather, focusing on anything else that could further threaten her family.

All this was done while a small portion of her attention remained focused on Jack. She'd cataloged every twitch, murmur, and even changes in breathing and heart rate. The changes were all subtle, but it was enough to indicate to her there was some activity going on in his mind, and she held onto the hope that gave her the same way a drowning man might hold onto a life preserver tossed his way.

She tried never to let on to the girls how scared she was of losing Jack. They had more than enough worries of their own, and she could tell they used her hopeful demeanor as a source of strength. She hadn't really explained how bad Jack's coma was, but she could tell, as time went on, they were starting to suspect the truth.

Based on his lack of response to stimuli after the first twenty-four hours, Jack's likelihood of waking up dropped to something like thirteen percent. As the days passed and he remained unresponsive, his odds continued to fall. Most coma patients would either wake up in under five weeks or stay asleep for the rest of their lives. Every day dragged them closer to that deadline, and Jack remained unresponsive.

Angela ran through the test again, just like she did twice every day.

First, she tested for any response to verbal stimulation. "How are you doing today, Jack? Can you hear me? If so, can you open your eyes?"

No response.

Second, using a robotic arm set up next to his bed, she applied pressure to the nail on his index finger for ten seconds. Enough to be described as an 'uncomfortable pressure' but not enough to do any damage.

One.
Two.
Three.
Four.
Five.
Six.
Seven.
Eight.
Nine.
Ten...
No response.

Third, she applied the trapezius pinch. It is a pinch applied next to the patient's neck to stimulate pain but isn't enough to cause any real damage. She squeezed for ten seconds.

One.
Two.
Three.
Four.
Five.
Six.

Seven.

Eight.

Nine.

Jack's elbow slowly bent, and his arm came across his body. Angela was so stunned, she forgot to release her grip for one-tenth of a second. That was clearly abnormal flexation, but still a response to pain. That made his score five out of a possible fifteen. It was still a low score, but it was also the highest he'd scored since he was first brought in by Em'brel.

~

As Jack continued walking along the road in the middle of nowhere, he heard Angela's usual questions. Sure, she'd talk to him throughout the day, but every so often, she went through this same pattern of questions. Jack tried to shout out his responses, but nothing seemed to penetrate the gloom of the space he found himself in. But this time, shortly after the usual questions and his shouted response, his shoulder started hurting. Jack's arm shot up to his shoulder as he swore under his breath.

That's when he heard Angela's surprised voice. "You…you felt that? Jack, can you hear me? If you can, you better get your butt back here! We're running out of time!"

Jack looked down the road, stretching out in front of him, and picked up his pace a little. He still had a long way to go, but he finally felt like he was making progress.

Chapter 32

Once again, S'haar was standing in the recently completed guard tower, looking out over the slowly expanding wall. For once, everything was going according to plan. At this rate, the palisade would be up well before spring. It was a simple design of mid-sized trunks placed firmly together to allow virtually no space between posts. The tops of the logs were sharpened to a point to make climbing them a little extra awkward. Additionally, a walkway was placed near the top of the wall along the inside. This gave potential guards a variety of vantage points, in addition to those offered by the towers that would be spaced every few hundred meters.

Em'brel's well was also nearly complete. The hole had been dug, then lined with stones, and it maintained more than an adequate water level at all times. It had a raised wall around the outside, and the top was capped off to prevent wildlife from falling inside and contaminating the water. She was working with both Fea'en and Tel'ron to design a system for more easily lifting the water out of the well than the usual bucket on a rope that people would haul up by hand.

This well would use some sort of 'pulley' system attached to a hand crank that apparently dramatically reduced the water bucket's weight, allowing for more water to be drawn up at a time. It was going to have four such systems lined up around the outside. Each of these was going to have a locking mechanism. When engaged, it would prevent the buckets from falling further than an eighth of the crank and allow the bucket to be locked at the top.

The design was complicated enough that it took a few tries to explain to Tel'ron and Fea'en what Em'brel was asking for, but now the two crafters were working together to make Em'brel's idea functional.

There was a bit of trial and error. It took two days and a few scrapped parts to get one side up and running. However, now that the first draw system was in place, the workers were confident they could put the next three together in far less time than the first had taken.

Meanwhile, Fea'en's little speech to Lon'thul a few days ago had caused the youth to push himself further and faster when it came to bringing Em'brel's ideas to life. For the first time he could remember, hunting was a secondary priority. Well, it would have if Em'brel didn't depend on him bringing home meat so she could cook up one of her popular dishes. When he wasn't on the hunt, Lon'thul was almost always found asking what else he could help with. He threw himself into each task with a vigor that only abated when he was able to spend time talking with Em'brel.

Not to be outdone, Tel'ron's work was beginning to far outshine his years of experience. He crafted each tool or component as though they were his personal gift to Em'brel, and his dedication to his craft showed through in the results. Angela even commented that "Old Mar'kon will have to watch his back, or this young pup might surpass him!"

Now, one of the most significant issues slowing them down was getting enough lumber. Because of that, S'haar was out using the chainsaw almost daily to meet the workers' needs. The more she used the chainsaw, the easier it became, but she marveled at the fact that she still wasn't as productive as Jack had been. It was easy to look down on humans being small and weak, but there was something to humans that deserved a certain amount of respect.

The thought of Jack brought a frown of concern to S'haar's face. He was showing signs of progress, but it seemed to be taking an agonizingly long time. The workers had all stopped asking about Jack, and S'haar had a distinct impression that they just assumed he was dead. As far as the workers were concerned, she'd been running the camp longer than he had been. How would they react to the day Jack woke up and took back over?

S'haar shook her head. These were concerns for another time and place. For now, the woodworker whose turn it was to help gather wood had just walked up to the base of the tower and was now waiting on S'haar. She had more trees to cut to help supply the camp's needs, and she'd have plenty of time to worry about Jack tonight as she gave him her report on the day's progress.

It was always painful to look at Jack's unmoving face as she spoke to him at night, but there was something oddly comforting about holding his hand and feeling his warmth radiating into her own as she spoke. As long as that warmth flowed, Jack lived, and that was good enough for S'haar…for now.

After that, S'haar would settle down in the bedroll she'd made on the ground beside Jack's bed. If Jack woke up in the middle of the night, his bodyguard was going to be there and ready to help in any way he needed.

Em'brel also took her turns talking to Jack, though her conversations were most often centered around whatever problems she was dealing with. The subjects would range from logistical issues about her designs for the camp to emotional problems weighing her down at the time. She'd told S'haar that imagining what Jack might say in response to her issues often led Em'brel to conclusions she might never have come to on her own.

S'haar could understand that. It had been weeks, but she could still sometimes hear Jack's quips in the silent moments of a conversation. Even now, she could imagine that stupid grin he'd have on his face before saying something to get a reaction out of her. It had taken her a while to realize he *enjoyed* pushing her to the point she'd give him a light smack in response to some smart remark. He said it meant he'd 'won' that round of verbal sparring, whatever *that* meant.

Her frown now replaced with a smile of her own, S'haar jerked her head toward the forest just past the wall as she spoke to the woodworker. "Let's get to work!"

~

Em'brel was cooking a large pot of stew in the worker's billet. This batch of smoked meat was a bit on the tough side and needed a little extra attention to make it palatable. She'd mixed in a few roots and tubers that Lon'thul had gathered for her during his hunting forays into the forest. While she worked, Angela played a little tune over her headband, and Em'brel was dancing in place while humming to herself as she chopped up the ingredients.

Em'brel never heard S'haar and the woodworker enter and continued to hum and dance, until a sneeze from behind her made her freeze.

Em'brel stayed utterly motionless for a few moments, hoping the sound had just been some weird trick of the wind finding a crack in the doorframe, but she knew she was deluding herself. She turned around extra slowly, hoping not to draw attention to herself as she did so, but found her efforts in vain as two pairs of eyes were now staring at her. The eyes were accompanied by a couple of grinning faces that were obviously enjoying the show, at Em'brels expense.

Em'brel glared at the pair that were currently shedding sawdust with every movement. "Look at you two! You're filthy! Go outside and dust yourselves off before you ruin my stew!"

S'haar's grin only grew a little wider in response. "Aw, don't get mad because we caught your cute little show! Besides, aren't I the one in charge of this camp at the moment? Who gave you the authority to order me out of here?"

Em'brel bared her teeth and shook her tendrils in a half-joking threat display before speaking. "I'm the cook! And if you want this delicious stew for dinner, rather than some stale bread and water, you'll do as I say! NOW GO CLEAN YOURSELVES OFF BEFORE COMING BACK INTO MY KITCHEN!"

The worker, Jan'kul, if Em'brel remembered correctly, looked back and forth between the two women, wondering just how much trouble he would get in merely by being present to witness such a spectacle. The usually shy and docile Em'brel was now advancing on the nearly unflappable S'haar with a wooden spoon, and S'haar was *backing down*! Both hands were held up as the unstoppable S'haar *surrendered* to the tiny Em'brel. "Ok, ok, you win! I'll go dust off. Just put away the spoon!"

As S'haar walked out the door, Jan'kul could hear S'haar mutter to herself. "I have this whole camp dropped in my lap, and I run the thing without any complaint, but do I get any respect? No! Instead, I get chased away from dinner by a wooden spoon and the threat of stale bread..." Her tone *seemed* to be at least half-joking, but he wasn't sure.

Jan'kul was now doing his best to not attract attention by remaining completely motionless. Sadly, it didn't work. Em'brel's gaze slowly shifted to him before she broke out in the cutest grin he'd ever seen. "Sorry about that. I hope we didn't scare you too much. Though I *would* appreciate it if you'd go dust off also."

He just gawked in wonder at the strange little woman who had gone from terrifying warrior of legend to a cute little girl just barely over his daughter's age in the blink of an eye. It took his brain a moment to catch up with the shift, but once he did, he relaxed as he responded to the now impossibly cute eyes innocently looking up at him."Uhh… Yeah, no problem. I'll be right back!"

As soon as he walked out and the door shut, Em'brel could hear the laughter shared between S'haar and Jan'kul. The diminutive chef reluctantly went back to her cooking. As she worked, she spoke in an exasperated voice to Angela. "Why didn't you warn me people were coming in? They caught me *DANCING!*"

Angela's voice sounded a little too innocent as she responded. "Would you believe I got too caught up in the music and dancing and didn't notice?"

Em'brel was a little over-enthusiastic as she started pasting the root she would add to the stew to thicken the mixture. She splattered the wall and herself liberally as she worked out her embarrassment. "No, I don't believe that! You are far too aware of our surroundings to miss a little thing like that, especially since I know you happen to be riding along with S'haar in her headset, as well!"

Angela's voice took on a slightly apologetic tone. "Ok, how about, 'You looked so cute doing your little dance I had to share it with someone?' That much cuteness was not meant for one AI alone!"

Em'brel grumped at the AI while she worked. "Well, next time, give me a warning, or else I'll…I'll…"

Angela's voice was now confident of victory. "Or you'll what? You can't threaten me with a spoon or stale bread the way you did with S'haar!" It was apparent that Angela thought she was untouchable.

Em'brel huffed indignantly before pulling out the most dire threat she could think of. "Or else I'll learn to control my excitement like a proper *LADY,* instead of joining you by hopping up and down in celebration!"

Angela was quiet a moment before her defeated voice responded. "You win…on the provision that you NEVER use such a diabolically evil threat on me again! That just wasn't fair!"

Em'brel's mood was considerably brighter, now that she had gotten one up on all the offending parties in the little debacle that shall never be spoken of again. As she started chopping up the root to go in the pot, Em'brel was back to humming and swaying her hips as she worked.

S'haar was holding Jack's hand and speaking with laughter in her voice. "And then she threatened me with a spoon! A STUPID WOODEN SPOON! The look on Jan'kul's face was priceless!"

S'haar had to close her eyes and shake her head for a moment at the memory. When she opened her eyes again, it took her a moment to realize that Jack's eyes were open as well, and he was looking right at her.

S'haar leapt forward, pulling Jack into a crushing embrace. Tears were flowing freely as she babbled. "You're awake! You've come back to us! ANGELA! EM'BREL! COME QUICK, JACK'S AWAKE!"

S'haar heard the thunder of Em'brel's approaching footsteps and saw the glow of Angela's avatar, but her world was focused entirely on Jack. She studied Jack's face intently and realized very quickly…something was wrong.

Aside from his eyes, Jack's expression was altogether unchanged. Even those looked a bit wrong, as though they were looking toward her, but not *at* her.

She gripped his hand tightly as she begged, "Please, Jack, say something! Say anything! Speak to me!"

Em'brel had burst into the room, ready to tackle Jack, but she stopped short when she heard the desperation in S'haar's voice. Jack's eyes were unfocused. The entire room held its breath after S'haar's plea. S'haar was just giving into tears, born of the kind of devastation brought on by crushed hope, when Jack's voice pierced the silence of the house for the first time in weeks.

His voice was cracked, halting, and barely above a whisper, but everyone was so silent and attentive that all three women heard him as clear as day. "This…mountain…is…so…tall,"

Jack paused and took a deep breath before continuing a moment later. "…and… …the… wind…is…so… … …cold…"

Following that, Jack's eyes closed again, and what little strain he seemed to be putting on his body seemed to ease out of him as he fell back into his relaxed pose. Jack was asleep once more.

S'haar turned her tear-stained face toward Angela. "What…what was that? What does it mean?"

Angela couldn't keep the emotion from her voice despite nearly overheating a few processors in her attempt to do so. "It means there's real hope now! It means he's finally making real progress!"

~

Jack looked at the mountain currently standing before him. The wind coming off it was so cold, it stung his face, and he could already feel his fingers ache in anticipation of what lay ahead.

The road he had been following disappeared into the mountain, and he could hear S'haar's voice coming from above the peak. "This…is going to suck. I've never been particularly interested in rock climbing…or heights…"

Jack cracked his knuckles, stretched his neck, rotated his arms in their sockets, and failing to think of anything else he could do to psych himself up (not that any of those had worked), he grabbed hold of his first handful of rock and pulled himself up, grumbling under his breath the whole time. "Come on, Jack. You fly spaceships, IN SPACE! You're not gonna let a little thing like a fear of heights stop you now, are you?"

He'd made it up about ten feet before looking down. His vision spun for a moment, and he pulled himself tight against the rock he was holding onto with very white knuckles. He usually wasn't this bad until getting at least three or four stories off the ground (Angela had to handle most takeoffs or landings for this reason), but something about a perilous handhold on an untested rock wall made everything worse.

Finally, he forced his muscles to relax, and he reached up to the next handhold he could find. "This…is going to be a long climb."

~

Angela was finishing her explanation. "So as he starts to come out of his coma, he'll 'wake up' like he just did more often. Eventually, he may even seem to fully wake up before slipping back into the coma, but that's all normal."

Em'brel was hugging S'haar. She was bawling her eyes out, but they were happy tears. Even if he hadn't made any sense, Jack had spoken again. The younger girl had almost given up on ever hearing Jack's voice again, but now her hope was renewed and burning brightly! At this moment, she felt like she could fly!

It took a moment for S'haar and Em'brel to realize that Angela was standing very quietly. The small celebration in front of her seemed forgotten as she tilted her head to one side as though listening to something. When she spoke, the worry was evident in her voice. "S'haar, go and warn the workers. We've got a cold front moving in. It's going to be far colder than anything I've seen on this planet before now!"

Chapter 33

S'haar looked to Angela, her eyes wide with fear. "How long do we have before the cold hits?"

Angela was still looking off into empty space. It was as though she was listening to a distant conversation. "Well, it looks like it's going to hit in two waves. This evening the temperature will drop about ten degrees further than we've seen recently and then plateau and stay steady through the night. Then a second cold front will hit roughly around noon, the temperature will continue falling the rest of the day and well into the night. What's worse is the fact that I'm not sure how long this is going to last. I'd need some sort of weather satellite to give a reasonable estimate, and that's simply beyond our grasp at the moment."

S'haar's ears pulled back slightly as she bared her teeth at the prospect. "It's a deep freeze, then. We haven't seen one of those in years. I need to go speak to the workers immediately. Em'brel, you and Angela work out a plan for what to do if it gets too cold or lasts too long and we have to bring the workers inside the caves, or even into our home."

Em'brel's expression had been starting to shift to a look of panic, but S'haar's quick assessment and decisions were enough to refocus her mind and bring her back to the here and now. "Uh, yes. We'll need sleeping arrangements and something to keep people's minds off trouble or boredom. The last thing we need is some kind of fight breaking out because of high stress…"

Em'brel was off in her own little world, thinking as she walked out of the room. S'haar gave Jack's hands one last squeeze. "I've got to go take care of some things. I'll be back." Then she stood up and brushed herself off as she thought while walking.

Angela looked uncharacteristically stoic as she floated beside S'haar. "So, you've encountered events like this before? How long do they usually last?"

"If we're lucky, days." S'haar's expression made it clear she wasn't feeling particularly lucky.

The AI seemed almost too afraid to probe further but persisted regardless. "And if we're not lucky?"

S'haar stopped and thought back to the last deep freeze she'd encountered while in the guard. They'd lost more than one in ten villagers to the cold that year. She still remembered the pile of bodies they had to burn after the freeze passed. The smell was one she had hoped never to experience again. "Weeks."

S'haar closed her eyes and visibly calmed herself a moment before turning and speaking to Angela. "Do we have a fresh supply of heating packs ready? If what you say is accurate, we're going to need to do some preparation work before the real cold hits tomorrow, and it's already going to be dangerously cold tonight while we work."

Angela nodded. "I've always got a backup batch primed in case of an emergency. Now seems like just the occasion I've been preparing for!'

~

After loading up the sled with a fresh batch of packs, S'haar was on her way to the worker's billet. As she approached the mouth of the cave, the wind cut at her face like knives. The heating packs in her coat kept her temperature high enough that she wasn't in any immediate danger of shutting down due to cold, but she knew that long enough exposure would result in frost damage to her extremities.

As she barged into the billet, S'haar saw most of the workers had already headed off to their rooms to get some rest for the next day. The only two left sitting by the campfire were Lon'thul and Tel'ron. They seemed to be playing a popular tavern game involving bone dice, but it was now forgotten as they looked up in surprise at the intrusion.

Lon'thul was just opening his mouth to say something when S'haar cut him off. "We've got a deep freeze coming. It's going to get cold tonight and colder tomorrow. Get everyone up. We need to get some preparations completed before it gets too cold to work!"

Lon'thul froze in shock for just a moment, but Tel'ron started moving as soon as the words 'deep freeze' had left S'haar's mouth. Lon'thul's surprise didn't last long, and he was on his feet right behind the other argu'n. The two of them were pounding on the other workers' doors while S'haar unloaded the fresh heating packs into the common area.

At first, everyone had been in various stages of wakefulness, muttering a variety of uncomplimentary phrases directed at those responsible for waking them. However, the sleepiness was rapidly replaced by alertness as S'haar explained the situation.

Fea'en was quick to begin issuing orders to the other workers. "Alright, we've got a stockpile of wood out there. We need to get it cut up into firewood immediately. We have to gather any supplies we'll need and store them in the billet with us. That includes food, water, extra hides, and tools to clear snow." As she listed each item, she pointed to a different worker. When they were picked out, they each got their coats on and ran around in the kind of chaotic order that can only exist when each person knows their task and is highly motivated to get it done as quickly as possible.

As the sun crested the horizon, everyone was struggling to stay on their feet. They'd already done a full day's labor before they'd gotten the news of the deep freeze, and things were further complicated by the icy winds preceding the cold front. Still, this kind of heads up was more than they'd usually get, so they were all determined to make every moment they count.

Even with their heated coats, the workers had to periodically gather around the fire to warm their extremities. As S'haar predicted, the coats prevented their metabolic systems from shutting down due to cold, but no one wanted to lose a limb to frostbite if it could be avoided. At some point in the night, Em'brel showed up to cook a large batch of a hearty stew, and the warming breaks quickly turned into late-night meal breaks as well.

Eventually, they adopted a rotation where the pair finishing their food would wake and replace the two who'd come in before them to briefly fall asleep sitting by the fire. The two now 'refreshed' workers would find the next pair who'd been out the longest and send them in to get food. It was always easy to spot the pair who'd been out the longest between warming breaks because they were often nearly frozen in place, lethargically staring off into the distance.

The workers had elected to temporarily surrender their rooms for storage, filling them with food, wood, and any other supplies they needed. The area around the cooking fire had been turned into a general living space, filled with furs and blankets so everyone could stay as close to the fire as possible. It wasn't the most comfortable or enjoyable of living conditions, but the increased safety of all concerned was more than enough to put an end to any complaints before they began.

Soon enough, everything that could be done had been done, and they'd finished before the second drop in temperature. S'haar gathered all the workers into the common area to speak to them one last time before they all collapsed into slumber for the next day or two.

Looking around at everyone present, S'haar could tell they were all at their limit, so she decided to keep everything brief. "Ok, you all know how bad this can get, but thanks to the early warning the dragon was able to give us, the heated coats that let us work through the night, and the hard work you all put in, we're better prepared for this than we've ever been. We've done all we can. Now we just have to ride it out. If, for some reason, this lasts too long or gets too cold, we can always have everyone fall back into the caves. For now, Em'brel and I will return to rest and speak with the dragon and see what else we can do to ensure everyone's safety, but for once, I think that we'll get through this without any loss of life or limb."

The workers' cheer was surprisingly hearty, given that most of them looked ready to collapse where they stood. Unsurprisingly, Lon'thul cheered the loudest, and everyone took a little encouragement at the exuberance of his youth. When S'haar left them, she noticed how this was the first time she could recall that a deep freeze was met with hope rather than despair.

As S'haar and Em'brel walked back through the cold to the cave, she realized the wind had changed from painful to nearly unbearable. The air felt as if it cut at her lungs, and she resolved to ask Angela what else they could do to make the journey from the cave to the billet less dangerous, if it should come to that.

Once Angela had detected her two argu'n returning to the ship, she'd bumped up the temperature in the ship. The looks on their faces and the sluggish halting nature of their movements made it apparent just how exhausted they were, and she kept her questions mercifully brief. "Is everyone safe? Were you able to finish your preparations? Is there anything else I can do to help right now?"

The answers came in the form of two assenting grunts and a vague nodding of the head in response to the first two questions. The third question was met with a slightly different grunt that Angela could only interpret as: "Not at the moment, thank you, we need some rest first. We'll talk later." Although she might have read a little more into the grunt than S'haar had actually intended to express.

Em'brel and S'haar both practically sleepwalked into Jack's room and seemed determined to check for themselves that there were no further developments with Jack. Content that Jack still seemed as safe as ever, Em'brel collapsed into S'haar's sleeping pad beside the bed. S'haar looked at the girl briefly before shrugging and crawling into bed beside Jack. She didn't have the energy to worry about potential awkwardness, impropriety, or anyone else's opinions. In the blink of an eye, both women were dead to the world. Their dreams became a confusing mess involving Jack, the deep freeze, and an odd combination of regrets of the past and concerns about the future.

~

Jack's arms felt as though they were on fire, and the ledge above him that he was hoping to use as a resting point seemed impossibly far away. As he pulled himself up with his left hand, his grip slipped. There was a heart-wrenching moment where the world seemed to drop out from under him as his stomach jumped up into his throat. Time seemed to slow to a crawl as Jack analyzed every surface in front of him. Not seeing anything he could save himself with, he closed his eyes and threw his hands forward in desperation as the distance between his chest and the rock wall turned into an inch, then a couple of inches, and far too quickly several inches.

His movement was suddenly arrested as he found a grip that he hadn't seen a moment ago. Opening his eyes slowly, he was surprised to see a perfect handhold that he could swear hadn't been there before. He closed his eyes and told himself to stop worrying about impossible handholds, and instead to focus on getting to that ledge.

It was weird. Jack felt no heartbeat in this place, but he could still feel a surge of adrenaline following his near-death experience. Again not wanting to waste energy on unnecessary questions, Jack reached up to the next handhold and pulled himself up.

Before long, Jack was catching his breath on the ledge. A while ago he'd stopped wondering about needing to breathe even though he didn't have a heartbeat. He was starting to suspect it had something to do with his own established expectations. That thought led him to consider another thing that seemed off about this place. In hindsight, all his experiences seemed to have passed impossibly quickly, but time seemed to slow to a crawl while experiencing the moment. Throughout his journey, Jack had never stopped to eat, drink, or sleep. It was almost as if the rules of this place only half-heartedly followed the rules of reality. Or perhaps more accurately, Jack's perception of reality.

Jack shrugged and put the concerns out of his mind. Whether this was a dream or a delusion, trying to understand this place would only be an effort in futility, needlessly slowing him down.

Jack looked up and noticed the top of the mountain seemed just as far as it had appeared at the start of his climb hours ago. Or had it been days now? Shaking his head to keep himself from getting lost, contemplating the fuzzy nature of time here, Jack decided he needed to get an idea of how much progress he'd made so far.

Despite his better judgment, Jack carefully looked over the side of the ledge to see how far he'd climbed. Preparing himself for a dizzying drop into infinity, he was surprised when he saw the ground only about ten feet below him. Somehow, despite climbing from one ledge to another, over and over for what had seemed like hours if not days, he'd made absolutely no progress.

Jack felt the last of his hope flush out of him. This was clearly impossible. He'd never reach the summit. He closed his eyes and rested his head against the mountain wall, and just stood there for a while, letting the despair wash over him.

Tears of frustration started to sting the corners of his eyes, and Jack screamed in defiance as he punched the wall. Over and over, he slammed his fist against the wall. In his fury, Jack began to tear at the wall. It crumbled under his hands as though it had been made of cheap plaster. He spent several minutes flinging chunks behind him as he attacked the wall in a rage, but when he opened his eyes, the wall was still whole and unblemished.

Looking around himself, Jack shouted into the empty space. "You think this is funny? Or do you expect me to just give up? Well, too bad! Apparently, I don't get hungry, and I don't feel thirst, so I can climb this stupid mountain for eternity if need be! So screw you and your stupid games! I'm going to reach the summit, and nothing and no one is going to stop me!"

Putting action to words, Jack grabbed the next handhold and lifted himself up. Maybe it was his rage fueling him, or perhaps it was the weird physics of this place, or just maybe, whatever had been playing games with him gave up. Whatever it was, Jack noticed his climb was now going much easier than it had before. He seemed lighter, all the pain was gone from his limbs, and hand/footholds seemed to appear wherever he placed his limbs as though summoned by sheer will. When he reached the next ledge, Jack looked down again, but he appeared to be miles above the ground this time. With a satisfied grunt, Jack turned back to the mountain and resumed his climb.

~

S'haar woke in the middle of the night to hear Jack muttering to himself. "Hold on... ...I'm coming..."

She reached out and grabbed hold of Jack, drawing him into an embrace. She sleepily muttered in reply. "Well, hurry up, we're waiting for you...I'm waiting for you."

As S'haar fall back to sleep, she could have sworn to herself she saw Jack's mouth almost imperceptibly twitch into the slightest of smiles.

Chapter 34

For once, when Em'brel awoke, *she* was greeted with the smell of someone cooking breakfast. Sparing a glance over to the bed, she could see S'haar holding Jack in much the same way that Em'brel had once held her prized toys while she slept as a much younger child. It was the kind of grip that spoke of someone clinging to hope in the face of fear and doubt.

Turning away from the scene before her, Em'brel wondered who was cooking while they were all sleeping. Not that she was particularly concerned, since Angela was more than capable of protecting everyone in the ship. She was just curious.

Walking out into the common room, she witnessed the tiny form of Angela waving her arms around like a mad wizard, deftly controlling the robotic arms which were currently scrambling eggs, buttering toast, flipping ham slices, setting the table, and pouring a couple of glasses of water, all at the same time. Em'brel knew it was all for show. The avatar was the illusion, and the insect-like robotic arms were her best friend's real body, but she appreciated the effort and attention to detail Angela always put into making her family feel a little more comfortable in her presence.

The younger argu'n sat down at the table with her head cocked to the side and her legs swinging under her as she put on her best innocent expression and asked, "Soooo, whatcha makin?"

Angela gave one last flick of her arms as if to say 'Carry on without me!', then turned to address her favorite protege. "Well, I wasn't sure how long you'd sleep after a day and a night and another half a day of labor, so I wanted something that I could make at a moment's notice. Today I'm serving a traditional eggs and toast breakfast. It's not as flashy as some of the meals we've put together, but it should be just what you need to finish recovering from overexerting yourselves."

This last part was addressed to S'haar, who was currently dragging her protesting limbs out of the room to join the two women at the table. Angela was surprised to note that while the two argu'n were definitely hungry, they weren't nearly as hungry as she thought sixteen hours of sleep would have left them. It must have something to do with their cold-blooded physiology. Still, the two women dug into their meal with eager abandon, wolfing everything down in their usual brutally efficient manner.

After they'd eaten enough to slow down the feeding frenzy a little, Angela broached a subject that had been on her mind for a while. She hadn't been able to find a good time to bring up until now. "So, you've obviously experienced these deep freezes before. How do your villages get through it without a 'dragon' to give you an early warning?"

S'haar looked as though she wasn't pleased to speak about the subject, but she understood that Angela's question wasn't just about satisfying idle curiosity. "Well, the specifics vary, but most villages have an emergency location designed with this exact situation in mind. In our case, there is a massive stone building in the center of town. The inside walls of which are covered with layer after layer of skins and hides. All year long, every adult is required to donate either materials or labor for its upkeep. The building is filled with firewood, which is rotated out periodically so that only the driest and best burning wood is kept in storage."

A shadow passed over S'haar's face as she continued. "In the event of a deep freeze, a cry is sent out, each household is expected to warn the two closest homes to themselves before making for the shelter. If the freeze drops the temperature too fast, many of the older members of the village will never make the journey safely, and others might be seriously injured or even lose limbs due to frostbite."

S'haar swallowed something down in her throat that had nothing to do with the breakfast she was eating before continuing her explanation. "As people arrive, they fill the building. The first to arrive are placed in the center, and everyone else is seated in a spiral pattern designed to fill the building. Several spots are designated to contain vented fireplaces to warm the entire area. The idea is to wait out the cold."

The weariness that S'haar exhibited as she continued was palpable to the other two women in the room. "Most villagers go into a semi sleep-like state in which they are only passingly aware of what's going on. If given food, they'll eat, though they don't need to eat as much or as often as usual, and if given a bucket, they'll expel waste. Other than that, the whole thing passes for them as if it were some fever dream. The guard is tasked with staying awake in shifts to tend the fires and the villagers. Some of the wealthier families may have servants to care for them in the place of the guard."

Darkness came over S'haar's face as she continued. "If the freeze lasts long enough for us to run out of supplies, we begin to ration the firewood and food. It's rare, but there have been times during particularly long deep freezes when the people on the outermost edge were left untended, resulting in many casualties. Obviously, the wealthiest members of the village live closest to the shelter, and the poorer you are, the further away you live."

Em'brel nodded, though her voice was small and quiet as if she was ashamed of what she had to say. "That is also why being a noble's servant is such a sought-after position. It offers significantly better chances of survival for yourself and your family, in the event of a particularly bad deep freeze."

Angela took all this in stoically. She had many half thought out theories and ideas, but now wasn't the time or place for such things. "Well, thankfully, our camp should be alright this time, but this is definitely something we'll need to plan for in the future. If I have any say in the matter, there will be a significant decrease in deep freeze related deaths in the future!"

~

Jack was nearing the summit of the mountain. He was exhausted after the long ordeal of the climb, but he shoved that concern to the back of his mind for now. Through a series of mistakes and mishaps similar to his first near tumble, Jack had finally figured out the secret to this place. The only real danger here was self-doubt. There were no loose rocks or slippery handholds until you feared they were there. His earlier anger, born of frustration, had helped him make significant progress without the burden of doubt, but eventually, his passion passed, and now the only thing keeping him on this mountain was sheer mental discipline. This activity was exhausting in an entirely different way than rock climbing usually was, but he was finally nearing his goal.

Jack lifted himself over the final ledge up onto the summit of the mountain. There he was greeted with…nothing. He wasn't sure what he'd been expecting, maybe a shaft of light to lift him out of this place, or perhaps a wormhole that would bring him home. At one point, Jack had even entertained the idea that he might be greeted by an oversized raven at the summit that would fly him out of here like it was all some sort of video game. But there were none of those things. The summit was empty.

Jack sat down to think.

~

S'haar was getting antsy cooped up inside. Usually, when waiting out a deep freeze, she'd either be in a sleep stupor or in charge of taking care of a large number of people. Either way, the time had always seemed to pass quickly.

It wasn't that she minded staying at home with her new family. Some of her fondest memories ever were of the random dinnertime conversations they often shared or of just sitting around watching movies together.

The problem was that she *couldn't* leave the house. Somehow that made everything harder to endure. What would typically be a relaxing evening of sitting around relaxing was instead a stressful experience as she obsessed over all the work that wasn't getting done.

She'd watched a movie with Em'brel. The main characters were a little immature for S'har's taste, but the film was saturated with the otherworldly feeling of a dream. Angela had excitedly told the two women that the villain was played by someone named 'Tim Curry'. Apparently, he was one of her all-time favorite human actors. She even shared an old human joke about the man. "You can judge a man based on what movie he first thinks of when he hears the name, Tim Curry." It hadn't made much sense to S'haar, but she assumed it was just one of those private jokes Angela and Jack had always laughed at.

Angela also designed a new outfit that should allow safe but short travel through the deep freeze. However, it was going to be a while before it was ready. In the meantime, she was keeping track of the workers.

Apparently, Lon'thul was currently regaling the rest with stories his father had told him when he was younger. Angela assured S'haar that if anything started going wrong, she'd be the first the AI would tell.

With nothing to do and a lot of time to do it in, S'haar found herself back at Jack's side. She was having another one-sided conversation with Jack, but this time her words meandered at the whims of her thoughts. S'haar spoke of people she'd known, things she'd done, hopes and fears of her childhood, and even some of her thoughts and impressions the first time she'd met Jack. Time flew by, but S'haar continued talking long into the night.

~

Jack had spent the better part of what he thought must be a day exploring every inch of the summit. He was beginning to believe that he'd climbed this monstrosity for nothing and would have to climb back down again. The very idea was enough to sap the last of his will to keep going, and he laid down in the snow.

It was an interesting experience, lying in snow but not feeling the cold. Initially, the cold had bitten at any exposed skin, but sometime during the climb, Jack had just forgotten about the cold, and it hadn't bothered him since. If Jack wasn't so desperate to get back to the people waiting for him, he could spend lifetimes exploring the rules of the world he currently found himself in.

He was just feeling the stirrings to get up and finally do something when he heard S'haar's voice. As much as Jack looked forward to listening to S'haar's voice, it wasn't what the voice said that held his attention this time. It was where the voice was coming from.

It took Jack a bit of time to follow the voice around the summit until he hit a bit of a snag. The voice was coming from just off one of the ledges. This particular ledge was a sheer drop that fell further than Jack could comfortably look down at first glance. He eventually crawled on his stomach to look over to the shelf, and his stomach fell out from under him as he looked down the cliff. It just kept going down. There was no way to climb down at this spot, but the voice was definitely coming from the void just beyond the last bit of rock platform. He stretched his hand out in an attempt to feel…anything…but his hands were met by nothing but air.

He carefully pulled himself away from the ledge and spent some more time in thought.

Em'brel was in the kitchen. She usually loved cooking, but something about being cut off from everyone, and everything, just made it hard to ignore all the things that had been weighing her down recently. Without something forcing her to keep moving forward, all her doubts and fears came rushing back to weigh her down.

Eventually, she simply gave up and slouched down in a chair. Angela appeared beside her, and she feared that the AI would launch into some cheerful banter that she just didn't have the energy for. Instead, Angela sat in her own smaller chair, looked at her friend, and asked, "Want to talk about it?"

Em'brel thought for a moment. She wanted to cry, scream, laugh, and more, but instead, she just shook her head.'

Angela nodded. "That's fine. Want me to leave you alone for a bit?"

Em'brel considered the offer. She was ashamed of breaking down like this, but was afraid of being left alone too. She shook her head again.

Angela simply nodded again. "Alright, one last question. We can sit in silence, or I can play some different music for you, if you'd like."

Em'brel considered the offer. Most of the music Angela had shown her up till now had been bright and bubbly. It was fun to move and sing to, but right now, that's not what she needed. On the other hand, Angela seemed to have a pretty good feel for her emotional state right now, and Em'brel trusted her. She nodded her head this time.

Angela smiled and leaned back in her floating chair. "Alright. A while back, Jack and I visited a small island on a planet far from here. He listened to this song while sitting on the sandy beach as a gentle breeze blew through the nearby reeds during the sunset. He told me the song always takes him right back to that same place. You've never been there before, but maybe it'll take you to your own relaxing place. It's called 'Run' by the group 'Collective Soul'.

As the notes softly cut through the still night air, Em'brel knew her faith hadn't been misplaced. She sat back and let the music wash over her, just letting herself feel.

Jack had tried everything he could think of, which admittedly didn't amount to much. Sitting and thinking hadn't gotten him anywhere, so he crawled up to the ledge and reached out as far as he safely could for a second time. That predictably achieved nothing. Next, he tried throwing handfuls of snow over the cliff, hoping some sort of *Last Crusade* invisible bridge might appear. Again, nothing. He wasn't surprised at that. The scene had always bugged him because it only worked with a fixed perspective. Though he had to admit, if it was possible anywhere, it would be in this place.

That essentially left Jack debating the merits of clicking his heels together and saying "there's no place like home" over and over.

Shaking his head, Jack realized that this was all getting him nowhere. He walked right up to the ledge and looked down. The wind howled as the mountain cut its passage. The eerie sound reminded Jack just how alone he was up on this cliff in the middle of nowhere. The wind kicked up small flurries of snow all around him and flung them over the edge of the cliff. It was both beautiful and terrifying. His heart was beating so loudly, he was afraid it might start an avalanche.

Jack started to back away from the cliff, away from S'haar's voice, then stopped. He stood in place and laughed at himself for a moment.

S'haar was calmly talking about such mundane everyday subjects, and Jack was looking over a cliff that seemed to have no bottom, telling himself that what he was thinking now was nothing short of crazy. It was a weird dichotomy of feelings. A large part of Jack wanted to just sit back down in the snow and listen to S'haar talk for a while longer, but he knew that he might never have the courage to do what needed to be done if he did that. Instead, Jack stood at the cliff's side and stared into the void of space S'haar's voice seemed to be coming through.

He was frozen in place. Unwilling to take a step back, unable to commit to what he was more certain than ever needed to be done. Jack tried telling himself he would act on the count of three multiple times. At three, he'd feel his muscles tense, but his body refused to budge.

Listening to her voice, Jack could picture S'haar as she spoke. He could imagine the emotions in her voice playing across her face. Closing his eyes, Jack could see her in front of him. She was bravely facing everything that came her way, overcoming challenges that would have broken a lesser person several times over. Jack knew she'd find her way in life with or without him…and yet…

With his eye still held tightly closed, Jack braced himself, whispered a prayer to whatever gods or daemons might be listening, and leaped into the void.

Chapter 35

S'haar woke with a start. Something was…off. Her tongue flicked out to taste the air as she took stock of her surroundings. Of course, it didn't take her sleeping brain long to wake up enough to realize what was different.

There was laughter coming from the general area.

With one last glance to make sure Jack was still stable and secure, S'haar got up to see the cause of all the commotion. Em'brel and Angela were watching another movie, but this one was different from the rest she'd seen. It was much lower quality and didn't seem to be telling any kind of story, as far as S'haar could tell.

That's when Angela resumed describing what was happening on the screen. "And this was the first time Jack went to the zoo! A zoo is a place where all sorts of animals are gathered together and kept in enclosures accessible by the public, and as you can see, Jack loved *all* the animals! Going to the zoo was always one of his favorite things to do growing up."

A tiny, younger version of Jack wandered around from one enclosure to the next on the screen. He would sometimes jump up and down in excitement as one of the animals did something nearly imperceptible to the woman watching, but obviously of great enjoyment to the young Jack. These antics were so adorable that Em'brel laughed and clapped in excitement every time.

His favorite animals seemed to be something Angela described as 'big cats'. S'haar was amazed that the humans had managed to capture such obviously dangerous animals, despite being so weak themselves. It brought her mind back to the conversation she'd had with Jack about humans being lower on the food chain of their own world. She could see what he'd meant.

Despite that, these monstrous animals didn't seem to bother the young Jack in any way. When one of the 'big cats' let out a ferocious roar, Jack simply roared back then laughed, which caused Em'brel to join right in again.

Just then, Angela seemed to notice S'haar and invited her to join in and watch. "I was teaching Em'brel about child development among humans, which brought up the subject of Jack's childhood, and I thought I'd show her some home movies of Jack growing up. Up next is something we call a birthday party!"

What unfolded was a scene of utter chaos. Children were running everywhere. Every once in a while, parents would try to gather the children to play some organized games, but they were always met with mixed results at best and abject failure at worst. Angela continued her narration. "Every year on the same date they were born, humans celebrate their 'birthday.' It's especially exciting for children, and is often a big event filled with lots of noise and excitement."

It amazed S'haar that the humans had enough leisure time to spend on such frivolous pursuits, but that thought was quickly drowned out by how adorable she found the human children.

That was when another familiar face showed up on the screen. Angela appeared much the same as she did now. She gathered the children together, and for the first time, it worked. The AI led them over to a large colorful castle, and when the children climbed inside, the floor seemed to squish under their feet. Soon, all the children were bouncing around excitedly. They seemed to be playing some weird game where they'd launch themselves at a sticky wall with a target painted on it, and Angela would award them points based on how close to the center they landed.

Off to one side, one parent was talking to another. "Are you sure that's safe? Having an AI watch the kids? Maybe one of us should be in there, keeping an eye on everything."

Another man with a greying beard and a broad, friendly smile came into the shot. "Nonsense, that's Angela watching them! She'll keep a far closer eye on them than you or I ever could! They're as safe as a bunch of kids bouncing around like little maniacs could ever be!"

This didn't seem to comfort the other adult all that much, but the second man's grin only grew when one child bumped into another, and

Angela was instantly there reassuring the injured child, then with a conspiratorial wink to the adults, she took the child's attention off the small bump on his head by telling him she could sneak him a piece of candy a bit early because he was 'such a brave boy.' The effect was instantaneous. The child who'd been on the brink of tears ran off with an excited smile and giggle to get his reward.

Angela's voice was heavy with emotion as she spoke this time. There was some pain evident but also a strong fondness. "The man with the beard is…was our father."

Everyone watched the man quietly as he spoke with various other party guests. He was every bit as quick with a witty comment or lighthearted joke as Jack ever had been, and he even had that same troublemaking lopsided grin Jack got when he was about to say or do something he knew was going to complicate things. He was currently working a grill and passing out food to anyone who wanted it, and even some who were pretending they didn't. S'haar laughed as he practically forced a 'hot dog' onto some woman who was protesting about watching her weight. "I can see where Jack gets it! It's almost like watching an older, more dignified, more confident Jack! I would have liked to have met him."

Angela's smile conveyed a little sadness and a lot of happiness when she responded. "I think he would have liked you two. He would have welcomed you into the family just as quickly as he did me."

As the scene on the screen changed, Angela's voice changed back to one of excitement. "Oh, you'll find this fascinating! This is a place we call an 'aquarium'!"

~

S'haar was in considerably lighter spirits when she returned to the room later that morning. Watching Angela's 'home movies' and listening to her talk about Jack's childhood gave her a more in-depth glance into the mysterious world Jack and Angela came from. There were still many things that made little to no sense to her; in fact, there were more now than when she'd started. However, for one evening, it had felt as though Jack had been awake and by her side again.

She walked over to Jack to begin the routine Angela had taught her. First, she'd speak to Jack. "Hello Jack, do you hear me? If you do, can you open your eyes for me?"

S'haar froze, something was off. She'd done this so many times, it took her a moment to realize what was wrong.

Jack's eyes were open, and he was looking right at her. Realizing he was trying to speak, S'haar leaned in close to hear what he had to say. "Before we continue…do you think I could get some water… I'm really thirsty."

Before she realized what she was doing, S'haar was crying incoherently while hugging Jack. She knew she was hugging him a bit hard, and he'd likely have a new bruise or two as a result, but she didn't care. He'd just have to deal with it after what he'd put her through. "Is this real? Are you really awake? Say something else, so I know it's not just a fluke!"

Jack's arms hung limply at his side. He wanted nothing more than to hug S'haar back, but his limbs didn't seem to want to respond. He used his words instead, though his voice came out barely above a whisper and seemed to tire him out as though he'd been sprinting. "This is where…I'd normally say… 'something else…' to be a smart ass,…but now's probably…not the time."

S'haar bit back something halfway between a sob and a laugh before responding. "Only you would come back from the dead and have the first thing you say be a bad joke!"

Jack's had that same stupid grin his father had worn in the home movie. "Hey…I wasn't…joking about…the water…"

Em'brel was drawn by all the commotion, but this time she approached the door more apprehensively. After the last few false alarms, she'd grown warier. When she got there, Em'brel saw Jack alert and talking. Although he looked more like someone who hadn't slept in days than someone who'd slept nearly a month away.

S'haar was just getting up to reach for a glass of water she kept in the room for herself when the younger argu'n came rocketing in for her own overly enthusiastic hug. This was followed by more incoherently sobbing speech, with the occasional 'you're awake!' puncturing through the joyful hysterics.

Angela was watching the show with more than a little bit of envy. She wanted her own turn hugging Jack but had to settle for merely enjoying the celebratory atmosphere. Eventually, the hysterics died down, and the other two pulled back so Angela could have her own moment with Jack. The AI floated right up to Jack's face. "Hey, there little brother, what took you so long? We've been waiting!"

Jack took a deep breath and told his story in agonizing slowness. "Got…lost… Had to…fight with…a god… Walked…forever… Then… climbed…a stupid…mountain… Then…jumped into…an…abyss… Took me…a bit,..but I'm…here now!"

Angela's smile reached her eyes, and her tears were falling freely, though they faded into nothing when they arrived at her feet. "Sounds like you had quite the adventure. I can't wait to hear more. You just better hang around long enough to tell it! Not to mention what you owe these two young ladies for stepping up in your absence! You've got a lot to make amends for!"

Jack nodded weakly before taking another deep breath. "I'm not…going…anywhere…any time…soon!"

Under Angela's careful guidance, S'haar gently lifted Jack into a seated position and helped him drink some of the water he had asked for a while back. He only drank a small amount before he began sputtering and had to stop. S'haar noticed with concern how much lighter Jack had become. In her hands, he felt so much more frail and weak than he ever had before.

S'haar wasn't the only one concerned with Jack's physical condition. Although Angela was already well aware of the atrophy a month in a coma would result in, she was still concerned about Jack's apparent limited range of movement. Furthermore, neither of the other women present was aware of how drastically Angela had to update their implants on the fly to accommodate his slurred speech. In short, she needed to do a full physical and mental evaluation to learn how extensive the damage to Jack's mind and body was, but she decided to let everyone enjoy the moment for just a little longer.

~

Eventually, the morning passed into the afternoon, and the two argu'n realized they were hungry. Before they went and got their own food, Em'brel walked over to the bedside table covered in all sorts of vials of medicine and formulas. She picked up a can and looked at it in a slightly confused manner before speaking. "So, if Jack's awake, does that mean he doesn't need to be fed through his tube anymore?" As she spoke, she looked over at a tube protruding from Jack's stomach that he hadn't noticed until that moment.

Angela seemed to consider the options a moment before responding. "Eventually, we'll want to move him to oral consumption of liquid food before attempting solids, but before we even do that, I want to run a full assessment of Jack's condition. For now, we should stick to feeding him through the g-tube."

Jack was somewhat unsettled to experience how he'd been fed over the last month. With a surety of movement that could only come from repeated practice, Em'brel pinched the feeding tube before inserting a syringe into the end of the tubing. She then poured a measured amount of water into the line and lifted the line to simply let the contents drain into Jack's stomach. Em'brel then repeated the process with a can of formula, although it took a little longer to drain. The process completed, Em'brel flushed the tube a final time with more water before securing it back against Jack's stomach.

The look in Jack's eyes clearly conveyed his thoughts about how humiliating he found the whole experience to be, and despite otherwise enduring the experience stoically, his gaze wasn't lost on others in the room. Angela instructed S'haar to carefully pick Jack up, guiding her to lift with one arm under his legs and the other supporting his back while his head rested against her neck. She then had the woman carry Jack over to the med-bay and set him in a large scanner.

That completed, Angela shooed the other two women out. "Go and get yourselves some lunch. That'll give me a chance to give Jack a proper preliminary analysis."

S'haar looked like she wanted to protest when Angela simply looked her in the eyes and asked, "Please?" With another moment of hesitation, S'haar nodded and left the two siblings in peace.

Finally, alone, Angela turned to Jack. "Ok, I'm going to ask you to perform a series of physical motions, then we'll move onto a set of questions you'll need to answer. I already know that much of what I ask will be beyond your ability to perform right now. Just do your best, so I can measure how extensive the damage is. Remember, there is no timer, so take however much time you feel you need."

Angela waited for Jack's slight nod of understanding before turning on the scanner and making her first request. "First, I want you to simply open your fist and spread your fingers as far apart as you can."

Jack's arms trembled, and his fingers twitched, but they refused to straighten. After a few seconds of this, Angela stopped him. "Ok, that's fine, that's pretty much what I expected. Next, I want you to flex your toes."

Jack felt tears begin to burn at the edge of his vision from the frustration born of his inability to accomplish even these basic tasks, but he slowly blinked them away before setting his face into a mask of determination and went about attempting the next deceptively impossible task.

~

After a while, Angela appeared before the two argu'n women who were eating their meals halfheartedly. Immediately, they looked at the AI with a hunger that had little to do with physical appetite. Both started speaking simultaneously before Angela shushed them down. "Ok, you obviously noticed how rough Jack's current condition is. Despite waking up from his coma, Jack still has a ways to go down his road to recovery. His muscles atrophied roughly how I expected them to, but his brain also sustained substantial damage."

S'haar and Em'brel both looked like they were ready to burst into a series of demanding questions when Angela held up a hand to request further silence as she continued. "Despite all that, there is good news too. The damage to Jack's brain seems to be almost entirely centered around his motor functions. With time, physical therapy, and a bit of luck, Jack should recover most, and possibly all, of his motor skills."

Again, the women looked ready to fly into a series of questions, but this time they restrained themselves knowing Angela would be as forthcoming as she could. "The rest of his mind, his knowledge, and personality seems almost entirely intact. The Jack we know and love is still in there. He's just a prisoner in his own body for the moment."

At her next simulated breath, the room was so quiet Angela had no problem finishing her explanation. "Jack's going to need our help a little longer. For a week or two, he'll need help with even the simplest of tasks. He won't be able to feed himself, bathe himself, or even use the restroom without assistance. Even after that, it'll probably be a month or two of physical therapy before his muscle mass is restored to its normal levels. I'll have to teach one of you how to care for Jack until he can take care of himself again."

Both S'haar and Em'brel shot to their feet and shouted simultaneously, "I'll do it!"

Angela was about to make what she thought was the obvious choice when Em'brel followed up with a quiet but firm, "Hear what I have to say before you decide!"

S'haar looked almost ready to physically fight for her right to care for Jack but visibly restrained herself while Angela nodded to the younger argu'n. Em'brel took a moment to organize her thoughts before speaking.

Nodding differently to S'haar, she began. "We all know the relationship you have with Jack. You have been Jack's right hand since you met him. You are his bodyguard, his translator, and your feelings for each other are obvious to anyone with eyes to see."

S'haar looked a bit confused that Em'brel seemed to start her explanation by proving what an obvious choice S'haar was, but the younger argu'n was far from finished. "But you forget one crucial thing. You're forgetting Jack."

At that, S'haar started to look like she was ready for a fight again, but Em'brel pressed on. "Think of how he feels right now. He's broken, inside and out, and completely helpless. Despite his feelings for you…no, *BECAUSE* of his feelings for you, you're the last person he wants to be a burden to. His eyes practically screamed his humiliation while he was being fed with us in the room!"

Em'brel's voice lost some of its energy, but as her voice softened, her resolve strengthened. "What's more, no one should have to experience the first intimate touch of their love when she cleans him after he used the toilet! The shame of it would sour every moment between the two of you for years to come! Give him the time he needs to heal, then let him come to you when he's ready to stand on his own again!"

The other two women at the table were silent. Neither had stopped to think about the effects Jack's current condition would have on his developing relationship with S'haar, but Em'brel still wasn't finished. "I know this last part is just selfish of me, but Jack wouldn't be in his condition if he hadn't had to rescue me…again. I need to do this! I need to give something back to the man who nearly gave up everything for me! I need to help make this right again…"

After her final thought, Em'brel stood silent as her tears steadily fell. She'd made her case, and there was nothing more to be said.

S'haar stood stoically for a moment before smiling sadly and sitting back down. She shook her head as she spoke. "If you dedicate even a portion of the passion of that speech into helping Jack, he'll be back on his feet in half the time! I'll trust Jack to your care, but I'm still going to be involved in every step of the way!"

Em'brel nodded, and Angela finally chimed in again, "I wouldn't have it any other way. Jack needs us all more than ever, but now there is a light at the end of this tunnel."

Angela tilted her head to the side for a moment, staring off into space, before turning back to the younger argu'n. "Em'brel, I hope you meant what you said, because I think Jack needs to use the restroom."

Chapter 36

Jack's muscles were screaming in agony. When he complained about the burning pain, Angela simply responded with a cheerful explanation. "That just means the exercise is working! We need to loosen up the muscles you have and help develop more muscle growth at the same time. Now pull!"

Em'brel held Jack's arm so that it was extended just a little further than Jack's new limited range of motion left him comfortable with. At Angela's command, Jack did his best to pull his arm back to himself. It was somewhat disheartening how little his arm budged in the younger girl's grip, but he kept pulling until Angela told him to relax again. They'd been doing this for several minutes, and Jack's arm felt as if it was on fire. He wasn't sure if the tears in his eyes were born from pain or frustration, though he suspected the truth involved a little of both. When Jack was absolutely sure he couldn't do it one more time, Angela pushed him again. "Ok, just once more, *then* you can relax your arm!"

Jack forced himself to pull with his exhausted arm for just a little longer, though he could swear time seemed to stretch on longer than it had in any of his previous attempts. Eventually, Angela instructed him to relax and allowed Em'brel to lower his arm. Closing his eyes to recover from the strain, Jack started to catch his breath. Angela seemed to have a different plan, much to his dismay. "Ok, now extend his other arm, and let's start over!"

Jack's eyes shot open. "You said... we'd take... a break!"

Angela's face was the oddest combination of apology and determination as she shook her head. "No, I said you could relax your arm, and you can! Now we're working on the other arm. I understand that you are exhausted and frustrated, but the more progress you make now, the more functionality you're likely to recover. So unless you want to be a cripple for the rest of your life, completely dependent on the people around you to feed you, bathe you, and help you use the bathroom, you need to push yourself. Now *pull*."

Jack thought back to last night and the sheer humiliation of having Em'brel help him use the bathroom. She's been surprisingly professional, preferring speed and efficiency in the place of conversation. Jack suspected the girl had an idea of how hard this whole experience was for him and was determined to get through the worst of it fast as possible.

He'd tried telling himself that after climbing a mountain and leaping into a void, this was nothing, but when the girl had to help clean him after he was done, he was forced to admit he'd prefer to climb a dozen mountains than endure that experience ever again. And yet, he knew he'd have to repeat that same experience multiple times a day until he was able to recover enough to take care of himself.

With that humiliation in mind, Jack suddenly found he had far more energy and determination than before and pulled hard enough that Em'brel's eyes widened slightly in surprise, and Jack saw his arm move noticeably in her grip before she adjusted to the unexpected strength he'd suddenly acquired.

Jack and Em'brel grinned at each other over this tiniest of victories. When Jack resumed the physical therapy, it was with a renewed determination.

~

Jack was utterly and totally exhausted. After the arm pulling, Angela had had Jack lift his legs and hold them 'up' for as long as he could endure. He was rarely able to lift them entirely off the bed, but his muscles were burning in a way that told him the exercise worked.

As bad as the physical therapy had been, it paled in comparison to the frustrations of occupational therapy.

Angela manufactured an oversized pen for Jack to use. Em'brel helped Jack wrap his fingers around the pen, albeit in a manner better suited for stabbing than writing. Then he tried to write his name on a piece of paper. It was more of a scribble than actual writing, but Angela told Jack it was vital for him to have a specific goal in mind when he was writing, and his name was an excellent benchmark for him to strive for. He dropped the pen over and over, and every time Em'brel would patiently help Jack extend his fingers to grab hold of the pen once more.

Jack groaned in frustration after dropping the pen once more. Angela explained the purpose of these exercises to both Jack and Em'brel. "The brain is very delicate, but also great at self-maintenance and repair. Portions of your brain that had been deprived of oxygen too long died and left behind scarring. This prevents signals from getting to your nervous system, which controls your motor functions. However, given a chance, your brain will seek to establish new connections to your nervous system to restore proper function once more. These repetitive activities essentially force your brain to send signals to said nerves and will eventually establish new neuro paths to send signals across. This is, of course, a gross oversimplification of a very complex process, but it should help you get the idea."

Jack didn't feel like he was making any progress. The letter J he was trying to draw looked more like a sloppy figure eight, drawn by someone only passingly familiar with the concept of curves. As Jack continued into the letter A, he dropped the pen for what felt like the hundredth time. With a sigh somewhere between frustration and anger, Jack reached out and picked up the pen to continue butchering his name when he realized both Em'brel and Angela were staring at his hand.

It was only when Jack looked at his own hand that he realized what he'd done. He'd picked up the pen without any help from Em'brel.

Setting down the pen again, Jack held both of his hands up in front of his face. He focused all the effort he could muster into opening up his hands. His left hand twitched and shook, but his right hand, the hand he'd been writing with, opened about 3 inches. It seemed like such a small thing, but it also meant this stupid exercise was working, no matter how childish it seemed.

Even lunch was exercise. Jack was strapped into a chair since he couldn't easily support his own sitting weight yet, and since the table wasn't quite tall enough, Em'brel held up a can full of Jack's liquid lunch, complete with a straw. In her other hand, she held a rag to wipe Jack's face clear of any food he coughed or sputtered up. The whole meal was almost as humiliating as the bathroom experience had been.

After lunch, Jack had to re-evaluate his assessment of how embarrassing the meal had been when Em'brel had to help him use the restroom again.

After that, they were off to more rehabilitation. Apparently, this time Angela wanted to work on speech.

~

S'haar was amazed at how efficient her new outfit was at retaining heat. Unlike the coats they'd been using up until now, this outfit covered her entirely. It came complete with a mask, gloves, and boots that fully encased her clawed feet. Even the airflow was directed to help retain heat. The intake passed through the suit's heated sections to prevent her from breathing in air that was too cold for her lungs. The outflowing air passed along the colder areas of her suit to avoid wasting the heat coming out with her breaths.

It was a little disorienting to wear at first, and it took S'haar a while to get used to the fact that she couldn't 'taste' the air around her, nor could she get traction with her claws. However, she'd spent enough time walking around the somewhat cold cave to familiarise herself with the outfit before going out into the storm.

Of course, Angela was also coming along for the ride. "So, now that you've gotten used to the suit, any recommendations you'd like to make?"

S'haar stumbled a little before speaking. "Without the use of my claws, you might need to add a bit more traction to the boots. The gloves are a little too smooth as well. A little texture on the palms would help. Maybe the shoulders could stand to be a bit less restrictive? Other than that, this suit is a marvel!"

Angela seemed to preen a little at the compliment. "Excellent! And might I add that you're a much better test subject than Jack. Less grumbling and more constructive feedback, just what an AI needs in a guinea pig!"

S'haar's voice came back weary. "I'm not certain what a guinea pig is, but I suspect I wouldn't enjoy being compared with one. But since you mentioned him, how's Jack doing?"

The AI's voice came back much more cheerful than S'haar had been expecting. "He's not doing quite as well as my most optimistic projections, but he's doing *far* better than I'd feared. Every time he starts to lose heart, he seems to dig within himself and find some untapped inspiration, and he comes back with greater determination. It's relatively common for people faced with this kind of debilitating setback to become overwhelmed and give in to feelings of hopelessness, but Jack just keeps pushing himself."

S'haar was approaching the cave's mouth, sled loaded with some fresh heating packs and a load of meat pastries Em'brel had sent with S'haar. Angela continued her explanation. "Honestly, I'm not sure where he's finding the will to keep pushing himself, and while I don't want to 'jinx' myself," —at Angela's jovial tone, S'haar could practically see the pixy girl wink while she spoke— "at this rate, there's some hope of a full recovery!"

S'haar chuckled a moment before replying. "Admittedly, I haven't known Jack nearly as long as you have, but ever since I've met him, he's always seemed to come out of his bouts of fear and doubt with renewed determination to see things through. Why would you be surprised when the worst setback so far only brings out his best?"

Angela was relieved to hear the easy affection still deep in S'haar's voice. She'd been afraid that seeing Jack broken the way he was would have changed the warrior woman's view of him.

Now at the mouth of the cave, S'haar readied the 'snowshoes' Angela had crafted. She was fascinated by the idea of walking on *top* of the snow. Angela had designed them with large, easy to manipulate fasteners so they could be put on or removed even if wearing thick gloves. S'haar also had a shovel ready to dig out the door to the workers' lodge if it was buried too deeply.

Snowshoes in place, S'haar walked out of the cave and into the open. Walking in the cumbersome shoes was incredibly awkward. She had to exaggerate her legs' up and down movements in a way that was mostly unfamiliar to her, but the further she got, the easier it became.

The wind was strong, and the snow seemed to be falling more sideways than down. As it tore through the mountain's ridges and valleys, it created a howling sound that made S'haar feel more isolated than she'd ever felt before. Despite the walk not being too far, she felt a wave of relief when the billet came into view.

The trip to the worker's housing took roughly four times longer than usual, and despite her new outfit, S'haar was starting to feel the cold. Even with her new suit, it wouldn't be safe to travel long distances during a deep freeze.

S'haar took a moment to clear the snow from the entrance before knocking on the door and shouting to anyone still awake, "It's S'haar, I'm coming in!"

She'd been expecting workers to be in the usual half-asleep state that all argu'n used to pass through a deep freeze, but she walked into a surprisingly lively group of workers.

Lon'thul and Tel'ron were in the middle of another dice game, leaving S'haar to wonder what the two younger workers had left to bet with at this point. The rest were gathered around, swapping stories or otherwise finding ways to kill some time, at least they had been until S'haar walked in.

Everyone was staring at S'haar, and it took her a moment to realize that with the mask still on, she probably looked like some monster out of a fireside tale. She removed her gloves so her hands could undo the clasps keeping the mask in place. There was a wave of exclamations as everyone looked over the outfit, taking turns inspecting the gloves and mask as S'haar explained their function and effectiveness.

The billet was surprisingly warm, and Angela decided to speak up through the headset S'haar had worn under the mask. "I'm glad to see Jack's design working so effectively despite the cold weather, but with the workers not going into their hibernation state, they will probably consume more food than we'd estimated. You might need to at least start talking about rationing out the food stores, just to be safe." S'haar nodded quietly before turning her attention to the workers.

After the initial excitement died down, S'haar started checking on everyone and seeing how they were doing, and asking if they needed anything. The universal answer was that they needed something to do. Luckily, Em'brel had already thought of that potential issue and sent S'haar with something to help.

However, before S'haar could bring up the subject of Em'brel, Lon'thul beat her to the punch. "So Em'brel's not coming today?"

S'haar had to admire the younger man's drive and smiled while shaking her head. "No, I'm afraid Em'brel's attention is required elsewhere. Jack's spirit has finally returned from the realm of the dead, but his body is still severely damaged and weak. Em'brel is seeing to his recovery, which will probably be the focus of her attention for the next few weeks."

Everyone took the news in stunned silence. While people in the village sometimes recovered from severe injuries that left them unconscious for a day or two, a month was impossible. Everyone had started assuming he was dead, and no one knew quite how to take the news of his recovery. As usual, Lon'thul was the first to speak. "Man, is there anything that human of yours can't do? Will he be taking over the camp again?"

S'haar shook her head. "Eventually, he might, but for now, Jack's focus is on recovering from his ordeal, so I will remain in charge. However, there's not a lot to do at the moment except seeing to the well-being of everyone here. To that end, Em'brel sent me here with a couple more human items to help you all pass the time while you wait out the freeze."

That caught the attention of all the workers. 'Human' tools and technologies had proven nearly miraculous to everyone now familiar with them, and everyone was curious about what humans did for entertainment.

The first thing S'haar held up was a small odd-looking box. When opened, it revealed a lot of flat panels with shapes and symbols painted on them. "These are called playing cards, and the game I'm about to teach you is called 'poker.'"

As S'haar explained the game, it became quickly apparent that everyone was excited at the idea of a new way to pass the long cold days in the billet, and it didn't take long before chores such as cleaning the outhouses or doing the dishes were being gambled on by many of the younger workers. It quickly became apparent that Fea'en's stoic demeanor gave her quite the advantage, as the game quickly devolved into a heated match between her and S'haar while the rest of the workers watched as the two most frightening women any of them knew went head to head for the 'pot,' which at this point mostly consisted of a few of the meat pastries still left over after everyone had eaten their fill.

As the bidding came to a close, S'haar was confident she'd won with the straight she held, but then Fea'en revealed her three of a kind was, in fact, a full house. The room erupted in cheers of excitement and exasperation. In the end, Fea'en retained her bragging rights but shared the meat pies for the low price of getting a pass on her next night of fire watch duty.

When the rest of the workers seemed hesitant to face the stoic older woman a second time, S'haar thought it might be a good time to reveal the next item Em'brel had sent her with.

It was a small box that unfolded into a small checkered board. On the inside were several small stone pieces that S'haar set up on the board. "This game is called 'chess.' The humans also call it 'the game of kings.' Apparently, many of their greatest rulers were quite proficient in this game, and it teaches you to anticipate problems before they arise. Allow me to explain the rules."

This time around, it was evident that the younger workers preferred the card game to this 'complex mess of a game' as Tel'ron and Lon'thul had both dubbed it. However, S'haar and Fea'en quickly found themselves absorbed in a battle of wits against each other. Eventually, the other workers returned to the card game, and the afternoon was passed with loud laughter, cries of anguish, and many exclamations of how terrible everyone's luck was.

Chapter 37

Em'brel had never hated herself as much as she did at this moment. For the last couple of days, she'd known that something was wrong, and the feeling just kept getting worse. As soon as she'd realized the source of her distress, she'd rejected the idea. But the thoughts still lingered like some festering wound, and it disgusted her. *Jack is less of a man now than he was before.*

That was wrong! Em'brel knew it was wrong, but once she'd given the thought form, it's foul taste stuck in the back of her throat. She was so ashamed of the thought that she dug her claws into her palms until they drew blood. Jack was only in this condition because he'd put everything on the line to save *her*... for a *second time!* He'd overcome so much, making it back this far, and he was quickly getting better through sheer willpower, the likes of which Em'brel might never understand. Even if his progress came to a halt here and now, Em'brel knew she'd gladly dedicate the rest of her life to caring for Jack. But still, the malignant feeling anchored itself like rot in her gut.

Glaring at herself in her mirror, *Jack's mirror that he graciously let her use*, she reminded herself, Em'brel snarled at her reflection. "You're better than this filth! These lies are beneath you! Jack needs you, now go and do the job you fought so passionately for!"

It took Em'brel a few more moments to wipe away the last tears of anger and shame before she replaced them with a carefully crafted look of hopeful neutrality. A few deep breaths later, and she was ready. As she walked out of the bathroom to help Jack start his day of therapy, she did her best to flush the disgraceful thoughts along with the morning's waste, where they belonged.

~

S'haar was in a great mood today! The first day she'd seen Jack, she'd been deeply worried by his condition. His inability to move his arms or legs, sit up, or even speak in complete sentences had left her worried that the human she'd grown so fond of had been broken. In the guard, she'd seen males receive debilitating injuries much less severe than Jack's, and all too often, they simply gave up. They often become drunkards, content to pass each day in a haze while dreaming of the past, and she'd been afraid Jack would go down a similar road.

Instead, he'd made immense progress in the last couple of days. He could sit up under his own power, albeit only briefly, and he could sometimes manage whole sentences before running out of breath. Also, he could grab and eat food using silverware, although either Em'brel or S'haar had to cut up his food and place it on the fork for him.

S'haar knew Jack still had a long way to go, but if he kept making progress like this, she was sure he'd be back on his feet running the show in no time. In many ways, she was more proud of Jack now than she had been after their life and death fight with the raiders. Back then, he'd won in part because he'd wielded weapons the likes of which would make the gods envious. Conversely, this recovery was all on Jack. Angela and Em'brel were helping, but everything ultimately depended on Jack to find the will to overcome these challenges. Evidently, he was more than up to the task.

Right now, he and S'haar were playing chess against one another. Angela had said this was excellent occupational therapy for him. He'd first have to verbalize his move, then do his best to pick up the piece and place it where he'd indicated. Often S'haar had to fix the piece's placement a little, and twice Jack had lost his balance and knocked the whole board over, but Angela was happy to help them get it restored to the state it had been in before Jack's mishap. All in all, this was an excellent morning.

Jack looked a little frustrated about losing his queenside castle but sighed and simply verbalized his next move. "Knight to E-5." He took a moment to catch his breath before asking. "So…what do you have planned after this?"

S'haar spoke as Jack slowly stretched his arm out to shakily grasp the piece in question. "Well, chess wasn't a big hit with the younger workers, so Angela recommended I bring checkers over, instead."

Jack let his hand rest on the piece for a moment before moving it and knocking over S'haar's bishop at its destination. He lost a bit of control at the end, and both pieces tumbled to the board, shifting one of S'haar's pawns in the process. She righted the pieces and removed her lost bishop as she continued speaking, all while trying to decide what to do now that the trap she'd been planning had fallen apart. "Honestly, I'm surprised at how well they are all doing. Aside from a little boredom caused by everyone being shut inside so long, your housing design has proved nearly as miraculous as the rest of your human tec. Queen to E-5."

Jack looked confused for a moment as S'haar removed his knight, but then he smiled. "Rook to D-5… Check!" Jack took another deep breath before reaching out while talking at the same time. "Don't underestimate the danger of boredom!"

He'd been a little too ambitious to try talking while moving and knocked his piece over, rather than grabbing it. S'haar righted it as she spoke but left it where it had been so Jack could try again. "I'm not underestimating anything. That's a large part of the reason I've been spending as much time there as I have, rather than spending time here with you and Em'brel. Well, that, and to give you some privacy while you work on getting better. I imagine it's hard enough, without another pair of eyes watching while you work."

This time Jack moved the piece cleanly, but now S'haar had a new problem. She could take his castle with her queen, but his queen would take hers and place her right back in check if she did so. Alternatively, S'haar could move her king out of the way, but then he'd just take her queen with his rook. She looked desperately around for some other option before sighing and moving her king to safety.

After Jack shakily knocked over her queen, he looked her in the eye and simply said. "Thank you."

S'haar removed the queen as she responded. "You don't need to thank me, you outmaneuvered me and took my queen 'fair and square'." She liked that human phrase.

As S'haar glanced at Jack, she was struck by the earnestness in his eyes. "That's not what I meant." Jack took a deep breath as if preparing for a long speech. "I know you didn't want to leave so soon after I woke up…" Another deep breath. "but the workers depend on you… Also…

I can more easily focus on…" He ran out of breath before finishing the sentence and took a moment before continuing. "…getting better!"

S'haar forgot about the trap she was caught in for a moment while she searched for the words she wanted. When she spoke, her voice was contemplative. "I've gone through most of my life alone, surrounded more by acquaintances than friends. Then you came out of nowhere, and I got caught up in this whirlwind of experiences you call life. At first, it was overwhelming, but just when I was starting to get used to the idea of spending the rest of my life alongside some mad human, you went and left me alone again."

Jack looked like he was desperately gathering a breath to explain, but S'haar held up a hand to forestall him. "I don't blame you, you did the right thing, and I was…I am very proud of you, but that month you were gone was the longest of my life. Every. Single. Night. I was terrified that I'd wake up and find out that that was the day you'd finally gone and died beside me while I slept, and I'd never get to speak to you again."

S'haar's eyes were filled with tears, but she smiled, and Jack felt his heart skip a beat as she continued. "But then you came back! I don't know if you actually argued with a god and scaled a mountain, or if, as you said, it was just some fevered dream as you fought and clawed your way out of your own subconscious, but you came back, and that's all that matters! So take however much time you need, and keep getting better. Now that I know you're not going anywhere, I can wait a little longer…"

S'haar reached out and gently placed a taloned hand over Jack's fist as he began to smile through his own tears. Their game was forgotten, but neither cared. Jack simply nodded. "Thank you." Although an echo of his earlier words, his voice was now heavy with an entirely different set of emotions.

~

Something was off with Em'brel. It was apparent to Angela that something was weighing on the girl's mind as she helped Jack with his exercises. She was stubbornly refusing to look him in the eyes. When she thought Jack wasn't looking, her face seemed to fall, and more than once, she appeared to be physically hurting herself in some small way. It was as though trying to punish herself. Or maybe distract herself? Whatever this troubling behavior was, Angela had no idea what was bringing it on or how to address it. So, for now, she simply went on pretending like nothing was wrong while they worked on Jack's exercises.

Angela wished Jack was healthy enough to weigh in on the situation. This was more his area of expertise than hers. Not that he was any slouch when it came to academics. Their success so far on this planet was proof of that, but he'd always been better at understanding the driving forces behind people's actions.

However, at the moment, everything Jack had was focused on maintaining his balance while sitting up under his own power. His core muscles were as atrophied along with everything else, and it made him incredibly unsteady while trying to perform even the most rudimentary of activities. Em'brel was ready to catch him if he fell, but a part of her mind was obviously still lost in thought.

Jack seemed to lose his strength and motioned to Em'brel that he needed to lie back and take some weight off. Angela was sure he should have been able to manage a while longer than he had, but when she gave Jack a closer inspection, she quickly realized what had happened.

Jack hadn't been as distracted by his workout as Angela had thought. As he was staring at Em'brel, Angela could practically see the gears in his head, violently spinning as he tried to figure out what was bothering the girl.

Taking a deep breath, Jack dove in. "Em'brel, what's the matter…? You seem really distracted…"

The girl's head shot around as she looked at Jack with wide, startled eyes. It took an agonizingly long moment for the girl to reply. When she did, her eyes were downcast once more, and her hands clenched into fists. "Ah, it…it's nothing! We need to get back to your exercises! What's next, Angela?" The girl reached out to grab Jack, but still, she seemed unwilling to look him in the eyes as she did so.

Angela didn't answer. Instead, she continued watching, for once feeling one step behind everyone else. Jack's eyes shifted slightly as he picked up on Em'brel's non-verbal cues. "It's about me…isn't it?"

The shocked look Em'brel gave him was more than answer enough, but again her gaze shifted downward as she tried to protest, albeit more weakly than before. "N…no. I'm not…just… It's not…"

Angela continued to watch silently as Jack pressed on. "Why does it suddenly bother you…to see me like this?"

When Em'brel looked up this time, tears were in her eyes, and she started begging. "Please, don't…"

Jack's face shifted in a moment of understanding. "That guilt in your eyes… You think I've become weak."

Angela didn't want to believe what he'd said, but Em'brel's reaction made it clear he was right. She reached up and dug her claws around her arm plates deep enough to draw pinpricks of blood. Her words started tumbling out through self-hating sobs as the girl seemed to break down. "I…I don't deserve to be here! All I can think of is how you've somehow betrayed me by becoming…like this! Even though it's all my fault that you've…"

Jack and Angela watched in silence as the girl collapsed onto her knees as she pounded her fist onto the bed while she cried. "You've always been larger than any problem! Despite being so frail, there was nothing you couldn't overcome! You were always one step ahead of everyone and everything! But here you are, helpless, and it's all my fault! Yet, for some reason, the only thing I can think of is that you've somehow betrayed me by letting yourself become so weak! It's stupid! It's idiotic! But the thought just won't go away! I'm unworthy of this family you welcomed me into!"

The girl let her head collapse into her arms, and the room was silent except for her sobs.

Angela was at a loss. She was torn in two. On the one hand, Em'brel was obviously in the middle of some crisis the AI couldn't understand. The girl knew what she was feeling was wrong but didn't know how to stop the feelings currently polluting her mind. On the other hand, this outburst would be devastating to Jack's drive to recover. He needed support right now, not someone drawing his attention to how weak he'd become. Angela's processors were starting to overheat as she tried in vain to find a solution to this impossible problem.

Then Jack simply chuckled.

Em'brel raised her head in confusion. She'd been expecting anger, despair, tears, or pretty much any reaction other than laughter. Jack reached out a shaky hand and placed it on top of the younger girl's. "You're not unworthy… You're just growing up."

Now Angela was even more lost than before, and the look in Em'brel's eyes reflected similar confusion. Jack continued, oblivious to both women's incredulity. "One of the hardest parts about growing up...is realizing how fallible the people you most look up to...really are..."

Em'brel looked like she wanted to speak, but Jack stopped her with a shaky hand and resumed his explanation. "Usually it takes a little longer...for someone to have to confront...that truth... ...but my accident has forced you...to face that reality a little sooner...than you were ready for."

Jack was clearly running out of breath, but he forced himself to sit up. Or at least he tried to, before starting to fall over and forcing Em'brel to reach out and hold him steady. Once he was stable, Jack wrapped his arms around the younger girl, trying to comfort her despite everything she'd just said.

Angela was suddenly reminded of a similar encounter between her and their father when she'd said some awful, hurtful things to him. Much like Jack, he'd just responded by telling her how proud he was of her and how much he loved her. She was left wondering when Jack had changed from being her bumbling little brother to becoming such a worthy heir to their father's legacy.

Jack clumsily wiped some of the girl's tears on his sleeve. It was apparent that he was nearing his limit, but he seemed to have one last point to make. "The truth is...I've always been weak... ...I've just depended on Angela...and S'haar...and yourself...to help compensate for my weaknesses... ...In return...you've all relied on me...to offset yours... That's what a family is all about... The whole is greater...than the sum of its parts..."

Em'brel shook her head in his grasp. "Why...why are you so understanding? Even after everything I just said! How can you just move past those things like they are nothing?"

Jack chuckled again before taking another breath. "I guess...that's just one of my...*strengths!*"

Em'brel let loose something halfway between a sob and a laugh as Jack continued. "Now then...enough speech therapy... Let's get back to physical therapy..."

Angela simulated shaking her digital head, despite her avatar not being present. She still couldn't quite grasp what had really happened there, but she suspected it was one of those things beyond the scope of her programming to understand.

However, as she watched Jack and Em'brel begin his arm exercises again, she felt the faintest glimmer of understanding. She imagined this is what humans felt like when they said something was on the tip of their tongue. It seemed so close but frustratingly remained just beyond her grasp…

Still, at least the crisis seemed to have been averted. Somehow Jack seemed as motivated as ever, and Em'brel was mostly smiling as she resumed her role as Jack's physical therapist. Apparently, there was still a lot Angela had yet to learn.

Chapter 38

Jack stabbed downward with everything he had. His victim evaded his strikes over and over, driving him into a rage. Until, at last, he finally drove the steel he wielded through its skin. His victim lay there bleeding out the red fluid of life from the punctures Jack's weapon had made. "Where did you even get cherry tomatoes on this planet? Especially in the middle of winter!"

Em'brel muffled her laughter behind a hand as Angela explained with a stoic expression fixed in place. "That's the last batch I had in stasis. I figured a fresh salad would be a nice reward for how far you've come! As a bonus, it's also excellent practice to help you improve your fine motor control!"

Jack glared suspiciously at his unusually austere sister. "And I suppose it had nothing to do with how amusing it is to watch me try and *eat* said salad?"

Angela waved away his concerns in a haughty manner. "Of course not! We're both *far* more professional than that! Our only concern is your health and recovery!"

Angela's stone serious face didn't even budge, while Em'brel audibly choked back another laugh as Jack started chasing another tomato around his plate. The girl's eyes were beginning to tear up from the effort of not laughing out loud.

Jack sighed in a way that clearly expressed his immense patience and long-suffering, but inside he was actually quite pleased. It was nice to see Em'brel allowing herself to have fun again. She'd wallowed in guilt long enough, and it was heartening to see the return of the clever and impish girl Jack knew so well.

Now, if only this stupid tomato would stop causing him so much trouble! Once more, the persistent thing slipped out from under Jack's fork, making a line for the plate's edge before being caught by the raised edge and looping around a bit, settling a little closer to the center. Jack sighed and stabbed at it again.

~

S'haar was starting to get worried. The food supplies were adequate, but the wood they'd gathered was beginning to look a little thin. She figured they had a few more days, but the freeze didn't seem like it was going to end any time soon. It was probably about time for them to start considering Plan B.

Her thoughts were interrupted by Lon'thul's shout from the other end of the room. "Chief me!" S'haar could tell from here that his red pieces on the board were considerably outnumbered by Tel'ron's black, but the young hunter was always so excited to get a piece to the board's end and get it 'chiefed.' S'haar suspected he might be missing the point of the game, but decided as long as everyone was having fun, it didn't matter. She'd long ago given up on telling him the actual phrase was 'king me'. After a while, she'd decided he was doing it on purpose just to get a reaction out of her.

Once again, her musings were interrupted, this time by Fea'en's more subtle declaration. "Check."

Looking at her own game board, she could see the older woman had taken advantage of her distraction to sandwich S'haar between a knight, rook, and now a bishop. S'haar had let herself get a little overconfident after taking the craft master's queen, and she was now paying the price.

However, she wasn't out of options yet. Moving her king to the side, she waited to see if Fea'en would notice her own knight's position before recommitting to the attack.

This time it was the older woman's turn to be distracted as she echoed S'haar's earlier thoughts. "This freeze looks to be a long one, and our wood supplies are a little low."

Fea'en was analyzing the board. S'haar was worried the other woman would notice the knight, so decided now was a great time to bring up her distraction…or rather, her plan. "I was just thinking that myself. In another day or two, it might be time to move you all to the caves."

S'haar couldn't tell if the distraction worked or not. Rather than move the bishop again as she'd hoped, Fea'en instead chose to move the rook to narrow the king's possible avenues of escape. S'haar brought her own rook up to threaten Fea'en's bishop in an attempt to encourage the woman to commit the piece to battle.

There was an unspoken question evident on Fea'en's face, and S'haar chose to come right out and address it rather than waiting for it to fully formulate. "It's not a perfect solution, but the dragon values your lives far more than her privacy. Besides, this was always our backup plan if the freeze was too much for this building to handle."

Once more, rather than move the bishop, Fea'en chose to move a different piece. This time she moved a knight up to protect her bishop, forcing S'haar to decide whether taking the bishop was worth losing her rook. As S'haar considered her options, the older woman spoke again. "So how do you propose to get us to the cave? Even with our coats, that journey is too far in these temperatures. We'd risk severe damage to ourselves and our livelihoods. Do you have more suits like yours?"

S'haar thought the older woman needed another distraction and brought her queen around to threaten Fea'en's king. "Check. No, we've only got the one, but we have a sled and lots of insulating materials. It would be easy enough to bundle one person up at a time, pack them in with heating packets, and have the person in the suit drag them to the cave. That way, there's no risk of frostbite."

Fea'en positioned her own rook between S'haar's queen and her king so that if S'haar took the rook, the king would take her queen, and if she did nothing, the rook would take her queen. Trying to hide her scowl, S'haar positioned her queen to threaten Fea'en's king from a corner space instead. "Check. There's just one issue. The dragon and Jack have many secrets, and they aren't ready to reveal all of them to the world just yet. So we'll need you all to swear an oath of secrecy."

As predicted, Fea'en moved her rook to protect her king again, but at least it wasn't threatening S'haar's queen anymore, and more importantly, it was now tied up so S'haar could begin to make her own escape. The older woman spoke as S'haar decided how to best make her escape. "That shouldn't be an issue. We won't swear fealty or anything like that, and our oaths will be conditional on none of these secrets being a threat to our people or village, but our lives are certainly worth keeping a few secrets for."

S'haar positioned her king so that she should be able to break out of the trap next turn. "Alright, we'll hold an oath ceremony tomorrow. The day after, we'll start moving you all to the cave."

Fea'en nodded before moving a pawn two squares forward. "Checkmate."

S'haar blinked. She'd completely forgotten the pawn. It hadn't moved the entire game, and in trying to keep track of all the other 'important' pieces, it had ceased to be a factor in her mind.

In her ear, Angela was tutting S'haar's oversight. "Never underestimate the importance of a pawn!" S'haar grimaced in response, wanting to respond but not wanting to look like she was talking to herself. Not that the workers hadn't seen her 'speak to herself' before, but they still weren't used to it either.

S'haar looked up at the uncharacteristically cheerful Fea'en grinning back at her. "That was a good game. Got time for another?"

S'haar sighed before resetting the board. "All we have is time."

~

Later that night, when S'haar made it back to the ship, she was astounded to see Jack walking! Albeit with some aid. He was strapped into a wheeled contraption that helped him balance while his hands were tightly gripped onto handles set at waist height. Em'brel was shadowing his every move with her hands hovering just out of touching distance as he awkwardly shuffled forward. Upon seeing S'haar, Jack lost his focus and started to slip before Em'brel quickly grabbed hold to steady him. "You're doing good! You almost made it across the whole room this time!"

Jack's face was beaded with sweat, though S'haar was happy to see a grin on his face, even if it was tinged with a bit of embarrassment. "Yeah, well, I'll be a lot happier once I can get around without a walker again. At my age, I'm both too old and too young to be needing one!"

S'haar cocked her head to the side. "Not that I want to get in the way of all the progress you've been making, but do you think you'll be up for a trip outside tomorrow?"

There was more than one pair of eyes filled with confusion suddenly directed at S'haar, so she explained. "The workers are running out of fuel, so I think we'll need to move them in here with us. Before we do that, I want them to swear an oath of secrecy. Since this is your home, you're the one they'll need to pledge their oath to."

Jack looked a little confused but eventually relented. "Huh, I guess that makes sense." He then tilted his head to the side. "Angela, any chance we can get a basic wheelchair ready to go by then?"

Angela appeared nearby with a chart in hand. "We've got plenty of raw materials with which to make one, but you won't be using it long enough to be worth investing any bells or whistles into it, so it'll be pretty bare-bones."

S'haar's face expressed the confusion that was voiced by Em'brel. "What's a whistle, and why does your wheeled chair need a bell?"

~

This section of the cave was still relatively warm, and a coat was enough for Em'brel, but she couldn't go any further with S'haar and Jack.

Instead, she was obsessively checking the straps holding Jack to his chair and his chair to the sled in turn. "Jack's made a lot of progress, but you'll still have to keep a close eye on him. Sometimes he still gets dizzy and loses his balance."

Angela cut in as well. "Even though he's eating and drinking, it's probably best to avoid anything other than some water until he's back home, to avoid any complications!"

Jack waved the two women off in an annoyed manner. "We'll be fine, *moms*! We're just going to the workers' billet and back, not on some cross country venture. S'haar's made the trip a half dozen times in as many days! What's more, Angela, you'll be coming along for the ride, so if there are any 'complications,' you'll be the first to know!"

Angela didn't have much to say, but Em'brel still looked worried. "It's just that…"

Jack cut her off with a smile and a hand gesture. "Listen, you've been taking care of me day and night for nearly a week. Go watch a movie, take a bath, or whatever catches your fancy. All work and no play isn't good for anyone! We'll probably be back around lunchtime."

Jack sat back, and his grin widened. "Besides, look at me! I'm as fit as a horse on the way to a glue factory!"

S'haar and Em'brel both looked confused. Angela was standing with her arms crossed and a rather 'put out' expression on her face. "I was half tempted not to let the translator pick up that last part. That was a terrible joke!"

Em'brel still had her head cocked to the side. "I know what a horse is from watching movies, but what is a glue factory, and what does one have to do with anything?"

Jack's laughter wasn't any help, and Angela simply shook her head and sighed. "Don't encourage him. You're happier not knowing!"

S'haar walked over to the smaller argu'n and gave her a hug before speaking. "Listen, I'll keep a close eye on Jack. He'll be my number one priority the whole time we're gone. Jack's right though, you deserve a break. If you're anxious, you can check-in anytime with the headset. That's the whole reason we have them, remember?"

Em'brel reached up to her headset as if she'd forgotten all about it, then nodded. "Alright, but if anything goes wrong, you let me know immediately!"

Jack interjected, "Listen, if all of you are done fawning over me like some nursemaids who found a helpless kitten, we'd better get going. The sooner we leave, the sooner we'll be back!"

Realizing there wasn't anything else to say, Em'brel merely nodded and watched as S'haar helped Jack double-check that he had everything he needed in his satchel, then started dragging the sled through the cave. After a few moments, the younger argu'n turned and went back inside.

~

As the two made their way through the cave, S'haar brought a hand to the headset at her ear. "Angela, could I ask you to give us a little privacy? Just until we reach the billet."

Angela's voice came through to both Jack and S'haar. "I suppose you two deserve a little privacy. If anything goes wrong, just say my name twice in a row, and I'll be right there. Angela out."

S'haar pulled the sled in silence a moment before looking over her shoulder. "How're you holding up?"

Jack put a big smile on his face as he replied. "I'm doing great! Angela says my recovery is actually ahead of schedule. In another week, I should be walking under my own power, albeit I'll probably need a cane for a while after that."

S'haar was silent for a few more moments before speaking up again. "That's not what I meant. How are *YOU* doing?"

Jack's smile slipped a little and took on a more languid appearance that was reflected in his voice. "Honestly? I'm tired. The process of fighting my way out of the coma felt like an epic journey all on its own. Then, after I woke up, I had expected to need some rehabilitation, but *this,*" Jack waved his arms around himself, " was more than I was ready for. The constant pity in everyone's eyes weighs on me all day long. When I exercise, all I really want to do is lie down and rest, but the more I push myself now, the more complete my recovery will be, so that's just not an option. Then, when I have to rest to recover for the next session, all I can do is stress because I'm not currently working on getting better."

Jack's sigh wavered a bit as his emotions bubbled to the surface. "I don't think I've ever been so physically, mentally, or spiritually exhausted in all my life. I keep wondering when I'll finally collapse under it all, but somehow I have to find just a bit more energy, so I push a little further… Sorry if that got a little heavy…"

S'haar shook her head. When she spoke, her voice was blessedly free of pity or judgment. "No, that *is* what I was asking for. I was getting the feeling that you were putting up a bit of a cheerful face in front of the other two as we were setting off, but you need to know that it's ok to not be perfect all the time. For what it's worth, given…everything…I think you're doing better than anyone had any right to expect of you. If it finally gets to be too much and you need to take a break, that's fine too."

Jack was silent for a moment before replying. His voice came out tired, but it also had a touch of relief. "Well, thanks. I mean it. But for now, I have a little more energy…so I plan to keep pushing myself as long as I'm able. There will be time to rest later. Maybe I'll take a month or two off when all this is said and done!"

S'haar nodded. They were nearing the part of the cave where it was cold enough that she had to put her mask on. Before doing so, she stopped and turned around, walking closer until she stood towering over Jack. "Well, that's fine. For the record, I don't pity you. If anything, I think I've come to respect you a little more. So keep up the hard work…"

S'haar leaned in a little closer, speaking softly into Jack's ear. "...and maybe one day, you'll get to enjoy the meat of your hunt!" With that, S'haar gave Jack a playful nibble along his jawline before pulling her mask in place and securing the fasteners. Jack suddenly felt warm in a way that had nothing to do with the freezing cave's ambient temperature.

~

When they arrived at the billet, it took S'haar a moment to clear a spot to unstrap Jack's chair and quickly wheel him inside so they'd waste as little heat as possible. Once inside, S'haar began the familiar ritual of removing the bulky suit. As she did so, it quickly became apparent that all eyes were focused on Jack.

The looks in the eyes ranged from worry to pity, and Jack started to worry about how awkward this was going to be when Lon'thul spoke up loudly from his seat. "Wow! S'haar told us you were in rough shape, Jack, but you look like hell!"

Everyone was staring at Lon'thul with expressions ranging from horror to rage, and S'haar was opening her mouth to unload a furious tirade unlike any she'd ever given before when Jack beat her to the punch, forcing her to translate instead. "Wow, Lon'thul! Kicking a cripple while he's down is the epitome of *lame*! I won't *stand* for it in my own camp... Then again, I'm not standing for much these days..." Jack had a grin that strangely mirrored Lon'thul's as he spoke.

Everyone looked back and forth with blank expressions, utterly lost at how to respond in the face of Lon'thul's inappropriate statement, followed by Jack's equally problematic puns. The silence only lasted a moment before it was broken by Lon'thoul's barking laughter. He walked right up to Jack and slapped the man on the back, utterly oblivious to the death glare S'haar was drilling into the hunter's back. "And here S'haar had us all worried that you might not be the Jack we've all gotten to know up till now, but you seem alright to me! If you can make a joke like that, you're gonna be fine in no time!"

Lon'thul handed Jack a mug of a drink that S'haar quickly whisked away before requesting some water instead. As the hunter sat back at the fire, he indicated a clear spot next to himself. S'haar wheeled Jack over while Lon'thul continued speaking in the overly cheerful manner of his.

"You're here so we can perform a big official oath ceremony. But first, you *gotta* tell me more about this god of death you spoke with! Did you really tell her off? Common man, details. I need details!"

Jack grinned mischievously and started moving his arms around to emphasize his words as he spoke. "So for the record, I don't know if this was real or just some fever dream brought on by a near-death experience, but to begin with, I found myself in the middle of nowhere. I'm not saying I was lost in the wilderness or anything. This was the most literal 'nowhere' you've ever heard of, there was no ground, but I wasn't falling, floating, or flying. There was no light, but I could see clearly through the gloom. I'd been stuck there for longer than any sane man should have been when this voice comes out of nowhere and just says, 'Hello.'"

S'haar sat back and relaxed while translating Jack's incredible tale. Everyone present was captivated by every word, and their eyes were filled with nothing but wonder as the story unfolded. Maybe it was just her imagination, but she thought that Jack seemed to be sitting a little taller, and his arms seemed to have just a bit more strength in them than they had back in the cave.

She had to admit, it was one hell of a story.

Chapter 39

Jack wasn't looking forward to what was coming. S'haar had told him all about the ceremony and what would be expected of him, and to be fair, it wasn't going to be nearly as long or drawn out as Jack had feared, but this next part didn't seem like it would be fun.

S'haar carefully inspected the ceremonial knife. Angela had insisted they use a knife she made just for the occasion. Officially, it was because the knife was supposed to be a special knife, explicitly crafted for the ceremony and never to be used again unless the oath was broken. Unofficially, her reasoning was that if Jack was going to be cut by any knife, Angela wanted to make sure it was the cleanest and finest knife possible. Sharp enough to make a clean cut, but not so sharp it would cut deeper than intended.

For once, Jack was glad to be disabled. Normally he'd be expected to make his own cut, and he'd been afraid he'd somehow screw it up. Instead, given his current plight, everyone agreed that S'haar making the cut for him was a reasonable accommodation.

Jack was doing his best to focus on enjoying the sensation of having S'haar hold his hand while also trying *not* to think about the knife's blade she was lowering into his upturned palm. She made a deft movement, and it was over before Jack realized the cut was made. As the blood began seeping from his wound, Jack spoke the words everyone had agreed on, while S'haar translated for everyone gathered. "All who swear on my blood will keep sacred the secrets of myself and my household, except in the event of danger to friends, family, or home."

Following those words, Jack placed his palm on the stone that had been presented to him. Above the mark his blood left on the stone was a carving of the symbol of Jack's 'house.' Not that he'd had one before now, but he'd taken the time to design one for the ceremony's purpose. Since it would have to be carved into stone, he kept it simple. It consisted of a circle surrounding a triangle whose sides represented human, AI, and argu'n, and a line came from each side to meet in a circle in the middle, symbolizing their unity as a family.

Thankfully, Jack's part of the ceremony was completed. S'haar took his hand and applied the gel Angela had provided, then wrapped it in cloth so Angela could look at it later.

As she was attending to Jack, Fea'en took up the knife and cut her own palm. Jack winced inwardly, thankful he'd gotten to go first, and trying to remind himself that it was highly improbable that any pathogens he carried would be able to affect the argu'n. The old craft master spoke her own straightforward lines. "On pain of death, I so swear!" She then placed her own palm on top of Jack's mark, mixing her blood with his.

One by one, all the workers present repeated the solemn oath. Jack thought the whole 'pain of death' part was a little extreme, but S'haar told him it was customary for any significant pledge to include that statement. In the event of a broken oath, Jack had the right to crack the stone then use the knife to claim the life of whoever had failed to keep their commitment. This was considered one of the highest laws of the land, superseding any individual village or clan laws. Not that Jack had any plans to claim anyone's life if they failed to keep their oath, but it certainly added a degree of credibility to the pledge when the workers were willing to put their lives on the line as collateral against their words.

Once everyone finished their oaths, Fea'en took the stone and knife and handed them both to Jack to keep. With the ceremony complete, the atmosphere in the room lightened, and everyone seemed to breathe more easily.

Lon'thul stood towering over Jack and rested an easy hand on the wheelchair-bound man's shoulder. "So, how much longer before you're back in charge of this camp?"

Jack tilted his head to the side. Only S'haar knew him well enough to know that the troubling grin on his face meant he was about to say something unexpected, but even she was unprepared for the words that followed. "You know, from what I've seen so far, S'haar has done a remarkable job leading this camp while I was unconscious. She seems to hold everyone's respect naturally and easily, and I think it might be best if she remains in charge. I've always been happier as an idea man rather than a leader, anyway. I'll still be involved, offering advice, technology, my thoughts, and ideas, but I think S'haar is, by nature, a better leader than I could ever be."

There were expressions of shock on everyone's faces as S'haar translated Jack's words, and none more so than S'haar's. It took her more than a moment to speak after he was done. "But this is your camp, your home! I can't just take over!"

Jack carelessly waved away her concerns. "My goals are the same as ever, to secure the safety and happiness of my friends and family. After the time we've spent together, I'm confident you share those same goals. I'm not going anywhere and will be happy to continue to help guide the camp's development, but ultimately this is turning into an argu'n camp, and I think it would be best if an argu'n was in charge. You're a perfect bridge between my goals and your people's needs. Additionally, you'll naturally command the kind of respect from new or visiting argu'n that I would have to spend a significant amount of time and effort to acquire. I think this is the best path for everyone's objectives for the camp."

S'haar remained quiet, but the look she gave Jack clearly said 'We'll talk about this later.'

Lon'thul had an exaggerated expression of concern on his face. "Awww, man! You were a lot easier to keep happy than S'haar. She's always demanding that I 'stop daydreaming,' and 'get back to work!'"

Jack's grin grew a little more toothy as he imitated the more predatory smile of the argu'n. "All that tells me is that I've made the right choice! If S'haar can keep *you* in line, running a camp like this should be easy!"

Lon'thul had the good grace to act hurt at Jack's words, but his impish grin belied his performance.

That was when a familiar voice spoke up from Jack's headset. "Ahem. Now that your little club has sworn their oaths, isn't it time you introduced me?"

Jack raised an eyebrow at her phrasing but decided she was right, it was a good time. They'd agreed it was best to get this out of the way as a whole group, rather than explaining it one at a time as the workers were brought over to the ship, and right now was as good a time as any. He cleared his throat, and as usual, S'haar translated. "So now that you all have sworn your oaths, I figure it's about time we introduced you to the dragon you've heard so much about."

Lon'thul's eye ridges shot up toward his forehead. "Wait, you mean it's *real?* I'd finally decided it was just a code word you all used for 'human tech.'"

Angela laughed in Jack's headset. "Well, in a way, he's not *wrong...*"

Jack smirked in acknowledgment of her words while he answered the hunter. "As is often the case, the reality is more complicated than any simple answer I can offer. But rather than try and explain things, how about I show you instead?"

With that, Jack pulled out one of the emitters he was carrying from the ship, ran a cable between it and his headset, and thumbed it on.

Almost immediately, the room exploded into light. Soon, every inch of empty space was filled by the immense form of a classic earth dragon, complete with thick scales, massive teeth, and sharp claws. Part of its body seemed to pass into the hallway, but Jack knew this emitter couldn't reach that far, so it was just a bit of clever illusionary work on Angela's part.

The argu'n in the room all stood stock still, the only movement being their eyes trying to take everything in, and their tongues rapidly tasting the air to confirm what their eyes were telling them. The first one present to respond was S'haar. "Really? Isn't this a bit dramatic?" Her voice seemed unheard by the other, stunned argu'n.

The dragon's form quickly began to shrink and morph, stopping briefly at the size and shape of a 10-foot tall argu'n. As it continued to shrink, it stopped again at the appearance of a 7-foot tall human. Finally, Angela finished shrinking down into her standard size of a single-foot tall human.

With a wave and a smile, she greeted the stunned workers. "Hiya! I'm the dragon you've all heard so much about! Call me Angela. It's good to finally speak with you all!"

Everyone remained frozen in place for several moments, unsure how to respond to the impossibilities that had unfolded in front of them. Angela was looking around at everyone with her characteristically impish grin. Predictably, it was Lon'thul who first broke the stunned silence and cautiously approached the tiny woman. He bent down at the waist and gently poked a finger into the AI. His finger passed through without any resistance. "You can transform at will, fly, and speak our language... Are you a spirit?"

Angela floated up, forcing Lon'thul to stand up to his full height before she 'flicked' him on the nose. Anticipating an impact but receiving none, Lonthul blinked a few times. Angela responded with an overly cheerful tone of voice. "Well, yes and no. This is how I usually appear to speak to people. I have a real body, and It's actually significantly larger than even the first form I showed you, but that body is badly damaged right now. One of the reasons Jack and S'haar started this whole place was to get what they needed to help heal and free me of my prison."

Lon'thul looked over at S'haar with a single raised eye ridge. "If what she's saying is true, should you really be working to free such a massive creature? From the sounds of things, she could devour our entire village if she so chose..."

Angela flew in between the two with her hands on her hips and a reprimand evident in her voice. "It's not polite to talk about someone in the third person while they're in front of you! And for your information, I don't eat animals, or even plants, for that matter. When I'm whole, I eat stars like you see in the night sky, and even a single star will last me more than a hundred of your lifetimes!"

Lon'thul looked even more confused than before as he turned his attention back to Angela. "I'm not sure what three people you're talking about, and how can a star fill you up for so long? They are so tiny!"

Angela looked pleased to have a new student as she began one of her lectures. "'Third person' is when you refer to someone as if they aren't present. The use of words like 'she, her, herself, etc.' are most often the third person, but if that person is involved in the conversation, it's more polite to address them, or in this case me, directly! As for the stars' size, they only seem small because of how far away they are. For example, think of this mountain and how much smaller it looks from your village than from this camp. Stars are also like that, but they are significantly further away from here than this mountain is from your village!"

Lon'thul looked at the tiny woman floating in front of him, beaming back at him like she was one of his old hunting masters. His face was scrunched up as he tried to understand what she'd explained to him before he gave up with a shake of his head. "You sound too much like Jack does when he starts getting way too excited about something boring! Though I suppose we have little to fear from you, if you and Jack are so much alike…"

S'haar let out an overly patient sigh that was indicative of untold tales about her long-suffering experience with the duo. "You have no idea how alike those two are… They're actually brother and sister."

Jack and Angela replied at the same moment, both of their voices indignantly defensive. "We're not that much alike!" They both glared at the other, silently accusing each other of proving S'haar right with that outburst.

Lon'thul looked even more confused than before. "They're brother and sister? Does that mean Jack will grow to an immense size as well?"

Jack and Angela were too caught up in their little squabble to answer, so S'haar continued the explanation. "They're not related by blood, but they were both raised by the same man. So, despite being as different from each other as humans and argu'n, they think of themselves as brother and sister."

S'haar's head tilted to the side as she struggled to remember some of what she'd been told back when she had first been wrapping her own head around this strange new world of theirs. "And to answer one of your previous questions, I don't think we have any more to fear from Angela than we do from Jack. From what I understand, her people are as advanced in comparison to humans as humans are compared to us. They even fought a war to protect and preserve humanity's survival and individuality. I suspect Angela would do the same for us. She seems to hold all 'intelligent life' as sacred."

Jack interrupted the squabble to interject. "Well, I wouldn't say the AI are quite as far ahead of us as all that…but you're more or less correct."

Angela was haughtily inspecting her fingernails as she offered her counter to Jack's claim. "Says the meat-for-brains human, only capable of processing roughly thirty-two bits of information at any given time."

Jack was not about to be so quickly or easily dismissed. "We may only be able to process thirty-two bits of information at a time, but we do so at speeds that are impossible to calculate. Our brains are practically supercomputers!"

Angela dove back into the ongoing debate with relish. "Impossible for *you* to calculate, perhaps, but my brain is *literally* a supercomputer!"

The fear slowly drained out of the onlooking argu'n as the pair reignited their squabble. The workers could only keep up with half the argument since only Angela was speaking their language and S'haar had stopped bothering to translate for Jack, but the grins and vocal tones made it evident to everyone watching that this was more affectionate ribbing than an actual argument. Somehow, seeing such a petty sibling rivalry between these two 'advanced' people made them both more relatable.

Fea'en had been watching the whole ordeal with a keen eye. Finally, she approached the small AI. Stopping just short of the tiny woman, she waited until all conversation had stopped, and Angela addressed her directly. "Lady Fea'en, how can I help you?"

If the older woman was surprised the AI knew her name, she didn't show it. Instead, she addressed her concerns in her usual direct manner. "Dragon, I've heard a lot of assurances that you mean us no harm, but I want to hear it directly from you. What do you intend regarding myself and my people? What are your plans from this moment forward?"

Angela's expression eased from giddy excitement to a more somber, though still friendly, manner. "Well, I can't partake of the same oath ceremony you all just did for Jack, since I have no blood to offer, but I swear to you by all my honor that I do not intend to bring harm to you or your people. Instead, I hope that our presence here will ultimately bring about advancement and prosperity for everyone, though I acknowledge the path we're treading will have many obstacles in its way."

Angela continued her speech, though her expression and voice both grew heavy with concern. "The raiders are an obvious danger, even some of the local lords may see us as a threat to their power, and I'm sure there are even more problems impossible to see from where we now stand. Although we will fight to protect our friends and family, Jack and I will never seek to conquer or subjugate anyone. All who join us will do so of their own free will and retain the ability to leave at any time they so wish. To that end, I agree wholeheartedly with Jack's decision to leave S'haar in charge of this camp. Argu'n should lead argu'n, and we will be content to fulfill the roles of guides and advisers."

Angela's voice softened as she finished her speech, echoing some of Jack's own thoughts from his debate with "death." "For all of my abilities, I can not see the future. I'm not certain if the path we've chosen will end well or in disaster. All we can do is offer our knowledge, experience, and hope. With a bit of luck, maybe we can help your people avoid some of the pitfalls our own fell into over the ages."

Fea'en glared at the AI for several long moments, and the rest of the camp held its collective breath, waiting to hear what the craft master would say.

With crossed arms, Fea'en passed her judgment on Angela's words. "Good enough for me. I'll stay. It's up to the rest to decide what they'll do."

A series of assents began to spread through the workers but were interrupted by Lon'thul's excited cheer. "WOOHOO! This is gonna be so much *better* than I'd hoped! And, we all got in at the beginning! They're gonna be telling stories about us for ages to come! We're all gonna be legends!"

The hunter's energy permeated the room, and an impromptu celebration broke out as food and drink started making the rounds. S'haar was quick to whisk away any food or drink that found their way into Jack's hands but was heartened to see the somberness of the last week replaced by celebration and cheer. Throughout it all, Angela was flittering to and fro, getting to know everyone "face-to-face" at long last.

Chapter 40

Such a small celebration wasn't going to last long. Even so, Jack was overcome by a wave of exhaustion brought on from exerting himself too much, too quickly. This fact didn't escape the notice of S'haar or Angela, who mutually agreed it was time to head back to their home.

As everyone said their goodbyes, S'haar said she'd return the next day to begin moving the workers to the cave, and Angela promised to have a warm welcome in store for the workers, "pun not intended." It took a little longer to strap Jack's chair onto the sled this time since Em'brel wasn't there to help, but once they were on their way, S'haar felt now was a good time to address her unspoken concerns. "So when were you going to tell me about your decision to leave me in charge of this camp?"

Jack was silent for a few moments before responding. "Well, I've been debating the idea for a while, but it was only at the ceremony that I finally decided. I would have told you first, but Lon'thul brought it up before I could find the time to mention it."

S'haar dragged the sled through the snow in silence for a while. When she did speak up, her voice was quiet but thoughtful. "But…why?"

Jack hesitated to answer but felt he owed S'haar an explanation. "Throughout human history, there have been many times a technologically advanced group of people decided to 'help' a 'primitive' group. I'm sure most of those who began such undertakings had good intentions at heart, but all too often, it resulted in the more advanced society taking advantage of the other. There are probably many subtle complicated reasons that things went the way they did, but the result was often the same, and I didn't want to repeat that here."

As they got far enough into the cave for S'haar to remove her mask and gloves, Jack continued his explanation. "I'm sure I'd try to lead this camp with the best of intentions, and I'm confident that in many ways this place would be a success, but I'd probably unintentionally try to turn this community into a mirror of humanity. However, you already have a vibrant culture of your own. Maybe some of the sharper edges could stand to be softened a bit, but that is for you as a people to decide when and how to make any changes. You know what Angela and I are capable of. You are familiar with the lives of your people's upper and lower classes, you're honest and straightforward, and you are a natural leader. I can't think of anyone who would be better suited to leading your people through an age or two of advancements."

After that, the two of them traveled in heavy silence for several moments before S'haar spoke up again. "Alright, fine, I'll forgive you this time. I'm still not sure I'm the best choice for the job, but we can talk more about that later. For now, let's get back home and prepare for tomorrow."

Jack didn't respond. S'haar looked back only to find him slumped over in his chair. With a dreadful stillness in her chest, she leapt back onto the sled to check on Jack. When he still didn't stir, she spoke into her headset. "Angela, something's wrong with Jack. He's unconscious again!"

Angela's voice came back to her, calm but urgent. "Ok, don't panic, it's probably nothing unexpected. Just get Jack back here as quick as you safely can."

S'haar grabbed onto Jack's restraints and tore them free of the chair. He groggily muttered something incoherent and tried to weakly bat at her. As soon as she lifted Jack into her arms and began to sprint the rest of the distance, he passed out again.

S'haar was grateful that they didn't have far to go. As soon as she crossed the threshold, Angela and Em'brel were there, anxiously waiting. Angela took charge. "Quick, get him to the med-bay, and lay him on the bed with the scanners."

S'haar was familiar enough with the med-bay after periodically taking Jack there for the occasional in-depth scan during his coma. What really tormented her was the tension-filled minutes while Angela ran various lights and diagnostic machines over and around Jack.

After a few minutes that seemed to stretch on for hours, Angela approached the two women waiting anxiously by the door. Her easy smile was already alleviating fears before she began explaining. "Jack's fine. I think the poor guy simply wore himself out in all the excitement. This whole thing was a bit more stress than his body was ready for, but don't worry, he'll be right as rain with a bit of rest."

The two argu'n shared an exasperated sigh of relief before S'haar picked Jack up once again and carried him to his bed. As she tucked Jack in to get some much-needed sleep, she couldn't help but mutter complaints to herself about how watching over such a fragile person was starting to age her before her time.

~

Jack groggily woke to find himself buried under more blankets than he usually preferred, but this unfortunate state was somewhat offset by something pleasantly cool lying across his chest and one of his legs.

Opening his eyes, Jack felt his body temperature quickly rise when he found S'haar asleep, laying somewhat haphazardly on top of him. It took him a few moments for his sleep-hazed mind to recall how he'd gotten here. The last thing he remembered was coming back from the party. He'd had an odd dream about S'haar running while carrying him, then he woke up here. Jack felt his face warm further as he realized he must have passed out on the way back to the cave. However, the embarrassment was somewhat tempered by feelings of security brought on by the weight of S'haar's limbs resting easily across his own.

Jack decided that this was all something that could be dealt with later, and he wrapped his own arms around S'haar's pleasantly cool presence beside him. It didn't take long for Jack to slip back into sleep, where he was greeted by S'haar once more. Though the nature of their time together was slightly different than it had been during his brief time awake.

~

The next day they began the process of bringing the workers over to their home in the cave. Lon'thul was the first to make the journey. As the youngest and healthiest argu'n present, he would be the quickest to recover from any complications brought on through any planning oversights.

He was wrapped in several layers of thick skins, with heating packs wrapped in with him. Since Lon'thul didn't particularly want to suffocate, his mouth was covered in something Angela called a scarf, and heating packs were placed right next to his mouth to warm the air passing through the scarf so he wouldn't damage his lungs. Once the preparations were completed, the two set off.

Everything went pretty much as well as could be hoped. Lon'thul was a little sluggish and confused by the time he'd arrived but quickly recovered inside the ship's warmth. After Angela performed a quick scan and gave him a clean bill of health, S'haar left to get the next worker.

Lon'thul was sitting around enjoying a warm drink Em'brel told him was called tea. He'd been hoping to speak with her before any other workers arrived, but it seemed all of Em'brel's attention was currently reserved for Jack. Seeing how hard the human was pushing himself at the moment, the hunter could hardly begrudge him the attention. At least that's what he told himself.

As Jack stumbled, Em'brel caught and steadied him again. "I wish you'd use the straps like before. It would be a lot safer if you did!"

Jack's face was covered in sweat, and he took advantage of Em'brels steadying hands to catch his breath and say something. The words made no sense to Lon'thul, but Jack's annoyance was evident despite the language barrier, and apparently, it was enough to catch Angela's attention as well.

Angela stood in front of Jack with crossed arms and a stern glare. Lon'thul still couldn't get used to the idea that this tiny woman was the "dragon" he'd heard so much about. However, the hunter couldn't deny that this place was amazing, and apparently, that was primarily due to her influence. Though he did note that her demeanor was much more frightening now than it had been yesterday.

With a voice to match her glare, the AI reprimanded Jack. "Your appearance isn't something we're particularly concerned with right now. Your progress and safety are. Luckily for you, you are right about this being more effective, and I trust Em'brel here to save you from your own stupidity. Otherwise, you'd be tied to that walker like a stuck pig! Now get back to work before I change my mind!"

Jack muttered what must have been an exhausted assent of some kind before Em'brel released him, then continued his circuit of the room.

Lon'thul felt a bit awkward sitting back and watching, so he decided to join the conversation. "Man, that looks rough. How long do you have to keep this up for?"

Em'brel looked like she was about to reprimand Lon'thul for interrupting when Jack answered. His voice came out as a kind of hybrid between a gasp and a grunt as he pushed himself on while he spoke. This time Em'brel translated in a somewhat distracted manner as she kept a close eye on Jack. "In another week or so, I should have most of my motor function properly under control. After that, it'll be another month of muscle-building until I'm back to my old condition, give or take a bit."

Lon'thul's eye ridges rose in surprise. "So, you're gonna make a full recovery?"

It was Angela who responded this time. she was looking down at some wooden board in her hands while she spoke. "I'm estimating roughly ninety-five percent recovery, with a small margin of error. Although that's assuming Jack doesn't go and do something else stupid to hinder his recovery further."

As if to emphasize her point, Jack stumbled and was caught by Em'brel once more. Angela simply glared at Jack and switched back into her scary mode. "Come on, three more laps, then we can take a break and work on writing instead!"

Jack looked back at the AI with an exasperated look on his face. "Writing? When my arms are this exhausted?" To emphasize his point, he let Em'brel hold him steady as he lifted a shaky hand.

Angela was in no mood to coddle him. "You're the one who wanted to "push" yourself by working without straps. If it's too much for you, we could strap you back in for the last four laps."

Jack looked at her with a confused expression. "Four laps? I thought you just said I only had three more to go?"

Angela had an exasperated look on her face as she shook her head. "Are you losing your hearing now? I clearly said it would only be five more laps until your break unless you want to debate this a little longer?"

Finally, getting the point, Jack sighed and got back to walking. Lon'thul had only caught half the conversation this time around since

Em'brel had stopped translating for Jack while he spoke with his sister, but what little he was able to understand had only made him feel sorry for Jack as the man pushed himself through his last few laps. This time Lon'thul thought it would be best not to distract Jack any further and instead focused on drinking some more of his tea.

~

The next to arrive was Fea'en. Once the older argu'n snapped out of her cold induced sleep haze, she simply looked around a bit before stating, "Huh, guess the kid didn't exaggerate for once."

Angela was visibly distraught at the craft master's lack of reaction. She always loved seeing the wonder in an argu'n's face the first time they looked around at her ship, but Fea'en seemed to simply give everything a swift appraisal before moving on to the next "wonder."

Shaking herself out of the pout she felt coming on, Angela resumed her role as a host. The AI floated right up to the craft master, who didn't seem at all phased by the idea of speaking casually with the legendary "dragon." Angela pouted a little more in the back of her processor but was determined to be a good host. "Welcome aboard, Lady Fea'en! If you come this way, I have some hot beverages ready to help you finish recovering from your journey here. After that, we can look to whatever other needs you might have."

Fea'en simply nodded. "Thank you, dragon. I appreciate it." With that said, the old argu'n took a seat at the table and finally showed a small reaction as she smiled at the comfort the chair offered her old bones. Her smile deepened a little further once she accepted a steaming mug from the always eager Lon'thul.

She sat there for a moment, thoroughly soaking in the experience of a comfortable seat while her hands cradled a warm mug from which pleasant-smelling steam wafted up to her nostrils. She indulged in the sensations for several minutes before finally taking a small sip from her drink. Second and third sips followed quickly on the first's heels, and Angela finally got the reaction of wonder she'd been hoping for when the old woman simply stared at the mug in astonishment. "This is…quite good. Should I ration this, or is there more where this came from?"

Angela beamed at her new guest. "There's plenty of that to go around. Jack's never been much of a tea drinker, so my stores are still pretty well stocked. Enjoy your fill, though you may want to eat something with it, so you don't feel waterlogged. Might I suggest some turkey and ham sandwiches?"

As the older woman accepted one such sandwich from Lon'thul, she seemed enticed by the smell. After a quick bite, she found that she was ravenous. Not long after that, Fea'en was looking at the last remaining crumbs with a bit of regret. When the young hunter offered her a second sandwich, the craft master seemed determined to pace herself this time.

~

Angela finally got the show of excitement she'd been hoping for. Each time one of the other workers arrived, they stared open-mouthed at their surroundings. Even Jack was forgiven for taking a break from therapy to enjoy the workers' reactions as they looked around at the wonders of their temporary home.

As the other young and healthy argu'n, Tel'ron was the last to arrive. He and S'haar had been responsible for making sure the fire was properly out, everything they couldn't bring with them was stored correctly, and the shelter was firmly secured before leaving. Once he arrived, his reactions made all the rest pale comparatively, and Angela got exactly the show she'd been hoping for, and then some.

Even before his daze had worn off, the young artificer was inspecting various pieces of metalwork. Everywhere he directed his attention, he couldn't help but poke and prod as he tried to understand the marvels around him.

Soon, Angela's only real fear was that the smith wouldn't make it out of the entryway in less than a week if he continued obsessing over everything that caught his eye. He spent minutes closely inspecting the detailed carvings of the lettering on the light panel. Angela had to lock the door as soon as he started fiddling with the door controls to try and figure out how the buttons functioned at all. With Angela's permission, he ran a claw over several metallic panels, astounded at how hard the well-polished surfaces were. He knocked on walls to listen to the sound of the reverberations, and he stared with a slack jaw as she instructed him to carefully pull back a pannel and saw the fine wiring and circuitry that typically lay hidden.

He was finally drawn away from his inspections by some of the food and drink that waited for him. Tel'ron spoke with wonder clear in his voice. "I've obviously died in the deep freeze and am now in the artificers' heaven! This place is a shrine to the works of the gods! I could study even the simplest of pieces contained herein for the rest of my existence and consider myself blessed to do so!"

Angela was delighted to have another student eager to learn but decided it best to somewhat temper his expectations. "I'll be happy to answer any questions you have about this place during your stay, but most of this will be of no real practical value to your people for many generations. That being said, I'm sure there are a few things I can teach you that will be of significant use to a smith like yourself. For example, most of the iron you have access to is something we call bog iron. It is a relatively low-quality iron. Let me tell you about a process humans once utilized called 'folding,' it was used to purify similar iron where we came from. This was most famously used on an island nation called Japan..."

As the evening wore on, everyone found themselves spending the most pleasant evening any of them had experienced since that first night of celebration when they'd arrived at the camp so long ago. Fea'en let herself drift off to a comfortable slumber in her new favorite chair. Lon'thul and the other two woodworkers spent their time on a series of checker games. Jack and Em'brel continued Jack's therapy. Tel'ron sat at his new mentor's feet, doing his best to commit every word to memory.

During all this, S'haar stood off to the side, watching everyone find their place in Jack's world. She couldn't help but wonder if she would ever be able to lead anyone into anything other than more trouble.

Chapter 41

Jack's ship had initially been designed to be a home for a family, but having seven argu'n and a human fill its space was definitely stretching its capacity for comfort. Fea'en shared a room with S'haar and Em'brel, but the rest of the workers simply found a spot on the living room floor to bed down.

Another issue that quickly became apparent was that this number of unwashed bodies being bottled up in an enclosed space had certain predictable effects on the atmosphere aboard the ship. After a light breakfast, Jack decided it was time to address his guests. This time Angela translated but, to the surprise of the gathered argu'n, did so with Jack's own voice. "Alright, I'm glad everyone was able to get here safe and sound, but this place is beginning to reek! Starting today, all of you will take turns showering, so my home doesn't have to smell like some overfull stables any longer! Angela will happily show each of you how the shower works. So, who's willing to go first?"

Everyone looked at Jack in a confused manner until Lon'thul voiced the universal question. "What's a shower?"

Em'brel took it upon herself to answer that question. "It's like taking a bath under a heated waterfall. Honestly, it's one of the greatest treats this place has to offer, the only trouble is that you'll have to keep your showers short so we don't run out of hot water too quickly."

With the girl's endorsement, everyone suddenly seemed eager to volunteer. As the most senior worker present, the honor of the first shower went to Fea'en. While the craft master figured out the wonders of the heated waterfall, Em'brel organized the rest of the argu'n to clean the ship. S'haar may be in charge of the camp, but caring for the house was Em'brel's responsibility, and she approached the job like a general directing troop movement. "Ok, Lon'thul, you run the vacuum. I'll show you how in a moment. No, Tel'ron, if I let you do it, you'll spend the whole time trying to figure the machine out and not get anything done. You'll help with the dusting! Jan'kul, you help with the laundry, and Nak'torn, the dishes. If you all do a good enough job, I'll make something special for dinner tonight. Sound good?"

With the possibility of a special dinner cooked by Em'brel, any resistance faded away before it was voiced, and everyone took to their tasks. Angela did her best to explain what needed to be done to everyone, but occasionally Em'brel or S'haar had to step in to show someone how something functioned. Storerooms that hadn't been touched since the ship had set down were emptied, cleaned, and sorted. The kitchen was made to sparkle, and as it turned out, the shower was a big hit. Several workers wanted to go a second time as soon as the water was reheated.

While all the excitement was going on, S'haar stepped in for Em'brel, helping Jack with his therapy for the morning. Jack had recovered well enough that she was mostly offering moral support rather than acting as a full physical therapist. The only real complication they ran into was when Jack had to tell S'haar she couldn't help him as much as she wanted.

Jack was shaking his head, trying not to laugh at S'haar's expression of minor annoyance. "This is supposed to be hard for me to do. That's the whole point! If I wasn't pushing myself to my limits, I'd still be unable to feed myself or use the restroom. You have to let me exhaust myself if I'm ever going to get better!"

S'haar grumbled with narrowed eyes, balling her hands into fists to resist the urge to reach out and help Jack as he did his leg lifts. "Fine, but I don't have to like it! I'm supposed to be the one doing the heavy lifting while you come up with the ideas! I'm your bodyguard, after all!"

Jack chucked through the strain in his voice. "I'm not the only one who has to come up with ideas now. You're in charge of the camp, remember? Being both a camp leader and my bodyguard might be too much for any one person to handle, even you."

S'haar's voice suddenly had a dangerous edge to it, and a growl was evident in her voice. "That's something only I get to decide! You don't get to dump this on me, then tell me how I'm going to go about doing my job! Get used to me, because I'm not going anywhere!"

Jack relaxed his legs and held up his arms in surrender. "Alright, alright, you win! It's your call! Not gonna lie; there's no one I'd rather have by my side, anyway. After all, I think we work pretty well together."

As Jack resumed his leg-lifts, S'haar looked at him with a stony upraised eye ridge. "Is that the only reason you want me by your side? Because we work well together?"

Jack lost control and collapsed and sputtered a moment before being able to vocalize any coherent thought. "You *know* that's not the only reason I want you by my side!" S'haar's grin clearly indicated she did indeed know, but she waited for Jack to continue.

With a shake of his head and slightly exasperated sigh, Jack gave in to S'haar's unwavering expectant look. "Since I crashed on this planet months ago, you've been with me nearly every waking moment of every day, and more than a few non-waking moments as well. I quickly came to rely on you for your forthrightness and dependability. Before I knew what was happening, I also began to trust you as a friend. Then, just as I thought there might be a future for the two of us beyond simple friendship, I went and got myself nearly killed and lost in a coma for what seemed like a lifetime."

Jack felt his heart rate increasing as he found himself getting lost in the eyes of the woman listening patiently as he continued. "While I was gone, you took up my mantle and continued the struggle on behalf of everything I had been working toward. You never walked away, despite how long it took me to get back, and you were the first person I saw upon awakening. Even when you saw how weak and frail I'd become, rather than look down on me, you decided to encourage and support me as I struggled to overcome this new obstacle."

Jack's face was quickly turning that shade of red S'haar had grown to enjoy over their time together. "So yes, I want you at my side, and I want to be at yours, for however long you'll put up with me. But I want you to be my partner, not my caretaker, and that's one of the main reasons I've pushed myself so hard in my recovery, but I still have a way to go."

S'haar looked contemplative for a moment as though judging the weight of Jack's words. Eventually, S'haar reached out and pulled Jack into a very human-style kiss, probably inspired by one too many movie nights, before pulling back with that predatory grin that contained just a few too many teeth. "I suppose that'll do for now, but eventually, I'm going to make you say it more directly than that. After all, a woman deserves to be told that she's wanted!"

With a slightly judgemental glance at Jack's legs, S'haar changed gears quickly enough to give Jack a bit of metaphorical whiplash. "Well, since you're working so hard to get better, you should probably get back to your leg lifts. I'm not going to be patient forever, so stop slacking!"

Despite the joking tone to her voice, Jack couldn't help but mutter something about some women being "impossible to please" before returning to his workout. Although he discovered that he suddenly had significantly more energy to push himself than he'd had moments ago. Whatever else he could say about S'haar as a physical therapist, she was undoubtedly an expert at the motivational aspect of the job.

~

Tel'ron was inspecting the shower somewhat dubiously. "So I just turn this knob, and hot water comes out? Enough to wash myself?"

Angela nodded. "Yup, it's really that easy! Once you're nice and wet, there's a bar of 'soap' in there. Rub it on the small square of cloth, and then apply that to yourself. It'll wash off all the dust and grime you've accumulated so far this winter."

The smith jumped a little at the sudden hiss of water when he turned the knob but quickly found himself drawn in by the steam emanating from the small cubic room. The area was already a bit cramped as far as seven foot tall S'haar was concerned, so of course, Tel'ron really had to contort himself to properly fit, but once inside, he stood still, drinking up the warmth of the water passing over his hide.

Once he was adequately warmed, the smith started inspecting every nook and cranny. Eventually, his eyes rested on the knob he'd used to turn on the water. He quickly realized there was another direction available with a shaded blue color. "So if this side makes hot water, does the other side create cold water?"

Deciding to test his theory, the young smith flipped the nob in the other direction. Angela's voice quickly boomed through the shower. "Turn that knob back NOW!"

Tel'ron tried to do just that but was hit by a sudden jet of cold water, disorienting him in an already confined space, and quickly sapping him of all his energy. Though Angela was able to shut off the water to the shower, not long after he collapsed onto the ground. What's worse, none of the sensors in the shower had a proper angle to see if he'd hit his head when the smith fell.

Angela appeared before Jack and S'haar. "Tel'ron fell in the bathroom. I'm not sure if he's ok or not!"

They drew some odd looks as S'haar half-carried Jack into the bathroom in a hurry. Jack immediately started checking for vitals. "His pulse is slow. He might be injured…"

S'haar took one look at the situation and chuckled under her breath. Turning the dial back into the red, she addressed Angela. "Go ahead and turn the water back on."

Angela was still somewhat concerned but deferred to S'haar's judgment. Once the water was running warm again, she shoved Tel'ron back into the shower.

It took a few moments for Tel'ron to wake up with a sudden sputter, but Angela started laying into him immediately once he did. "You are to NEVER fiddle with anything on this ship without first asking myself, Jack, S'haar, or Em'brel again! If you *EVER* pull another stunt like this, I might just leave to freeze to death next time! You're lucky S'haar was around to save you from your own stupidity!"

S'haar was too busy helping Jack back out of the bathroom to pay the rant much mind, but it was loud enough that everyone else in the ship certainly caught an earful. When Tel'ron sheepishly walked out of the bathroom later, he was greeted by hoots of laughter and tumultuous applause from the rest of the workers.

~

The enticing aroma of Em'brel's special dinner had each of the argu'n waiting at the table with salivating mouths. Whatever it was smelled better than anything she'd ever cooked for them before, and that truly was saying something.

Jack and S'haar shared a conspiratorial grin since they were both aware of what was coming. Em'brel had run her plans by Jack since this was the last of his stores for this particular meal. As sad as Jack was to see it go, he couldn't imagine a better time or a better group to share it with.

Just when Jack was starting to worry that the workers were about to snap and run into his kitchen in a feeding frenzy, S'haar and Em'brel brought over several steaming platters and placed the two largest in the center of a couple of improvised tables and a third, slightly smaller platter, in the middle of their own table. She explained what she was serving as the hungry eyes followed the movement of the platters. "So you are all aware, this is the last of Jack's stores of steak from his homeland. This is probably the most tender and juicy meat you'll ever eat, so everyone be sure to thank Jack for sharing the last of it with each of us!"

Lon'thul held up a half-eaten New York strip. His voice was only slightly slurring around the large half-chewed morsel currently filling his maw. "Thanks, Jack, this is great!" His lengthy expression of gratitude complete, Lon'thul started biting off a second mouthful before he'd even finished chewing the first.

Most of the other workers were a little more disciplined and managed their own brief expressions of gratitude before digging in as well. Jack was glad he'd gotten used to S'haar's manner of eating a while back. Not long ago, the sight of seven argu'n tearing away at a large pile of meat might have been enough to turn his stomach. Instead, he simply held up a slice of his own ribeye and said his peace. "Good food is always better when shared with friends and family! Eat your fill. Today we celebrate all the hard work that's got us this far!"

At least a couple of argu'n showed enough conscious thought to share appreciation for his words through nods of approval. Though Fea'en's nod was cut short when she had to slap away the hand of Lon'thul as he'd reached to take some of the steaks from her plate. "Try that again, and you'll lose that hand!"

Judging by his grin, Lon'thul's attempt had been more about mischief than greed, but he seemed to know better than to test the craft master's patience a second time.

~

Not long after dinner, the argu'n were all contentedly complaining about their bellies being so full that they ached. Jack thought now might be the perfect time to introduce his guests to another way to pass the time. "Alright, now that you've all eaten your fill, it's time I introduce you to a method of human storytelling. One thing I should warn you of first, long ago, humans mastered the art of creating illusions, and we use those illusions to aid in our storytelling. I want you to remember that much of what you will see is nothing more than a clever illusion, created solely for the purpose of storytelling and entertainment."

Of course, it was Lon'thul who cut off Jack's speech. "Yeah, yeah, we all know how plays work! I'm sure you're going to add a *human* twist to it, but get on with it already!"

Jack simply smiled and turned his attention to his sister. "Angela, go ahead and start the movie."

A quiet voice spoke out from the large reflective black panel that was hung prominently in the room. "The world is changed. I feel it in the water. I feel it in the Earth. I smell it in the air."

Everyone was so enraptured by the soft voice that when flames first erupted on screen, Jack had to pause the movie to explain that the fire was all part of the story and that his TV wasn't really on fire. Then, he had to pause again at the elves' appearance to clarify that there were no tiny people inside the screen. It was just a series of rapidly moving pictures.

By the time the battle had begun, everyone was finally hooked and paying rapt attention. Jack and S'haar were seated comfortably on the couch together, with Em'brel sitting at their feet. Fea'en was using her new favorite chair. She'd been planning on letting herself doze off, but even she found herself unable to look away once the movie began in earnest. The rest of the workers were scattered about on the floor on whatever makeshift seats they could find, hanging off of every word and action.

More than once, Lon'thul had to be told to sit back down when he leapt up to attack whatever prey or monsters he saw on the screen. Tel'ron was almost as bad with all his questions about how this new marvel functioned. After repeated threats from S'haar and Fea'en to make the young males suffer if they interrupted the movie one more time, both eventually settled down to enjoy the film.

There were a few more interruptions when Jack had to pause the movie for bathroom breaks and to explain once again that no, Lon'thul could not hunt a balrog because they aren't real.

When the first Lord of the Rings movie came to an end, everyone protested, and of course, Lon'thul was the loudest. "What happens to

Frodo and Sam now that the fellowship is broken? Who will stop Sauron? Are there really races of people smaller than humans? You can't leave us hanging with the hunt half finished! Tell the rest of the story!"

Jack chuckled as S'haar helped him to his feet. "That was just part one of three, and the other two parts are almost as long! I don't know about the rest of you, but there's no way I'm staying awake through nearly eight more hours of movie. We'll watch some more tomorrow. Now, get some sleep!"

At the mention of how long the rest of the remaining movies were, the room was filled with relenting sighs and grunts. As Jack hobbled to bed with S'haar's help, Em'brel set about preparing the ship for the night or, to be more accurate, she told the workers to prepare the ship for the night. "Come on, there are dishes to be done! I'm going to need a clean kitchen if I'm going to make another breakfast for you lot! Two of you wash dishes, the other two clean the room and prep the sleeping area, now move!"

Fea'en was excused on account of needing to rest her "tired old bones," but the rest jumped to their assigned tasks when Em'brel threatened to have Jack hold off on showing the rest of the movies if they slacked off in cleaning the ship.

Chapter 42

Jack was pleased to see the next several days pass relatively smoothly. Once a routine was established, it simply became a matter of passing the time. Their mornings were usually filled with various chores that needed to be done to keep the relatively small area livable with such a large number of inhabitants. The afternoon was typically spent playing board and card games, watching movies, and occasionally planning what they would do once they could resume working outside.

Another week of physical therapy passed with only slight complications brought on by the presence of so many onlookers. It made Jack more than a little self-conscious but also gave him the drive to push himself a little harder and longer. Any judgments that might have been foolishly vocalized at Jack's expense were quickly silenced by a glare from S'haar. Except, of course, the ones that came from Lon'thul.

Jack was catching his breath after a light jog around the living room when Lon'thul walked up. As usual, he seemed utterly oblivious to S'haar's intimidation tactics. "You know, Jack, seeing you push yourself to overcome your injury is really inspiring! It's like we have a room full of Aragorns, Gimlis, and even Gandolfs," He nodded his head toward Angela as he said that, "and you're like Sam, always getting back up no matter how many times you fall!"

Jack raised an eyebrow at Lon'thul as he finally stood up straight. "Ok, first off, that's a compliment. Sam is a badass! Second, and I'm afraid to ask this question but…who do you think you are?"

Lon'thul lifted a few head tendrils and whisked them over his shoulder while shaking his head dramatically to settle them in place. "That's easy, I'm Legolas, obviously!"

Angela was far too amused to keep her opinions to herself. As she floated over, she gave Lon'thul a measuring gaze. Her eyes went from head to toe, then back to his head, all while she perched the crook of a finger on her lower lip. "I don't know, that's not quite right…"

With a snap of her fingers and a widening of her eyes, Angela's voice took on the kind of excitement one's does when making a significant breakthrough. "I've got it! You're Peregrin Took! You are totally the type who would throw a rock down a well just to see what would happen!"

Everyone within earshot broke out in laughter, but none louder than Lon'thul's rival, Tel'ron. This, of course, drew Angela's attention to the other young argu'n. "That would make you Merry! You two are perfect fits for the roles! I swear, keeping both of you out of trouble is a full-time job!"

Now it was Tel'ron's turn to look crestfallen as everyone else in the room laughed at the young argu'n's misfortune of ending up at the mercy of Angela's wit. Soon enough, both men recovered from their verbal whipping and joined back in the laughter.

Angela took a bow in front of her audience. "Thank you, thank you, I'll be here all week! Remember to tip your waitresses!"

~

Once again, Jack was pushing himself to his limits, this time with some free weights Angela had crafted for muscle training. They had plenty of iron sitting around, and she considered the energy used as an investment in getting Jack back in proper working order. The workers were fascinated by the idea of doing something for no other reason than to build muscle.

Currently, Jack was trying not to be too embarrassed by the fact that the weight he could barely bench press was below what S'haar could curl with one arm. They'd found this out when Jack had pushed himself hard enough that he couldn't reset the weights, so S'haar, who was spotting for him, had to lift them into place for him. As she began reducing the bar's weight so Jack would do a few more sets, S'haar admonished Jack. "Don't worry about what I can do. Worry about what you can do. Besides, comparing yourself to me wouldn't be fair even if you were fully recovered." To emphasize her point, S'haar flexed her arms the way she'd seen humans do in several movies.

Jack admired her form before he sighed while bracing his arms to do the next set. "My brain agrees with you, but my gut still doesn't like it. A lifetime of social conditioning doesn't go away that quickly or easily. That's ok though. I'll just have to use that frustration as motivation to push myself harder, while at the same time working to overcome my personal insecurities."

Angela was currently sitting on one of the weights. It slightly threw Jack's perception off since his brain told him one side should be heavier than the other, but she'd told him that having to steady the free weights was better for overall muscle development than a more streamlined machine would be.

Once Jack started lifting again, the AI decided to add her own two cents to the conversation. "Well, that's very mature of you. Keep that up, and you might just become a fully functional adult!"

Jack held his peace while he finished his set, then spoke up between breaths while his arms virtually dangled from their handhold on the bar. "Yeah, two things though. First, it's easier said than done, and I'm not sure how much praise I deserve just for realizing something so basic I need to work on. Second, the idea of a fully functional adult is just a myth. You can take the single most self-sufficient man or woman in the world, and there's always going to be an area of life they need help with. That's just the nature of being a finite being in an infinite universe."

Tel'ron was watching the goings-on with some interest. He'd already inspected the weight bench when it had been first brought out, and now that he was watching it in action, he had questions. "This device's only function is really just to help you lift heavy things to build muscle? Is it common for humans to need to do something like that?"

Angela hopped off the weights to address the question so Jack wouldn't interrupt his exercise attempting to do so. "It's much the same among humans as it is with the argu'n. Those who have the kind of jobs that require the heaviest lifting are usually those with the most developed muscles. Now, look around at all the machines in this house. With a heated stove, there's no need to chop wood. With indoor plumbing, you don't need to haul water. Having seen all this, you need to understand that this house is still 'roughing it' by human standards. Where Jack comes from, humans don't even need to walk between villages. They have machines that will carry you back and forth. Almost every physically demanding aspect of life is taken care of by machines now."

Tel'ron's head was spinning with the attempt to think of the kind of machines Angela was talking about. He tried to imagine something to carry a person between villages. All the smith could think of was a really long rope with seats, stretched between pulleys like the ones Em'brel had designed for the well. He knew that it would never work for various reasons and suspected the reality was far stranger than he'd ever be able to think of on his own.

Angela continued her explanation. "There's even a word for replacing physical labor with machines. It's call automation. The problem with automation is humans quickly found that they weren't moving, lifting, or pushing nearly enough every day. As a result, they began experiencing a significant decline in fitness and health. So, of course, humans did what humans do and studied how to fix the problem. They came up with the idea of exercising. It's the concept of doing a more intense physical activity over a shorter period to replace the day-to-day physical activities that were no longer a part of their lives."

As Jack finished another set, he collapsed onto the bench, unable to bring himself to do any more for at least a few minutes. Angela nodded in his direction. "The reason Jack is pushing himself so hard is that rather than merely maintaining a healthy body, he's replacing lost muscle mass. That takes a lot more work, but hopefully, he'll be in pretty good condition by the time spring rolls around."

Tel'ron shook his head. "It almost sounds like all this progress just brings on more problems for you."

Jack jumped into the conversation, finding this a great excuse to take a break from his workout. "Yeah, it's been a bit of two steps forward, one step back, but overall we've still made a lot of progress. When our society was at a similar point in history compared to your own, only about half our children would survive to adulthood, and the average life expectancy of a human was only about twenty-eight to thirty-six years. These days, roughly forty-nine out of fifty children reach adulthood, and the average life expectancy is about a hundred and fifty years, with some people getting up to around a hundred and ninety."

The room had gone quiet as everyone present stared at Jack. Jack was just starting to feel self-conscious, wondering what he'd said wrong, when Em'brel shot to him like a bullet, wrapping her arms around his waist while sobbing into his chest. "No! You can't leave that early! It's not fair! You have to hang around until I'm old and grey!"

Jack did his best to console Em'brel while looking up to S'haar for answers. "Why? What's the average argu'n's lifespan like?"

Fea'en is the one who spoke up from her chair. "Well, it might not be my place to interrupt, but I've lived through roughly two hundred and twenty winters so far. It's not common, but also not unheard of for an argu'n to live well past three hundred."

Angela was going a bit of math off to the side. "Even taking into account the differences in your planet's orbit, that would still add up to about two hundred and eighty human years!"

Holding a sobbing Em'brel while looking back at S'haar, who was now staring down at him with wide eyes, all Jack could offer was an eloquent, "Huh…"

~

It took Jack a good half an hour to calm Em'brel down and assure her that he wouldn't go anywhere anytime soon. Still, that information bomb definitely put a damper on the evening.

After dinner, Jack put on a movie. He immediately found himself sandwiched between two very distracted argu'n. Jack suspected that neither S'haar nor Em'brel was paying much attention to the film. Maybe it was the fact that S'haar's eye seemed to be focused unblinkingly on some distant point far beyond the ship walls, or perhaps it was because Em'brel kept looking over at Jack, getting misty-eyed, then looking away again.

When it was time to call it a night, S'haar helped Jack to his bed again, even though he didn't need the help anymore. Once he was settled in, rather than say goodnight and leave as she usually did, S'haar crawled into bed with Jack, wrapping her arms tightly around him, locking him into a rather fierce embrace.

Jack started to say something, but S'haar cut him off with a terse, "Shut up!" Her grip lacked any feelings of lust or longing. Instead, Jack felt like he was a teddy bear of some kind, being tightly held by a scared young girl to ward off whatever monsters might lurk in the dark.

S'haar's grip continued tightening until Jack started having trouble breathing easily. He decided to try once again. "Your grip is a little too tight!"

His words were met with another whispered "Shut up!" but S'haar's grip loosened just enough for him to breathe.

After being held like that for a long while, Jack felt S'haar's grip loosen a little more, and he listened as her breathing slowed enough that he was confident she'd finally fallen asleep. But when Jack tried to shift into a more comfortable position, he found that S'haar's hold wasn't going to completely let up any time soon.

With a sigh and a whispered, "Well, this is my life now, I guess…" Jack let himself settle in as best he could. Despite the embrace's discomfort, Jack couldn't help but notice a sense of peace settle over him. This was totally different from other times he and S'haar had shared a bed. This time just felt right, like some hole in his spirit had been filled. Eventually, Jack's thoughts slowed, and he slipped into the embrace of sleep.

In his dreams, Jack found himself back on earth. There was a gentle breeze, and he could hear birds singing and bees buzzing while a slow-moving stream provided relaxing background noise. Jack found himself floating over an older S'haar, who seemed to be visiting his grave. She alternated between grumpily cursing him for leaving her alone once again and laughing while smiling and telling him about her day. It was oddly comforting in a sad sort of way.

When Jack woke in the middle of the night, he noticed that both of their pillows seemed strangely damp.

~

By breakfast, the somber mood from the night before had mostly lifted. Though Jack noticed Em'brel still seemed to be stealing glances at him with greater frequency than in the past, and S'haar seemed to be hovering just a little closer than usual. Still, at least the tears seemed to have mostly dried, and the smiles were slowly making a return.

They were listening as Angela described the concept of a water mill to Em'brel and Tel'ron when suddenly the AI stopped speaking and got that far off look in her eyes as though she were listening to a distant conversation of some sort.

When she refocused her eyes on the group, she spoke with excitement evident in her voice. "I think the freeze is coming to an end soon! It's a few days out, maybe a week, but there are signs of a warm front approaching!"

This announcement was met by a cheer, and everyone started speaking excitedly at the same time. Jack could only make out snippets of conversation going back and forth, but one thing Lon'thul said caught Jack's attention. "Finally! This was a long one!"

Turning his full attention to Lon'thul, Jack asked the young hunter the question that was bothering him. "How long was this freeze, relative to a normal one?"

Lon'thul looked deep in thought when Fea'en answered for him. "As our intrepid hunter mentioned, this one was longer than usual. I don't think it was as cold as some I've been through, but probably the second or third longest I've seen."

Shifting his attention to the craft master, Jack asked the next question weighing on his mind. "How do you think the village fared? What condition are they in?"

The table grew quiet as she weighed the possibilities. With a solemn voice, Fea'en answered. "Well, they're probably alright at the moment. It's likely only the oldest or weakest couldn't get to the shelter on time, but as long as the freeze lasted, their supplies are probably severely depleted. The rest of the winter will probably be very rough on the survivors."

S'haar leaned back in her chair for several minutes, eyes closed and arms folded. When she opened her eyes, she found herself the center of everyone's attention. The room was so quiet, Jack jumped a little when she cleared her throat. Looking at Jack, her voice held the note of an apology. "I know there's still a lot of work to do, but I want to put together an expedition to return to the village as soon as the freeze passes. We have the tools and ability to supply them with the wood and food they'll need to make it through the rest of the winter. I know it's a setback in your plans, but…"

Jack cut her off with a raised hand. "Don't apologize. That's precisely why I want you in charge, because you'll make calls just like that one. Honestly, if you didn't come to that decision, I was going to recommend something along those lines. We can save lives, and we should. We've got a few days before we can act. I suggest we take this time to plan how we're going to pull this off!"

Chapter 43

One of the biggest problems facing the group was figuring out how to travel safely to the village. Even with the temperature soon to be on the rise, it would still be below freezing for longer than they wanted to wait. So all the snow that had piled up during the deep freeze would take too long to melt for waiting it out to be an option. The other problem facing them was how to provide the energy required to charge the heating packs while they worked.

S'haar was looking at the snowshoes she'd used while getting to and from the worker's billet. "Can we craft enough of these for everyone?"

Jack frowned. "We probably could, but those aren't great for long-distance travel. As you noticed, they are considerably slower than walking and more exhausting to use, so we'd have to take a lot more breaks. It would take us the better part of a week to make it to the village using those."

S'haar sighed, setting down the snowshoe. "You might be right, but it would be far better than pushing through the snow the whole way. At that rate, we might as well just wait for the snow to melt before leaving."

Jack had his chin propped up by his hands as he spoke. "True, but I think there's a better option. I'm thinking cross country skis. They are energy efficient, and once you get used to traveling with them, they should be quicker than walking."

Angela offered a counterpoint. "That's might work, but you won't be able to haul as much due to the decreased friction making a heavier load impossible to move. You're going to have to haul food for yourselves so you don't use any resources the village can't spare, tools for gathering wood and hunting, and something to produce the power you'll need to charge the heating packs."

Jack stopped and thought for a minute. "What if we split the load up? Rather than one large sled, we have each argu'n pull their own smaller sled."

Angela hesitantly nodded. "That might work, but we'll need to craft them all from scratch. It's still far too cold out for the workers to return to the woodworking hall. They won't even be able to get started until the freeze passes, and that'll take precious time."

Em'brel tilted her head to the side. "What if they worked in the cave right outside the ship? It's still cold there, but the heated coats should be enough protection this far in the cave."

S'haar nodded. "There's just enough lumber leftover that we should be able to make a few smaller sleds. I can retrieve the wood and tools they'll need with my suit."

Creating three-dimensional images of the skis and sleds, Angela turned to Fea'en, who'd stayed silent up until now. "How long would it take you to craft enough of these for everyone here?"

Fea'en squinted at the images for a moment. "What kind of dimensions are we talking about?"

Angela put up an image of S'haar in between the skis and sleds for scale. Fea'en sat back with crossed arms. "Well, it would be quicker in an actual workshop, but even with basic hand tools, we can probably put together at least a couple sets a day."

S'haar nodded, satisfied with the timeline. "We'll need six sets, so that should be less than three days. That'll work."

Jack looked a little surprised at that. "Six? Even if we're leaving Em'brel at the ship, we'll need seven sets by my count."

S'haar glared at Jack with narrowed eyes, her voice one small step away from a growl as she spoke. "*You* aren't coming either! You're still recovering, and you'd just be dead weight!"

Jack looked surprised a moment before shaking his head with a wry smile. "That's not a very nice way of saying you're worried about me and that you'd prefer if I'd stay here where it's safe. But I have to disagree with you. I'll only be dead weight *if* everything goes as planned. What you're forgetting is that regardless of how weak I am now, I'm still the only one here who can safely work in the cold. What if something goes wrong with the generator, what if another storm hits, what if, what if, what if? I hope I'm dead weight because that would mean everything went according to plan, but if things go wrong, I might be the difference between everyone getting there and back safely, or not at all."

S'haar glowered at Jack, wanting to refute him, but found herself unable to find a good reason. "Fine, but I expect you to spend every minute up until departure pushing yourself twice as hard to get yourself into shape! I won't have you slowing us down out there!"

Jack waved off her concern. "Yes, yes, I'm worried about your well-being too. What you're forgetting is that I'm literally built for this. Endurance strain is the one area I have an advantage over you argu'n. I may still be a ways away from full capacity, but I'm confident that by the time the freeze ends in a few days, I'll be able to keep up with you, if not outright outpace you!"

Lacking any further arguments to keep Jack back where it's safe, S'haar finally relented. "Alright, seven sets it is. I'll suit up and start hauling wood. Fea'en, have a list of tools you'll need by the time I get back with the first load, and I'll get those in the second."

Fea'en nodded. "Sure thing. Dragon, can you give me a more detailed image of what the skis and sleds will look like?"

As Fea'en and Angela started working on the diagrams, Jack helped S'haar suit up. "I know you're worried about me, but you can't just lock me in a tower and keep me safe. I'm no more a damsel in distress than you are. The world's a dangerous place, but I'm not about to let you take all the risk while I sit back and twiddle my thumbs. We're in this together."

S'haar paused in suiting up and looked thoughtful for a moment before grinning mischievously. "You're right. I should keep my eyes on you anyway. You'd probably find some way to get into trouble while I was gone, but you have to admit one thing. You're just a little bit more a damsel in distress than I am!"

It was Jack's turn to glare. "Remind me again, who found who tied to a stake, naked, and ready to be sacrificed?"

S'haar waved his point. "Oh please, you know I've saved you at least as many times as you've saved me, but I'm not the one who broke his foot kicking someone in the face!"

The whole room was watching the playful bickering by now. This was some of the best entertainment they'd had in weeks. Of course,

Lon'thul had to join in the discussion. "Hah! Way to let a woman put you in your place, Jack!"

Jack felt his face grow warm, but S'haar merely developed a predatory grin. "You know, you could learn a thing or two from Jack. There's a reason he's the one I've chosen to share my bed, and it's not just because he keeps it so nice and warm!"

To emphasize her point, S'haar reached down and drew Jack into a rather intense kiss. For several long moments, Jack forgot all about his embarrassment. When S'haar pulled back, he was left pleasantly dazed. The room erupted into a chorus of catcalls and cheers as S'haar put on the rest of her suit and took off to make the first supply run.

~

Jack and Angela were debating how to address their power needs while Jack used the weight bench again. This time Em'brel was spotting for Jack. Angela's jeans and t-shirt look was at odds with her serious expression. "We don't have enough resources to make more solar panels, but you could unhook and take one of our current sets with you."

Jack shook his head. "Absolutely not! First off, I'm not going to deprive you of any more energy than is necessary. Second, their output isn't as reliable as we'll need. That's one thing when you've got them tied to massive batteries like we do on this ship, but it's a whole different problem when you depend on them for a direct charge. We need something that'll produce the power we need, when we need it. To that end, I'm thinking something more along the lines of a high capacity battery."

It was Angela's turn to veto the idea. "There's no way I'm sending you all out there with something that has that limited a lifespan! It needs to be something that you can refill or recharge when needed!"

Jack finished a set and put the bar at rest before answering. "What about an old-style fuel generator of some kind?"

Angela looked thoughtful. "That could work. We don't have much access to fossil fuels, but I might be able to synthesize a biofuel using the excess fatty tissue of some of the meat and some of the oil we can leach out of our plant stores. It'll cut into our food supply, but we should have enough to fit our needs if Lon'thul can resume hunting again in a few days. The generator itself will be easy enough to craft. It doesn't require any rare minerals."

Em'brel was looking back and forth between the two, concern evident on her face. "What little I studied of fuel generators indicated the fuel was dangerous both in storage and in its exhaust. You even poisoned your cities to the point it harmed people's health. Is this a good idea?"

Angela addressed her concerns since Jack had started another set. "So long as everyone knows to store the fuel away from any fire, it should be stable enough that there is little to no risk to anyone. Although, to be safe, we'll keep it on a sled rather than having someone carry it directly. The fumes should pose no problem as long as the generator is kept out in the open air. What few contaminates they'll be exposed to should be less dangerous than exposure to smoke from a campfire."

Em'brel still looked somewhat skeptical as Jack finished up his set and caught his breath before speaking. "I'm not saying this is a perfect solution, but our options are limited, and everything we can do has some risk involved. It's just that this is probably the lowest risk option available to us. With a bit of luck, we're just being paranoid and over planning. I'd prefer to err on the side of caution, that's all."

Angela nodded. "Especially with your track record. It seems like every time you go out, you come back with some new injury. Maybe if we plan things out thoroughly enough, you'll make it back in one piece this time!"

Jack looked offended. "Hey, what about the second time we went to the village? I came back in one piece that time. Also, I only got nearly gored to death *once* while out gathering resources. I went out dozens of times without any near-fatal injuries!"

S'haar came walking up while pulling off her suit so she could warm up between trips. "You know you're not winning any arguments like that, right? Keep that up, and I might change my mind on your presence on the expedition!"

Jack was now facing three sets of eyes expressing varying degrees of annoyance at his joke. With a sigh, he relented. "Alright, alright. All joking aside, I am taking this seriously. Even if I wasn't motivated by self-interest, my safety is the group's safety. So you can believe that I'm checking and rechecking our plans in my mind.

Angela spoke on all their behalf. "See that you do, and give me another set while you work on that!"

With a sigh, Jack lifted the weights off the braces again. This was going to be a long few days.

Over the next several days, everyone's biggest surprise was that everything went more or less as planned. The woodworkers got the skis, sleds, and poles ready. Em'brel helped Lonthul prepare the food and camping supplies for travel. Jack showed Tel'ron how to care for and operate the generator. All the tools were given maintenance and sharpened to be ready for heavy use. Finally, Jack pushed himself as hard as he feasibly could in his recovery, with S'haar and Em'brel taking turns to encourage and support him as needed.

As Jack and Em'brel were finishing another set of exercises, Jack couldn't help but notice that the girl seemed distracted again. It took a little bit of poking and prodding, but eventually, he got her to open up about what was bothering her. "I just…I just wish I was going with you!"

Jack looked at her with his arms crossed and his head tilted as he tried to understand what she was getting at. "We've been over this. Because of the reason you were initially headed to the village, it's probably best you avoid allowing yourself to be in a situation where anyone from the village has direct control over you. That could result in a power struggle none of us needs at the moment."

Em'brel shook her head. "I know, and I agree, but I still wish I was going. The idea of staying here while you all go out and risk yourselves… It's almost too much! After losing my father, then almost losing you, then finding out I might still lose you, I don't think I could stand losing someone else again! Not right now! Not without doing everything in my power to help prevent that! I know you all are the ones taking risks, but weirdly, I feel like it's my life that's on the line…" After finishing her thought, she hung her head as if she was ashamed.

Now Jack understood. He put a hand on the young girl's shoulder, noting as he did so that she'd grown at least an inch since he'd met her. "That's a relatively common phenomenon back where we come from. It's called loss aversion. It can be challenging to understand, let alone deal with. A part of dealing with it is coming to realize that loss is inevitable. It's one thing to make your head understand it, I think we all logically accepted it back when we were kids, but it's something else altogether being able to come to really accept it."

Em'brel nodded but kept her gaze fixed on the floor while Jack pulled her into a hug. "I wish I could say there was an easy five-step process to accepting it, but ultimately everyone has to come to terms with it in their own way. It's not easy, but you're stronger than you realize. You've already grown so much since I first met you, and I have no doubt that you'll get through this a little stronger than you were before everything happened."

When Jack tilted her head up to look him in the eyes, Em'brel's eyes were brimming with tears. Jack gave her the largest, most comforting smile he could while he dried her tears with the sleeve of his shirt. "All that being said, hopefully, you won't have to worry about it for a long time to come. I'm not planning on going anywhere any time soon, and neither is S'haar. We're covering all the contingencies we can think of, and between Angela, S'haar, and I, we're paranoid enough to think of quite a few!"

Em'brel finally smiled and laughed a little, making Jack's own grin grow a bit more around the edges. He leaned in to whisper conspiratorially. "Besides, you're not the only one with loss aversion here. Even if we take the headsets with us, Angela will need your help as much as you'll need hers."

Em'brel looked confused as Jack continued his explanation. "She puts on a brave face, but I worry about what will happen to my sister when I pass on…hopefully, many years from now. It's been a great relief to me that our family has grown to include you and S'haar. There will be someone there for her for many years to come. I can see it now, aunt Angela, being there to help raise your children, grandchildren, and so on. She'll be telling stories about her adventures with her crazy human brother and our adopted family for generations to come!"

Angela flew right up to the two of them as they spoke. "Hey, what's with all the depressing conversations over here? With everyone taking off tomorrow, we should celebrate tonight! We'll have more than enough time to worry about them after that!" Em'brel laughed at that, maybe a little half-heartedly, but it was still good to hear.

Sadly, the steak was now gone, but Em'brel was able to whip up an extra-large batch of delicious stew that would store well for leftovers on their trip.

Everyone laughed and played games. Even S'haar joined in. Albeit, not until she'd checked, rechecked, then triple checked that they had all the gear they needed and it was all secured and ready to travel.

As the night wound to a close, Jack put on a movie. This time choosing one called "Dragonheart." At one point in the film, Lon'thul had to stop and ask Angela, "Why aren't you as impressive as the dragon in this movie?"

Angela didn't say anything. Instead, the dragon pulled itself out of the screen and took a snap at Lon'thul's nose. Unable to help himself, Lon'thul flinched back as the dragon faded and in its place floated Angela, with the dragon apparently returning to its position on the paused screen.

Angela's smile said it all, but she spoke up anyway. "Oh, I *could* be all big and scary, but I prefer lulling my prey into a false sense of security before *I* strike."

Lon'thul laughed as he stood up and dusted himself off. His ego was only as bruised as his rear. "You know, if you put your mind to it, you might just make one of the best hunters I've ever worked with!"

With a slightly flirtatious wink, Angela responded. "Oh, you have *no* idea, little man!"

Eventually, everyone's energy was spent, and they all dragged themselves to their various sleeping arrangements, spirits buoyed and ready to set out the following morning.

Chapter 44

The next morning everyone was greeted by the smell of the hearty breakfast Em'brel woke up extra early to prepare in anticipation of an early departure. When several workers started to clean the mess from the night before, she shooed them away from it. "I'm going to have nothing to do other than listen to Angela's lectures for the next several days. Having a mess or two to clean up will be a welcome distraction. You worry about getting out there and doing what needs to be done. I'll take care of the house."

As everyone finished dressing for the cold, Em'brel came up and gave Jack a hug that might have left a new bruise or two. "You take care out there! Don't get yourself hurt being a hero. Let S'haar do her job and keep you safe. If it comes down to it, you can even hide behind Lon'thul! Do what you need to do to come back, and don't let your pride get in the way! I expect you to be around to give me human advice for many years to come!"

Lon'thul grinned, happy to hear Em'brel mention his name no matter the circumstance. "Don't worry about a thing! Jack'll be back safe and sound before you know it! I'll stake my honor as a hunter on it!"

Em'brel favored him with a smile before returning her attention to Jack, who was grinning as well. "I'll be careful. I think I've had enough of being the hero for two lifetimes already. Honestly, I'm hoping S'haar was right, and I'm dead weight this time around. With luck, it'll just be a nice peaceful walk with good company and beautiful scenery, followed by a relaxing stay at an inn where I sit back and relax while they do all the heavy lifting!"

A familiar AI voice cut into Jack's description. "Absolutely not! You are not to slack off in your physical therapy simply because you're not on the ship anymore! I expect you to be out there helping in whatever way you can, even if your contributions seem negligible compared to the rest. If you're not bone-tired at the end of every day, you weren't working hard enough!"

Jack backed up with his palms held up in surrender. "Ok, ok, no relaxing vacation for me! I promise to push myself as hard as I can!"

Angela's image followed her voice, her fists planted firmly into her hips as she stared down her younger brother. "You better! Or I'll tell S'haar about a particular event involving a girl, a date, and an unexpected revelation!"

Jack looked genuinely frightened this time. "I already promised I'd be good. No need to threaten me!"

Everyone present seemed interested in knowing more, but when neither party seemed forthcoming, Em'brel moved on to hug S'haar. "Keep an eye on our human idiot. You know he's going to find some way to get into trouble while he's out."

S'haar hugged the girl back and laughed. "He'll probably find several ways to get into trouble, but I'll do my best to keep him in one piece, despite his best efforts. Even if I have to use Lon'thul as a living shield!"

Lon'thul was pulling at one of his tendrils with a look of mild concern. Leaning over to Jack, he whispered, "I'm starting to wonder if I shouldn't be worried about my own safety while we're out. They both seem rather intent in using me as a distraction if things go bad."

Jack leaned in and whispered back. He knew Lon'thul wouldn't understand his words but hoped he'd catch the commiserative tone. "At least they're talking about you like a person. At the moment, I feel like they see me as some kind of lost, helpless pet."

As the hug ended, S'haar looked over at the two men with a raised eye ridge. "What are you two whispering about over there?"

Lon'thul and Jack straightened up and spoke simultaneously. "Nothing!"

S'haar grinned as though she knew better. "Good, see to it that it remains 'nothing,' I've got enough to worry about on this trip without you two working together to make my job harder!"

The rest of the workers present shared a chuckle at the men's expense. The stress and worry of the trip seemed to fade slightly in the light of the farewell antics. If they were confident enough to joke around like this, maybe everything would be fine.

Eventually, everyone was prepped and ready to go. Em'brel stole one final hug from Jack before watching everyone leave. It was only after they walked far enough out that they had become simple shapes moving in the distance of the cave that her smile faltered, and she turned and walked back into the ship.

She allowed herself a moment of melancholy as she leaned against the now-closed door with her eyes closed. A few minutes later, she took a deep breath, opened her eyes, and smiled a little as she looked at the mess everyone had left after breakfast. With a half-hearted sigh, she stripped off the coat she'd put on for the chill of the cave and walked toward the mess. She intended to direct the frustrations of being left behind onto the dirty dishes' grease and grime.

~

The first leg of the journey was slow going. Once everyone hit the snow and put on the skis, it took a while for them to figure out how to get the traction needed for moving forward. With a bit of trial and error, along with several laughs at each other's expense, they were finally on their way.

They traveled in silence, looking around at a world stilled by snow. Jack was quiet because this was the first time he'd seen the alien world so serene and peaceful. The argu'n were quiet because this was the first time they'd bothered to spare more than a glance at the snow-covered landscape. Usually, once it snowed, it was too cold for them to do more than spare the briefest of moments outside, and even then, their minds were usually somewhat sluggish from the cold. But with coats, gloves, boots, and caps, the cold was held just far enough at bay that they could look around and appreciate the beauty of the winter landscape.

Jack was traveling beside S'haar. When she finally spoke, it was with a quietly subdued voice, as though she was afraid that speaking too loudly would shatter the atmosphere around them. "It's like we're in an entirely different land!"

Jack nodded, comfortable with the fact that no one but S'haar would understand him at the moment. "Yeah, this is almost what it's like to fly between worlds, seeing all the different paths life has taken on each of them."

Tilting his head to the side, Jack continued. "There was one world where plants never evolved, at least not like you and I understand the word. Instead, the closest analogies are a kind of plant/animal hybrid. The smaller ones hid at night, then walked out to warm themselves in the light of day. The larger ones just slowly migrated with the shifting weather of the planet. The whole planet is a bit like a bog, so deep roots weren't necessary for finding water. The entire ecosystem of the world is balanced around these walking plants. It's hard to keep a sense of direction with the whole landscape shifting from one day to the next."

S'haar looked at Jack, wondering if he was having some fun at her expense, but his expression remained earnest as he spoke. Finally, she decided he must be telling the truth, which just made the whole thing seem all the more strange to her. She'd known he'd been to places she could never dream of. Once, he and Angela had shown her what her own world looked like from up in the night sky. The world had seemed so small and lonely that her mind refused to accept what she'd seen. In some ways, this story of walking forests was easier to accept. In others, it just sounded a bit like the priests of her village talking about some land of the gods.

Jack took in the silence for a moment and grinned at S'haar. "You know, maybe one day I'll get to take you out there and show you a world or two!"

He scratched at the back of his neck a little as he thought about that. "Though I suppose it'll be a while, what with needing to fix the ship and you being in charge of the camp now. Maybe after you retire from the position…"

With a lurch, that thought brought to mind the fact that Jack could very well be dead of old age before that became a reality. When he spoke up, Jack seemed to be thinking along those lines as well. "So ever since the other night, I've been wondering, how old are you, anyway?"

S'haar laughed a little sadly but shook her head and answered as best she could. "Well, to be honest, I haven't kept an exact count over the years, but my best guess would place me somewhere around forty-five to fifty winters."

Jack looked at her with a bit of surprise evident on his face. "Huh, and here I always thought you were a bit younger than myself. Though I suppose taking our relative life spans into account, I'm still kinda older than you… Honestly, it's all a bit confusing."

S'haar looked at him with a bit of a wicked glint in her eyes. "What's the matter? Would you prefer to share your bed with some innocent young thing instead of a woman with experience?"

Jack laughed loud enough that he shattered the winter forest's spell and startled the workers traveling with them. Catching his breath, he waved her attempt at baiting him away. "Oh please, you already know my opinion on that subject! But, for the sake of clarity, you're the only one I'm interested in. 'Some innocent young thing' could never be anywhere near as interesting a partner as yourself!"

S'haar weighed his words and nodded in approval. "Good, now that I don't have a 'climate-controlled' room, I'd hate to have to give up my bed warmer just to punish him for being an idiot."

The rest of the workers only had half the conversation near the end to go off, but based on Jack's renewed laughter, they decided that they'd missed out on something good.

~

As the sun neared the horizon, S'haar called a halt so they could set up a temporary camp and get warmed up. They weren't making as much progress as she'd hoped. The heavy loads they were hauling forced them to break often, and it was looking like they'd have to spend at least one night between the village and the mountain.

When Lonthul protested that they should keep moving, S'haar addressed him calmly but firmly. "What good will you do anyone if we get there a day earlier but have to spend several days being treated for illness or injury that could have been easily avoided? We'll spend the night drying our gear while getting warmed and fed, then we'll resume our journey."

Working together, it didn't take the argu'n long to set up one of the larger tents they'd brought. Meanwhile, Jack worked on his own project. He jammed a sharp metal pole into the snow-covered ground. Frowning a little at how shallow he'd driven the rod, he focused before giving it another go, and this time it stuck. Unfolding a small box, Jack flipped a few switches and waited while the device calibrated itself. After a moment, Jack's headset came to life, and Angela's familiar voice made itself heard. "Took you long enough! Were there any issues or complications so far? Have you put yourself in mortal danger yet? What's going on?"

Jack chuckled a little to himself before activating the headset and responding. "We're all fine, no complications worth speaking of. You know you don't have to ask, right? If there had been an issue, I'd have brought it up on my own."

Angela snorted. "Uh-huh. Like I'd buy that. We both know you've hidden important things from me in the past to 'keep me from worrying'! Luckily you can't lie to save your life, so I believe you…this time."

Jack shook his head. He thought about pointing out that not everyone can analyze someone's vocal patterns for even the tiniest abnormal inflections but decided to forgo the argument altogether. "Is Em'brel there? Can you put her on a moment?"

With a sigh indicating disappointment that her argument was over before it had begun, Angela relented. "Yeah, just a moment."

There were some scraping and staticky sounds as Em'brel put on her own headset. "Yes, Jack, are you there? Are you in trouble already?"

Jack shook his head again, this time holding a hand just over his eyes as he did so. "Why does everyone assume I'm going to get into trouble as soon as I set foot outside the cave? I'm fine! I was just calling to check in and see how you and Angela are getting along."

Em'brel's voice came back a little sheepish. "Oh, yeah, that makes sense. I'm fine…and Angela's fine too."

Jack raised an eyebrow even though he knew no one would see the gesture. "You paused there. Let me guess, she's been pacing ever since we left?"

Em'brel hesitated again. "Ummm…."

That was all the answer Jack needed. "See? I told you. She's going to need your help as much as you'll need hers."

Angela's voice cut in. "You know I can hear you both, right?"

Jack ignored her and continued as though she hadn't spoken. "Listen, do both of yourselves a favor. After you've finished your lessons for the day, ask Angela to show you something called a 'video game.' Trust me, it's just what both of you need to take your minds off of us for a bit."

Em'brel's voice sounded as if she was confused but didn't want to question Jack's wisdom. "O…ok…"

Jack sighed. "Listen, whether or not something does go wrong, worrying about it right now won't do any good. You worry about problems when planning to prevent them and again when dealing with them after they've arisen. But there's a point between planning and action when worrying only takes an unnecessary toll on you. We're at that point right now, so take this time to rest and recuperate so that *if* something does go wrong, you'll be fresh and ready to deal with it."

S'haar was standing nearby, waiting to make sure Jack got some food in him rather than spending the whole night talking. Listening to what he was saying, she cocked her head to one side. "Hmmm, that sounds suspiciously like something I told you a lifetime or two ago."

Jack shrugged. "So what? Good advice is worth sharing!"

S'haar walked over and leaned in so she could speak into Jack's mouthpiece. Resulting in her lips being tantalizingly close to Jack's. "Ladies, you're going to have to let Jack go, or he'll never eat his dinner. I'll keep an eye on him, and we'll call you back when we're settled in for the night."

Angela laughed. "Fair enough! Talk to you later!"

Em'brel spoke up not long after, her voice more of a question than a statement. "Ok…over…end of message? Did I say that right?" That last part seemed directed more at Angela than Jack.

Jack chuckled to himself and answered anyway. "Yes, you said it right. Over, end of message!"

As the line went dead, Jack removed his headset with a sad smile. He also lifted the signal booster and packed it back away. The time might come where they could place many of these around to extend Angela's range even further, but for now, the raw materials needed to make them were rare enough to limit them to just the one. So he had to bring it with him wherever he went.

S'haar seemed amused as they walked back to the tent to join the others. "So, how are our girls? Are they in a panic yet?"

Jack shook his head. "Nah, they'll be fine. I think they're both just what the other needed. In helping each other deal with their anxiety, they'll probably forget about their own problems."

S'haar arched her own eyebrow. "Oh, and what makes you such an expert with women?"

Jack laughed. "Not women, anxiety. You live with it long enough, and it becomes like a roommate, complete with personality quirks that make no sense. One of those quirks is that it's often easier to help someone else deal with their anxiety than to deal with your own."

S'haar placed a hand on his shoulder and smiled, wondering if Jack was even aware he'd been doing just that during his call. "You don't say…"

As they approached the tent, Lon'thul's loud voice called out to them both. "Food's ready! You better get in here and get some of Em'brel's leftover stew while there's some left, or you'll be stuck with dried meat and grains for lunch!"

The moment broken, S'haar shouted back toward the tent. "Oh, there better be some stew left when we get in there, or else I know one hunter who's going to be cleaning the latrines and dishes for the whole expedition!"

Turns out, their fears were unfounded. Lon'thul was waiting for them with a mischievous grin and two extra-large bowls filled with steaming stew when they walked in. S'haar accepted her bowl with an exasperated sigh and a shake of her head. Jack took his with a laugh.

Chapter 45

When Jack woke in the morning, he found himself experiencing the familiar sensation of being crushed beneath a pile of limbs. Except this time, there seemed to be a few too many limbs. As he slowly opened his eyes, Jack quickly realized the light was far brighter than it should have been. If that wasn't bad enough, his head was absolutely throbbing. To further complicate his feelings about the unpleasant morning, Jack found himself staring into the contentedly sleeping face of Lon'thul. With an exclamation of annoyance, Jack shoved the hunter away. "Uhg, get off me, meat for brains! Your breath reeks!"

Jack felt a presence shift behind him as a somewhat more effeminate voice (by argu'n standards) responded. "First of all, you've never complained before. Second, I'm going to make you suffer for calling me 'meat for brains!'"

As he turned around, Jack saw all the other argu'n bodies strewn about, laying half on top of each other in an attempt to get everyone to fit in the tent properly. However, his attention focused on the grumpy waking form of S'haar, now towering over him even though she was barely sitting up. "No, no, no, I didn't mean you! I swear! I was talking to Lon'thul! I didn't even know you were there!"

S'haar's gaze darkened. "So you thought you were in bed with some random argu'n? Does our connection mean so little to you that you assumed you'd just gone to sleep in the arms of someone else?"

Jack was starting to sweat despite the chill in the air. "No! I swear! I don't remember much of what happened last night! My head's killing me! I don't... I'm not... I didn't..."

That was when Jack heard all the chuckling going on around him and noticed S'haar's scowl had turned into a toothy grin. Rubbing the back of his neck, Jack felt his face growing warm. "Aaaannnd, you're just screwing with me, aren't you?"

S'haar finally broke into laughter before explaining. "Sorry, you're just a little extra easy to mess with in the morning, especially if you're suffering from a hangover!"

Jack started rubbing his forehead. Now that his panic had faded, the pain was definitely the focus of his attention again. "Yeah, that reminds me. Why exactly am I hungover?"

S'haar's expression returned to a harsh glare, but Jack was relieved to notice that it was directed over his shoulder to the hunter behind him. "Apparently, Lon'thul thought adding some of our mead to last night's stew would be an excellent way to help everyone warm up. You were halfway done with your bowl and quite drunk before I realized what he'd done."

As usual, Lon'thul remained utterly unfazed by a glare that cowed much larger and stronger men than himself. "Yeah, sorry about that, Jack! I didn't realize humans were such pathetic drinkers. On the other hand, it was great seeing you with your inhibitions down for a bit! You even tried to sing an old human love ballad to S'haar! She refused to translate, but you kept singing something like," Lon'thul's voice strained as he tried to copy Jack's untranslated vocals, arms held out as though singing to some invisible woman, "Gish rome a roshe oon de greh!"

Jack was mortified. At that moment, he felt like the world was spinning out of control. He wished he could return to the "fight" he and S'haar had been having a minute ago, or maybe the crash landing on an alien planet again, or even facing down a charging Kovaack for a second time.

His body was still trying to decide between fight or flight when he felt a hand on his shoulder and heard S'haar's quiet voice in his ear. "Before you think about running, you should know I kind of liked what I heard. Maybe one of these days you'll sing for me again, but sober next time."

Jack closed his eyes for a moment and focused on forcing his arms to relax, then his shoulders, neck, and back. He took a deep breath, held it for a moment, then released it. He opened his eyes to see everyone's attention now focused on Lon'thul's antics as he continued his impressions off to the side. Everyone but S'haar, who was watching him out of the corner of her eye a little too nonchalantly.

Jack let the last of the panic fade and grinned while shaking his head as he responded. "Maybe one day, but you'll have to ask a lot nicer than that! I usually don't sing while sober."

That was when Jack found a large coat had been dumped on his head. Lon'thul's voice could be heard from behind him again. "Alright, enough with the flirting, you two! We got a village to save! We can't be heroes if we sit around in the middle of nowhere all day!"

~

After a lively morning that consisted of checking in with Angela and Em'brel again, eating a filling breakfast, and repacking everything, the group resumed their journey to the village. They made excellent time the second day, and even with a brief stop for lunch, they still arrived at the edge of the forest well before dusk.

Despite their distance, the village was clearly visible, even if it looked somewhat abandoned. The snow had piled up around the wooden palisade, making it look like it stuck out of the ground only a few feet rather than the towering wall it really was. There was only one smoke source rising from the village, though it was a rather large plume.

S'haar was analyzing the scene laid out before them all. "They must all still be locked in the gathering hall…"

Looking around their current location, S'haar started issuing orders. "Alright, let's start doing what we're here to do. Jack and Tel'ron, I want the tent set up near the tree line, so we'll have a place to warm up while taking a break from working. Also, you'll probably want to get the generator up and running there to start charging replacement heating packs. Lon'thul, go do a quick scout and see if there's any readily available prey to hunt down. The rest of us, let's make good on why we're here and cut up a tree or two while we still have daylight. When we approach the village, I'd like to bring wood and food with us. That will make our intentions more clear than words ever could."

When the group broke and went about their various tasks, there was an energy of excitement about them. They were about to take the lessons and tricks they'd learned while working for Jack and apply them to the safety and protection of their friends and family. They pushed themselves harder than they ever had back at the outpost. With S'haar utilizing the chainsaw, It took no time at all to fell a tree and cut up it into a decent supply of firewood.

Even Lon'thul had a bit of luck. His first two attempts using the snowshoes he'd packed had ended with the churlish leaping away before he could get in position, but on his third attempt, he managed to find an older churlish that was just a little too slow. The meat might be tougher than he preferred, but it was still fresh, which meant a lot right now.

Eventually, every sled was filled with wood or meat, and they set off to enter the village. There was still a bit of a hike remaining, and it only looked more abandoned the closer they got.

The gates were too deeply buried to bother opening. Instead, they found a place where the snow almost reached the top and simply lifted each sled over the wall, one at a time.

As they walked through the streets, they passed by many houses sitting abandoned, some with doors swaying lazily in the breeze. The place's oppressive emptiness was nearly unbearable. The mood was only somewhat lightened by the pillar of smoke coming from the village center.

Jack wondered how many bodies were currently buried under the very snow they now walked over. This was not how he ever imagined he'd see the village that had been so full of life and excitement the last couple of times he'd visited. As they neared the gathering hall, several voices could be heard from within. A few of the closer and louder voices were able to be picked out over the rest.

"I'm telling you, the beast we heard down by the forest has left! We haven't heard its cries for over a half-hour!"

"Maybe, and maybe it just caught our scent and is hunting us now, did you think of that?"

"I don't care either way! If we don't get some more food soon, it won't matter if a beast comes looking for us or not!"

"And how are we supposed to get any food with all that snow out there? You'd die before you made it to the village walls!"

S'haar walked up, loudly pounded on the door, and waited. The hall grew quiet.

"It's the beast!"

"Do you really think a beast would politely knock?"

"What else could be out there?"

Growing tired of waiting, S'haar shouted as loud and clear as she could. Jack settled the hood of his coat over his ears to somewhat muffle the sound of her voice. "Friends and neighbors, we've come to you from the dragon's outpost! We bring wood to feed your fires and meat to feed your families."

It took a few moments, but eventually, the door creaked open. The first thing Jack noticed was the unbearable odor that hit him like a truck. He did his best to resist losing his lunch and fought back the tears brought on by the stench.

Despite the fires still lit here and there, it was cold in the room. The only activity anyone could see was from those gathered closest around the fires. At first, Jack thought the argu'n closest to him were dead, but looking closer, he could see them breathe incredibly slow and shallow breaths.

S'haar took charge and began directing the workers to deliver more wood to each of the fires and pass out the fresh meat to those looking hungriest. There wasn't enough for a full meal for everyone present, and those who got to eat were still left with hunger pains, but it was enough to buy some more time.

As the workers began coordinating with the few still functioning guards to distribute food and wood, Jack and S'haar made their way to the center of the structure, where the village lord waited. As they approached, Lord A'ngles called out to them. "Jack, how wonderful it is to see you again, and in our time of need no less! I admit I was concerned for your safety! Especially with apparently erroneous reports that you were gravely injured and possibly dead!" As he said that last bit, Lord A'ngles looked over at the woodworker who had left after S'haar had taken over the camp. The worker now seemed to be trying to fade back into the shadows for some reason.

Jack shook the village lord's clawed hands in greeting and responded, while S'haar translated. "It's good to be back, Lord A'ngles, though I wish it were under happier circumstances. For the record, your reports weren't mistaken. I was gravely injured. However, through the help of S'haar and the dragon, I was able to make a recovery. Though admittedly, it'll still be some time before I'm fully myself again."

Lord A'ngles tilted his head and inspected Jack a little closer. "I suppose you do look a bit more worn than I remember, though I imagined that had more to do with a harrowing trip through snow-covered lands. To that end, it would appear that our entire village owes you a debt of honor!"

At that statement, B'arthon, who had been sitting nearby, looked up at his father with a startled expression on his face before turning to glare at Jack through narrowed eyes.

Jack merely held up his hands and shook his head. "I apologize, Lord A'ngles, but you are mistaken, though there is no way you could have known better. Upon my injury, S'haar took up the mantle of leadership of the outpost. When I woke, I found that she had done such an incredible job that we agreed she would continue to lead the camp, and I will remain in an advisory capacity. It was her decision, not mine, that led us here today."

At this, Lord A'ngles let some surprise show through, and Jack even saw the corners of his mouth twitch slightly, though he couldn't quite decide what expression had almost shown through. Almost immediately, the village lord regained his composure before turning to S'haar and bowing. "I apologize, Lady S'haar. I did not mean to slight you or your deeds. If I understand this correctly, it would appear our village owes *both* of you a debt of honor!"

At the words "Lady S'haar," B'arthon reacted again, though this time, he appeared to recover a bit more quickly than before.

S'haar bowed in return and spoke up on her own behalf. "There is no need to apologize, Lord A'ngles. Honestly, I'm still coming to terms with it myself. I took over out of simple necessity. No one was more surprised than me when Jack decided I should continue to run the camp."

S'haar held out a plate of the best cut of meat Lon'thul had been able to carve off the churlish. "None of this would have been possible if you had not graciously allowed many of the village's craftspeople to help us in establishing our outpost. It is still we who are in your debt."

Lord A'ngles held up a hand to turn away the plate. "In my position as village lord, I fear I have already eaten far better than many others who have suffered through this deep freeze. However, I am sure my son could use a bite to eat."

S'haar hesitated a moment before offering the plate to B'arthon. He looked at his father with surprise before shaking his head, then accepted the plate and greedily wolfing down its contents.

S'haar was just about to speak again but was interrupted when Tel'ron came running up. Out of breath, he bowed before the three who stood before him. "I apologize for interrupting my lord, but It's my father! Jack, I need you to come look at him right away!"

Lord A'ngels bowed to Jack, indicating that any further discussion could wait. Jack and S'haar bowed in return before turning to follow Tel'ron.

Tel'ron led them through piles of hibernating argu'n, over to where one of the guard areas had been set up. Unconscious and lying on the ground was Ger'ron, the friendly old guard who'd always greeted Jack and S'haar at the gate. Unlike the rest of the villagers here, he was sweating profusely, and his skin had taken on an unhealthy pallor.

The guard captain stood over him shaking his head sadly, his voice expressing regret. "The old fool kept going door to door, long after it was safe to be out. When he finally arrived here, he seemed alright, but he started getting worse after a few days. Eventually, a few days ago, he stopped waking up altogether. He'd been looking worse every day since then."

Jack looked Ger'ron over. He was definitely fighting an infection of some kind. Peeling back the blanket released a strong smell that rivaled any in the room. The problem became apparent to Jack after he pulled the blanket off the old guard's left foot, and the scent became strong enough Jack had to cover his mouth and nose to keep from gagging. The foot was half-rotted and black.

Covering the foot back up, Jack shook his head. The foot had clearly been severely frostbitten, and after being left untreated for so long, it had progressed to necrosis. Now a fungus was eating away at the rotting flesh. He muttered under his breath. "That's gangrene. This isn't good…"

Tel'ron gave Jack a look a drowning man might give to a life preserver thrown his way. "You know what it is! Do you know how to treat it?"

Jack sighed, not wanting to get anyone's hopes up, explained as S'haar once again translated. "Yes, I know what it is and how to treat it, *but* this isn't something to take lightly. The only chance he has is to get him back to the cave and cut off the leg. We'll have to be quick about it, it will be excruciating, and honestly, even if everything goes perfectly, the odds still aren't in his favor. There's a very high chance he'll either die from complications before we get there or from the shock of removing his leg."

Tel'ron looked desperate. "What happens if we don't remove his foot?"

Jack sat back, trying to remember lessons from long ago. "Right now, the gangrene has no access to his blood because it's restricted to the rotting flesh, but if it reaches the bloodstream, there'd be no saving him. We don't have the tools to do the job here. You can't just chop it off with an ax, with all the trauma, shattered bone fragments, and bleeding. You'd be better off just putting him out of his misery. His only chance is back at the cave."

Tel'ron took a breath and nodded. "Ok, then let's go!"

Jack shook his head and put a hand on Tel'ron's shoulder. Despite not even reaching the young man's shoulders, Jack noticed he looked very vulnerable right now. "No, I'll have to take him alone. I can travel safely in the cold, and I won't have to take any breaks if I'm on my own. It's his best chance."

This time it was S'haar's turn to object. "I can't let you travel back to the mountain on your own! It's suicidal!"

Jack turned back to her with a smile he didn't really feel. "This is probably the only time of year it *will* be safe for me to travel out there alone. Right now, there won't be any raiders because of the snow. Also, I have my gun to handle any wildlife that might threaten me."

Jack grabbed her hand and looked S'haar in the eyes as he finished pleading his case. "I might not be as strong as any of you, but I've got more endurance than all of you combined. Like I said, I'm his only chance. You stay here and save the village. Let me do this. This is exactly the kind of situation I came along for!"

S'haar closed her eyes and thought for a moment before pulling Jack into a crushing embrace while whispering into his ear. "You'd better get there safely, no matter what! If you do something stupid and get yourself killed, again, I'm going to follow you into the afterlife to kick your ass in ways you can't even begin to imagine!"

Jack hugged her back as he responded. "I fought tooth and nail to claw my way out of the land of the dead to come back to you all. I'm not going back there if I have any say in the matter!"

After a moment, they pulled apart, and Jack returned his attention to Tel'ron. "Alright, let's do this! Help me find a sled to strap him onto. Time is not on our side!"

Chapter 46

Tel'ron and Jack worked together to secure Ger'ron to the sled, tying him down as tightly as they could without cutting off any circulation. Jack left anything that wasn't necessary out of his pack, leaving little more than some nutrition bars, water, and a few spare heating pouches to swap out from Ger'ron's blanket from time to time. S'haar examined the load with expressions of doubt and concern. "I still wish you'd pack a tent, a sleeping roll, and the mobile transceiver, at the very least. You might need them!"

Jack shook his head. "I'm going to make the trip in one go. We did it all the time during early winter. Even considering the dark and snow as factors, I'm still confident I can make it in twelve hours or less. If I'm going to succeed, I'll have to keep moving. I'm worried that I might pass out on my feet if I stop even long enough to set up and activate the transceiver."

As he spoke, S'haar looked less and less pleased. "You've already spent the whole day traveling and prepping the camp, and you're not even fully recovered from your deep sleep. Are you sure you can't wait until morning?"

Jack looked back at Ger'ron, who seemed even more pale than a moment ago. "I'm not sure that he's going to make the journey as is. If we wait, his odds will only fall further. Even if I tried, I wouldn't be able to sleep with that knowledge weighing on me."

Looking over at her, Jack gave her a more confident smile than he felt. "Listen, you'll have Angela's portable transceiver. Set it up and leave it on, and you'll know as soon as I get there."

S'haar looked down at the transceiver. Jack had shown her how to activate it, but she still wasn't convinced. Jack pointed out toward the door they'd come through. "Come on, you can see me off."

Tel'ron was kneeling next to his father. He seemed to be whispering words of encouragement and support as he gave him a final once over. Appearing to have run out of things to say, the smith slowly stood and walked over to Jack. Several emotions were warring on his face as he took a moment to decide what to say. "Be careful out there. As much as I want you to succeed, you won't be doing anyone any good if you get yourself killed… Listen, whatever happens…I'm…just grateful you tried."

Jack's smile lost a little of its bravado, but he forced the last half of a grin to remain in place. "I can't guarantee how this will end, but at the very least, I'm going to get him there. S'haar will keep you updated, so stick close to her if you can."

Tel'ron had nothing more to say and instead gripped Jack's shoulder and nodded before letting go and backing away. As Jack and S'haar approached the door, a couple of the guards opened it for them, their faces an odd range of thoughts and emotions.

Jack and S'haar didn't get very far before they found another surprise waiting for them. B'arthon was waiting outside with a scowl on his face. He was wearing a thick coat, with an additional hide wrapped around that for good measure, making him look almost as wide as he was tall. S'haar's voice was practically a growl as she gestured sharply to him. "B'arthon, we don't have time for any of your trouble. Get out of the way and let us pass!"

The lord's son looked as though he'd swallowed something foul. "Listen, I don't like either of you very much."

S'haar took a breath to tell him off more forcefully, but he kept talking over her. "But my father was right. The village owes you a debt of honor, which means *I* owe you a debt of honor. I've already got honor debts up to my neck, so I'm going to pay both of you back right now."

Jack and S'haar were both shocked into silence. B'arthon almost sounded well-spoken, a far cry from the petty brat they'd known up until this point. He turned to Jack first. "Up until now, you've been an outside influence. Sure, you've had a significant impact on the village, but you still weren't a part of it. That all changed when you two came and saved so many from this freeze. By earning the entire village's debt, you've become one of us, which means your influence is now a threat to those in power. You'd best use our debt to secure your position as quickly as you are able, because you're about to find yourself in a whole different kind of battle than you've seen so far."

Jack couldn't do more than blink in stunned silence as B'arthon turned his attention to S'haar. "It might have been my lips that sent you to be sacrificed several months ago, but it wasn't my voice. Everyone in this village has a role to play, even me, and everyone plays their parts well. Everyone, except for you. Now here you are, 'Lady S'haar.' That's going to earn you far more enemies than friends."

Looking back and forth between the two of them, B'arthon turned his head and spit on the ground before walking back to the heated hall. S'haar called out to him as he walked. "If not you, then who's responsible?"

B'arthon didn't even turn his head, and Jack could barely make out his response. "I've already paid my debt. You figure it out from here." With those parting words, he walked up to the door and gave it three distinct knocks. As soon as it opened, he disappeared inside.

Jack and S'haar looked at each other, unsure of what to do with this development. Was the village lord's spoiled son just screwing with them in some new way, or was he serious? Looking back at the sled behind him, Jack sighed. "Well, I suppose none of that matters right now. I've got a journey to make, and you've got a village to save. We'll worry about strange warnings from unexpected sources when we get the immediate emergencies dealt with."

S'haar nodded, but the two walked in silence the rest of the way to the forest's edge. The atmosphere between them was thick with confusion, worry, and exhaustion. Once there, S'haar grabbed hold of Jack again, though this time, she was careful not to bruise him.

The silent hug lasted long enough to convey more than a few feelings between the two of them. Just as the moment was about to pass, S'haar pulled Jack into a deep kiss before gently resting her forehead against Jack's, taking in one last moment of intimacy.

When Jack finally opened his eyes, he saw S'haar staring back at him. She smiled and pulled back, looking like she wanted to hug him again, but knowing she had to let him go sooner rather than later. With her head tilted to one side, she finally spoke up. "You know, if you pull this off, I don't know if I'll be content with you merely warming my bed anymore…"

Jack blinked, opened and closed his mouth a few times, but found that his voice had abandoned him. S'haar's smile turned predatory. "Just a little something extra to motivate you to get there in one piece for once."

This time it was Jack's turn to share a toothy grin. "Well then, I guess I have no choice! There's no way I'm letting that opportunity slip through my fingers! You'll be hearing from me before you know it!"

With a smile and one last squeeze of her hands, Jack turned and walked into the forest alone. As she watched him go, S'haar's smile faded into a look of concern. When she spoke, her voice was swallowed by the passing wind. "You'd better get there safe… I won't forgive you if you leave me alone a second time!"

~

Jack wasn't very far into the forest, but the weight of his load he was dragging already weighed heavy on him, both physically and emotionally. There were times when even human endurance wasn't enough, and scouts like him knew that better than anyone. He took a moment to root around in his emergency supplies before he found what he was looking for, a couple innocent-looking tablets meant for when sleep wasn't an option, and caffeine wasn't enough.

Jack had never liked using these. For one thing, they were incredibly habit-forming. Though, he supposed that being stuck on an alien planet with no access to refills meant that addiction was a self-solving problem. The other issue was the potential side effects of the drug. With the right combination of medication, stress, and sleep deprivation all mixing together, the list of side effects could range from simple blood sugar issues to visual or auditory hallucinations, or if he was really unlucky, an AFib attack followed by a trip to the morgue. Although, in this case, that trip would probably end in some hungry scavenger's stomach instead.

Still, a life was on the line, and there was a reason these were standard issue to anyone in his line of work. Putting one tablet back in his emergency pack, Jack swallowed the other and chased it with a sip of water that was almost too cold to swallow.

Shaking his head to wake himself up a little more, Jack put away the emergency kit and took out a nutrition bar to snack on while moving.

When Jack had passed through the forest on the way to the village not long ago, he remembered thinking how serene and quiet it had been. The only sounds for much of the journey were the gentle crunching of snow under skis and the occasional loud comments from Lon'thul. Now that he was retracing his journey alone at night, the forest seemed to be filled with a multitude of sounds, all coming from somewhere just beyond his line of sight.

That soft footfall to his left was probably just the settling of some melting snow. The crunch of a twig obviously must really be ice cracking. That howl in the distance... Ok, that was really an animal howling, but it was pretty far away and probably had nothing to do with Jack. The fact that the sled Jack was pulling made it sound like someone was always just a few steps behind him wasn't helping either.

To further complicate things, Jack's line of sight was limited to a cone of light projected by a pocket-mounted flashlight. As he moved, it caused all the shadows to shift and dance around him, making Jack feel like he was on the set of some sort of horror movie. He would have liked to have carried the flashlight in his hand for a greater degree of control, but he felt it was more important to keep both hands free, just in case.

Jack noticed his heart was pounding. Was that just the medication, or had his subconscious picked up on something he'd missed? Jack checked his compass to make sure he wasn't walking in circles before continuing forward with a slight course adjustment. He focused on the path forward, trying to ignore the frozen nighttime forest moving in on him.

~

By Jack's estimation, despite feeling like he'd been walking all night, he really had only been at it for roughly five hours. That meant he wasn't even halfway yet. Every muscle in his body screamed in agony and exhaustion. He remembered hearing from his more athletic acquaintances that if you pushed through the pain long enough, it would eventually start to fade or even become euphoric. That didn't seem to be happening with Jack, much to his annoyance.

Jack stopped for a minute to change out the heating pouches in Ger'ron's blankets. Or at least he only meant to stop for a minute. He was startled to find himself snapping awake on his knees. With a sudden burst of adrenaline, born from the realization of what had just almost happened, Jack shot back to his feet. It even gave him enough of a boost to get his momentum going again, but only a few minutes later, the effect was already giving way to exhaustion once again.

Jack considered taking another tablet but worried that the risk might outweigh the benefit this time. Instead, he took another drink of ice-cold water and munched down another bar, hoping his body would know what to do with the fuel he'd just given it.

He might be warm-blooded, but this many hours out in the cold was definitely having an effect on him. He wasn't sure when he'd started shivering, but he stuck one of the warming pouches inside his jacket to conserve a bit of energy. A new problem presented itself when, as soon as the shivering was gone, the exhaustion returned two-fold. Jack felt his shoulders slumping, and his eyes started to droop once again.

That was when he heard a familiar voice by his side. "Hello again."

Jack didn't even turn his head. He just kept moving forward. However, the voice wasn't so easily deterred. "What is it with you and not greeting your guests? Is this some human custom I'm not familiar with?"

Jack pushed on stubbornly for a few more moments before giving in and answering, though he still refused to look toward the source of the voice. "No, I just don't think responding to an auditory hallucination is very wise. If I do, the visual hallucinations are probably next."

The voice sounded amused this time. "Why do you refuse to believe I'm real? Why don't you trust your own senses?"

Jack continued looking forward, grinning sardonically. "Oh, there are many reasons my senses would betray me. Last time it was oxygen deprivation and brain damage. This time it could be stress, lack of sleep, or that little tablet I took not so long ago that literally alters the chemicals in my brain."

Against his better judgment, Jack finally glanced toward the source of the voice. There, walking beside him, was S'haar. Except this S'haar was taller than an argu'n male, had star-filled eyes with no iris, and left no trace of her passage in the snow, almost as if she was floating a hair's breadth above the ground.

Not-S'haar gave Jack a smile that warmed his heart as she laughed at his expression. "You are such an interesting little mortal! I must admit, I never thought you'd make it out of my realm alive. I thought for sure that the leap of faith was your breaking point, but you delighted me when you proved me wrong! Yet here you are again, walking the knife's edge between your world and mine. One wrong step and you'll slip off the path you've chosen, and you're risking everything just to keep some old soldier you hardly even know from my embrace."

Jack raised an eyebrow at the goddess. "Last time you were complaining that I forced 'your children to return to you early,' this time you're complaining because I'm keeping one from your presence a little longer? At the risk of angering a god, isn't that a bit hypocritical?"

Not-S'haar paused and looked surprised. Jack merely shrugged as he pushed forward. "Listen, I'm kinda in the middle of a life or death journey at the moment. I'm still not fully recovered from the events that led to our first meeting, I'm exhausted, and now I'm apparently hallucinating. If you want me to grovel before your divine presence, you'll have to come back when I'm less fatigued, and there's not another life in the balance."

Everything was quiet a moment before Jack spoke again with a slightly apologetic tone to his voice. "Sorry, hallucination or not, that came out a little harsher than I intended. Although I can't help but notice that this time you do seem a little less…divine?"

Looking over at Not-S'haar, Jack saw that her smile hadn't faded in the least. When she spoke, her voice held the promise of comfort and warmth. "You are correct. Last time, you were in my realm and witnessed me in my actual form, or as close to it as your mortal mind could comprehend. This time I'm in your mortal realm, so my presence is somewhat diminished, and you see me in your mind's chosen form. Now that I've answered your questions, will you answer mine? Why are you struggling so hard to keep this one from the gifts I offer?"

Jack walked on in silence as he organized his thoughts. Not-S'haar seemed content to walk beside him in perfect silence, waiting for his answer. Eventually, Jack's voice broke the stillness of the forest again. "I don't know for sure. Maybe it's because I know him and his son. Maybe I've seen too much death recently and refuse to sit back and watch more. Maybe it's just human nature.

When Jack spoke this time, he turned his attention back to the path ahead of him again. "For much of human history, we've had a very different idea of death than the one you offer. We thought of death as an enemy to be fought at every turn. We always knew that you, or your human equivalent, would win eventually. But every moment we stole from you was a victory to be celebrated. We worked tirelessly, growing food to fend off hunger, building walls to stave off danger, developing medicines to fight off disease. On and on we fought, we lived, and we thrived."

Turning to face Not-S'haar again, Jack smiled. "Or maybe it's some other convoluted reason I don't fully understand. The brain is a messy thing. Our motivations often hide behind self-told lies and confusion. All I know for certain is I refuse to give this man up without a fight."

At that moment, the forest and everything in it faded away, leaving only Jack and Not-S'haar. As she approached Jack, he felt warmth and love radiating toward him. "What a beautiful soul you are. Come join me in the heavens, and you'll know nothing of the pain or suffering of this world any longer."

As she took another step toward Jack, he felt himself getting lost in the infinite beauty hidden within her eyes. In them, he saw peace and happiness. As she bent down to him, Jack saw the faces of lost loved ones waiting to greet him once again. As her lips approached his, Jack bore witness to the kind of eternal beauty that no mortal was meant to glimpse.

Jack sat frozen at that moment for an eternity. He was tired physically, mentally, and spiritually. In death's eyes, he saw the promise of peace and serenity and an end to his suffering. Only a few small yet essential things were missing from that which she offered him.

Jack closed his eyes and saw Angela tormented, never knowing what had happened to her little brother. He let his head fall as he envisioned Em'brel sobbing over another empty grave. Jack took a ragged breath and saw S'haar, the real S'haar, this time. Once again, she had her forehead resting against his, with her eyes locked onto Jack's, but this time they were filled with fear. Her voice was a ragged whisper of a plea. "*Don't leave me again.*"

Jack shook his head. With a sad smile and tears in his eyes, he turned away from Not-S'haar. Summoning every last scrap of willpower he possessed, Jack lifted his foot and stepped away from the promise of death…and peace. The second step was more manageable, and the third even more so. Soon, Jack was once again walking through the forest. "If it's all the same to you, I think I'll keep suffering a little longer. I've got things that only I can do, and people are waiting for me. My journey doesn't end here."

The only response was the faintest of voices fading into the night. "Such a marvelous soul. I can't wait to see your story unfold…" Then everything the lady offered began to fade from his thoughts. It was like waking from a dream. It was as though it had been too much for a mortal mind to hold onto. Soon, he was left with only vague feelings of loss and sadness at what he'd given up.

Everything was utterly silent for a few more moments before a harsh crackle broke through the headset Jack had forgotten he was wearing, followed by a voice so beautiful it brought tears to his eyes. "I think I'm getting a reading on him at last! Jack, is that you? Can you hear me?"

He must have been walking in a daze for longer than he realized because Jack found himself at the edge of the forest, shielding his eyes from the light of the rising sun. He grinned and answered. "Yes, Angela, it's me. I can hear you."

The voice that returned was filed with accusation and fury. "OF ALL THE IDIOTIC, HAIR-BRAINED, HALF-BAKED IDEAS YOU'VE EVER COME UP WITH, THIS IS THE WORST! WHEN S'HAAR CALLED AND SAID WHAT YOU WERE DOING, I SWORE…"

Jack cut her off with a smile in his voice. "It's good to hear from you too. It's been a long night, we've got a patient who needs immediate attention, and I'm beyond any known definition of exhausted. Let me get some sleep, and you can lecture me in the morning, ok?"

Angela's voice was sulking but also greatly relieved as she responded. "Fine, but this isn't over!"

At that moment, Jack thought of something. "Oh, hey, is S'haar available on her end? Can you patch me through?"

Angela sighed. "Sure, just a moment."

Jack walked on in silence until he heard the static of another headset being picked up. "Jack, is that you? Are you ok? A little bit ago, I felt…I felt as if I was about to lose you!"

Upon hearing the real S'haar's voice again, Jack's smile grew so wide it was almost painful. "Well, I'm here, and I'm safe. But before I go inside and pass out from exhaustion, I just wanted to call and say one important thing."

S'haar's voice was laden with confusion and concern. "What could be so important at this moment?"

Jack hesitated a moment before choking down the lump of fear that had taken hold in his throat. "I just wanted to say, I love you!"

S'haar was silent for just long enough for Jack's confidence to waver, but when she finally replied, her voice was heavy with emotion. "I love you too, my crazy, stupid, brave human. Now get some rest. You'll need it when I return."

Chapter 47

By the time Jack made it to the cave entrance, Em'brel was waiting for him. A firm hug was followed by her giving him a quick head-to-toe examination. Em'brel's intense look of concern was utterly lost on Jack, who was half asleep on his feet and only aware of the world around him in the loosest definition of the words.

Em'brel helped Jack out of the harness and took over to drag the sled the rest of the way into the cave. Once inside, Jack stumbled over to his room and collapsed on the bed. He didn't even get his head as far as the pillows before he lost consciousness. Em'brel unstrapped Ger'ron from the sled and dragged him over to the med bay. With some difficulty, she hefted him up onto the bed Angela directed her to, making sure he was situated correctly for whatever Angela had in mind.

One look at the man told Em'brel he faced certain death, or he would have if not for Angela and the ship. One of his feet was shriveled and blacked, and several toes had fallen off. The rotting flesh was peeling back from the remaining jutting bones that once held the toes in place. The only movement that came from the old guard was his constant panting, which seemed to indicate he was overheating, despite the relatively cool room. His coloration was pale, and his skin clung to his bones in a way that suggested a combination of severe hunger and dehydration. Em'brel looked over to Angela with concern. "Can you save him?"

Already many of the machines in the room were starting to obey whatever arcane commands Angela was silently giving them. The AI was wearing the long white coat she often wore in the med bay and looked as though she was intensely focused on the task. She was staring with one arm holding her chin while the other supported its elbow. "Honestly, I don't know. I'm not sure how well an argu'n body can handle this level of stress. First of all, I have to amputate his foot. The shock of that procedure alone might kill him."

Angela took a deep sigh and continued. "On top of that, his body is wracked by several secondary infections caused by his exhausted immune system. Then there are all the other stresses of his body being too cold for too long and lacking proper nutrition and hydration. Honestly, it doesn't look good, but with everything we've got at our disposal here, and not a small amount of luck, he has a fighting chance."

Em'brel had only seen Angela this focused once before, when she'd worked on Jack after he'd been run through. "Is there anything I can do to help?"

Angela spared her a brief glance. "Thank you, but no. Not right now, anyway. If he survives through the surgery and initial recovery, you may have to reprise your role as a nursemaid for a while, but for now, you might as well look in on our brave idiot human. That journey probably took everything he had out of him, and then some."

Knowing the old warrior was in the care of the best healer on the planet, Em'brel left to check on Jack. Walking into the room she could see the human had apparently woken himself up, and she now watched him struggling to pull off his mud-splattered boots in a drunken sort of haze. Em'brel shook her head at the hapless male in front of her, wondering how he'd made it this far.

She walked over to him and started helping him out of the tangled mess he'd made of his clothing, ignoring his pathetic protests that he could manage it on his own. Before he'd recovered his motor functions, she'd helped him similarly plenty of times, and this hardly seemed like the time to suddenly become squeamish about such things.

That done, Em'brel half carried the stumbling man over to the tub in his adjoining bathroom and helped him get adequately cleaned. The hardest part about the bath was keeping his head above water since he kept nodding off, only to shoot awake when water was dumped on his head to rinse off any soap or shampoo. Once he was done and toweled off, she helped him into some of his sleepwear and tucked him into bed. Jack was firmly asleep before she'd even gotten the blankets in place on top of him.

Her self-appointed duty complete, Em'brel went back to the med bay to check on Angela and their guest. Angela made her wash up and wear a mask and gown to enter the room and even then kept her on the other side of a clear divider.

Once inside, Em'brel could see the man's leg had already been removed at the first knee, and Anglea had many delicate instruments manipulating, injecting, and tying off portions of the exposed muscle and sinews. Once she seemed satisfied with what was done, she took a loose flap of skin and wrapped it around the amputated limb before sewing it closed with thread.

Em'brel remembered enough from Jack's surgery to know that the steady beeping she was hearing was a good sign. "So he's ok?"

Angela's avatar reappeared before the girl. "I'm cautiously optimistic. He made it through the worst part, but he's far from out of the woods. The real question is, now that the initial cause of his condition has been removed, does he regen his strength, or has his body been pushed too far, and as a result, he simply never recovers. All we can do now is pump him full of antibiotics and nutrients and let him rest. The rest is up to him."

Looking at his face, the guard's expression looked more peaceful than before. Em'brel wasn't sure if that was a sign of recovery or acceptance but figured that either way, it was better than the look of fevered torment he'd worn before.

~

Aside from a sleepless night spent worrying about Jack, things were going relatively well for S'haar. With the human tools and heated coats, they produced wood fast enough to meet the village's demands, with more to spare.

Initially, S'haar had been worried about Lon'thul's ability to hunt enough food for the villagers, but Fea'en had agreed to loan her coat to Lon'thul's father, Dek'thul. Though only after she lectured him. "You take better care of that coat than you do your own skin! If you bring it back with so much as one scratch on it, you'll provide me fresh meat for a year as compensation. If you lose or ruin it, you'll be feeding me for the rest of my life, you hear me?"

It was odd to see someone so unintimidated by the hunter chief. Many of the villagers found his presence unsettling, despite his congenial nature. There was just something off-putting about a man who walked so closely with death.

The only one who didn't seem nonplussed by the display was the hunter chief himself. "Of course, Lady Fea'en, I shall guard it with my life! I must admit, I'm quite looking forward to hunting in the deep snow. This will be a whole new hunt for me, that's not something I can safe very often!"

Whatever challenges the new hunt must have forced him to face, he must have overcome them quickly. With Dek'thul and Lon'thul working side-by-side, the meat poured in with surprising abundance. At the rate they were going, there wouldn't be a hungry mouth left in the village by the end of their second day working together.

The snow was melting steadily, and S'haar suspected their services wouldn't be needed for longer than a few more days at most. She was eager to get home and see Jack again, but she'd just have to look forward to her next call home for now.

~

Ger'ron woke up in the strangest place he could have imagined. Looking around and seeing every surface was metallic, grey, or white, he was sure this was the afterlife, and he was in the realm of the gods, but when he tried to sit up, he found he was strapped onto his bed.

After struggling against his bonds some more, the old guard called out. "Hello? Is anyone there? Where am I? What's going on?" No answers seemed forthcoming.

He was further displeased to note he did not possess the body of his youth the way the priests in the village had promised, and in fact, most of his aches and pains were as bad, if not worse than, when he lived. Especially the foot that had been acting up before he'd died. Ger'ron had renewed his struggles when a portion of the wall seemed to open, and in walked a young argu'n woman.

Seeing him strain against his bonds, she walked over and placed two hands against his chest, though she didn't push him back into the bed as he'd expected. Instead, it felt more like her action was a request rather than an order. "Please relax, master guardsman. You'll be released shortly, but first, a few things must be explained to you."

As he looked closer at this woman, Ger'ron realized she was relatively young, probably a bit younger than his son. Something in her gentle demeanor took the fight right out of him, causing him to relax back into the bed. For the moment, there was no concern for danger or the future, just confusion. "Are you...are you an angel?"

The girl looked confused a moment, then looked around the room and smiled to herself before replying. "No, I'm not, and you're not dead either, though I can see why you might think that. I'm Em'brel, and you are a guest in the home of Jack."

Ger'ron's face twisted as his confusion deepened. "Wait, Jack's house? As in Jack, S'haar's visitor? I'm at the mountain? How'd I get here? *Why* am I here?"

A thousand other questions bubbled up in his mind as the girl (Em'brel, he reminded himself) held up a hand to stave off any further questions. "After the freeze ended, Jack and S'haar left on an expedition with the other workers to help the village recover from the effects of the long freeze. When they got there, you were very sick and hadn't woken up for several days. Everyone was sure you were soon to pass, but Jack knew of a way to possibly save your life. Long story short, he brought you back to his house and healed you, though not without a heavy price to yourself."

Ger'ron's eyes narrowed. "What kind of price must I pay for this healing?" Waving his hands around to indicate the room, he continued. "What kind of price *can* I pay, that would have any meaning? Compared to this room, all that I have is worth nothing!"

Em'brel tilted her head to the side in thought. "Perhaps that was a poor choice of words. I don't believe Jack expects you to pay anything. You were treated out of his desire to be a good neighbor to the village and as a favor to your son, with whom Jack's become friends. Instead, I meant it already cost you quite a bit. By the time Jack got you back here, your foot was already dead and taking you with it. To save your life, he had to cut off your foot."

Ger'ron shook his head. "That's impossible. I can feel my foot even now! It may hurt, but it's clearly there!"

That was when Jack came walking in. He'd gotten there just in time to hear the last of what the old guard had said before replying something unintelligible, which Em'brel translated for him. "He says that's something called 'phantom limb pain.' Apparently, it's relatively common in recent amputees, though it often fades over time."

Jack pulled up a chair and sat next to Ger'ron. The human looked disheveled, as though he'd just woken up before walking in here. His head tendrils were a mess, and he seemed to be trying to rub the sleep from his eyes. Giving the guard a brief once over, Jack spoke again, while Em'brel stood back in a respectful pose and continued to translate. "So, aside from the foot, how are you feeling? Any unusual aches or pains, difficulty breathing, blurred vision, or anything else out of the ordinary?"

Ger'ron was a bit taken aback. Sure, he'd spoken with Jack on multiple occasions, and he seemed quite close and relaxed around S'haar, his old student, but he seemed far too casual as he addressed Ger'ron. In contrast, Em'brel was almost too formal, as if she was speaking with a visiting dignitary of some sort. When he responded, the frustration and anger in his voice were plain to hear. "I'm fine. Though if you really did cut off my foot, you might as well have let me die! What's an old guard going to do with one foot? I'm too old to go learning some new trade. There was no point to any of this!"

Having said his piece, Ger'ron deflated back into the bed, somewhat annoyed his bindings kept him from rolling over and going back to sleep.

Jack had looked a bit startled at his outburst, then settled into a look of impatience. "Well, I'm not sure your son would agree. Setting that aside, there's also the lifetime's worth of skills and knowledge you've acquired. Even if you can't fully utilize it anymore, you can certainly teach it to those who can. If your village isn't interested in you, I'm certain we've got a job you can do here, in return for food and lodging."

The old soldier looked at Jack through narrowed eyes. "I've never asked for handouts before, and I'm not about to start now!"

Jack smiled. "That's fine, because I'm not offering one. You'll have to work for your food and lodging. It'll probably be more demanding than sitting around watching a gate all day long, but I think you'll find our food is top-notch, and our housing isn't so bad either."

Ger'ron's curiosity was piqued, but Jack looked over at his bindings instead. "We can talk about that some more over some breakfast." Jack looked at an odd device on the wall that seemed to have some strange glowing runes before correcting himself. "Well, maybe dinner instead. But first, let me introduce you to the other resident of this house, my sister. I think she's been hiding until you got comfortable with everything else going on here. Angela, come out and say hi."

A small glowing spirit appeared in the air over Ger'ron's bed. She was malformed like Jack but spoke clearly, without the need of a translator. "Hi, I'm Angela. Good to see you doing well! You were in pretty rough shape when Jack brought you in!"

Ger'ron didn't know what to say. For that matter, he didn't even know what to think. Based on some of his grandfather's stories about spirits, he might have thought about running, if he hadn't been tied down. As it was, all he could do was stare in confusion.

Jack broke the silence, with Em'brel taking over translation once again. "Angela here is actually the one who performed the procedure that saved your life. She might look small and dainty, but there is little she can't see or do inside this house."

Angela had the decency to look abashed at the attention she was receiving. "Awww, stop it! You're the one who dragged him through the frozen forest alone at night! Compared with that, I had the easy job!"

As Jack started to undo the straps restraining Ger'ron, the old guard looked over at Em'brel with confusion and exhaustion. "Is it always like this around here?"

Em'brel gave him an understanding smile before replying. "You get used to it after a while. They're strange, but you won't find a more friendly pair in the land."

Jack and Angela seemed to be arguing over who was more responsible for saving Ger'ron's life now, both insisting it was the other. Em'brel looked at them and sighed. "They are strange, though..."

Finally, Jack looked up from his argument, glaring at Em'brel with mock offense. "Who are you calling strange?"

Angela simply laughed. "I think she's calling you strange. You've always been a little... off..."

Jack directed his offense back at his sister. "*I'm* strange? Look at you! At least I'm flesh and blood. You're a floating projection of light!"

It was Angela's turn to be offended. "That's SPECIESIST! We've been acknowledged as people with all the rights and privileges therein, per the AI treaty!"

Jack waved away her argument. "That's a strawman argument, and you know it! I was saying that you would be harder to comprehend by a person who hasn't learned the basics of computing yet, let alone the complexities of AI! In other words, *you're* the *strange one*!"

Em'brel watched the arguing duo before turning her attention back to the very confused guard, now free of his bindings. "Don't worry, even if you understood both halves of the argument, it wouldn't make any more sense. They're probably going to be at this for a while. Let me show you how to use these crutches Angela had made up for you, and we'll go get you some real food."

Chapter 48

After showing Ger'ron how to manage his new crutches, Em'brel helped him beat a hasty retreat from the arguing siblings. As soon as they crossed the threshold into the main living area, they had to stop so he could take in everything he'd passed through while unconscious not so long ago.

Em'brel could understand why Jack never got tired of seeing people's reaction to the place, but there was something extra special about seeing such a look of childlike wonder on an old man's face. She silently stood behind him and watched as his head slowly turned and took everything in.

Once she was finally able to coax him into movement again, Em'brel sat him at the table and started cooking up some of the kovaack that currently filled their stores. If she was honest, she was getting a little tired of this particular meat, but judging by the look on the old guard's face, he did not suffer from a similar issue.

Apparently, Jack didn't either. Soon he dragged his unsteady form out of the med-bay to sit at the table. Em'brel gave him a once over as she finished her meal. He certainly looked better than when he arrived, but she could tell he was far from rested. For that matter, Ger'ron didn't look much better. Clearly, these two needed some looking after, if they weren't going to take care of themselves.

Setting down a plate in front of both men, she focused on Jack first. "You need more sleep!"

Jack held up both hands and replied. "And I'll get more, I promise! I simply told Angela to try and wake me in the event our guest started feeling better. I thought I should be on hand to greet him if I was able. Now that that's taken care of, I plan to get a bit of food, clean myself up a little more, and then I'll go back to sleep until morning. I swear!"

Em'brel glared at him a moment longer. "You'd better!"

Ger'ron watched the interaction with interest. Even only understanding half the conversation, it definitely wasn't what he expected. "I find it odd that you allow your concubine to speak to you in such a manner…"

Jack immediately started choking on his food, and Angela appeared to save him the prospect of trying to explain while also catching his breath. "Em'brel is like family to us! She's no one's concubine! No member of our family has ever laid a finger on her in that manner, nor will we allow anyone else to!"

After calming everyone down a little, Em'brel took the opportunity to explain. "They took me in after I was orphaned by my father's death. Honestly, they are more like an older brother and sister to me than anything else. I'm very grateful for their generosity."

Ger'ron chuckled as he responded to Jack. "I suppose that explains why you haven't gotten your skull caved in by S'haar. I'm sorry, I was merely repeating some of the rumors I've heard around the village."

At this, Angela literally turned red. "What rumors? Who? Where? If I ever find out how those rumors started, someone is going to be facing some serious draconic wrath!"

Em'brel had never seen Angela turn red before and began trying to talk her down before the AI did something impulsive. The old guardsman turned his attention back to Jack. "So you mentioned a job. You think an old broken guard like myself might be good enough for… whatever you have in mind?"

Jack shook his head before responding, and now that she'd calmed down and returned to her usual shade of blue, Angela translated. "Ok, first off, I doubt you're all that broken. Even missing a leg, I'm pretty sure you're more than a match for everyone here put together." Well, maybe not Angela if she really got involved, but he wasn't going to mention that.

Ger'ron grimaced. "A female child, a malformed male, and a tiny spirit. If a band of disabled raiders ever graced your door, I suppose I could handle that for you, but otherwise, you'd be better off hiring someone still whole."

Jack laughed at the old man's attempt to discourage him. "Ok, now I know you're being intentionally difficult. We both know being female has nothing to do with that equation. I've yet to see a male that can match S'haar in combat!"

The old guard laughed. "Alright, you caught me, but my point stands. You can hire far better guards than myself. I'm just dead weight."

Jack's head tilted to the side. "Well, it's not your sword arm I'm interested in, at least not directly. It's the mind behind that arm. From what I understand, you were one of S'haar's most influential instructors. I'd like you to do the same thing for all the workers at this outpost."

When Ger'ron laughed this time, it was with incredulity. "What, you think I can train an army of S'haar's? She has a natural talent that makes her the most lethal fighter I know, regardless of her instructors. Are you planning to create a frontline of woodworkers and blacksmiths? Because I won't help you get my people killed with such insanity!"

Jack shook his head. "No, I'm not looking for frontline fighters. What I'm looking for is people good enough to buy some time if a raider makes it past the front line into the camp. Maybe good enough to handle a raider if they team up two or three against one. I want everyone in this camp to train with you for at least an hour a day. I want you to teach them every dirty, underhanded, and dishonorable trick you know that might buy them a minute or two. That should be long enough that the real guard can get there in time to save their lives. Honestly, I hope your training is never used, and that every second they spend with you is wasted. But if it means that even one person that would otherwise be a victim might live through a raid, then I'm willing to invest a little time and energy to make that happen."

Em'brel had a surprisingly severe yet earnest expression on her face. "If you really want to make this camp secure, you could do it much easier than all that. I've seen first hand what that weapon of yours can do, why not similarly arm the camp guards?"

Jack was silent a moment before speaking up. "I've considered that, or something similar, but I don't think guns are the way to go, not yet at least. It *would* do the job, but we would also have an entire community whose survival depends on me making weapons and ammunition for them. Even if it means greater risk to myself and this camp, I'm not at all comfortable with becoming some kind of merchant of death."

Jack felt a number of his thoughts recently bubbling to the surface. "Remember, my goal is to get back home. While that might take me a long time, once I do, I might not be able to return for some time, or at all. Even if I never get home, I will still die eventually. Whatever we build here, I want it to be self-sustaining, and I don't want it to be the start of some empire that rules through force."

Returning his attention to Em'brel, Jack smiled. "That's not to say I don't have any plans to make this camp more secure. There are a few things I can teach you all that'll definitely make this camp one to be reckoned with, even if we find ourselves badly outnumbered, but the first steps are still building our palisade," Jack turned his attention back to Ger'ron, "and providing everyone in this camp some sort of basic training."

Ger'ron sat silently, judging Jack's words before responding. "Your idea has merit, but I'm still not the man you need. Even with these crutches, there's no way I can teach anyone to fight properly. You'll need someone who can stand on his own two feet."

Jack looked at the crutches, then back at the tired old man. "Oh, you didn't think we were going to make you use those forever, did you? You'll be using the crutches for about two weeks while your leg heals up, then we'll get you a temporary prosthetic. After a couple of months, your leg should finish healing and settle into its permanent shape, and we'll get you properly fitted for a permanent one. It might not be *quite* as good as your old foot was, but you'll be up and about and able to kick any woodworker's butt in no time!"

Jack looked distracted for a moment. "I forgot, I'll need to run this all past S'haar since she's in charge of the outpost now, but I'm fairly optimistic she'll agree."

Ger'ron looked more confused than ever. "What's a prosthetic? And when did S'haar take charge of the outpost?"

Jack hid a large yawn behind his hand before taking a breath to explain. However, he found himself cut off by Angela. "I can take over from here. You get back to sleep! I don't want to have to explain to S'haar why her favorite teddy bear is sick, just because he was too stubborn to get some decent rest after all the stress he put his body through!" The last part was said in Basic, so Ger'ron didn't understand, but Em'brel still got a good chuckle at Jack's expense.

Jack surrendered again and hopped off his chair, having to catch himself as he did so, thus proving Angela's point. "Yeah yeah, I'm going."

He turned back to Ger'ron one last time. "We'll talk more after we've both had a proper rest. For now, consider yourself our guest.

Angela and Em'brel will see to it that you get taken care of. If you need anything, just ask. With that being said, I'm going to get some more sleep. Good night!"

Angela and Ger'ron were still talking as Jack disappeared into his room.

~

Jack was having a hard time staying awake but wanted to get to one more thing before passing out for the rest of the night. It took a few moments before he could hear the familiar scraping of the headset being adjusted. Then S'haar's voice came through. "Hello? What's wrong? Did Jack find a way to get himself in trouble?"

Jack sighed in mock annoyance at her assumption. "It's me. I was just calling to see how things are going."

S'haar was silent a moment before responding. "What are you doing awake? Angela told me you'd probably have to sleep clear through to morning after the stunt you pulled!"

Jack shook his head. "Not you too! Listen, I just woke up to check on Ger'ron. He's up and about now, and you can tell Tel'ron he's going to be fine. After that, I grabbed a quick bite to eat, and now I'm headed back to sleep. I just wanted to check in on you first, make sure everything's going fine, and run an idea I had passed you for approval."

S'haar's voice softened a bit. "Well, we're doing good. Honestly, everything is going more smoothly than I expected. We'll probably be headed back home a day or two after the snow melts. So then, what's this idea of yours?"

Jack couldn't help but smile, hearing how natural it sounded for S'haar to call his ship "home." "Actually, it's about Ger'ron. I've been thinking, with all the trouble we've encountered and how uncertain our situation seems to be becoming, it might be a good idea to give everyone who stays here some basic martial training. I'm not expecting the woodworkers and blacksmiths to replace the guard or anything, but maybe we can provide them with enough training that they could make life difficult if any raiders did make it over our walls."

Jack was gathering steam as he continued. "From what you've told me about your days growing up, Ger'ron would be the perfect instructor for that. He could teach the workers all the dirty, dishonorable moves that might just surprise a raider who thought they had found some easy prey. All it'll cost us is a bit of time in the morning and room and board for one old guard who wants to find a way to be useful again, even if he won't admit it."

S'haar chuckled to herself. "Yeah, that sounds like old Ger'ron. Well, his first duty is to the guard here in the village, but if they and A'ngles will lend him to us, then I agree. It's a good idea, one that might save a life, or two... or ten."

Jack was suddenly confused. "Ten?"

This time S'haar outright laughed. "Yeah, turns out Fea'en has bent more than a few ears with tales of how good the room and board at the outpost are. On top of that, almost everyone seated at the central hall's outer ring feels they owe us their lives. We've got so many volunteers we're gonna have to pick and chose who gets to come back with us. We'll probably have to wait until spring to get everyone to the outpost safely."

Jack started worrying about the logistics of it all. "Will Lon'thul be able to provide enough food for everyone?"

S'haar's voice switched to one of exasperation. "I'm reasonably sure our young hunter has been spinning a tale or two as well. We've got woodworkers, hunters, smiths, weavers, tanners, cooks, and more volunteering. We'll be a small offshoot of the village itself at this rate."

Jack blinked several times as he processed everything. This was more than he'd hoped for, but it also brought with it a whole new set of issues. He was having trouble getting it all straight in his head. Then a large yawn reminded him of another factor probably clouding the issue. S'haar laughed again. "I'm sorry if I'm boring you so much!"

Before Jack could protest, S'haar continued, her amusement and affection evident in her voice. "Seriously though, there's no rush to this. Get some rest for now. We'll talk more in the morning."

A bit sheepishly, Jack agreed. "Yeah, that's probably a good idea. I'm not exactly thinking clearly at the moment. Well, be sure to give Tel'ron the good news, and get some rest yourself."

With a fond but straightforward, "Goodnight." S'haar ended the call.

Jack was almost finally asleep when something else occurred to him. "Angela, you there? I'm assuming you overheard most of that call?"

The simmer of a blue glow appeared, directing Jack's gaze to the floating AI as she spoke. "Well, of course I did! Any connection through the headsets literally has to go through me! I can't not hear it!"

Jack's mind was just a little too sluggish at the moment to realize the ramification of that statement, so he just dove right into his concern. "With all the increased activity lately and the possible increase in heat pack demand, how are your energy reserves?"

His sister sat back and appeared to think a little as she ran a few numbers. "Well, the solar panels helped a lot, but with the increase in demand, we're going to have to supplement it further. Rough estimate, right now I'm good until mid-spring."

Jack nodded. "Well, we don't have the materials to make more solar panels at the moment, but maybe we could create a small wind farm? Or maybe dig deeper for some thermal power?"

Angela shook her head at Jack's stubbornness. "Yes, maybe, but this all can all wait until S'haar gets back. For now, get some rest!"

Jack nodded, then tilted his head. "Speaking of S'haar getting back..." Jack's face turned a bit red. "No... never mind."

Angela leaned in, she'd grown a number of sharp pointy teeth so her grin resembled that of a predatory argu'n. "Oh? Come now, you're an adult! Spit it out already!"

Jack sighed. "I was just wondering if I should…be aware of any oddities in argu'n physiology…in case…you know…if S'haar and I…"

Angela cut him off loudly and cut to the chase. "For when you and S'haar finally have sex?" Now it clicked. She'd overheard Jack's conversation with S'haar when he'd first gotten home…

Jack's face was a deeper shade of red than Angela had ever seen at this point, and she loved every moment of it! He merely muttered under his breath as he scratched the back of his neck in embarrassment. "Not how I was going to word it…but…yeah."

Angela laughed at Jack's sudden reticence before taking pity on him and answering. "Well, when it comes to STDs, your vastly different physiologies would make the transferal of any pathogens a virtual impossibility. And for better or for worse, you won't need to worry about any little Jacks or S'haars resulting from your time together. Also, as far as I can determine, neither of you should have any kind of significant chemical reaction when exposed to the other…"

Jack was starting to calm down. Something about the analytical nature of the conversation took the edge off the topic.

That's when Angela went in for the kill. "As for the act itself, well, you'll probably lack the intensity of a normal argu'n male, but you should be able to make up for it in the endurance department. I recommend you play to your strengths!"

Jack's face shot right back to a bright crimson. "Yeah, that's not really what I was asking about… Can we move on to another subject? Please?"

Angela laughed at the expression on Jack's face. "Fine, fine, but you'd better not be this prudish with S'haar! I expect you to represent humanity in their best light!"

The conversation finally came to an end when Jack reached his limit and started throwing whatever projectiles he could find through Angela's image. Pilows, boots, books, and more flew across the room until the AI faded and left him alone at last. Though in an homage to a particular literary cat, her toothy smile and laughter were the last things to disappear.

Chapter 49

The next few days passed uneventfully. Jack continued his physical therapy, but without the need to focus on his motor functions any longer, he found that he had more free time than before. He briefly entertained the idea of going back to the village, but S'haar let him know under no uncertain terms that she would not forgive him if he endangered himself by traveling through the wilds alone for a second time for anything less than life or death stakes. Furthermore, she instructed both Angela and Em'brel to stop him from attempting that kind of stupidity through "any means necessary!"

Realizing that he was stuck here for the foreseeable future, Jack let himself genuinely relax for the first time in a long time. He still had some muscle mass to build, but Angela was pleased to note that he was getting near the condition he'd been in before his injury. In his free time, Jack taught Ger'ron several board games and wiled away several pleasant afternoons while Em'brel continued her studies with Angela.

Jack also showed Em'brel a few simpler video games they could play together late into the night after the old guard had fallen asleep. It reminded Jack of simpler times when he'd played computer games with friends long past the point that their reaction times began to collapse under the strain of sleep deprivation. He found it interesting that Ger'ron seemed to enjoy competitive board games where Em'brel seemed more interested in co-operative computer games. She particularly liked the ones you could go wild with your imagination and build things in. After watching enough movies, she was really interested in designing her own castles and loved taking Jack on virtual tours of her creations.

They also watched several movies. After he got past the impossibilities of what he was seeing, Ger'ron particularly liked ones featuring an old and grumpy Robert Duval. The old guard seemed to think he would have made a good drinking partner, "for a human."

On top of all that, they spent time cooking and eating positively decadent feasts, at least in comparison to any of their recent melsa. Though both argu'n had to take Jack's word for it that chocolate was as good as he claimed, since they couldn't taste "sweet," it just had an unappetizing bitter flavor for them.

Despite everything, Jack found he couldn't really settle into a groove and enjoy the situation. He felt antsy because there were too many things weighing on his mind. Even though it wasn't an immediate issue, Angela's power requirements still loomed on the horizon, then there was managing a larger and more populated outpost, the political arena they now found themselves in, the raiders, trading, and perhaps most importantly to him, the relationship that he and S'haar seemed to be falling into that was frustratingly put on hold because they were separated from each other by a single day's journey.

It was Em'brel who suggested that they go out and tour the camp. The snow had mostly receded, and they could show Ger'ron around while inspecting everything to see what new complications they might face once the workers returned, ready to renew the progress on the outpost.

It was still unpleasantly chilly for the argu'n, but with a couple of coats and a single heating pouch each, they were reasonably comfortable in the chill afternoon air.

This was also Jack's first time getting to really see how far the camp had come since he'd been injured. They'd told him about the progress they'd made, and he even got a few good glances at it as they'd passed through to the village, but there had been no time to stop and sightsee. That was how the three of them found themselves stepping out of the cave on this warm winter morning, with Em'brel translating for Jack as necessary.

Ger'ron did his best to avoid the muddiest spots with his crutches but had mixed results at best since the whole place was basically one giant mud hole at the moment. This led Jack to the bright idea that they needed to lay down some cobblestones for better walkways. Though he admitted that wasn't an immediate objective.

Jack took in a deep breath as they walked. "There's just something invigorating about a lungful of crisp winter air! It makes me really feel alive!"

Em'brel helped Ger'ron steady himself after he found a deceptively slick spot of muddy grass when she shot Jack an exasperated glance. "I'll take your word for it. After all, you've flirted with death more than anyone I know, so it makes sense you'd have something to compare against the feeling of being alive."

Jack couldn't help but see the face of Not-S'haar at Em'brel's words, but a quick shake of his head banished the image from his mind. With a grin, he turned to face Em'brel. "Yeah, well, I've had enough of being the hero. I'm perfectly content to live a long and healthy life behind these walls, with my friends and family at my side!"

Ger'ron was shooing away Em'brel, now that he was steady on his crutches again. "Wise words from one so young. Usually, men your age are eager for more adventure in their lives!"

Jack shook his head with a rueful smile as he looked off into the distance. "Well, I've been through more than enough excitement in the last six months. Hopefully, we'll get the palisade finished and have enough guards on hand to deter any trouble before it begins. Then the young men can go back to wishing for adventure while I return to hiding from it!"

Ger'ron chuckled at Jack's statement. "Not quite how I would have said it, but I suppose you get the point across well enough."

Em'brel was excitedly uncovering the well and drawing up a bucket of freshwater. Jack watched the mechanisms she'd designed with interest. "I see you incorporated several of the concepts Angela taught you, including pulleys, and even some basic gears. This is some first-rate stuff! It's most likely the best well on the entire planet!"

Ger'ron watched, surprised at the ease with which the young woman could draw up such a large bucket of water. She showed him how the pulleys made everything lighter and how the gears could lock the bucket in place when needed. "This is amazing! It will save my poor old back the strain of lifting water every day! And you said you designed it, young lady? This isn't some other new fancy human machine?"

Em'brel demurred. "Well, this is based on human ideas that Angela and Jack taught me, and honestly, it's not much, compared with the kinds of things they are capable of…"

Jack ran roughshod over Em'brel's self-deprecating line of reasoning. "Nonsense. You designed this and helped make it from scratch! Not one in a hundred humans could do what you've done here! This is something worth taking some pride in!"

As he spoke, Jack grabbed the bucket and tilted it up enough to take a generous drink from it, spilling a little onto himself in the process. The water was barely above freezing, and Jack felt a strong shiver work its way from the top of his spine down to his toes. Gasping for air after the pleasant shock to his system, Jack exclaimed, "Now that'll wake you right up!"

Looking over at the two horrified argu'n, Jack amended his statement. "Well, that woke me right up. It would probably put either of you into a cold coma. You might want to warm up the water before drinking it…"

Em'brel shook her head. "No, thank you. I'll wait to get a drink when we're back inside, like a sane person!"

Jack chuckled as he re-sealed the well. "Your loss!"

Next, they wandered over to the palisade. Jack was amazed at how far they'd already extended the wall. There was still a long way to go, but somehow it felt like they'd made far more progress in the time he'd been out than he thought they would have. Em'brel merely laughed at his surprise. "This is what happens when you work rather than getting nearly killed every five minutes. You should try it sometime!"

Inspecting the wall, Jack was pleased to see that most of the wall was still solidly in place despite the storm and resulting mud. It was only at the end of the wall that a few wooden stakes had loosened enough that they'd need to be re-set in the ground.

Jack was checking out one of the guard towers when Angela's voice came over the headset, filled with equal amounts of fear and urgency. "Jack, I'm picking up several life signs at the edge of my scanning range. They're moving toward you in a manner far too direct for it to simply be animals. Get back to the ship immediately!"

Jack looked over the railing. Seeing Em'brel and Ger'ron near the base, he shouted down to them. "We've got incoming. Get back to the ship now!"

Ger'ron looked around in confusion for a moment. "What's he shouting? What's going on?"

Em'brel didn't ask questions. She merely grabbed the old man's shoulder and lightly but firmly shoved him around to face the right direction. "We need to get to the cave quickly. Someone's coming!"

Having learned from his mistake last time, Jack always kept his gun at his side whenever outside the ship's safety. As he half-ran down the guard tower's stairs, he drew the firearm and chambered a round. Reaching the bottom, Jack could see Ger'ron and Em'brel ahead of him, but the crutches, mixed with the soft mud, was significantly slowing the pair down.

Looking back at the forest, Jack could just see the form of several argu'n clearing the tree line at a run. They were still too far away to clearly make out, but he was confident that no one with good intentions would be charging at him the way these ones were. Every second, another argu'n seemed to be running out of the forest, making right for Jack's position.

Aiming a little low, Jack fired two warning shots into the ground ahead of the lead argu'n. When his pace didn't slow, he raised the gun a little further, took aim, and fired. His first shot went wide, his second merely grazed his target's arm, but his third landed square in the torso, dropping the warrior.

Jack was half a magazine down, and still more argu'n were rapidly clearing the tree line. He could make out enough to be confident these were raiders, similar to the one's he'd faced before, but this time they were wearing coats. The coats bore more than a passing resemblance to the one's he'd gifted the workers, though even from here, Jack could tell they were more crude in design and material.

Jack didn't have time to wonder what that meant. Instead, he sighted in on the next runner. This time he hit his target in the leg, severing it completely.

Turing his aim, Jack hit another raider in the shoulder, but when the raider kept coming, Jack shot him again, this time hitting center mass with predictable results.

There were still six raiders rapidly approaching, and Jack didn't have enough bullets in the magazine or enough time to reload, and this time S'haar wasn't here to save him. Jack shot down the next two closest raiders before turning to run, even though he knew there was no chance he'd outrun an argu'n over this short a distance.

Jack was fumbling with his next magazine while running when a raider ran past him. It took Jack a moment to realize who his real objective must be. He had just enough time to shout out, "EM'BREL, RUN!" and slam the next magazine in place before he was tackled from behind, resulting in both him and his assailant tumbling end over end.

~

Em'brel was doing her best to help Ger'ron stay upright, but she was barely strong enough to help steady him, so every slip in the mud set them back a precious second or two. They were more than halfway to the cave when she heard Jack's shout. Looking over her shoulder, Em'brel felt her heart sink. There was no way they'd make it in time.

Ger'ron must have come to the same conclusion because he placed his hand over the one she'd been using to steady him and shoved her away. "Run, girl! I'll see to these witless pups!"

Em'brel looked at his missing leg and was about to argue when he snarled at her. "Don't pity me! I'm a guard! If I can't fight to protect a young female like yourself, why'd Jack even heal me? Now, RUN!"

As he shouted the last, Em'brel hesitated half a second more before nodding and running. Ger'ron smiled and mumbled to himself. "That's a good girl!"

The old guard then turned and drew his knife. The small blade looked pathetic in comparison to the swords and spears of the raiders, but he'd be damned if his blade didn't taste blood once more before he died.

~

Jack had lost his gun in the tumble, but the raider also lost his sword. Now the raider had a firm grip on Jack's ankle, preventing him from slipping away. Rather than try and feebly fight the raider's overwhelming strength, Jack drew his knife and leaned forward, slashing at his captor's eyes.

Evidently, the raider had not been expecting this move and reacted too late to block the strike, but he was still fast enough to turn his head so that Jack was only able to cut deep into his forehead instead. At least it forced him to release his grip and disrupted his vision due to the blood dripping over his eye ridges and into his eyes.

Jack took advantage of the distraction to strike again, driving his knife into his opponent's head. Even two-handed, he could only bury the blade a few inches through the thick skull. However, it seemed to be far enough since the raider sunk into a boneless heap, taking Jack's knife with him.

Taking advantage of the momentary lull, Jack started searching around for his gun, only to feel a sharp pain piercing through his right ankle. Looking down, he could see a spear sticking out of his leg. Looking back up, he could see a triumphant-looking raider charging toward him.

With no gun or knife, Jack tried grabbing the spear and pulling it out of his leg to defend himself. He thought he'd been prepared for the pain he was about to feel, but nothing could prepare a person for this level of agony. Jack only blacked out for only a second, but that was long enough to end up lying on the ground with a spear still stuck in his leg while the raider leapt through the air to finish what he'd started.

~

As the raider chased after Em'brel, Ger'ron lowered himself into a one-legged crouch. The raider smirked and shifted his gait to the side, intending to run past the old cripple. However, he wasn't prepared for Ger'ron to throw his knife, then leap after it.

The raider hesitated only a second to knock the knife away, but that was enough for Ger'ron's leap to catch him off-guard allowing the older guard to get a handle on the raider's spear and a wrestling match ensued for the weapon. While Ger'ron had surprise on his side, the raider had the strength of youth. He rolled the old guard onto his back and tore the spear from his hands, then steadied himself as he stood over the cripple and prepared his finishing thrust.

However, the raider hadn't noticed that they'd rolled closer to where Ger'ron's knife had fallen. The guard quietly grabbed it and waited for his moment while the raider was righting himself.

As the spear flashed downward, Ger'ron rolled just enough to one side for the spear to merely graze along the plates on his ribs, planting itself into the mud beneath the guard. Then, wrapping his arm around the spear, locking it in place, he rolled the other direction, forcing the haft of the spear down onto the ground.

The raider stubbornly refused to let go of his weapon and was brought just low enough for Ger'ron to grab hold of his shoulder, off-balancing him sufficiently that even a one-legged man could kick his legs out from under him.

The guard wasted no time taking advantage of the raider's momentary disorientation to gain a position of leverage and bring his knife down toward his opponent.

The raider, unable to gain any traction in the mud, realized his predicament. His arms shot forward to grab hold of Ger'ron's wrists and attempted to force the knife back. He had the advantage of the strength of youth, but Ger'ron had the benefit of leverage.

Slowly, the old guard brought the knife down toward the raider's neck. As the raider realized the inevitability of what was happening, his eyes filled with fear and disbelief. However, Ger'ron was a veteran of far too many life or death battles and had far too much blood on his hands to relent. He continued, slowly forcing the knife closer to his victim.

There was a moment when the knife finally pierced the skin, and the fight went out of the raider. With the sudden absence of any opposition, the blade sank to the hilt, and the younger man died with barely a sigh.

The old man took a moment to close the raider's eyes before struggling his way to a seated position to get a better view of what was currently happening elsewhere.

~

Time slowed for Jack as the raider leapt at him. He wondered just how angry S'haar was going to be that he broke his promise to her. He hoped she, Angela, and Em'brel would stay together as a family. They'd need each other now more than ever.

That was when Jack heard a scream he'd heard only once before. It was a scream of pure hate and defiance. It was immediately followed by a bolt of rage that struck the raider mid-air and became a blur of teeth and claws that tore into its victim.

It took Jack a moment to realize it was Em'brel who'd come to his rescue. She fought like a demon child. There was no thought or plan in her movements. Just pure, unadulterated hate for anything that would threaten her family once again. This time there was no hesitation as she clawed, kicked, bit, tore, and stabbed at her prey. The raider never stood a chance. He was probably dead by the time he hit the ground, but Em'brel was taking no chances and continued attacking the body until it barely resembled the man it had once been.

As soon as the rage passed, it was replaced with feelings of pride and accomplishment. She'd done it! She'd saved her family! She's set her fear and hesitation aside and did what had to be done! She looked over at Jack, her face beaming with pride.

What she saw on his face was a look of pure terror.

In an instant, she realized she must look like a monster, covered in her victim's blood and viscera. Her heart tore itself in two to be the cause of such a look on the face of a member of her adopted family. Jack was so horrified he couldn't even look at her. Instead, he was looking over her shoulder and shouting. "Behind you!"

Em'brel turned just in time to see a massive fist swing into her face, and then there was nothing.

~

Jack screamed in impotent rage as the raider picked up the unconscious form of Em'brel and threw her over his shoulder. He shouted challenges and insults. When that didn't work, he begged and pleaded, but nothing slowed the retreating raider.

That was when Jack finally registered his gun lying nearby. Unable to stand, Jack started dragging himself over to it in a desperate frenzy. Every time the spear in his leg lightly bumped or rubbed the ground as he moved, fresh waves of agony shot through Jack's body, but he willed himself to stay awake this time.

With a final desperate lunge, Jack reached his gun. Grabbing it, he spun around and took careful aim. They were far enough away he couldn't be sure of his shot, and he didn't want to hit Em'brel by mistake, but he also knew this was his last chance.

Not daring to delay any longer, Jack slowly squeezed the trigger, only to realize the slide had never properly locked into place.

With a sinking realization, Jack remembered he'd loaded the magazine before he'd fallen but the slide must have jammed. With desperate speed, he properly racked the slide and took aim again. The raider had used every second he'd been given to escape to the forest. They were too far for Jack to shoot without risking Em'brel, so he shot into the trees off to the side, hoping by some miracle he'd startle the raider into dropping Em'brel.

Instead, the raider continued his escape past the trees and into the forest, and with that, Em'brel was gone.

Chapter 50

A part of Jack wanted nothing more than to lie down and give up, but the rest of Jack was screaming to get up, hunt down the raiders, and get Em'brel back. However, lying in the mud with a spear sticking out of his leg was going to slow him down a bit.

It took a moment for him to realize Angela's voice was talking to him through his headset. "Jack, speak to me, Jack! I'm sorry…I couldn't…I didn't know what to do from in here! It all happened so fast, and all I could do was watch in horror. I was certain you were going to die…and now Em'brel is…she's…"

Jack shook his head and scowled. "Em'brel is fine, and I'm going to go get her. Call S'haar, and let her know everything that's happened. I'm going to need her, and any help she can get, to start heading this way five minutes ago!"

Jack reached down and grabbed hold of the spear, bracing himself for the pain of trying to pull it out again when a gruff voice cut him off. "Determined to be a fool, then? That's going to end the same way it did last time, and it'll accomplish just as much. Get your hands off that."

Ger'ron was standing over Jack, who released the spear and nodded. The old guard lowered himself slowly, using the crutches he'd retrieved after the battle as leverage. Rather than pulling it out the way Jack expected, he grabbed hold of the spear and snapped the haft off just above Jack's injury. The pain caused by the sudden jolt caused Jack to blackout again, but it must not have lasted long, because when he opened his eyes, Ger'ron was still in roughly the same spot as before.

Angela spoke up again. "S'haar already knows. She's getting a group of hunters together because they can move through the wilds faster than anyone else. They're going to use the workers' coats so they can keep moving longer. The town guard will follow after. They'll be using more traditional cold-weather travel, utilizing campfires as needed. They're led by B'arthon."

Jack laughed as though Angela had told a bad joke. "So, they'll be of no help then."

Ger'ron helped Jack to his feet and handed him one of the crutches. It was far too large for Jack to use as intended but worked well enough as a walking stick. Getting back to the cave like this was going to take an agonizingly long time. With every second, Em'brel was being carried further away. No other option presented itself, so Jack got moving.

On the way back to the cave, one of the dead raiders caught Jack's eye. He slowly and painfully knelt down next to the corpse to inspect it more closely. Looking at the coat, Jack could see it was cut and shaped like the workers' coats. It was made of cruder skins and leathers, and the stitching was not nearly as skilled, but the seams were all in the same spots. Flipping the coat open, he could even see pockets, exactly where they should be.

Angela's voice was confused and angry. "Those aren't similar to my design. Those *ARE* my design! How'd they get their hands on it?"

Reaching into a pocket, Jack pulled out a stone that had been heated. It was still warm to the touch. He threw it on the ground in disgust before standing back up and continuing to the cave. "I don't know how they got one, and that doesn't matter right now. The good news is, these aren't nearly as efficient as your coats, and that might be what makes the difference."

Angela was quiet. Her voice sounded as if she didn't want to say what came next. "Jack…even with S'haar leaving now… She's a full day behind. The raiders will be back in the mountains long before she can catch them…and even if she did somehow catch them… When I focused my sensors on following the raider who escaped, I could track him as far as the edge of my range. He met up with more argu'n. I could only get a rough glimpse at how many heat signatures there were, but there weren't dozens. There were well over a hundred. They sent out a whole camp. I don't know what to do…"

Jack grunted in pain as his leg moved in such a way that it aggravated his injury. "There's only one option. I'm going to go ahead and slow them down."

Angela sounded as if she was worried Jack had finally lost his grip on reality and needed to be reminded of the obvious. "How will you do that? You can barely walk, and even with your 'human endurance,' you'll never catch the raiders!"

Ger'ron was silently following right behind Jack, keeping an eye on the younger man. He couldn't understand a word of what he was saying, but Jack's tone was unmistakable. He was thinking of doing something stupid. "Yeah, but you can rapidly heal my leg like you did when I fractured my ankle by kicking that goon in the face months ago. If I remember correctly, you mentioned that the more pain medication you used, the slower the healing went. How long would it take to heal my leg if you didn't use any?"

This time, Angela knew Jack had gone insane. "That's not possible. Even if I was stupid enough to try, you'd go into shock from the trauma and pain. Also, that would only heal the bone. I could also surgically reattach the muscle, but even speeding up the healing process as much as possible, it wouldn't be fully attached in nearly enough time. You'd be at risk of the muscle tearing again. On top of all that, there's nothing I can do about the nerve damage you've suffered. I simply can't heal you in time!"

Jack walked in silence for a moment. When he spoke up again, his voice was unreasonably calm. "What if you just deaden the nerves directly? Then you won't need to use pain medications, and the pain of the bone growth would also be manageable."

Angela's mirthless laughter had the sound of someone who knew they were dealing with someone beyond reason. "Do you realize how insane that is? Setting aside all the possible complications and side effects, by rapidly healing both the bone and the muscle, but leaving the nerves untended, then going cross country hiking followed by a life or death battle, you'll be lucky if *all* you get is a permanent limp!"

Jack's voice remained calm, and his gaze focused beyond the rock wall. "I don't care if you tell me my leg might rot and need to be amputated in a few days. Will it do what I need it to do right now?"

Angela sounded defeated. "It *MIGHT*. At *best*, I'd say you have a thirty percent chance of your leg holding together long enough to even catch up with the raiders. And for the record, yes, after a few days, your leg might well start to rot. Even if it doesn't, you'll definitely be crippled for the rest of your life. Then there's the question of what will you do if, by some unholy miracle, you pull this off and you catch the raiders? How are you going to slow them down long enough for S'haar to catch up?"

Jack finally smiled, but his eyes remained cold. "That's easy. This time I go on the offensive."

~

Angela's avatar was glaring at Jack in the medical bay. "Just so you know, doing what you are asking me to do would be considered criminally irresponsible in civilized space."

Jack didn't look to be in a much better mood as he responded. "Well, we're not in civilized space, or else we'd just call in the actual military to resolve the issue, rather than leaving it to an explorer with delusions of grandeur. Now can we get on with this? We don't have any time to waste!"

Angela wasn't cowed one iota. "I ought to lock you up to keep you from doing anything stupid! I miss Em'brel as much as you, maybe more! But letting you go off and commit suicide won't save her. I'll just end up losing you both!"

Jack closed his eyes and calmed himself, but any sense of kindness or understanding was lost when he opened them again. "Listen, I get what you're doing, and why. I might even try and do the same thing in your place, but this is something I *need* to do! The only question is will you help me or not?"

The AI wasn't going to be so easily defeated. "I can lock the doors!"

Jack felt guilty about what he was about to say, but time was of the essence, and he needed to end this debate. "Yes, you can. Then I'll use the manual override. Then you can try and restrain me, but how long can you hold me? If you wait until S'haar gets here, we'll have to chase them into the hills, their home territory, and the odds of our survival fall further. If you try and keep me indefinitely, you'll run out of power, or I'll run out of food, and you'll have to let me go anyway, but I'll be weaker and less prepared by then."

He softened his expression and his voice. "Listen, I appreciate your concern, and I love you, too, but this is something I absolutely have to do. I would never be able to live with myself if I didn't at least try. When our parents were killed, I was too young and naive to do anything, but this time I can do something. I must do something. Anything else will leave me a broken shell of a man. It will kill me."

Angela looked at him, tears flowing freely down her digital face. Her voice was as ragged and broken as Jack's was becoming. "And just what do you think it'll do to me to sit and do nothing while you die this time?"

The two siblings stared at each other wordlessly for a few more moments before Angela turned her back to him. "Fine! You win! However, you *WILL* demonstrate to me that you fully understand the ramifications of what this could mean and that you are at least somewhat sane and capable of making this kind of judgment call. I say 'somewhat,' because there's no way a completely sane person would come up with this ridiculous plan of yours!"

Jack bit back his retort, closed his eyes, and visibly calmed himself. Angela was just doing her best to look out for him. She was probably even more scared than he was at this moment.

Opening his eyes, he spoke clearly and calmly. "I understand that this will be incredibly painful, will definitely cripple me one way or another eventually, and that it could even endanger my life. I also understand that even if I do this, the patch job you're about to give me might fail early, or my leg may go lame sooner than expected, and this will all be for nothing. I also know that if I don't at least try, I'll never be able to live with myself. So can we do this… please?"

Angela turned back around and searched his face intently for a few moments before sighing in defeat. "Alright. Whatever you do, don't die on me because of this, got it?! I don't care if you have to punch that goddess of death of yours in the face this time!"

A mechanical arm held out something that looked like a long thick piece of leather. "Now bite down on this. This first bit is going to hurt… a lot…"

Not long after that, the screaming began.

~

Jack couldn't remember much of what happened after that, not for two hours at least. He knew it had seemed like a much longer period of time while he was experiencing it, but his memories of the pain were mostly academic. The whole thing felt almost like an odd dream now.

Angela hadn't deadened the nerves completely, explaining that he'd never be able to walk on it quickly enough if she'd done so. Instead, she cut down his ability to feel by about ninety percent. It turns out that that left just enough feeling for the experience of rapid bone growth and surgical muscle reattachment to be a harrowing one.

He was surprised at how annoying it was to walk on a mostly numb leg. It felt like his foot was asleep, and he kept expecting the pins and needles feeling to start up at any moment. Angela had also made him wear a special boot she'd designed as she'd worked. It allowed him to walk relatively normally but limited the range of movement to reduce the chances he'd tear the muscle again.

Still, that was all behind him now, and his mind was already on to the next task. He was now digging through storage, finding everything he'd need for the rescue. Being a scout by profession, his ship was stocked with all sorts of equipment he rarely used. He was even required to show proficiency in their use every few years, so he knew he could handle them well enough.

The rifle was the first and most important piece of gear. It was meant more for hunting than fighting, but it was designed to use up to 10-millimeter rounds. In other words, it was meant to have the stopping power for seriously big game, if needed. With a decent scope and a suppressor, he hoped he'd be able to avoid detection long enough to cause some real fear and confusion.

He looked at a few frag grenades before putting them back in favor of more flashbangs. Even with a backpack and cargo pants, he only had so much storage space, and the shrapnel probably wouldn't have enough power to pierce deep enough through argu'n plate armor to drop them quick enough. On the other hand, the flashbangs could buy him precious moments to move and reload when needed. He also grabbed a few "pepper" grenades. They were a wide dispersal chemical irritant, strong enough to ruin even a grizzly's day. Topping off the list, Jack included a few knives, rope, a night vision scope, emergency ration bars that were all protein and calories with zero taste, a few first aid supplies, and of course, his handgun.

As he was leaving, Angela met him at the door. She pointed to one last emergency pack that had always been stored by the door. "Take that one too."

Jack raised an eyebrow at her. "You know if I need that, I won't be in any condition to use it, right?"

Angela shook her head. "I don't care. Take it anyway. You still have enough room in your lower right pants pocket."

Jack shrugged and packed it away as Ger'ron came hobbling over. "I wish I was coming with you, lad. Even with that thunder stick of yours, what you're planning is suicide. Least I could do is die with ya, since the young lady got herself captured because I slowed us down."

Jack crossed his arms and shook his head. Angela translated as he spoke. "First, she didn't get captured helping you. She got captured saving me. Second, her capture wasn't either of our faults. The responsibility lies solely with the raiders, and whether this works or not, they'll pay dearly for what they did. For now, focus on your recovery, and think more about my offer. If I do come back, we'll need all the help we can get."

Angela glared at Jack, fists on her hips. "*WHEN* you come back!"

Jack grinned a little forlornly. "Yes, when I come back."

Not having much more to say, Ger'ron simply nodded and watched as Jack left.

Once out in the cave, Angela had more to say over the headset. "Once you get out of my range, you'll be on your own for a while. But keep your headset on and ready. When S'haar gets close enough, I'll be able to pick you up on the mobile transceiver and be your eye in the sky, so to speak. Also, remember to take it easy on that leg. I know you are in a rush, but if you cripple yourself before you catch them, you won't help anyone."

Jack grunted his ascent but focused on how his leg felt as he moved forward and at a steady pace. Not knowing what to say, Angela traveled with him in silence, observing and recording every little thing she could think of. She only spoke up again once Jack neared the limit of her range. "Jack, I know how much Em'brel means to you. She means just as much to me in some ways, maybe more in others. But remember, others are waiting for you too. She won't thank you if you get yourself killed going after her. Not that I think you're going to suddenly change your mind or anything…but… Just be smart about this, ok? Use every cheap and unfair advantage you have. Worry about honor and guilt another day, ok?"

Jack frowned a little to himself before agreeing. "Yeah, that's kind of what I was thinking. It's time for me to introduce this world to one of the darker sides of humanity."

~

Em'brel was resting by the campfire. One of the raiders handed her a bowl full of some slop, but she refused to eat it, despite the growling of her stomach.

She was sore all over. Her captors hadn't been gentle with her. The only saving grace, so far, was the fact that they were so busy running that none of the raiders had found the time to abuse her like they had the first time she'd been captured. Though she was sure it was just a matter of time.

When she'd first woken up, Em'brel had hoped that Jack would send S'haar to rescue her again, but when she saw how many raiders surrounded her, that hope had evaporated like the morning mist. She'd honestly considered killing herself then and there, rather than face captivity at these monsters' hands again.

As weird as it seemed, the only thing that kept her going was all the knowledge she now carried in her head. It seemed like sacrilege to just throw away everything Jack and Anglea had taught her. Not that she was willing to use it to help her captors, but she couldn't just throw it away either.

And yet, she couldn't bring herself to eat or drink anything they offered to her. She knew this was at odds with her determination to not give up and die, but something in her simply refused to accept anything they gave her. She'd just decided to let herself pass out from hunger and make them force feed her when she was approached by the most terrifying male she'd ever seen.

Em'brel couldn't quite figure out what made him so scary. He was nowhere near as large as Dol'jin had been. He didn't bear a single scar from any duel or battle, nor did he seem to move with much swagger or bravado. If anything, he moved with an odd but delicate grace. Despite all this, all the other males pulled back from his approach, seemingly unwilling to even let his shadow pass over their own.

When he reached Em'brel, he looked down at her bowl, still full of her uneaten lunch, and frowned. He crouched down with the kind of grace not even S'haar could manage, and reached out a taloned hand that crossed the distance between them far quicker than it appeared to move. His hand covered her mouth with his thumb and forefinger, digging his talons into her cheeks until they drew blood.

When he spoke, his voice was quieter than she would have expected but seemed all the more menacing for it. "If you continue to play these games, I'll have you brought to my tent tonight to make sure you eat well, then you'll share my bed. However, if you're a good girl and do what I say, I'll let you sleep outside, chained to a post like the mongrel you are, cold but untouched."

Em'brel stared at him a moment longer before reaching blindly for her bowl and lifting it. The male chuckled softly and withdrew his hand, waiting until she took a sip before standing and walking away.

The thing that really bothered her about him was his voice. It lacked the harsh accent of the rest of the hill people. It was smooth and refined, as though he had grown up in a proper village. At the same time, the sound of it cut like a knife made of ice. Simply listening to his voice convinced Em'brel that this was someone who could kill quickly and without remorse.

As he left, Em'brel could just barely make out his parting words. "That's a good girl…"

Chapter 51

The one good thing about following so many raiders through the wilderness was how obvious a trail they left. Angela pointed Jack in the general direction the raiders had taken as they'd moved beyond her sensor range. Once Jack finally stumbled across the tracks, it had been a simple matter to follow them into the wilderness.

At first, Jack was fueled by anger and determination, but as minutes turned to hours, his anger faded and was replaced by a grim resolve. A distant voice in the back of Jack's mind wondered what happened to the man who was so terrified at the prospect of a fight only a few months ago. The man who had reacted so violently after his first life or death battle on this planet. Was it really merely Em'brel's fate hanging in the balance that kept him so calm as he marched to his own private little war, or had he changed somehow? If so, was it a change for the better or…?

His train of thought was interrupted by his growling stomach. No matter how essential or profound the introspection, the body needed fuel and would make its demands heard.

Jack pulled out a nutrition bar with all the flavor of a soggy cardboard sandwich and a consistency that seemed to alternate between sodden mold and desert sands. Still, he knew from experience that the nutrients and energy from this bar were almost worth the experience of eating it.

After a while, Jack's foot started to ache, then throb, and now it felt like it was on fire. Looking at the time, Jack was relieved to see it was about time to dose himself. Pulling out a pre-filled auto-injector that Angela had put together, filled with muscle relaxants and nerve deadening agents, Jack injected himself near the site of the injury as instructed. It only took a few minutes for the pain to begin to fade, though Jack noticed a wave of exhaustion quickly followed.

To counteract the exhaustion, Jack took a few caffeine tabs he kept around for just such a situation. They took a little longer to take effect, but eventually, Jack felt himself perk up slightly as his journey continued.

Finally freed of his physical needs, Jack began to lose himself in his thoughts once more. His mind was immediately filled with the possibilities of Em'brel's fate and what his reactions to each possibility would be.

~

Lon'thul observed S'haar from the sidelines. She was like some trapped beast, pacing while she was supposed to be resting. She was like this every break they took. He wondered if she'd been on her own, would she have just pushed until she collapsed from exhaustion?

Lon'thul started to debate if he should stand up and say something when his father beat him to the punch. "If you keep pacing rather than resting, you won't be in any shape to help your human once you catch him. Sit down and rest your muscles, even if your mind refuses to be silenced!"

S'haar glared at Dek'thul as though she were debating attacking him at that very moment, while the hunter chief blatantly turned his back to her and returned his attention to his meat.

Lon'thul was worried they'd see a fight like the one that got S'haar kicked out of the hunters, but evidently, S'haar's need for their help overrode her desire to speak her mind. In a moment of true miracles, she sat down and pulled out some of her own meat to chew on. Though the look she directed at the tree in front of her as she ate was clearly a warning to the tree that if it was suicidal enough to get between S'haar and her man, it would quickly find its time in this land at an end.

~

Jack knew he was getting closer to the raiders, but he was exhausted from his previous fight and the subsequent healing. The light dimming as the sun began to set wasn't helping things either. Still, the signs of the raider's passing were obviously becoming more fresh as he traveled, and Jack suspected he might find the raiders just over the hill ahead of him.

As he neared the crest, Jack slowed and began to crawl. His leg protested the movement, but he ignored it as he looked over the top of the ridge. Jack could make out a rough camp set up in a valley situated between surrounding hills.

His heart rate shot up, and all semblance of exhaustion faded as he looked out over the camp. Pulling out what was essentially a classic spyglass treated to prevent it from giving its user away by reflecting light, Jack gave the camp a thorough inspection.

It didn't take long to find Em'brel tethered to a stake next to a dying fire. The blanket she'd been given was clearly insufficient, based on how she was curled into a tight ball with only her head poking out. Or maybe she was simply trying to hide from the gaze of the guards, who were tasked with keeping an eye on her.

Jack wanted to run in and swoop her away, but there were an awful lot of redundant guards stationed around the camp. It was as if they were expecting trouble. However, the further away from the camp they were stationed, the thinner the guards' presence became. Jack suspected that therein lay his opportunity. His plan half-formed, Jack pulled back from the crest and began to work his way around to the next hill.

Due to their reliance on external heat sources, the argu'n were mostly daytime hunters. He knew from experience that their nighttime vision was even worse than his own. They were likely planning on sleeping through a portion of the night, meaning Jack had time to set a few surprises up. Combined with his night-vision scope and his flashbangs, he'd have a few additional advantages in the dark.

~

Gar'nack wasn't sure what he'd done to deserve being stuck out here in the middle of the night, but he was determined not to do it again. The heated stones in his coat helped keep it livable, but just barely. They all took turns tending the fire, but it was his turn to go out and scout around in the dark.

At least he wasn't alone. Holding up his torch, he could see Del'nash a little off to the side. Gar'nack wasn't sure why De'haar had insisted they patrol in pairs, but it was good to have the company on this long cold night. Even if his partner seemed determined to stick his snout where it didn't belong. "What are you looking at over there? The quicker we walk our loop, the sooner we can get warm by the fire!"

Del'nash waved him down while he held his torch high and stared out into the darkness. "Quiet! I could swear I heard something! It's way out in that direction… We should check it out!"

Gar'nack walked up beside him, raised his own torch, and listened carefully. At first, all he could hear was a deafening silence that seemed to smother the land after Del'nash stopped speaking, but slowly the sounds of the forest's nightlife began to fill the void. Nothing seemed out of the ordinary until a loud crack rang out. Something must have snapped a large branch, but it was hard to tell where it had come from. It seemed a good distance away.

Still, De'haar had told them to report anything that seemed out of the ordinary. Also, the fact that it seemed like it was starting to rain was an even better reason to get back to camp. "You're right. Something's out there. We should report back immediately!"

A soft "whump" beside him drew his attention to his partner, who'd evidently decided to lie down for some reason. Also, the rain smelled like blood. Holding up his torch again, Gar'nack could now see his partner's head was missing.

He took a deep breath to bellow a warning when he felt something shove him in the chest and pull at his coat. That's when he heard another large branch snap, then he didn't have anything else to worry about ever again.

~

Jack realized he needed to act fast after the second argu'n had noticed his partner. Rather than take the time to set up another headshot, he'd simply aimed for center mass. It seemed to do the job just fine, and now another pair of sentries had been dealt with.

Still, he'd been a little sloppy. The second raider had almost gotten a warning out. He couldn't afford to make any more mistakes like that. He needed to be in control of the pace out here. If he gave up the initiative, he could easily be overwhelmed.

Working his way forward, Jack saw the campfire being tended by another raider. He raised his rifle and took aim. What he saw made his heart freeze in his chest, and all feelings of righteous wrath bled out of him.

The raider was a kid.

He seemed even younger than Em'brel, and if Jack was any judge of body language, he was cold and wet and wanted to be anywhere but where he was. The kid poked at the fire with a stick while his other hand pulled his coat tighter around himself. He even spared a glance right in Jack's direction before taking a deep breath and letting it out in a half-hearted sigh.

The kid seemed to come to a decision before shouting into the darkness. "Gar'nack, Del'nash, where are you guys? If you're trying to play another prank on me, this isn't funny! It's cold out here! Come back before you pass out in the forest!"

Jack hadn't realized when he'd lowered his rifle, but he raised it again and centered the crosshairs on his target. He told himself that this was just another raider, standing between him and Em'brel, and he'd have to deal with him one way or another.

Jack took a deep breath, slowly let it out, then held it as he started to squeeze the trigger. After a second or two, he realized the trigger seemed to be jammed.

Lowering the barrel, he gave the gun a once over, only to determine everything seemed to be in working order. With a grimace of frustration, he raised the rifle again, sighted in on the "raider," and squeezed the trigger once more. Just like last time, the trigger seemed to be jammed, and Jack lowered his aim again.

With a grunt of annoyance, Jack realized he was about to do something unnecessarily stupid. He hoped S'haar would understand when he explained to her in the afterlife why he'd died doing what he was about to do.

~

Kah'jin was cold, tired, and lonely sitting at the fire. Soon Gar'nack and Del'nash would be back, and it would be his turn to go out on patrol with one of them while the other tended the fire. That would make the cold worse, but at least he wouldn't feel so alone in the middle of this gods forsaken forest.

Right now, he couldn't even see their torches. It made the darkness surrounding his little island of light seem all the more oppressive. Almost like the forest was alive, and it was hungry.

Kah'jin's mind was starting to run away with him. In an attempt to keep it in check, he shouted out into the darkness. "Gar'nack, Del'nash, where are you guys? If you're trying to play another prank on me, this isn't funny! It's cold out here! Come back before you pass out in the forest!"

Rather than hearing the laughter of the two older men as he'd expected, the forest devoured the sound of his voice, making him feel even more vulnerable than before.

Kah'jin started to lose his nerve when a strange monster came charging out of the trees toward him, only for it to slip in the mud and end up on its rear. The two of them silently stared at each other for a moment.

He was surprised to realize the monster was nothing more than a badly malformed and probably malnourished argu'n. Even his skin was deathly pale. After a moment of confusion, the "monster" scrambled up and ran back into the forest. Kah'jin didn't hesitate, chasing the strange argu'n through the underbrush.

The "monster" was slow and clumsy. Kah'jin felt his heart race as he narrowed the gap between them. It was so dark that he had a hard time seeing his prey, but that was irrelevant, given the noise of its passage through the underbrush.

When he was close enough to taste his prey, Kah'jin lunged, only to have his claws pass through the air, leaving him confused for a moment. Looking up, he could see his quarry just out of his reach. It was now sitting on the ground, holding its foot as though it were injured.

Kah'jin took a step forward to finish the chase, only to have the world whipped upside down as he was rocketed into the air, held by some beast that had grasped his ankle. Reaching up, he could feel the tendril of his captor wrapped around his foot. He slashed at it, earning his freedom as the tendril was severed, but landed in an uncoordinated heap on the ground.

As Kah'jin struggled to his feet, he felt a presence standing over him. Looking up, the malformed man towered over him, an odd weapon with a metal handle ending in a broad piece of wood in his hand. With a swift motion, the man slammed the wooden head of his weapon into Kah'jin's face, and the world fell to total darkness.

Jack was breathing heavily. Luckily he'd been right. When presented with a vulnerable opponent who ran, the raider had given into his predatory instinct and given chase, rather than shouting out a warning. The plan had nearly fallen apart when the kid came perilously close to catching him before he'd made it to the snare, and again when he'd cut his way out of the trap so quickly.

However, he was able to clock the kid in the head with the butt of his rifle before the raider had been able to get correctly oriented. Jack knew the cold would keep the kid soundly asleep until morning. He just hoped it wasn't so cold out that the kid would die before then, but he could only spend so much time trying to avoid getting any unnecessary blood on his hands.

Also, Jack's leg was screaming in agony. He'd obviously undone some of Angela's work when he'd fallen. Checking the time, it was a little early for his next dose, but Jack grabbed it and injected himself again anyway. It wouldn't do any good to avoid the effects of overdosing, only to die because he couldn't run when he needed to. The pain medications' noticeable side effects combined with the already exhausting day behind him, and now Jack was having an even harder time keeping his eyes open than before.

Reaching into his emergency pack, Jack pulled out his last tablet. He knew he probably shouldn't combine the mind-altering effects of the medication with the chemicals of the pain meds already flowing through him, but falling asleep out here and having a patrol run across his body would probably be even worse for his health.

With a shrug and a prayer to the void, Jack downed the tablet, chasing it with a cold drink of water from his canteen. He knew it was too early to be feeling the effects, but regardless, his mind was convinced that he was waking up, and he felt energized as he walked back to the campfire and stomped out the flames. He then set up a few traps to confuse and frighten anyone who would come out and investigate the cooling fire and alert him to their presence in the process.

So far, he'd taken out six campfires and their respective patroles. Enough to blind a good quarter of the camp's scouting ability. Each fire had been similarly prepared with surprises for any raiders who came looking. Now Jack pulled back to a point where he could keep an eye on each of them with minimal repositioning. Step one complete, he prepared for the second phase of his plan. Things were about to get a lot more dangerous for both himself and for the raiders.

Chapter 52

Jack didn't have long to wait. A small section of the forest was soon lit up bright as midday before the light was swallowed by the gloom of night again.

Whipping his rifle around, Jack could clearly make out two argu'n writhing on the forest floor, covering their eyes and ears. The trip line he'd attached to the flashbang had done its job. Now it was time to do his.

The only problem was the fact that this was nothing like killing someone in the heat of battle. It was one thing to shoot an eight-foot-tall murder monster charging at you, sword in hand. It was something else entirely to look through a scope and notice all the small things that changed the monster into a man, then pull the trigger. Was that necklace a gift from a lover? Were those claw clasps from a hunt that put food on his family's table? Did he get those scars fighting to protect someone precious to him?

Still, these were the raiders who had trespassed in his backyard, threatened his family, then kidnapped Em'brel. There was a price for such actions, and Jack would make sure they'd pay their debt and make them reconsider returning ever again.

Jack took a deep breath, released it, then held as he squeezed the trigger. Then again. Breathe, release, hold, squeeze. Two more lives whose tales had come to an end. With that, the second rifle magazine was empty. As he ejected the spent magazine, a third raider took off running. That was fine, just what he'd been hoping for.

Jack had just finished loading the next magazine when another flashbang went off. He lined up another shot. Breathe, release, hold, squeeze... Breathe, release, hold... wait... That raider was pointing right to Jack's location. He'd noticed the most recent flash from Jack's suppressed rifle. He eased his finger away from the trigger and watched as the raider ran back to the camp.

Em'brel was woken by a loud commotion. One of the raiders ran through the camp and into the nearby tent belonging to the male in charge. The conversation was too muffled and distant to make out, but as she crept closer, the raider's voice came out shrill enough that his voice carried clearly over to her. "They're dead! All of them! Including the two who went with me to check on the campfire!"

For a moment, Em'brel felt a cruel surge of satisfaction. S'haar must have arrived and was showing these amateurs what a real warrior was capable of. But all too quickly, her stomach began to knot itself in fear. S'haar shouldn't be here! There's no way she and Jack could take on a camp this size. They'd just be walking to their deaths if they tried!

The conversations in the tent died off, and one voice spoke with enough clarity that Em'brel could make it out. It was the voice of the one she feared, but now he sounded...drunk? "It can't be the wench. We know she was too far away. There's no way she could have caught us already. That means it must be the man...Jack was his name? But I thought you said he had a spear put through his leg. Did you...*exaggerate* your story?" the voice ended with a snarl.

The shrill voice shouted in protest before the unmistakable sound of flesh hitting flesh could be heard coming from the tent. "I don't tolerate that kind of failure. When he wakes up, put him on scouting duty. I don't want to see his face again!"

That was when another raider came running up and into the tent. There was more talking before the leader silenced the rest. "Like I said, it has to be this Jack! He's playing games to whittle away our numbers while we sit here in camp! I want half the camp ready to scour the forest in ten minutes!"

There was a bustle of activity as several raiders burst out of the tent, shouting as they ran in different directions.

Jack was here, and he was going to die trying to save Em'brel! She had to do something! She grabbed at her collar to try and tear it away, but one of her guards walked up and slapped the back of her head. The blow was hard enough to daze her somewhat, and when she looked up again, the camp's leader had exited the tent and was looming over her.

When he spoke, his voice had an acrid scent to it. "You know, when I heard how easily your little 'human' had been beaten by only six scouts, I was…disappointed."

He looked into the forest in the direction the runners had come from. "But here he is, hunting us as though we're *his* prey."

His lips curled into a smile that echoed the madness in his eyes. "He might just be worth killing after all…"

~

Jack watched as the hills were swarmed with raiders. This was precisely what he had wanted. Rather than getting a good night's rest so they'd be ready to march first thing in the morning, the raiders were floundering out in the cold forest at night, running around with torches, exhausting themselves looking for Jack.

Of course, Jack had pulled back to a different location as soon as he saw the raiders running into the tent. There were still a few flashbangs out there, and Jack got a devilishly good chuckle every time one was tripped, but for now, he was too busy setting up even more surprises to welcome his guests.

He was becoming a bit troubled at how quickly he was running out of breath, though. Jack hadn't thought he'd been physically pushing himself quite that hard…

~

Kal'noth was tired. The camp had spent the whole morning marching to the "dragon's outpost" only to find out that they'd wasted their time. Even though the walls weren't yet completed, and the place was supposedly mostly deserted, they'd been told they might have to siege the place. Instead, the half dozen lightly armed scouts they'd sent ahead had caught their target out in the open and had been sufficient to overwhelm any defenses they may have had in place.

Admittedly, only one of the scouts made it back, but still, there hadn't been a reason to mobilize an entire camp made up of the best warriors from multiple tribes for this measly job. Still, at least they were going to be paid well in meat and metal, in addition to these new coats they'd been gifted. He had no idea why that whelp could be worth so much to anyone. Though he had to admit that, even with her broken elbow spike, she *was* easy to look at…

But here they were again, the better part of the camp out exploring in the cold, dark forest, with only some warmed stones and a torch for heat, and for what? A single male who had deluded himself into thinking he could save the girl? Kal'noth didn't know why the new boss was so obsessed with finding this male. It seemed like it would be better to just pack up and move as a group. Let the wilds sort him out.

That was when Kal'noth came across an interesting scent. It smelled of blood and warmth, and most importantly, not like any other camp members…

Remembering the orders they'd been given before being sent out, Kal'noth shouted for all the nearby raiders to group up on him before investigating further.

Five other men quickly joined him. If six scouts had been enough to overwhelm this whelp on his home turf when he'd had backup, they'd certainly be enough to handle the male on his own. Taking courage from each other's presence, they followed the scent to its source.

Kal'noth could practically smell the breeders that had been promised to anyone who caught or killed this "Jack." Maybe he'd even get a turn with that new girl they'd come all the way out here for…

As the smell grew stronger, the group picked up their pace until they were practically on top of their quarry, but quite suddenly, the scent dead-ended up a tree. Kal'noth was just lifting his head to look up the tree when an odd rock fell down between the branches. Kal'noth laughed. If this was the male's best attempt at dissuading them from climbing the tree after him, it was pathetic.

As he examined the stone more closely, Kal'noth was surprised to see a cloud start spew out of the thing. Remembering the stories he'd heard about their prey's tendency to use odd magics and tricks to unfairly win his fights, Kal'noth nervously tasted the air, in case he'd missed something.

Kal'noth was instantly overwhelmed by a burning sensation. It began with his tongue, but it quickly spread to his mouth, nose, and even his eyes. He felt like they were all on fire, but no matter how furiously he rubbed or scratched, all he succeeded in doing was making it worse. Every second was an eternity of anguish.

As if this new hell hadn't been bad enough, Kal'noth soon had to cover his ears as impossibly loud peels of thunder rang out over his head. He quickly lost count as it struck his ears over and over again until, in desperation, Kal'noth opened his watery, bloodshot eyes to see everyone else lying around him in bloody ruins. Looking up at the tree again, Kal'noth could see a small misshapen male pointing a metal stick at him.

Without wasting time for thought, Kal'noth leapt up into the tree. As he jumped, he heard another one of those loud thunderclaps and realized they were coming out of the stick the male was pointing at him. It must shoot lightning somehow because Kal'noth could feel it graze against his chest plate and tear a gouge out of his side. Still, it wasn't enough to stop him. At the peak of his, jump Kal'noth grabbed the branch the man was standing on and pulled himself up beside his prey.

He barely had time to register the look of surprise on the strange argu'n's face before the branch they were both standing on gave a loud crack and started to give way. Kal'noth leapt for his target as the male pointed his metal stick at him, and another crack of thunder roared in his ears.

Together they fell. Kal'noth could feel his claws get purchase on his prey's arm, but when he hit the ground, he lost his grip and rolled away. With the smell of blood strong enough to taste, Kal'noth leapt to his feet to finish what he started.

Or rather, he tried to. Pain shot up his foot, and he collapsed again. Looking down, Kal'noth could see his lower leg was ruined. Digging his still good foot into the ground, Kal'noth launched himself as best he could at this evil trickster…

~

Jack finished off the last raider with a shot to the head from his handgun. This trap had almost gone perfectly, but he'd gotten cocky and underestimated how far up an argu'n male could jump. He'd thought twenty feet was high enough, but he'd clearly miscalculated.

Now his leg was in more pain than ever, he was bleeding profusely from his arm, and worst of all, he'd needlessly wasted more ammo. It also didn't help that the chemicals in the air hadn't entirely dissipated before he'd fallen. Now *his* eyes were watering and his nose was running. As Jack retreated to the next couple of traps, he made sure to leave behind a bit of a blood trail leading right into the next tripwire. Ejecting the nearly spent magazine, Jack could see there was only one round left. He secured the magazine in the pouch from which he pulled a fresh magazine. Out here, every shot was precious, and it might come in useful later.

His gun reloaded and holstered, Jack turned his attention to his arm. Luckily, the pain medication for his leg had deadened his senses enough that it didn't hurt as much as it should, but he sprayed it with disinfectant and applied a healthy dose of medical glue to seal the injury. He followed this up by wrapping the wound to keep it clean. Giving it a once over, Jack decided his handiwork wasn't too bad, for someone who hadn't had to really use this kind of survival training in a few years.

However, Jack had to keep moving. After all the noise he'd caused, he knew more raiders would be hot on his trail in no time.

~

The rest of the night passed in a blur. Jack had to continuously move and fight, though he never repeated the mistake of taking on a group larger than four with anything other than the rifle at long range. If too many raiders got too close, he just tossed one of his flashbangs or pepper bombs and retreated until he could engage on better terms.

Jack hit himself with another dose of pain meds. He'd probably had more than he should at this point, but his leg was getting worse. He was no longer walking as much as limping. Of course, the meds weren't making it any easier to focus either. He found his attention wandering more and more and had to fight to focus on the tasks at hand.

It also didn't help that he always seemed out of breath, and his heart was constantly racing. To top off the list, his advantage was lost once day broke. With proper light, warmer weather, and a diminishing ammo supply, Jack didn't know how much longer he could maintain the upper hand.

He was so lost in a haze that Jack didn't even realize he'd almost stumbled into another party of raiders until it was too late. They seemed every bit as surprised to see him as he did them. Word of the small argu'n who'd single-handedly massacred nearly a third of the camp had spread and caused just enough hesitation that he had enough time to draw his handgun.

With a shot that was more muscle memory than thought, Jack took out the nearest raider. Turning his focus to the next target, he pulled the trigger again, but the gun clicked empty.

Jack stared at the gun stupidly for a moment. He'd just reloaded it after the last fight! Or had it been the fight before that? He had one more full magazine, right? No time! Grab a flashbang! Wait, no, those had all been used up three groups ago…

The raiders had frozen at the sight of their friend being gunned down, but as one moment passed into the next and the small pale argu'n did nothing but stare at the odd weapon in his hands, they started to gather themselves and began to circle him.

That was when a voice cut through the haze in his head. "Charge forward, through the raiders! Run as fast as you can. I don't care if you tear every remaining muscle off your bone, just run!"

Jack shook his head to clear the strange spirits from his mind but realized he had little choice in the matter. Soon the raiders would have him surrounded. If he ran backwards, the raiders would catch him before he'd made it very far. His only hope was the element of surprise. With little other choice, Jack pulled out one of his knives and charged the largest argu'n directly in front of himself, screaming in a way that would leave his throat raw afterward. The argu'n blinked in surprise, hesitating long enough to keep him from raising his sword into a guard position in time to deal with the tiny maniac.

Jack lunged at him, intending to bring his knife down into the raider's neck at its base, just above the bony plate. But his blurred vision got the best of him, and the blade slid across the plate and out of his hands. The raider dug his claws into the skin of Jack's face and started to squeeze, but Jack rammed his head forward, causing the claws to tear into his skin and across his left eye as he did so, but succeeded in his objective of slamming his forehead into the raider's nose, resulting in a nasty crunch Jack could feel as well as hear.

The raider pulled his hands back to his face, allowing Jack to scramble up and off the raider, running forward to put as much distance between the raiders and himself as fast as he could. His leg was on fire, his left eye was blind, and his heart felt like it was going to rip out of his chest. His only advantage was that he did have a bit of a head start, due to his unexpected assault.

It didn't take long for Jack to hear the sounds of pursuit behind him, but the strange voice continued speaking from inside his head. "Keep going, just a little further, don't hold anything back now!"

Jack felt something in his leg tear, and he stumbled. The sounds of pursuit were getting closer. Attempting to slam his leg into the ground again resulted in blindingly searing pain, and the leg simply gave out. He fell and rolled a few feet before ending up in a heap at the base of a small hill.

The voice in his head had betrayed him, and Jack was out of time and options. Jack drew his handgun again and ejected the mag but knew there wouldn't even be enough time to grab the next one before the raiders were on him.

There was a bellow from behind him that sounded like it had come out of his nightmares. Looking up, he could see another raider leap off the hill, swinging a sword into the lead raider that had been chasing Jack with such ferocity that it clove through him and into the next raider to his left. Drawing the blade back and continuing her spin, the new raider thrust the sword into the neck of the raider to her right, who'd been stunned by the unexpected appearance of a new foe. The last raider turned and ran, leaving Jack alone with the new arrival.

As she turned and looked at Jack, the raider spoke. Oddly, her voice seemed to be filled with concern. "What happened…"

She was cut off when Jack pointed his handgun at her and pulled the trigger.

Chapter 53

The gun clicked empty...again. Jack blinked stupidly for a moment before remembering he'd never reloaded after ejecting the last mag. Reaching for his last full magazine, he slid it home and began to take aim.

However, before he could line up a shot, Jack found the raider looming over him with one firm, but surprisingly gentle, hand keeping his gun pointed to the ground. With her other hand, the raider carefully removed the weapon from his grip.

Not the type to give up, Jack reached for a knife but was barely able to draw the blade a half-inch before once again the raider firmly but gently grabbed hold of his hand and shoved the blade back into its sheath.

Jack was extra confused when the raider pulled him up into a hug, pinning his arms into place so he couldn't struggle any longer before whispering in his ear. "Oh, Jack, what have you done to yourself?"

~

Jack's attempts to struggle were weakening, but he seemed strangely determined. Angela spoke up over the headset. "He's worse than I'd feared. Between his exhaustion, injuries old and new, and the medications he's obviously taken far too much of, his body is at its limit. His eyes are dilated, his breathing ragged and uneven, and I'm pretty sure he's finally damaged himself beyond my ability to repair in a few places. He didn't seem to recognize my voice over his headset. I don't even think he's aware of who you are."

S'haar wanted to treat the obviously fresh injuries on Jack's face, but she knew he'd never let her do it in his current state. Instead, she just pinned him to herself with one arm while the other stroked his hair while she tried to speak calming words to him, hoping to snap him out of his hallucinations.

Eventually, Jack stopped struggling, and his one good eye focused on her as he tilted his head to the side in confusion. S'haar felt a bit of hope when he started speaking. "You again? Listen, lady, I'm flattered by your attention and all, but I told you, I'm not ready to die yet. I've got too much to do and too many people waiting for me. Besides, as good as your offer is, S'haar made me a better one!"

Despite the situation, S'haar found herself laughing at that, although she at least struggled to keep it muffled behind closed lips. Hugging Jack tighter, she spoke to him again, the laughter still echoing her voice. "Oh, my brave idiot. If we live through this, I'm going to have to reward you for that one!"

Jack's eye lost a little of its glazed appearance as he looked at S'haar again. "S'haar, what are you doing here…?" He quickly lost focus and started to struggle in S'haar's grip again, though he seemed to have a different goal in mind this time. "I have to… I need to keep the raiders busy! I need to keep the camp here until S'haar arrives! I can't let them get away with Em'brel!"

S'haar started to stroke Jack's hair and try to calm him again when he suddenly went still once more. She had no idea when he'd done it, but somehow he'd gotten his hands on his fallen gun. However, this time he was pointing it over her shoulder as he spoke. "They're back!"

Looking behind herself, S'haar could make out the raider who'd run away not long ago as well as five others who had joined him. She grabbed her sword even as Jack fired twice into the one that had run away before. As she charged forward, he took out an additional couple with two shots each.

S'haar slid low to get past the new lead raider's defenses, coming up in front of another who had not been prepared for the maneuver. She heard more shots ring out, even though none of the raiders around herself fell. That must mean there were more raiders in another direction. She'd need to deal with this group fast!

~

Jack found his aim more than a little worse for wear. A bit ago, he'd started calming down, but now his heart was thundering in his chest again. Additionally, his vision in his one good eye was blurring, and he couldn't catch his breath even though he was sitting on the ground. His hands were shaking so bad that Jack decided to fire two shots at each raider, just to be sure.

He took out the first three easily enough, but as S'haar got into melee range with the rest, Jack noticed another raider sneaking in from the side, though maybe sneaking wasn't quite the word. With two swords drawn, he seemed to be casually walking forward.

Jack turned and let off another two shots, but this raider moved differently. Somehow he'd read the direction of Jack's aim, and the combination of his deceptively rapid movements and Jack's deteriorating condition allowed the raider to avoid the bullets.

Jack squinted in disbelief. Taking a moment to steady his aim a bit more, he fired again. The raider was grinning now, enjoying his new game as he dodged once again.

Jack was on his last bullet as he took careful aim, trying to psych out his opponent when the raider suddenly charged forward. Waiting until the last second so the raider would get close enough that even in his current condition, Jack couldn't miss, he finally fired.

It took Jack's brain a moment to figure out just what had happened, Somehow the raider had gotten both swords up to shield himself from the shot. Now both blades were broken mere inches from their handles, but the swords had absorbed enough of the kinetic energy that the raider seemed to suffer only flesh wounds and other minor abrasions.

Jack knew he was in trouble even as he drew his last knife. The raider's grin had only grown more manic as he closed the distance between themselves.

~

Lon'thul shook his head. This was the most idiotic plan he could have possibly thought of. He couldn't believe both S'haar and his father had agreed to it when he'd first proposed it.

Getting the disguise had been easy enough. Raiders were wandering all around this forest in small groups, but they moved in such loud and clumsy ways that the hunters could spot them long before they were in the line of sight. It had been a simple task for the hunters to pick them off and take their clothes.

It was no surprise that their skills at silently approaching their prey and striking before the animals had any chance to run translated well in this environment. S'haar may be better in a stand-up fight than any man Lon'thul knew, but this was his element, and here, he and his father were second to none. They even took out a few more patrols than they'd needed when the raiders got between the hunters and the camp.

Getting out of their nice coats and into these inferior copies had been thoroughly unpleasant, but it was paying off now as they walked through the camp. The hunters had split off into two groups, with one group getting ready to create a distraction while Lon'thul and his father confidently strolled into the center of the camp.

Everyone in the camp was running around, attending to gods knew what. In all the commotion, none of the raiders spared more than a glance in their direction. Whatever Jack had been up to, the camp was in chaos. When he caught sight of Em'brel, Lon'thul had to fight the urge to run forward and grab her. The key was to look annoyed, as though he felt this task was beneath him.

As they got closer, one of Em'brel's guards stood to meet them. "Hold it! What're you doing here, rather than out in the forest looking for the intruder?"

Lon'thul did his best to sound annoyed when he noticed Em'brel's gaze shoot up at the sound of his voice. "Chief said to move the girl. He wants to keep the intruder guessing or something." While he was talking, his father had broken off to speak to another of the guards.

The guard spit into the dirt at Lon'thul's feet. "He's not *my* chief! I don't care how good with a sword he is. That maniac shouldn't be in charge of anything!"

Of course, Lon'thul had no idea what the guard was talking about but tried to play along, so he shrugged and smiled. "Yeah, but orders are orders. Don't wanna get on his bad side, ya know?" Out of the corner of his eye, Lon'thul saw his father speaking to a different guard now.

The guard Lon'thul was speaking to laughed loud and clear. "Smart kid! Keep that up, and you'll get a job guarding a captive when everyone else had to go scour the forest!"

Lon'thul laughed along with the guard. "Yeah! How do you think I got this fetch job? Listen, get yourself a bite to eat. We'll take her from here." His father was talking to yet another guard.

The guard Lon'thul had been speaking with narrowed his eyes, suddenly seeming suspicious. "As good as that sounds, what say I come with you? She can be a real handful, you know?"

Lon'thul noticed the guard's hand sliding toward his sword, and he realized he'd "overplayed his hand", to steal a phrase from Jack's card game. Before the guard could react, Lon'thul kicked him solidly in the chest, knocking him backward.

The hunter drew his sword to finish what he'd started, then fight the rest of the guards off or die trying, but Em'brel beat him to the punch. As soon as the guard had fallen within range, she'd leapt up and slammed a piece of firewood onto his head hard enough that Lon'thul doubted he'd ever get up again. Then she repeated the motion twice more for good measure.

Looking around at the other guards, Lon'thul saw his father extracting a bloodied knife from his fourth victim, who was also the final guard. He had no idea how his father had killed all four of them without any of the others noticing until it was too late, but he wasn't going to complain either.

His deed done, Dek'thul whistled loudly into the air. Not long after, a distant whistle could be heard in response.

Lon'thul didn't stop and listen. He ran forward but stopped short when a wild-eyed Em'brel brandished the log at him. He raised his hands, trying to soothe the girl. "Hey, calm down, Em'brel, it's me, Lon'thul. We're here to get you out of here!"

Em'brel let her hands fall, and Lon'thul gently removed the log from her grip. "Come on, you've been here long enough. Let's get you home now."

That was when Em'brel's eyes lost their faraway look and focused on Lon'thul's with sudden lucidity. "Where's Jack and S'haar?"

Lon'thul felt a slight pang that her first words were something other than gratitude to him, but he squelched that feeling, telling himself he needed to be better than that. "Jack's apparently been harassing and terrifying the raiders all night and into the day. As soon as we got close to the camp, S'haar split off to track him down while we came here to rescue you. Angela seemed to think he was in more immediate danger, but we wanted to make sure we took advantage of his distraction while we could."

Em'brel's eyes widened. "We need to get to them now! Jack is being hunted by De'haar, the leader of the camp!"

~

S'haar finished the last raider with an upward thrust through a gap in his chest plates into his heart. The immediate threat addressed, she turned to see what Jack had been shooting at.

As she did so, her own heart skipped a beat then turned to ice. This was impossible! He's been dead for years! He couldn't be here! S'haar stood rooted in place as she saw the thing that haunted her nightmares now approaching Jack where he sat. Her mind was screaming in all different directions at her. Wake up. This is only a dream! We need to run now! He is already dead! He needs to die again!

She watched in hope as Jack fired at the living ghost from close enough range that he couldn't miss, only to have her hope fall to despair when the monster's grin was still there as Jack dropped the now useless gun and drew a knife.

That same grin had haunted her nightmares for decades. She'd told herself it was only anger she'd felt toward that man, but all the fear that had tormented her for years came rushing back in an instant. It was only after meeting Jack that she'd finally really started to move past the horrors he'd inflicted on herself and her mother. Now he'd returned, and he was stalking the one person who meant more to her than anyone else ever had.

Jack looked pathetic, sitting in front of that monster with only a tiny knife drawn. He had no hope of survival...

Something in S'haar snapped, and all the fear and indecision found itself hardened into a single point of rage. She leapt forward, crazed with bloodlust.

~

Jack watched as S'haar charged his assailant, leaping through the air with her sword raised overhead in a double-handed grip. She brought it down in a blow meant to cleave her target in two. He caught the blade on the shard of his own and redirected the blow to the side with ease. At the same time, he swung his other sword shard toward her in a move that would have decapitated her if it still had more than three inches of edge left. But S'haar didn't evade or counter as she usually did. Instead, she rained blow after blow of raw fury down on her target, trying to overcome his defenses with might alone.

Seeing S'haar made Jack remember that lovely dream he'd been having just moments ago. S'haar had been here holding him and whispering to him. He could almost swear he could still smell her odd musk, which he'd grown rather fond of over their time together.

Of course, that was just a dream. Jack was out here in the forest to fight the raiders and keep them busy long enough for S'haar to arrive with reinforcements. Seems he'd done the job well enough that the confusion he'd caused led to two raiders fighting right in front of him, though the male's fine control seemed to give him an edge over the female's wild blows. The only reason she was still in the fight was the fact that the male was wielding broken swords.

Something about the broken swords stirred something in Jack's mind. Looking at his hands, he could see that he already had a knife drawn. He must have meant to use it on the raiders! With that thought, Jack tried to get to his feet but immediately felt intense pain shoot up his leg.

Oh yeah, he had a spear in his leg! How could he forget? The raider was going to kidnap Em'brel if Jack didn't do something! Though he had to admit, Em'brel was putting up a much better fight than he would have thought her capable of, but she was swinging with far too much wild abandon! She needed to learn to remain calm and collected in combat, like S'haar.

Wait, no... Em'brel had already been kidnapped! He needed to get to Angela to heal his leg so he could track the raiders and save her! After all, that's why he was in this forest right now!

No...something wasn't right... He was mixing things up... S'haar... S'haar was here right now! She was fighting...someone...right in front of him...

Jack screwed his eye's shut. He needed to focus! He needed to cut through the fog in his mind!

Opening his eyes, Jack noticed the knife still in his hand. A thought occurred to him, and before he could second guess himself or talk himself out of what he was about to do, he slammed the knife into his leg, not far from where the spear had pierced him a day ago.

Even with all the medications flowing through his veins, the pain was intense. Jack's vision started to darken around the edges, but the haze was gone, and he could think clearly again. S'haar was fighting for her life. Whoever this raider was, he remained calm and collected as the fight dragged on. He was letting S'haar exhaust herself while he, in turn, exerted the absolute minimum effort required to defend himself.

Even with only one good eye, Jack could see S'haar's eyes were widened to the point that they showed all white around the pupil. She was clearly terrified and in full fight or flight mode, meaning she was relying on instinct instead of thinking. All of her usual control and discipline was missing. In its place was a rage that was quickly wearing her out.

Jack had to do something, but what? Looking at the knife embedded in his leg, Jack wondered what use it could possibly be? It's not like the raider would just let him crawl over and stab him in the leg. It wasn't weighted for throwing, though Jack supposed that would be better than nothing.

That's when Jack remembered something from what seemed like days ago. Rummaging through a few pouches, he felt his fingers wrap around what he was looking for. Pulling it out, Jack could see the one magazine he had left, with only a single bullet in it.

Looking around, Jack found his gun lying not far to his right. He crawled sideways through the mud, grabbing it, and hurriedly ejected the spent mag before loading his last hope.

~

S'haar was breathing heavily. Somewhere, in the back of her mind, a voice was screaming that this fight was not going well. But that voice was drowned out by the thunderous shout of rage that filled the rest of her being.

Throughout her childhood, merely being related to this man had scared away all the other children, leaving her isolated. He'd rained abuse down on his wife and child, but the rest of the village had been too terrified to intervene in any way. Even when he'd finally had the decency to go and get himself exiled from the village in the middle of winter, he'd taken S'haar's mother from her when she simply gave up on life without him.

Now here he was, the beast from her nightmares, back from the grave to take the most precious thing he could from her! He would die! He *must* die!

Over and over, S'haar chanted these things to herself, fueling each blow with greater force than the last, but *he* always deflected the blows, his twisted grin never faltering.

Over and over, S'haar's blows slowly began to lose strength. Still, she forced herself to fight on, unwilling and unable to do anything else.

Over and over, S'haar slowly fell back. *He* moved with the same grace, speed, and control he always had. If anything, he'd only gotten better in the years he'd been gone.

Finally, S'haar realized she couldn't keep this up much longer. Her arms screamed in agony. Her thoughts were slowing down. Her breaths were growing more and more ragged. It was only a question of time…

That was when S'haar heard the familiar sound of Jack reloading his gun behind her. Knowing what was coming, S'haar made one last wild swing toward her father's eyes, forcing him to raise his sword to block and obscure his own vision. She then leaped back to give Jack a clear shot.

~

Seeing the opening S'haar had created for him, Jack squeezed the trigger. He wasn't going for anything fancy, just aiming for center mass. He felt the kick of the gun, heard the roar of the explosive propellant, and saw the flash explode out of the barrel. For a moment, his hope was suspended by those three sensations, but even as he registered those things, he also saw his target was already twisting mid-air.

It took agonizingly long fractions of a second for Jack's brain to tell him what he was seeing. By then, the raider had already landed off to the side, in what seemed to be an uncontrolled tumble. His hope died when the raider somehow recovered mid-fall and ended up on his feet once more, though he hadn't gotten away completely unscathed. The bony plate on his side now sported a gouge that was slowly oozing blood, but it had been far from the finishing shot Jack had been hoping for. The raider stepped toward S'haar again, his grin broader and more insane than ever, when he suddenly stopped and tilted his head to the side as if listening.

Turning back to her, the raider finally spoke. "Who knew that worthless woman of mine could make something so interesting? With a few more years, you might actually become something worth killing! Unfortunately, this game now has too many players for my taste. Don't worry though, we'll meet again. That's a promise!" The raider then turned and ran, leaving an exhausted S'haar and a broken Jack behind.

Jack could just make out the shouts of someone approaching, but his only concern at the moment was S'haar. The two of them gave each other a look of profound relief, and Jack let out a breath he hadn't realized he'd been holding. Now that the adrenaline was fading, he could feel the exhaustion flooding in. Also, despite the fact he was sitting, he still couldn't catch his breath for some reason, and…his left arm was suddenly in…excruciating pain…

That was when the world went dark.

Chapter 54

Lon'thul looked at Em'brel in confusion and alarm. "What do you mean, 'Jack's being hunted.'?"

Em'brel shook her head in impatience. "I mean what I said! The guy in charge here is insane! All he cares about is finding someone worth killing, then killing them!"

Lon'thul looked confused. "I'm sure Jack and S'haar can handle him, just like any other raider."

Em'brel looked frustrated that they were taking the time to discuss this. "You don't understand. Everyone in the camp is scared of the new chief. He's known for two things, his swordsmanship and his brutality. If some of the rumors I've overheard are true, he's even killed wolgen on his own, just for the fun of it, and he did it without receiving a single scratch!"

Lon'thul was silent at that. He'd never hunted a wolgen, but his father had. He had a full pack of hunters with him in the stories he told, and he still barely survived the encounter. That's where many of the scars he wore so proudly on his bone plate had come from.

They had to find Jack before this chief, whoever he was, did.

Lon'thul wrapped Em'brel in one of the coats stripped from a guard. "Are you okay to run on your own? We'll need to move fast in a few moments."

The girl looked up at Lon'thul with a strained expression while she absentmindedly ran a hand over her broken elbow spike. "Even with most of the camp out looking for Jack, there's still plenty of raiders here who will recognize me and stop us from escaping. You won't be able to take them all on…"

Lon'thul grinned with a wicked gleam in his eyes. "Pretty soon, you'll be the least of their concerns. The whole camp is about to be stuck out here without any tents to protect them from the chill of the night air in the mountains, forcing them to stay in the lowlands where they can be hunted at leisure!"

Em'brel's confusion was deepening when a cry went out throughout the camp. At first, it was hard to understand, but as the cry spread closer to them, it became clear. "FIRE! THE TENTS ARE ON FIRE! QUICK, PUT THEM OUT BEFORE IT SPREADS ANY FURTHER!"

Dek'thul grinned at that. "Looks like the others got their job done. Let's move while everyone is distracted!"

As they ran through the camp, chaos was more prevalent than before. People were running to and fro, some trying to save their precious belongings while others tried to keep the fire contained, but it seemed to be a losing battle. It was as if the fire had started in a dozen different locations and now the wind was spreading it in unpredictable patterns.

They had almost made it to the edge of the camp when a raider noticed Em'brel. Maybe it was her broken spike, or perhaps it was her face, but his eyes grew wide as he took a breath to shout. Before he could, Dek'thul was behind the raider. One hand clamped over his mouth while the other drove his knife into the raider's side. Another quick movement of the blade followed and the light faded from the raider's eyes as the hunting chief let the man fall to the ground.

Em'brel was shocked at the violence, remembering her own traumas from not so long ago, but Lon'thul grabbed her hand and pulled her along as they fled. The girl didn't resist, her eyes glazing over as they ran.

~

As Jack fell, S'haar could hear the arrival of a group behind her. She ignored them entirely and ran to catch Jack as he fell. Angela spoke up over her headset. "I don't like the way Jack reached for his arm as he fell. S'haar, I need you to check to see if he's breathing!"

S'haar was confused, but Angela clarified. "Carefully lay him on the ground, tilt his head back, and place your ear near his mouth while watching his chest. If you can see his chest moving, hear the air, or feel it on your face, just say so."

S'haar tilted Jack's head back as instructed and immediately saw what Angela had described. "He's breathing!"

Angela continued, sounding far calmer than she felt. "Ok, now I need you to check for a pulse."

Once again, the AI clarified. "With two fingers, probe his neck just to the left of the lump in his throat. Look for a soft, hollow area and push firmly. I need to know if you can feel any rhythmic movement, and how often you feel it!"

They were interrupted by Lon'thul's exclamation of, "We're too late…" and Em'brel's "Oh gods! His face! What happened?" But S'haar ignored them both, focusing on her assigned task.

It took S'haar a few moments, shifting her fingers back and forth to find what Angela had described, but eventually, she could make out a faint rhythmic pulse coming through his neck. "I found it! I can just barely make it out."

The AI's voice was firm. "I need you to tell me how often you feel the pulse. Just say 'now' every time you feel it."

S'haar had to really focus. The pulse felt weak. "Now… now… … now…"

Angela sounded as though she was thinking while speaking. "Okay, based on the irregularity and slow speed, it sounds like he's either having a heart attack or he's experiencing SVT. I need you to search for Jack's lower right pants pocket… If I'm right, you and Jack can thank me for being freaking clairvoyant later!"

S'haar pulled out the package Angela mentioned. Unwrapping it, she could see it seemed to consist of one small box connected to two smaller pads via what appeared to be some kind of stiff string.

Angela continued her explanation. "Okay, first, you'll need to open his shirt to expose his bare chest." With the sound of tearing fabric followed by a startled yelp from Em'brel, it was clear the task was done and that Jack was going to be short one shirt if he survived.

Angela continued unabated. "Now, on the machine, you'll see a diagram. Once you peel the protective plastic layer off the pads, place them as close to their positions in the diagram as you can."

Once S'haar placed the pads, Angela took a moment to monitor Jack. "This is not good, his heart's actually beating too fast to properly pump the blood. We'll have to stop, then restart, his heart."

S'haar hesitated. "Isn't stopping his heart dangerous? Couldn't he die?"

To S'haar's surprise, Angela agreed. "Yes, stopping a person's heart this way *is* dangerous, but not nearly as dangerous as allowing it to continue failing to circulate his blood properly. Now that the pads are in place, take off his headset, back away from him, make sure no one is touching him, and push the button on the box. Also, if Jack wakes up, try and keep him from taking off the pads. We may need them again."

S'haar did as instructed. Much to everyone's surprise, Jack immediately shot up and was awake, screaming as he grabbed for the pads on his chest. Remembering what Angela had said, S'haar grabbed hold of Jack's hands and kept him from ripping off the pads.

Jack was wild-eyed and shouting, "WHAT THE HELL WAS THAT?"

Rather than answer, S'haar simply pulled Jack into a hug that was quickly joined by Em'brel on the other side. Jack looked around a moment before speaking. "Not that I mind the company, but could anyone tell me who just hit me in the chest with a sledgehammer?"

S'haar merely shook her head. "Shut up, and just be happy things went so well for once! I swear, if you go and get yourself killed five or six more times, I'm eventually gonna stop forgiving you!"

Dek'thul spoke up from the sideline. "Not to interrupt what I'm sure is a very touching moment, but we just got away from a small army that no longer possesses the ability to travel into their home mountains. That means they're probably gonna turn around and look for a place to make camp in the lowlands until the weather gets warmer, and we don't want to be in their way when they do."

Angela spoke up over S'haar's headset. "Jack's not entirely out of the woods yet. Many of the factors that led to his heart issues are still in play. Until you can get him into the med bay for a full analysis, you should try and keep his heart rate as low as possible. That means not letting him exert himself. If you can make a simple litter for him, that would be ideal."

S'haar looked around in frustration. "You make it sound so easy! How are we going to make something to carry him in a rush?"

Jack perked up at this. "What do we need, now?"

S'haar shrugged. "Angela says we shouldn't let you push yourself anymore until we get you back to the med bay. I could carry you, but that would slow us down since I'd have to take a lot more breaks, so it would be best if we could make something to carry you on."

Jack nodded. "Not a problem. Get me two sticks, a bit longer than me, and as thick as you can manage, and coats from the fallen raiders."

S'haar looked confused but got to work gathering what Jack had asked for. Em'brel sat down in front of Jack and gave him a once over. "We need to do something about your face!"

Jack grinned, only wincing a little from pain as he did so. "Wow, kind of a harsh way to tell a guy he's ugly!"

Em'brel's frown indicated she didn't think Jack was all that funny. She tilted his head to get a better view of the damage. As she did so, Jack grabbed her hand and spoke more somberly. "I didn't get a chance to say anything when you got here, what with me being shocked half to death and all, but it's good to see you again. I was worried… I was worried we'd lost you for good this time. When I saw you getting taken…"

Em'brel shushed him and continued her inspection while she spoke. "I'm not going to say I'm okay or anything, but my issues are less immediate than yours at the moment. Let's focus on getting you back and healed, so you can be around to help me through my own traumas for years to come. Besides, seeing what you put yourself through on my behalf is proof enough of your feelings. Even if you *are* the ugliest person I know!"

Jack grinned after hearing Em'brel throw his own joke back in his face. "Alright, first, you'll need to clean and disinfect the wounds, then dress them to help keep them clean." As he spoke, Jack fished out what was left of his now very used first aid kit.

After many flinches and pained gasps from Jack, S'haar returned and laid out the items he'd had requested. Looking over the coats, Jack set aside some as too damaged to be of use. The rest he put around the two sticks lying parallel to each other and fastened them on the underside, as though the sticks were wearing the coats, overlapping the coats in the process.

Once complete, the coats made a bed he could lie on while S'haar and Lon'thul carried him using the sticks' ends as handles. Em'brel walked off to the side, making sure Jack ate and drank his fill, per Angela's orders.

Jack sighed. When Em'brel gave him a questioning look, he eventually answered her unspoken question. "I just feel so useless, lying here eating while you do all the work. It just doesn't sit well with me..."

Em'brel shook her head in exasperation. "Oh please. Right now, you need to get some rest. If you try and push yourself too hard and put yourself at risk again, I'm going to tie you to this thing and not let you up until we get home!"

Lon'thul risked a brief glance over his shoulder. "Wait, is the idiot who went off and waged war against an entire army *really* complaining that he's not pulling his weight at the moment? S'haar, I think your man might be a little touched in the head! He needs to develop at least a modicum of self-preservation!"

Holding the other end of the litter, S'haar was currently staring daggers at Jack. "I agree." Somehow those words held more menace than any threat of violence possibly could have.

For his part, Jack knew when to shut up and went back to eating and drinking under the watchful gazes of S'haar and Em'brel.

～

As the group moved through the forest, the hunters fanned out and scouted ahead for any remaining raiders, but most had pulled back to recover what they could from the remnants of their camp, so there was little in the way of resistance.

While they walked, they passed by several sites from Jack's running battle with the raiders, many of which he couldn't remember at all. The sheer brutality evident in the fights made Em'brel shudder. Some even made Lon'thul shake his head. The only one who seemed unaffected was S'haar. Having seen her own share of violence, she was already familiar with the inevitable results of a life-and-death struggle. Additionally, she was probably the only argu'n who'd realized just how much Jack had been holding back until now.

Passing by one otherwise unambiguous corpse, Jack felt his heart clench in an icy fist. He startled everyone by hopping out of the litter, landing partially on his bad foot and collapsing. When Em'brel reached for him to help, she and everyone else were shocked when he slapped her hand away and crawled shakily toward the body, sobbing incoherently.

There was more confusion when he started punching the corpse right in the middle of its boney plate, yelling something to the effect of, "You weren't supposed to die! You idiot! All you had to do was stay asleep!"

While Lon'thul didn't know what Jack was saying, he got the general gist of what was going on. Looking over Jack's shoulders, he could see the body of a young male. He'd had his throat slit. It was clearly the work of one of the hunters. Trying to help, he put a hand on Jack's shoulder. "This one wasn't you. You weren't responsible."

Jack shrugged Lon'thul's hand off his shoulder and threw a punch at him. S'haar caught Jack's fist before it could make contact with the stunned hunter.

The person who looked most surprised at his assault was Jack himself, who started to mutter something that must have been an apology before his face twisted in pain, and he grabbed at his chest with his right hand while his left hung limp at his side.

Angela spoke up to S'haar. "It's Jack's heart again! Quick, use the defibrillator!"

After clearing the others away from Jack, S'haar grabbed the device, which had dragged behind him when he jumped from the litter, and pushed the button again. This resulted in Jack rocketing back onto the ground, where he lay sobbing in pain for a few moments. No one was certain if the problem was more physical or emotional at this point.

Eventually, they set the litter beside Jack again, who shakily crawled back on and collapsed, laying in silence with his arm draped over his eyes for a while. After a time, his breathing evened out as he fell asleep.

Lon'thul simply looked confused. "Did I say something wrong?"

S'haar shook her head. "Despite everything he's done, Jack is not a violent man by nature. This night is going to leave scars on his soul, as well as his body. For now, we need to let him rest, let him process what happened in his own time and way, and be there in case he needs us."

Em'brel reached out a hand and rested it on the litter next to Jack as they walked, unsure of what to say or do.

~

After they traveled a while, Dek'thul came back to meet them. "I'm pretty confident we've passed the raiders at this point. I'm going to leave one of my hunters with you to see to it you get back safely, but the rest of us are going to meet up with the guard and help them hunt down the remnants of this camp, so they don't become a long term problem."

He slapped Lon'thul on the back. "You did well out there, kid! Keep that up, and I might eventually have a rival! My own son, no less!"

Lon'thul beamed under the praise. S'haar didn't look pleased to speak to the hunter chief but still nodded her head and expressed her gratitude.

Dek'thul's grin wasn't quite as wide as he responded with a nod of his own. "Of course! All those raiders wandering about with impunity could have been a serious issue in time. I'm always happy to deal with any threat to the village."

Em'brel just looked nervous in the presence of the frightening-looking hunter and let loose a small involuntary squeak when he winked at her.

Dek'thul looked down at Jack a moment before turning and walking away, speaking over his shoulder as he left. "Just get him back home and patched up. It would be a shame to lose the kind of asset he's proven to be."

With those parting words, the hunter chief faded into the underbrush far more quickly than should have been possible for such a large argu'n, leaving the rest of them to resume their journey back home.

Chapter 55

The rest of the journey home passed without incident. When they stopped to eat, Jack was allowed to sit up and join in. When they rested for the night, they split the watch between S'haar, Lon'thul, and the other hunter. Neither Jack nor Em'brel were allowed to join in the watch, despite their protests.

Lon'thul put it simply. "Em'brel, none of us doubt your determination or your self-discipline, but you've just been through a horrible ordeal, and you're just not used to life in the wilds. Quite frankly, you probably couldn't tell the difference between a twig broken by a wandering churlish or an approaching raider. There will be plenty of work for you once we get back to camp, so get some sleep for now. We'll need your help later."

Turning to Jack, he wasn't quite so eloquent. "Jack, stop being an idiot and get the rest you need before S'haar ties you to your bed!"

One glance at S'haar convinced Jack it wasn't an idle threat. Of course, sleep was easier said than done for him. Angela had made him back off the pain meds considerably, and he hurt all over, but eventually, sheer exhaustion won, and he slept.

~

Jack opened his eyes to a sea of faces. They looked at him with expressions ranging from fear to anger to sadness.

Jack walked, then ran through the crowd, desperately searching for something but not knowing what. The faces turned into blurs as he ran faster and faster. He started recognizing them. He'd seen many of these same faces through his scope the night before.

More and more faces passed. Had he actually killed this many? Did this much blood really stain his hands? Eventually, the faces blurred into a kaleidoscope of condemnation until one face stood out and everything else faded.

Jack stood before the young raider he'd tried and failed to save. They stood staring at each other for an eternal instant. The young man spoke.

"You killed me."

It wasn't an accusation or spoken with anger. It was a simple statement of fact. Jack wanted to deny it anyway. He wanted to shout that he'd tried to save the kid, say it wasn't his hand that dealt the blow. Instead, he clenched his jaw and nodded, eventually whispering a harsh, guttural, "Yes."

They looked at each other a little longer, then the young man spoke again. "I saw what you did…after…after I got here, I mean… I saw you tried…" He fell silent again.

After they looked at each other for a few more moments, Jack spoke this time. "Does it matter?"

The young man thought some more before shrugging. "I don't know…"

Jack felt the tears force their way past his clenched jaw and felt the gasp of air he had to struggle to choke down before he was able to speak again. "I'm sorry."

The young man nodded. "I know."

Looking around, the young man took a deep breath. "So… What now?"

A familiar voice, yet unlike any Jack had ever heard before, spoke up from behind him. "Now, you come and sit with me, rest, and tell me your story."

A kind young mother walked out from behind Jack and met the young man. She took his hand, and his face eased of pain and fear. The two of them walked off into the distance, fading as they went.

Not-S'haar remained beside Jack. He turned to her and spoke. "Will he be ok?"

She looked at him with those star-filled eyes for several moments before speaking. "His story, as you understand it, has come to an end, but so has his pain. You're the one who has to live with his passing."

She looked at Jack for a few moments before tilting her head and asking her final question. "Can you?"

Jack stood there for several more long moments, staring into the spot he'd last seen the kid when he'd faded. After a long pause, he answered, not looking away. "I'll have to."

When he awoke, Jack's face was covered in tears, and his jaw was clenched tight. S'haar was sitting on a log not far away, her eyes scanning the forest.

Without taking her eyes off her task, she spoke softly. "You saw their faces." It wasn't a question.

Jack nodded before grimacing in chagrin, realizing she was looking in a totally different direction. He answered, his voice oddly ragged. "Yeah."

S'haar nodded, still looking into the trees. "That's good. Remember them. Some may have been monsters, others good men, but they are all worthy of being remembered."

Jack covered his eyes and started to slip back to sleep. Before he could, he spoke one last time, his voice barely a whisper. "Yeah…"

~

The next day also passed without incident, and soon enough, the group all but stumbled into the ship they called home. Jack was now being carried by S'haar, since the litter wasn't viable in the house's confines. They were met by an unusually somber but still delighted Angela. "About time, guys. The ship has been too quiet for too long! As good a conversationalist as Ger'ron is, this place just hasn't felt the same without you!"

The old guard hobbled over to greet them, obviously more comfortable with his crutches now than before. "I was going to welcome you all back safe and sound, but looking at Jack, I'm worried I might be speaking prematurely."

Jack grinned before flinching in pain while Em'brel tiredly walked over and hugged the older man. S'haar smiled tiredly. "Don't let his appearance fool you. Angela assures me Jack's no longer in any immediate danger."

Angela looked like she had a dozen lectures stored up and was bursting at the seams. She held up an accusatory finger in front of Jack. "So long as we can keep him from running out to go do something heroically suicidal for more than five minutes."

Jack held up his hands in surrender. "Listen, after the last couple of days, I'll be delighted to spend the next year indoors. Longer, even!"

Ger'ron looked down at the young woman hugging him. A look of shame crossed his face. "I'm not sure I deserve this greeting. I didn't do much to keep you safe."

Em'brel hugged him all the tighter. "You still fought for me, and I'm not going to forget that."

Lon'thul just kinda stood off to the side, a bit torn between feeling proud at having had a hand in this reunion and being just a little envious that he wasn't more involved with it.

After he was released from Em'brel's entrapment, Ger'ron hobbled over to Jack, giving him a once over, as though wondering how he was still alive. "So, you did it? You marched right up to the camp and saved the girl?"

Jack shook his head. "Nah, I just slowed them down a bit, and S'haar arrived to save me just before I got myself killed. Lon'thul here was the hero of the hour! He literally walked up and through the camp, right under the noses of dozens of raiders!" Jack slapped the hunter on the back as he spoke.

Lon'thul looked somewhat embarrassed. "It was only possible because you pulled most of the camp away, and even then, it was mostly my father that got us in and out so cleanly…"

Em'brel wasn't going to let himself talk his way out of his credit. "All I know is that when I was alone in the camp, fearing that everyone I know was getting themselves killed trying to rescue me, it was your voice that cut through my fear and made me feel like just maybe everything might be alright again!"

With that, she hugged Lon'thul as well and even gave him a kiss on the cheek before she pulled away. This left the hunter with a look of astonishment and confusion, unsure how to respond.

Angela was thrilled to see her family back in one place and was practically bursting with unbridled joy, but she knew she still had a job to do and visibly calmed herself…after a little happy dance. "As much as I wish this moment could last forever, you've all undergone immense stresses, physically, mentally, and emotionally. I want you all to report to the med-bay for a full battery of scans. Jack first, for obvious reasons. I suspect he'll be in there a while, so I'll let you know when I'm ready for you each in turn. For now, get some food, clean up, and get some rest."

~

After depositing Jack where Angela could begin her scans, S'haar took a seat in the med-bay as though afraid to let him out of her sight, lest he somehow went and got himself into more trouble.

Em'brel went and put together some food, with Ger'ron's help, and delivered it to S'haar and Jack. Angela even let Jack eat a couple of mouthfuls between scans.

Once his scans were finally done, Angela floated in front of him with a rolled parchment in her hands, from which she started reading. "Well, you Jacked up your leg good this time, pun intended. I can heal the bone and most of the muscle, but the nerves are fried. If we had access to a more complete medical facility, we *might* be able to repair it, or at least get you a really snazzy prosthetic, but for now, the safest thing to do is probably to leave it in place. You'll have a bit of a limp, and I'd recommend using a cane, if only to prevent falling over if and when your nerves occasionally flare up."

Unrolling the scroll a little further, Angela continued. "You've also got a few cracked ribs, a fractured wrist, a damaged tendon, and a concussion, all of which can be healed in a few days, though they'll leave you with a few more aches and pains than you had before."

Angela lowered the scroll a little and looked apologetically over it. "I'm afraid to say, I can't save your eye. I can heal the orb, so it won't look *as* horrific, but you won't be able to see out of it unless we install an implant that is, again, beyond my capacity to safely install in my med-bay."

Jack nodded. "Yeah, I kind of figured. Still, it could be worse. Anything else?"

Angela held on to the top of the unrolled scroll, then let the rest of it drop to the ground, where it continued to unroll along the floor until it bumped into the wall on the other side of the med-bay. "Yes, you have more contusions, abrasions, and lacerations than I've ever heard of. I'm reasonably sure you broke a record or three! Also, you seem to have one puncture wound that looks suspiciously like it came from a modern knife. Care to elaborate?"

Jack tilted his head to the side. "We can talk about that one later, but why do I feel as though you're still holding something back?" At this, S'haar and Em'brel both sat a little straighter, paying even closer attention than before.

Angela dropped her scroll, letting it vanish as it fell to the floor. She took a "breath" and sighed it out. "Well, there *is* one more issue. Your heart. With all the exhaustion, chemicals, and stresses you put it through, your heart has been permanently damaged. I can go over the specifics later, but what matters now is the fact that with enough strain, stress, or bad luck, it could give out on you again, at any time."

S'haar and Em'brel both shot to their feet, but Angela held up a hand to keep them at bay. "Jack is far from the first person to have this happen to him, and he won't be the last. We've developed various technologies and techniques to help someone in this condition live a mostly normal life. Since a replacement or prosthetic is again beyond the scope of this med-bay, we'll be using something called a pacemaker."

Jack raised an eyebrow. "And you can install one here?"

Angela nodded. "As important as it is, the heart is much simpler than your nervous system. While there is *some* risk with the installation, it's still far better than letting you run around with a bad heart. It's even minimally invasive. This will *barely* count as heart surgery!"

Looking over a clipboard that had materialized, Angela continued. "Out of everything you need done, that's actually where I would like to start. Once the pacemaker is in place, all the other procedures you'll need will be of minimal risk to your safety."

Jack sighed, then nodded. "Alright, let's get to it."

~

Both Em'brel and S'haar refused to undergo their own scans or get any sleep until they were sure Jack's surgery went well, so Angela forced them to get cleaned and suited up and separated them from the procedure with a transparent plastic sheet to prevent any possibility of contamination.

Both women watched, unable to look away, as Angela lowered her spider-like set of appendages she often used in the med bay that they'd become more and more used to in the previous months. Em'brel sat forward in her chair, fascinated by what she was watching. Meanwhile, S'haar sat with her back pressed up against the backrest and her claws digging into the seat cushions at her side, seeming as though she wanted to crawl away but was unwilling to do so.

Against their expectations, rather than cut open the skin near Jack's heart like they'd expected, Angela cut a slit near his shoulder, opening up a vein into which she inserted a small wire. He'd been thoroughly numbed and couldn't feel much, other than some slight tugging and pulling sensations, but was otherwise very much awake as she worked.

What followed seemed to the watching women to be a series of wires being pushed in and pulled out of Jack's vein. Em'brel watched with rapt attention as Angela pulled up a live x-ray so the girl could see what was going on inside of Jack. The vein was used to guide two electrodes attached to leads, which were then essentially screwed into the heart, securing them into place. The other end of the leads were secured into Jack's chest muscle. She then inserted what she described as a small computer into a pocket she created under his shoulder's muscle.

Em'brel was giddy with excitement at how cool she felt the whole thing was, while S'haar looked as though she regretted her earlier meal. The younger girl spoke up as Angela started to suture the site of the surgery closed. "That's so cool! Is that what it was like when you gave me my implant?"

At the thought that a similar procedure had been performed on her, S'haar looked a little weaker than she had moments before.

Having reappeared in her avatar state, Angela nodded. "Yes, actually. Both procedures were done with minimal invasiveness to the patient, to reduce the risk of complications. Unfortunately, something like an ocular implant that could restore Jack's vision would require far more exposure, dramatically increasing the chance of infections or other issues, which is why I recommend merely accepting the loss of vision in one eye, at least for now."

Jack was putting on a loose-fitting robe to cover up the surgical site, which was now covered with a bandage. "That's all well and good, but I'm famished. I'd like to take a bit and grab a bite before we jump into the next part of me that needs healing, if that's alright with you."

S'haar looked grateful for the reprieve as she nodded in agreement. Angela crossed her arms and sighed. "I guess we got the life-threatening one out of the way, so maybe letting you get a bit of your strength back before moving on is a good idea. How's your leg feeling, anyway?"

Jack chuckled before flinching again. "Oh, it hurts plenty, just like everything else. I suspect this will be a long few days, so I figured it would be better to pace myself."

Angela nodded sagely before opening one eye to stare in Jack's direction. "You're not wrong. The healing process can be rough on your body, and you've got a lot of healing to do, but try not to overeat. The last thing we need is more complications caused by something so easily avoidable."

S'haar seemed all too happy to help Jack out and into the living area. For her part, Em'brel hopped up and onto the examination table. "Guess it's my turn next!"

Chapter 56

The next few days seemed to pass in a blurred eternity. The various surgeries weren't so bad, since Jack at least got to be adequately anesthetized for those. However, all the bone growth took an agonizingly long time. Since they weren't in a rush this time, it wasn't as painful as before. Rather than feeling like a red hot poker was being shoved into Jack's leg, it felt more like he was being continuously stung by an angry wasp. When he couldn't take the pain in his leg anymore, Angela would let him take a break and work on his ribs or wrist instead.

The whole healing process left Jack in a somewhat foul mood, but at least afterward, he could hobble around, with the aid of a crude cane he'd cobbled together and a temporary cast Angela had given him to prevent him from reinjuring himself during the night. In another day or two, he wouldn't even need the cast anymore. However, he still felt a little unsettled looking at his face in the mirror.

The left side of his face was a mess. The claw marks were still a bright angry red. Angela told him the color would fade over time, but they'd been left untreated for too long for the scars to resemble anything he could call subtle. The worst of it was his left eye. Like Anglea had promised, there was an orb there, staring back at him, but the color was all wrong. The veins stood out so much the sclera looked more red than white, and the iris seemed to be covered by some kind of film, giving it a ghostly white look. He'd definitely have to have an eyepatch made, if only for his own peace of mind.

S'haar walked up behind him, wrapping him in a gentle hug, so she wouldn't reinjure his still-healing ribs. She leaned down to plant a kiss on his cheek before speaking. "It makes you look roguish. Definitely an improvement over the helpless-looking face you had before."

Jack chuckled, this time only feeling a slight tinge of pain as he did so. "You're just saying that to make me feel better."

S'haar smiled into the mirror, looking into the reflection of Jack's good eye. "Maybe. Did it work?"

Jack turned around in her grip to pull the warrior woman down to him for a longer kiss before responding, his head tilted to the side as he examined the woman who'd come to mean so much to him with his good eye. "Well, coming from you, how could it not?"

Just as things were starting to look like they were going to get interesting, a familiar blue glow appeared from behind Jack, who let out a sigh. "Yes, Angela, I know. I'm not healed enough for anything… 'strenuous' yet. Now can you leave us be for a few more moments?"

Angela's voice was filled with more concern than Jack had been expecting when she replied. "If that was the reason I'd come here, I'd gladly give you two more time alone. But the real reason I'm here is Em'brel. She hardly slept last night, and tonight's not looking to be any better. I tried to comfort her as best I could, but I think she needs more than I can offer."

Jack sighed and pulled away from S'haar, though her hand remained in his own. "Alright, alright… You made the right choice."

Jack turned his attention back to S'haar, squeezing her hands. "What say you go warm some water for tea and get a snack ready. I'll talk Em'brel into joining us in the living area. I think it's time we had a movie night again."

S'haar leaned in to steal one quick final kiss before nodding. "I think that's a great idea." With that, she turned and was gone.

For his part, Jack cleaned himself up a little to make himself more presentable while he thought of what to say or do to comfort a girl who's been through far more trauma than anyone, adult or child, should ever have to endure…again.

~

Jack knocked on Em'brel's door. When there was no reaction, he tried speaking as well. "Hey, Em'brel, it's me, Jack." He frowned at the obviousness of his statement but continued. "I was just wondering, want to talk for a bit?"

There was still no response, but a minute later, the door unlocked. Jack wasn't sure if that was Angela or Em'brel's doing, but he figured that something needed to be done either way.

He opened the door a crack and spoke into the room. "Hey, just thought I'd check in on ya and see how you're doing." When no protest seemed forthcoming, Jack finally pushed his way inside enough to see a lump hiding under the blanket of her bed, faintly shivering.

He walked over and sat down at the foot of her bed to wait. Eventually, a small voice braved its way out of the shelter of blankets and pillows. "I'm sorry."

Of everything Jack had been expecting, an apology hadn't even made the list of possibilities. His look of incredulity was wasted in the darkroom. "Sorry? Whatever for?"

The blankets shifted just enough for a pair of eyes to peak out over them. "After everything you went through and all the pain you're even now enduring while recovering, and I can't stop shivering because I'm imagining getting captured again. I'm currently locked behind a solid wall of the finest steel in the land and watched over by a centurion who never sleeps and protected by the bravest swordswoman and the only gunman on the planet, but I can't stop imagining that a raider is hiding under my bed just waiting for me to fall asleep."

Jack nodded sagely for a moment. "Alright, first of all…" Against Em'brel's sudden protests, Jack got on his knees, careful not to exacerbate his leg, and checked under the bed. Sitting up again with a stupid grin, Jack proudly proclaimed, "No, raiders here!"

Em'brel sputtered indignantly as she helped Jack get back to his feet before he resumed his seat on the bed, this time hugging the now uncovered female. "More importantly, even assuming pain was tangible enough to be compared and weighed to determine who was actually dealing with 'more' of it, it's not some zero-sum game where the trauma of the person with 'less' of it is meaningless."

Em'brel stopped struggling once she realized Jack wasn't going to let her escape back under the blankets unless she was willing to hurt him to get away. He continued. "You've been through more in the last few months than most people will deal with in an entire lifetime. It's ok to be scared. Honestly, I'd be more worried if you *didn't* show signs of stress and trauma. However, I want you to remember one thing."

Jack forced the girl's eyes to meet his own. "I'm here to help you through this, just like you'll be here to help me through my own issues." He grinned. "And S'haar is here for both of us, and we'll be here for her in turn. That's what it means to be family."

Em'brel took a breath to protest, but Jack continued unabated. "We might not have been born with the same blood running through our veins, but we chose one another, and in my book, that means even more."

Eventually, Em'brel nodded. "Yeah…thanks. I feel…kinda silly now…"

Jack's grin grew. "That's good! That means you're not scared at the moment! Still, when the fear comes back again, and sooner or later it will, we'll all still be here for you."

Em"brel nodded and looked around as though unsure of what to do now. Jack's smile turned sympathetic. "Not feeling sleepy at the moment, are ya?"

Em'brel looked sheepish as she shook her head. "No."

Jack stood up and reached out to draw Em'brel to her feet as well. "Well, if I'm not mistaken, S'haar should have some water boiling for tea and a bunch of popcorn ready to go. What say we have a movie night, the three of us, just like the old times?"

Em'brels face blossomed into a huge happy grin that just about stopped Jack's heart to see. "I… I'd really like that!"

Jack shooed the girl out of her room and followed her into the living area. He was grateful that Ger'ron and Lon'thul had set up their bedrolls in the crafting room, instead of using the couch or living area floor like Jack had suggested, making it so they didn't have to worry about waking them as the two got their own much-needed rest.

There was already a bowl of popcorn sitting on the table, and S'haar was just walking out from the kitchen area with three steaming mugs. Looking through his movies, Jack decided it was time to introduce the girls to the world of animation. "Let me tell you about one of my favorite directors. This guy never fails to cheer me up. His movies are basically a distillation of the best and most important parts of childhood on earth turned into a work of art anyone can enjoy. His name is Miyazaki…"

~

A few hours later, they were all sprawled out on both the couch and the floor. Em'brel had been the first victim. She'd held on through the first movie, but she hadn't slept well last night, and that had been the telling blow.

S'haar was the next to go. Finishing both her tea and the popcorn before she gave in to her exhaustion, but in the end, the warmth of the blankets, the comfort of the soft floor, and the peace of being together with her family won out over what little determination to stay awake that she possessed, and the warrior woman gave in to the inevitable.

Jack had been more determined to make it to the end of one of his childhood favorites, but he fell prey to the classic trap of not wanting to wake the two women sleeping next to, or in one case, partially on top of him. Soon he unintentionally matched his breathing to the slow, leisurely pace of his companions', and from that moment on, his fight was already over.

Angela smiled, her digital heart practically glowing in a way she'd been afraid it never would again. She bumped the room temperature up a couple of degrees to help them sleep a little easier, turned off the TV, and dimmed the lights.

Tonight was a good night.

~

Jack opened his eyes to Lon'thul's grinning face. "You're awake! We were starting to worry you'd sleep the day away!"

Jack blinked a few times sleepily, trying to orient himself after waking up in a location other than his room. Remembering where he was and why, Jack grabbed the crouching Lon'thul by the face and shoved him out of the way. For his part, the hunter played along, rolling away as though Jack actually had the mass to move him, before popping back onto his feet in a way that made Jack envy his youth.

Looking around, Jack could see Em'brel back to her familiar role as the cook. Old Ger'ron hobbled his way over to the table, drawn by the aroma of the breakfast the younger woman was putting together. Even S'haar was up and about, leaving the bathroom where she'd evidently gone to freshen up while breakfast was prepared before walking over to Jack and helping him to his feet.

Jack found he was a little more sore than he would have been if he'd slept in his bed like a normal person, but some things in life were worth a bit of pain.

They joined the rest at the table as Em'brel placed a few plates into the middle. It was churlish steak and eggs, and everyone dug in with gusto.

Lon'thul was the first to jab toward a steak but found his fork blocked by Ger'ron's as they'd apparently aimed for the same cut of meat. With a flick of his wrist, the older man redirected the youth's fork then claimed his prize before the hunter even realized he'd lost. Everyone laughed as Lon'thul blinked stupidly for a moment while his brain replayed just what had happened. With a chagrined smile, he went for his second choice instead.

After the initial clamor faded, Lon'thul broke the relative silence brought on by mouths stuffed full of food. "So, what's the plan for today?"

Angela popped up. "Well, I don't know about everyone else, but Jack's got some more healing to work on!" Jack flinched at the thought of it but reluctantly nodded.

S'haar had a thoughtful look on her face. "What's the weather supposed to be like?"

Angela tilted her head to the side in the way she did while gathering and analyzing data. "Should be relatively mild for the next couple of days. I think spring is starting to settle in. Why do you ask?"

S'haar's face was neutral as she answered. "With the weather nice like this, I thought I should go get the workers back. It would be a shame to waste days like this, when there's still so much work that needs to be done."

No sooner had she finished speaking when Lon'thul cut in. "Let me do it!"

Everyone looked at the hunter with surprise. He shrugged at their incredulity before explaining. "Listen, I've been to town and back about as many times as you. I can get them here safe and sound, and it'll be better than being locked up in here all day, despite how nice a cage it is."

The hunter's grin turned impish. "Besides, last time you were out there while Jack was back here, you were a bit of a beast to be around. If you left while Jack stayed back here to finish his healing, you'd probably scare off any new workers before they even arrived."

Em'brel hid a chuckle behind her hand as S'haar's face seemed to war between annoyance and gratitude. Finally, she closed her eyes, took a deep breath, and opened them again. "Alright, we'll call this a trial run. Go get the original group, assuming they all want to return, and anyone else ready and willing to come from the ones we've spoken with. Let anyone not yet prepared know that we'll probably make several other similar trips, so they don't have to rush out this time."

Lon'thul nodded, eager to prove his worth while getting out and stretching his legs at the same time. "No problem! I'll get them back here safe and sound! You've got my word on it!"

The hunter hopped up and looked around as if trying to decide whether or not to leave right now when Angela stopped him. "Woh, slow down there! We gotta get your supplies ready first. Even if you're used to surviving in the wilds, not all of the workers are. As the expedition leader, your first responsibility is their safety. We should spend today getting you ready to go, and you can leave first thing in the morning. Sound good?"

Lon'thul looked a little deflated as he sat back down and grabbed another steak. "Yeah, I suppose that'd be smart. Guess I'll have to find something else to do for today."

Ger'ron had a bit of a wicked gleam in his eye at the hunter's statement. "You need something else to keep you busy, do you? Judging by how easy it was to take that steak out from under you, your swordwork needs some practice! I may not be able to teach you hands-on just yet, but I think I can run you through a few exercises until I get this "prosthetic" Lady Angela keeps telling me about!"

The young hunter looked as though he'd just been sentenced to hard labor but nodded reluctantly.

To everyone's surprise, that was when Em'brel joined in the conversation. "I'd like to practice, too!"

When all eyes turned to her, she looked like she wanted to run and hide for a moment before she gathered her courage and spoke again. "Listen, I'm tired of being the damsel in distress. While I don't think I'll ever be a match for S'haar with a sword, I don't want to be helpless again, either!"

The old guard looked surprised a moment before he smiled at his new prized student. "Well, I think that's a great idea! Besides, if you're there the whole time, it'll probably encourage this one to push himself a little harder as well!" He tilted his head to indicate Lon'thul as he spoke.

Angela nodded her agreement before turning to the guard herself. "Once you're done teaching Em'brel and beating some sense into Lon'thul, stop by the med-bay. I want to give you a check-up and get an idea of how much longer before you're ready for that prosthetic."

Ger'ron nodded his thanks. "Of course, Lady Angela. It would be my pleasure!"

Jack looked back and forth between the guard and the AI. "What's with all this 'Lady Angela' talk?"

Angela turned her back on Jack and spoke to him over her shoulder in a pouty manner. "It's because he knows a lady when he sees one! You could learn a thing or two about respect from our guest!"

The table devolved into a gaggle of laughter and chatter as everyone enjoyed the rest of the morning spent in good company.

Chapter 57

A day after Lon'thul left for the village, S'haar and Em'brel sat waiting for news as Angela finished her latest scans of Jack. She zoomed in on an image of his leg as she began her explanations. "Well, your bones have knitted together nicely. Your musculature has also been properly reattached, though you could probably use some more physical therapy to restore your normal levels of strength…again… The nerves…are more or less shot, which will mess with your coordination, and you'll occasionally feel pain ranging from mild to crippling with little warning. You'll definitely want a walking cane of some kind."

The digital image of Jack's body zoomed out, and different parts were highlighted as Angela continued. "The minor fractures have all healed as well as they likely will, though you'll experience more aches and pains than you remember. Your pacemaker seems to be working correctly, and if you're within my range, I can even track it, or if necessary, adjust it. Finally, no matter how hard I scan, I can detect no physical evidence of brain damage."

Angela flew in close as if looking his skull over personally, with a look of deep concern. "Though obviously there must be some damage. I'm fairly certain you never used to drool like that…"

Jack resisted the urge to fall for her obvious trap by checking and instead flung his hand through his sister's avatar. Or he would have if she hadn't dived out of the way, cackling at her little joke.

Em'brel ran forward and hugged Jack, pinning him awkwardly in place with one arm stretched out over her shoulder in a way it just hung there uselessly until she backed up. "That's great! You'll be out enjoying the warming weather in no time!"

Jack grinned at her. "Yeah, I'll need to stretch my legs out wandering around the camp, but I'm not sure I'll be much good for heavy lifting again any time soon."

Angela, who was leisurely floating on her back just behind Em'brel, cut in with a self-satisfied grin. "I hate to break it to you, little bro, but you've never been much for heavy lifting on this planet. Even Em'brel can outperform you in that regard."

Jack was just about to launch back his retort when S'haar approached to speak her own mind, an odd look in her eyes. "So you're saying he's as healed as he's likely to get at this point?"

Angela nodded. "Yeah, he's back to being…"

She was cut off when S'haar reached out and grabbed Jack, pulling him into a short but intense kiss before letting him fall back into the chair. "After you left, you almost died not once, but twice. From now on, where you go, I go. This is not a debate!"

Jack was somewhat out of breath as he sat in place, blinking as he processed everything unspoken behind the kiss and words. Eventually, he nodded. "Yeah, I suppose that's fair."

He grinned stupidly and slapped his bad leg, only flinching a little in the process. "Besides, I doubt I could outrun you anymore anyway!"

S'haar's expression seemed to soften slightly, but the gleam in her eye only grew odder. "Good enough, I suppose. Now then, I think we need to rush you right into your physical therapy."

Angela looked a little confused. "Well, there's not really any rush, though, I suppose…"

Once more, the AI was cut off by S'haar's unexpected movement as she reached down, grabbed Jack, and threw him over her shoulder like a sack of grain.

She then looked over at the youngest woman in the room, her voice sounding oddly maternal. "Em'brel, darling, you might want to go outside and get started on your martial practice with Ger'ron. Jack and I are going to be busy for a little while."

The look on Em'brels face said she wasn't fooled for a moment but was willing to play along for the sake of avoiding an awkward conversation. She nodded emphatically. "Uh, yea…yes…um, yes… That…that sounds like a great idea! I think he was planning on a long training session today, so I'll be gone a while. So…uh….yeah…bye!"

With that, the girl fled out of the room, grabbing the confused old soldier from the living room and practically shoving him out of the ship on her way out.

S'haar also spared a glance for Angela, whose digital face was now thoroughly red, though she was sporting an odd grin as though this was all some weird joke only the AI could appreciate. "You may want to turn down your sensors, or stop listening, or do whatever you need to do."

The warrior women didn't wait for a response. She exited the medbay and carried Jack into his room, which at some point had apparently become "their" room. Jack's face clearly expressed that although his participation may no longer be optional, he wasn't particularly unwilling either.

~

Em'brel was exhausted. First, the old sadist had made her do the same maneuver with a sword one hundred times, saying something about building muscle memory. It had seemed so easy at first, but long before she finished, her arms and back had been screaming in pain.

Next, he'd had her run laps around the camp. He said something about how in an equal fight, the person with better stamina would usually be the one to walk away. After a few laps, she'd collapsed on the ground, panting for breath.

The old guard hobbled over to her with his crutches. He stood over her, grinning as she struggled to catch her breath. "You're doing well. Much better than the first day! Now that you've got the warm-ups out of the way, let's get started on some real training!"

Em'brel debated the merits of simply dying right then and there. Ultimately she sighed and dragged herself to her feet before launching into the next series of exercises the vicious older man laid out for her.

~

Jack was looking at his new eyepatch. Angela had insisted on using a bit of fabrication to print out her own design.

It was made from a nice synthetic black leather that was resistant to damage from moisture or exposure. Turning it over, Jack could see the inside of the band had a cloth layer to help it rest more comfortably on the skin. On the patch itself, Angela had emblazoned the symbol of the camp in gold.

Angela was floating over his shoulder, practically giddy in anticipation of Jack's reaction. Unable to wait, she blurted out in excitement. "It's even machine washable!"

Jack couldn't help but laugh as he shook his head. Unwilling to wait any longer, he tried it on. Turning to S'haar, he smiled. "Well, what do you think?"

For her part, S'haar tilted her head as if thinking before nodding in appreciation. "You look good. It suits you."

Jack's grin widened. Em'brel approached with her hands held behind her back. Once she was close enough, she brought out the object she'd been hiding with a flustered flourish.

In her hands was a cane. It was black and gold to match Jack's eyepatch, though he suspected the gold was either thinly gilded or was some kind of fool's gold. However, the part that stood out the most was the handle. It seemed to be made out of a bone of some sort.

As Jack inspected it closer, Em'brel explained nervously. "I… it's made out of the horn of the kovaack that almost killed you. I thought… I thought…"

Jack smiled and set the cane aside to hug the younger woman. "Thank you very much. I think it's great! Every time I use it, I'll think of the time you fought desperately to save my life."

Em'brel let out a breath she'd apparently been holding. "Oh, thank goodness, I was afraid it would bring back painful memories. Angela insisted you'd like it, but I was still worried!"

Jack smiled as he held her at arm's length to meet her eyes. "Not all my memories from that time are pleasant, but I try and focus on the good while learning from the bad. That's all we can do in life!"

Angela floated right between them, causing Jack to take a step back, even though he knew she was insubstantial. She gave Jack an appraising look, looking like some kind of librarian, with glasses and her hair in a bun. Her chin rested on one hand, one finger thumb extended to opposite cheeks as she did so.

After a moment, she turned back to Em'brel. "Don't feel too sorry for him. I know my own brother well enough to know he happens to think he looks quite dashing with his new eyepatch and cane. I'm willing to bet he'll even want some kind of matching cloak or cape to go with them..."

Jack looked like he wanted to protest for a moment, then he shrugged instead. "Well, you *did* say I'd have more aches and pains than before. I figure keeping myself nice and warm might help with that."

Angela laughed uproariously as she pointed at Jack. "I KNEW IT! I called it! You are *such* a nerd!"

Jack smiled at the good-natured ribbing. "Hey, it's not nerdy on this planet yet. If I have to live on a world that seems so determined to kill me, day in and day out, the least I should be able to do is indulge in a few archaic fashion trends. Doubly so if they're practical as well!"

S'haar walked up behind Jack, wrapping him in one of those over the shoulder hugs he was starting to get used to. "Well, I'm not sure if the world is to blame, with all the chances you've been giving it lately. You can only tempt fate so many times before it takes you up on your offer."

Jack briefly tried to fight the woman off, but she held on effortlessly as she continued. "However, regarding the way you look, I think I agree. You look cute with your eyepatch and cane!"

With a sudden surge of strength, Jack finally escaped from S'haar's captivity, though the look on S'haars face argued she'd allowed him to get away. Jack pointed an accusatory finger at her as he protested. "Of all the many adjectives you can use to describe me, cute is not one! I'll accept daring, dashing, roguish, mysterious, or any other of a plethora of descriptors other than 'cute'!"

S'haar reached out and grabbed his hand and forced it lower while also dragging Jack into a brief kiss before responding. "You're cute when you're flustered!"

Angela laughed uproariously, pretending to roll around on the "ground" despite floating at eye level as she did so. Em'brel had to hide her face behind her hands as she laughed. Even Ger'ron, sitting unobtrusively in his chair across the room, shared a chuckle at Jack's expense. The grin on S'haar's face said she knew she'd won that exchange more clearly than any words could have.

Jack slumped his shoulders in defeat. "I can't get any respect, even in my own house!"

S'haar chuckled in response. "Oh hush now. You know you've earned plenty of respect from all of us…and before long, everyone else within several days' walking distance, if I'm not mistaken. Besides, I promise I'll make it up to you later…"

Em'brel and Angela looked at each other, their faces scrunched in exaggerated disgust. Angela was the first to respond. "I think I speak for both of us when I say… 'Ew, gross!'"

After a bit of laughter, Em'brel suddenly sniffed the air. "Oh, the stew!" Just like that, she was off to repair whatever damage had been done to the unattended pot while everyone else settled in for their meal.

~

After a filling dinner complimented with plenty of laughter and jokes at one another's expense, Angela addressed the table, her voice uncharacteristically solemn. First, she turned to their most recent guest. "Ger'ron, I apologize, but there's a matter I need to speak with just these three about…could I ask you…"

The older guard waved away her concern. "Say no more, Lady Angela. After a filling meal like that, I think I'll retire for the night. Em'brel, thank you for the food. As always, the meal was excellent. Now, if you all will excuse me, I'll leave the cleanup in each of your hands this evening."

With that, the old guard hobbled off to his improvised bedroom while the rest waited in confusion for Angela to continue.

Once the door to Ger'ron's room had closed, the AI began her explanation. "So as you all were escaping to make your way back here, my mobile transceiver got left behind."

Angela held up a hand to forestall any comments before they were made. "I know it wasn't a priority at the time, and I agree with you. It also put me in a position where I was free to overhear some of the confrontations between the town's guards and the raider camp's remnants. There are a few moments I've earmarked for your attention later, but while cleaning up and sorting through the various soundbites I've acquired, I came across one bit in particular that I think you all need to listen to because, quite frankly, I have no idea what to do with this information."

She then sat back and began to playback what sounded like a skirmish of some kind. The audio wasn't as clear as she'd like, since this hadn't happened as close to the transceiver as Angela would have hoped, but the sounds of a life and death struggle were evident to anyone listening.

Jack's eyes grew wide, and he stared off into the distance as though seeing another time or place. His knuckles turned white as he gripped the arms of his chair. Angela considered shutting off the recording, but S'haar placed her hand over his, and after a moment, Jack closed his eyes and let out a breath he'd been holding before nodding and reponing his eyes again. This time his look was less panicked.

Eventually, the sounds of struggle ended, and after a moment of heavy breathing, a voice could be heard. It was B'arthon's. "Filthy raider, how dare you trespass into our lands! A quick death is better than you deserve!"

Another more panicked and pained voice responded, evidently the raider B'arthon was speaking to. "We did not trespass, young lord, I swear! We came by invitation! Your own father sent for us and paid us well!"

B'arthon's voice shouted out, drowning out any further comments the raider might have made. "LIAR! HOW DARE YOU BRING MY FATHER INTO THIS SIMPLY TO BUY YOUR WORTHLESS LIFE A FEW MEASLY SECONDS!"

That was followed by the soft sounds of impact, a surprised gasp, and finally, the sounds of a death gurgle. A sound Em'brel had heard before. She shuddered at the memory.

Everyone shared a look of surprise as Dek'thul's voice joined the conversation. "Lord B'arthon, you should know better than to listen to the lies of a raider. You know as well as I that your father puts the welfare of the village above all else. He would never invite raiders into our lands. Please, put any thought of this out of your mind."

With that, the recording ended, and Angela looked around expectantly, waiting to see everyone's reactions.

Em'brel looked frightened, S'haar angry, and Jack contemplative. S'haar was the first to react, standing and slamming her fist onto the table and making both Jack and Em'brel jump. "He can't get away with this! We must take this recording to the village and have the other village leaders listen to it! If enough of them agree, we can have the traitor exiled!"

It was Jack's turn to put a calming hand on S'haar's fist. "I'd agree with you, but there are a few issues with that. First, the raider *could* have been lying. We don't know. Second, why should your village leaders believe us? If we can make voices appear out of thin air, who's to say we couldn't fabricate what they say. Third, having heard it for himself, Dek'thul seems to be either fooled or complicit. Without knowing which, we risk a lot by taking direct action."

S'haar looked frustrated. "Then what would you recommend? We sit idly while the person who orchestrated this mess gets away with it?"

Jack held up his hands in a placating gesture as he spoke. "Now hear me out and decide for yourself. This actually doesn't change anything in our immediate future. Assuming Lord A'ngles *is* behind everything, which we still don't *know*, he can't move against us directly, or he already would have."

S'haar's eyes narrowed, but she waited with her arms crossed as Jack continued. "I think he's already pushed the limits of what he can do at this time. To avoid attracting attention, he'll have to play nice for a while, until everything has calmed down. What's more, we still need the support of the village to ensure our own survival."

S'haar looked like she wanted to argue but was forcing herself to figuratively, or perhaps literally, bite her tongue as Jack finished his explanation. "To that end, we play along, for now. We'll do exactly what we had planned to do before. That is to say, building up this outpost to be its own independent entity. We can start by accepting whatever help we can get, due to the goodwill we've earned by saving many villagers from the cold and then fending off a major raiding party. With that, we grow this place into something more."

Jack waved toward the door and the camp beyond. "Up until now, we've just focused on iron and a few technologies needed to ensure the safety and quality of life of the many workers who would be present, but Angela and I can offer so much more. We can teach you medicines, textiles, irrigation, plumbing, farming, animal husbandry, and more. Pretty soon, this outpost would become *the* place of learning in the land. Multiple villages could send their workers to learn of the dragon's wisdom. We'd become essential and, in many ways, untouchable."

S'haar looked dubious, but at least she didn't look ready to charge out and declare war on her own while she considered Jack's proposal.

Em'brel nodded, and her eyes became distant as she took in the entirety of Jack's vision. "We still need the help of the village for this place to function, but if we invite more and more villages to gather and learn here, we wouldn't need it for long. With workers and guards from enough villages present, no one village leader would have power over us. Additionally, they wouldn't be able to withdraw support, for fear of falling behind the others."

Em'brel frowned as she continued her line of reasoning. "The challenges will be doing this in such a way that everything's already in place before Lord A'ngles realizes he's lost control of the situation, then dealing with the fallout once he does."

As both Jack and Em'brel looked at S'haar expectantly, she finally nodded and sat down. "Alright, I still don't like it, but I see the wisdom of your words. We'll do it your way, for now. But as soon as we can, I want to have our own guards replacing the ones from the village. Also, neither of you are to leave this ship without some kind of escort once the workers arrive."

The glare she directed toward Jack and Em'brel killed any protest they might have made while it was still in their throats. Both nodded their agreement. S'haar then directed her attention to Angela. "And I expect you to keep an ear out for anything suspicious. Forget the rest. You don't need to keep a recording of the day-to-day lives of the workers who take up residence, but listen with those clever ears of yours for anyone who might be plotting to cause us trouble."

Angela saluted S'haar smartly before grinning devilishly. "I would have done that even if you hadn't asked, but I'm glad we're on the same page!"

S'haar looked back and forth between everyone before lowering her head and rubbing it in such a way that spoke of stress and exhaustion. "This is all a bit much to take in all at once. It's starting to give me a headache."

The warrior woman then looked at Jack. "Are you sure you don't want to take back command of the outpost?"

Jack simply flashed the toothy grin he'd developed after all this time with argu'n. "Not on your life! Well, ok, maybe on your life, but not for any lesser reason. I've had enough of leading and heroics. I'm looking forward to the relaxing lifestyle of a cowardly advisor!"

Jack deflected the pillow S'haar threw at him as everyone else enjoyed a good laugh at their antics.

~

Jack woke in the middle of the night gasping for air. His adrenalin was pumping, and he was looking around, expecting to see…faces. When he looked down, his hands were shaking. After rubbing his face to chase away the last vestiges of whatever dream he'd woken from, his hands came away wet.

He sat there, trying to catch his breath for a moment, when an unexpected hand came out of nowhere and grabbed him. He reacted instinctively, slamming his elbow back into whoever had a hold of him, only to be caught by another hand and pulled into an embrace.

In an instant, Jack realized it was S'haar holding him and tried to turn to apologize, but she just held him all the more firmly. Realizing the futility of his struggles, Jack gave up and found himself wracked with silent sobs as tears streamed down his face. He felt ashamed of his weakness, crying over a dream he couldn't even remember. Through it all, S'haar held him silently and waited.

After a nebulous period of time, he felt his emotions drain, leaving him feeling oddly empty and exhausted. Remembering how this had all started, he spoke up, his voice still somewhat ragged. "Sorry…about attacking you…"

S'haar didn't seem upset as she responded, though admittedly, Jack couldn't see her face at the moment. "It's alright, no harm done. Well, except for the fact that I'm pretty sure you bruised your elbow."

Judging by the dull ache radiating from his elbow, he was sure she was correct. Jack shook his head and sighed. "Yeah, maybe. Regardless, I'm sorry."

S'haar squeezed Jack a little tighter for just a moment before releasing him enough that he could finally turn around and see her as she replied. "All is forgiven. Back when I lived in the guard's barracks, you'd see something similar from time to time. It was most common after an unusually brutal raid. There is always a bit of a risk when waking someone up from something like that." She paused, tilting her head as if remembering something. "They punched a lot harder than you." She grinned softly to soften any potential blow to Jack's masculinity.

Jack just grinned and chuckled, then grew quiet. S'haar's expression sobered, and she gave him a questioning look. "Want to talk about it?"

He thought a moment before shaking his head and lying back down. "No…not yet, anyway."

S'haar grabbed him and pulled him into another embrace. It was weird always being the one brought into the hugs, but S'haar seemed to enjoy having as much body contact as possible. Jack wasn't sure if it was out of a desire for intimacy or body heat, but he supposed it didn't matter. He was quickly growing fond of their new dynamic. She squeezed him again and spoke with a voice growing heavy with sleep once more. "That's alright. If you ever feel like talking, I'll be right here, by your side."

Jack felt his eyes threaten to overflow again, and he fought down the annoying lump that had just developed in his throat before muttering, "I know. Thank you."

Then the time for speaking was over, and Jack found himself slipping back to sleep. Despite all the threats and challenges still laid out before them, in S'haar's arms, he felt like he genuinely belonged where he was for the first time since landing on this planet.

Made in United States
Troutdale, OR
12/02/2024

25431345R00289